THE GARDENS OF SATURN
by Paul J. McAuley

SOLDIERS HOME
by William Barton

LEGACIES
by Tom Purdom

MOON DUEL
by Fritz Leiber

SAVIOR
by Robert Reed

GALACTIC NORTH
by Alastair Reynolds

MASQUE OF THE RED SHIFT
by Fred Saberhagen

TIME PIECE
by Joe Haldeman

ON THE ORION LINE
by Stephen Baxter

Space Soldiers
Edited by Jack Dann & Gardner Dozois

Edited by Jack Dann & Gardner Dozois

UNICORNS!
MAGICATS!
BESTIARY!
MERMAIDS!
SORCERERS!
DEMONS!
DOGTALES!
SEASERPENTS!
DINOSAURS!
LITTLE PEOPLE!
MAGICATS II
UNICORNS II
DRAGONS!
INVADERS!
HORSES!
ANGELS!
HACKERS
TIMEGATES
CLONES
IMMORTALS
NANOTECH
ARMAGEDDONS
ALIENS AMONG US
GENOMETRY
SPACE SOLDIERS

Edited by Terri Windling

FAERY!

SPACE SOLDIERS

EDITED BY
JACK DANN & GARDNER DOZOIS

ACE BOOKS, NEW YORK

SPACE SOLDIERS

An Ace Book / published by arrangement with
the editors

PRINTING HISTORY
Ace edition / April 2001

Cover art by Lee MacLeod

For information address: The Berkley Publishing Group,
a division of Penguin Putnam Inc.,
375 Hudson Street, New York, New York 10014.

The Penguin Putnam Inc. World Wide Web site address is
http://www.penguinputnam.com

Check out the ACE Science Fiction & Fantasy newsletter
and much more on the Internet at Club PPI!

ISBN: 0-441-00824-0

ACE®
Ace Books are published by The Berkley Publishing Group,
a division of Penguin Putnam Inc.,
375 Hudson Street, New York, New York 10014.
ACE and the "A" design
are trademarks belonging to Penguin Putnam Inc.

PRINTED IN THE UNITED STATES OF AMERICA

10 9 8 7 6 5 4 3 2 1

Acknowledgments

ACKNOWLEDGMENT IS MADE FOR PERMISSION
TO REPRINT THE FOLLOWING MATERIAL:

"The Gardens of Saturn," by Paul J. McAuley. Copyright © 1998 by Interzone. First published in *Interzone*, November 1998. Reprinted by permission of the author.

"Soldiers Home," by William Barton. Copyright © 1999 by Dell Magazines. First published in *Asimov's Science Fiction*, May 1999. Reprinted by permission of the author.

"Legacies," by Tom Purdom. Copyright © 1993 by Bantam Doubleday Dell Magazines. First published in *Asimov's Science Fiction*, January 1994. Reprinted by permission of the author.

"Moon Duel," by Fritz Leiber. Copyright © 1965 by Galaxy Publishing Corporation. First published in *If*, September 1965. Reprinted by permission of the author's estate and the agents for that estate, Richard Curtis Associates, Inc.

"Savior," by Robert Reed. Copyright © 1998 by Dell Magazines. First published in *Asimov's Science Fiction*, August 1998. Reprinted by permission of the author.

"Galactic North," by Alastair Reynolds. Copyright © 1999 by Interzone. First published in *Interzone*, July 1999. Reprinted by permission of the author.

"Masque of the Red Shift," by Fred Saberhagen. Copyright © 1965 by Galaxy Publishing Corporation. First published in *If*, November 1965. Reprinted by permission of the author.

"Time Piece," by Joe Haldeman. Copyright © 1970 by Universal Publishing & Distributing Corp. First published in *Worlds of If*, July 1970. Reprinted by permission of the author.

"On the Orion Line," by Stephen Baxter. Copyright © 2000 by Dell Magazines. First published in *Asimov's Science Fiction*, October/November 2000. Reprinted by permission of the author.

CONTENTS

PREFACE

If a realistic appraisal of human nature and the lessons of history leads you, as it has led us, to the reluctant conclusion that as long as human beings are still *human beings* as we understand them, then war—of one sort or another, on one scale or another, in one arena or another—will probably always be part of the human condition . . . and as long as you postulate that our high-tech civilization will remain intact and keep on growing and evolving (instead of suffering some kind of disaster or societal crash—such as a too-catastrophic war, for instance—that dumps us back to the Dark Ages or wipes us out altogether) . . . and if you then assume, as seems likely, that in that high-tech future the human race will continue to expand into space, with more and more people living on the moons and planets of the solar system, and eventually perhaps even reaching toward the stars . . . then, inevitably, one is led to conclude that the future will include *war* in space as well . . . and that therefore *soldiers* will be needed to *fight* those wars in space.

Space soldiers. The poor bastards who will have to put their lives on the line to enforce policies made by politicians millions of miles—or perhaps even millions of light-years—away, the ones who will do the actual fighting, and the dying, whether it's in deep space, on an alien world, or on the airless surface of some frozen moon or asteroid. The ones who by battle's end will be just as dead as their distant comrades on uncountable battlefields back to the dawn of time, no matter that they're killed by a high-intensity plasma burst or the impact of an antimatter pellet rather than by a stone ax. The ones who will have to try to kill some *other* soldier before *they* can succeed in killing *them*, no matter if the weapon they take in hand to do that is a bronze spear or a laser gun. The ones who will wonder if they'll live to see another dawn, whether they're in orbit around a star in the

Vega system or trudging across the frozen surface of one of Jupiter's moons.

These space soldiers will be fighting on battlefields totally unique in the bloody history of warfare, facing tactical problems and technical challenges that no soldier has ever had to face before, wielding weapons that it may be literally impossible for us to imagine, even here at the threshold of the twenty-first century . . . but the nine science fiction writers in this book, daring and expert dreamers, take their best shot at imagining these unimaginable futures *for* you, in the process delivering some of the most exciting, suspenseful, action-packed, and intensely imaginative science fiction ever written.

So turn the page, and enjoy the fictions you'll find here while they *are* still fictions, before they're drafting *you* to take part in a campaign in Luna's Sea of Tranquility, or around the rings of Saturn . . .

(For other stories of high-tech futuristic warfare, try the Ace anthologies *Future War, Invaders!, Hackers,* and *Isaac Asimov's War.*)

THE GARDENS OF SATURN

Paul J. McAuley

Born in Oxford, England, in 1955, Paul J. McAuley now makes his home in London. He is considered to be one of the best of the new breed of British writers (although a few Australian writers could be fit in under this heading as well) who are producing that sort of revamped, updated, widescreen Space Opera sometimes referred to as "radical hard science fiction," and is a frequent contributor to Interzone, *as well as to markets such as* Amazing, The Magazine of Fantasy and Science Fiction, Asimov's Science, When the Music's Over, *and elsewhere. His first novel,* Four Hundred Billion Stars, *won the Philip K. Dick award. His other books include the novels* Of The Fall, Eternal Light, *and* Pasquale's Angel, *two collections of his short work,* The King of the Hill and Other Stories *and* The Invisible Country, *and an original anthology coedited with Kim Newman,* In Dreams. *His acclaimed novel,* Fairyland *won both the Arthur C. Clarke Award and the John W. Campbell Award in 1996. His most recent books are* Child of the River, Ancient of Days, *and* Shrine of Stars, *which compromise a major new trilogy of ambitious scope and scale,* Confluence, *set ten million years in the future.*

In the lushly inventive story that follows, he shows us that sometimes the aftermath of war can be every bit as deadly as the conflict itself . . .

Baker was in the pilots' canteen, talking about the price of trace elements with a couple of factors, when someone started making trouble at the servitor. A tall skinny redhead in baggy flight pants and a tight jumper with the sleeves torn off had hooked her left arm around one of the servitor's staples and was kicking hell out it with her bare feet, bouncing hard each time and coming back, shouting at the machine, "You want how much for this shit?" and kicking it again.

Obviously she hadn't been on Phoebe very long, or she would have known that for all their girder-up-the-ass morals the Redeemers were gougers of the worst kind. It was Baker's nature to try and like everybody, but even he had a hard time being charitable about them. His collective could afford only basic environmental amenities when visiting other habitats, and on Phoebe those were very basic indeed—tank food and a coffin not much bigger than the lifesystem on the scow. If you wanted a shower you paid for two minutes and a hundred liters of grey water; beer or any other luxury goods were available only at premium rates. It was take it or leave it, and everyone had to take it because Phoebe's orbit and the Redeemers' expertise in cargo-handling and routing made it the prime resupply, rendezvous and transfer site in all of the Saturn system.

Baker could have stayed on board his scow, of course, but even he needed to get out and about occasionally. At least here you could raise your arms over your head, and sculling about the public areas cost nothing. And besides, he liked talking to people. He had a lot of friends. He had friends everywhere he went in the system. It was the way he'd been rebuilt.

People all around the canteen started to cheer every kick the woman gave the servitor, happy to get some free entertainment, to see someone vent the frustration they all felt. "That feisty little old thing could come and work me over anytime," one of the factors at Baker's table said; her partner, a scarred and wrinkled woman about a hundred years old, cracked a grin and told her that it would be like setting a Titan tiger against an air cow.

At the same moment, Baker got a tingle of recognition.

Like most of the public areas of the Phoebe habitat, the canteen was a basic microgravity architectural sphere, and Baker was tethered to a table upsidedown above the woman, like a bat hung from the ceiling, but there was something familiar about her . . .

"I have called for help," the servitor said in a monotonal foghorn voice. "Please desist. I have called for help."

The woman grabbed a black cable studded with lenses which had snaked out to peer at her, said "Fuck you," and got a round of applause when she broke it off. People, mostly men, started to shout advice to her, but then everyone fell silent, because one of the supervisors had swum into the canteen.

The creepy thing about the Redeemers wasn't that they all had been chopped to look alike, or that you couldn't tell which had once been male and which female, or even that they all had grey skin the colour of the thermal paint that goes over a hull before its final finish, but that they provided no cues at all as to what they might be feeling.

This one was as long and skinny as the rest, in a one-piece suit that looked as if it was made out of bandages. It moved swiftly, flowing through the air straight at the red-headed woman, who recoiled and said loudly, "This fucking machine sucked the credit out of my chip and won't give it up."

Everyone was looking at her as she hung with one arm casually locked around the one of the staples in the servitor's fascia, her head turned up now to glare at the Redeemer, who kept his place in midair with minute swimming motions of one long, spidery hand, like a reef barracuda wondering whether to attack or pass by, and Baker unclipped his tether because now he knew that he knew her.

Jackson. Vera Flamillion Jackson. Colonel Jackson.

Don't do anything dumb, his sidekick said, and when Baker told it that she was an old friend, it added, Everyone's your friend, but it isn't good to get involved.

The woman was talking fast and low now, stopping when

the Redeemer said something, shaking her head and talking again, her words lost in the hum of the fans which were pushing warm stale air about and the chatter of the people all around. Baker kicked out from the table, turning neatly in midair so he landed right-side-up by the woman, hooking an arm through the same staple from which she hung and seeing her turn and grin, recognizing him at once, as if the past thirty years had never happened.

They exchanged life stories over a couple of bulbs of cold beer. Baker's treat because Jackson had no credit on her. It pretty much wiped out the small amount he'd set aside to spend here; against the advice of his sidekick he'd also paid the fine the Redeemer had insisted on levying. He'd have to check out of the coffin hotel and go sleep on the scow, but he didn't mind. Jackson was an *old* friend, and if he remembered her then once upon a time she must have been important to him.

They'd been teenagers in the war and although Jackson was pushing 50 now, she still looked good. Maybe a little gaunt, and with lines cross-hatching her fine-grained milk-white skin, but she still had a flirtatious way of looking at him from beneath the floating fringe of her red hair. Baker didn't remember too much about his life before the accident, but he remembered that look, and seeing it now made him feel strange. There were black tattoos on her neck and upper arms, crude knotted swirls lacking animation, and she was missing her little finger on her right hand, but, yes, she looked good. She'd been married, he learned, her way of joining a collective that had built a habitat inside a hollowed-out asteroid. That hadn't worked out, she wasn't exactly clear why, and now she was here.

Once or twice their fingers brushed together and he got a tingle as her net tried to access his, but his sidekick blocked the attempts easily. Her net hadn't been modified, it said, and just as well, because she's dangerous.

She's an old friend, Baker insisted, irritated by the sidekick's paranoia. I'm not going to do anything crazy. Just talk about old times, about who I used to be.

What's the point of that? the sidekick said. She's trouble, and don't say I didn't warn you.

"I got bored with it," Jackson was saying, meaning the collective she'd left. "Spending most of the time worrying about stabilizing the ecology. Might as well have settled down on a rock."

"Instead of in one," Baker said, and laughed at his own joke.

"In, out, same thing. Too many people to deal with, too much routine. I mean, have you ever tried to *grow* plants?" Before he could answer, she leaned at the rail of the promenade and added, "You ever get claustrophobic in a place like this?"

They were on one of the upper levels of the Shaft. It had been bored two kilometres into Phoebe's icy mantle with a singleshot fusion laser and was capped with a diamond dome; you could look up through webs and cables and floating islands of plants and see Saturn's small crescent tipped in the black sky. Each level was ringed around with terraced gardens glowing green under sunlamps, neatly planted out with luxury crops, even flowers, level after level of gardens ringing the well of the Shaft. Parts of the upper levels were open to visitors, but most was exclusive Redeemer territory, unknown and unknowable.

Baker said, "I used to help in the farms, but I like what I do now better."

He was married into a collective, but he didn't think he needed to tell her that. It was a business thing; he hardly saw any of his wives or co-husbands from one year to the next and he certainly couldn't fuck anyone in the marriage—or vice versa—without permission from one of the elders. There'd been a sweet honeymoon week with the youngest of the collective's wives, but that had pretty much been it.

That isn't what counts, his sidekick said, and Baker brushed at his ear in annoyance.

Jackson said, "In the war we could go anywhere. That's what I miss."

"Well, we went where we were told."

"Yeah, but we did it our way. We fucked the enemy up pretty good, too. You still see any of the guys?"

"No, not really."

"Me either. Remember Goodluck Crowe? He must surely be dead the way he was going."

Baker shrugged and smiled.

"That time he came in with his bird's venturis fucked, spinning eccentrically? Crashed into one of the ports and the last of his fuel went up and bounced the remains of his ship straight back out? And then he's found down in one of the cargo bays in his p-suit, lost in pitch darkness because his suit light got smashed. The explosion shot him out and he was so dazed he didn't know where he was? He banged up his knee I recall, floating about in there, but that was all."

"Well," Baker said, still smiling, "I guess he went back to Earth."

"How many missions did you fly?"

"I think six." He knew exactly because he'd once paid a data miner to look up his combat record.

She said, "Do you still do that counting thing?"

"Counting thing?"

"You know, with potatoes. One potato, two potato. To count seconds. Three potato, four. You don't remember?"

He had done it out loud, she said, while suppressing the clock functions of his net, claiming that it helped him concentrate on the essential moment. They'd timed him once; over ten minutes he'd deviated by less than a second.

"You don't remember?"

Her gaze was steady, and Baker felt a touch of embarrassment and looked away. She clearly remembered more about him than he did; it was like suddenly finding yourself naked. He said, "It sounds stupid to me. What's the point of trying to do something better than a brainless machine?"

She said, "It's funny. You were listed missing in action,

one of the few casualties on our side. But here you are, and you don't seem much like the man I used to know."

He told her the story. He'd told it so many times now that it was polished smooth and bright. He'd told it so many times that he believed that he remembered what had happened, even though it was a reconstruction. He'd been so badly injured that he had no memory of the accident which had nearly killed him, and only patchy memories of the times before.

Like all combat pilots in the Quiet War, he had been a teenager, picked for his quick reflexes, multi-tasking skills and coolness under pressure. He'd been zipped into a singleship, its lifesystem an integral pressure suit that fed and cleaned him and maintained his muscle tone with patterned electrical stimuli while he flew the ship and its accompanying flock of deadly little remote control drones. Each singleship took a different orbit, swooping through Saturn's rings in complex multiple encounter orbits, attacking flyby targets with the drones when the timelag in the feedback was less than a second, never using the same tactic twice. Like all the combat pilots, Baker had been essentially a telepresence operator infiltrated into the enemy's territory, spending most of his time in Russian sleep with the singleship's systems powered down, waking an hour before the brief high-velocity encounters between drones and target, making a hundred decisions in the crucial few seconds and then vanishing into the rings again. It had been just one front of the Quiet War between the Outer System colonists and the Three Powers Alliance of Earth, less important than the damage done by spies, the economic blitz, and the propaganda campaign.

Saturn's rings were a good place to hide, but they were dangerous, the biggest concentration of rubble and dust in the Solar System, shepherded by tiny moons and tidal resonances into orbits 100,000 kilometres wide and only fifteen deep. Baker's singleship passed and repassed through the rings more than a hundred times, and then a single pinhead-sized bit of rock killed him. It smashed through the thick mantle of airfoam that coated the singleship's hull and punched a neat hole in the hull, breaking up into more than a dozen particles that had all penetrated the six layers of Baker's lifesystem and the gel which cased his sleeping body. Some shattered the artificial-reality visor of his facemask and left charred tracks through his skull and brain; others smashed through the singleship's computer; one ruptured a fuel line.

He'd died without knowing it. but the singleship's computer had saved him. Nanotech in the lifesystem gel sealed ruptured blood vessels; the lifesystem drained his blood and replaced it with an artificial plasma rich in glycoproteins, lowered his body temperature to two degrees. Although the singleship's automatic systems were only partially functional, they powered up its motor, ready to expend its fuel in a last burn to accelerate it into a long-period orbit where it might be retrieved. But most of the fuel had already leaked away and the burn terminated after only a few seconds, leaving the singleship tumbling in a chaotic orbit.

The Quiet War ended a few days later; in the aftermath, there was only a cursory search for the missing singleship. Fifteen years passed before it was spotted by a long-range survey. A collective retrieved it a year later, looking for scrap value and finding Baker. They revived him and used foetal cells to regrow the damaged parts of his brain, upgraded the neural net through which he had interfaced with the singleship and the drones. He had worked for the collective for two years, paying off the debt, and then they had let him marry into their extended family.

At the end of the story, Jackson said, "Well, I guess that out-does Goodluck Crowe. So now you're working for them?"

"I'm a partner."

"Yeah, right. Funny, isn't it? We helped win the Quiet

War, our own governments encouraged us to settle here, and then we were shafted. What do you pilot?"

"A scow. I do freight runs."

"That's just what I mean," Jackson said. "Most of the freight in this system is rail-gunned. You used to be a hot-shot pilot and now you're working the edge, picking up part-cargoes, trading margins on luxury items. I bet they'd use a chip instead of you if they could."

"I choose my own routes. I do business on the Bourse."

"Puttering around, making half a cent a kilo on the marginal price difference of vitamins between Daphoene and Rhea. Hardly the same as combat, is it?"

"I don't remember too much from before my accident," Baker asid amiably. "Are you still a pilot?"

"Well, I guess I'm sort of freelance."

Baker felt a twinge of alarm. His sidekick said, If she asks for credit, you will not give it. I think that she was in the prison farms—the tattoos suggest that. I told you that this was a bad idea.

Something must have shown on his face, because Jackson said, "I have credit. Plenty of it—I'm staying in the Hilton. But, see, it's all *room* credit."

Baker didn't understand.

Be careful, his sidekick said. Here it comes.

"See," Jackson said, her bright blue eyes fixed on his, "I thought I'd walk about for a while. Stretch muscles. Then I wanted a beer, and the fucking machine sucked all the credit from my chip and wouldn't give anything up. Tell me about your ship."

"Hamilton Towmaster, prewar but reconditioned. Daeyo motors, 80,000 kilos thrust. She's a good old flamebucket. She'll probably outlast me."

"You get where you're going?"

"Pretty much anywhere in the system."

Although mostly it was runs back and forth between Titan and Phoebe. The collective was one of the contractors on the Titan project. Titan was lousy with organic, but it was presently one vast storm and would be for another century, until the terraforming began to stabilize, so fixed carbon and other biomass for the construction crews had to be imported from Phoebe's vacuum farms, and that was what Baker mostly hauled.

Jackson sucked on the last of her beer; the thin plastic of the bulb made a crinkling sound as it contracted. She said, "It's a pretty sorry state. Here we are, both of us on the winning side of the war, and the tweaks have got us fucked."

Baker looked around, but luckily none of the incredibly tall, stick-thin people ambling about the promenade with the slow shuffle required by sticky shoes seemed to have heard her. Calling an Outer System colonist a tweak was like calling one of Baker's ancestors a nigger. The original colonists had undergone extensive engineering to adapt them to micorgravity; incomers like Baker made do with widgets in their blood and bones to maintain calcium balance and the like, and in most places in the Outer System medical liability laws ensured that they weren't allowed to have children.

Jackson said, "Ordinary people like us have to stick together. That way we can show the tweaks what real humans can do. The way I see it, the war is still going on."

Baker said, "What is it you do now?"

Jackson crumpled the empty bulb and dropped it over the rail; it fell away slowly towards one of the nets. She said, "Come see where I live these days."

The hotel was two levels down, a terrace landscaped as rolling parkland, with lawns and colorful flowerbeds, and clumps of trees grown into puffy clouds of leaves the way they did in micorgravity. Little carts ambled here and there between the cabins. Baker had been to Phoebe 50 or 60 times but he had never before been here. This was where vips from Earth stayed, along with *novo abastado* industrialists and miners who rendezvoused here to make deals because the Redeemers were scrupulous about commercial confidentiality.

Jackson had to sign Baker in. Blinking on the flash of the retinal print camera, he sat next to her on a cart which took them deep into the level. A sky projection hid the rocky ceiling high above; in the middle air, a couple of people were trolling about on gossamer wings. The guests could hunt here too, Jackson said, although the meat remained the property of the Redeemers.

"You buy a licence to go out and shoot one of the little cows or mammoths they have here, and then you pay all over again if you want a steak."

Baker said, "You ever done it?"

"I've other fish to fry," she said.

He was very aware of her warmth, next to him on the bench seat of the cart, hips and shoulders touching. He was also aware of his sidekick's unhappiness; it hadn't stopped complaining since he'd accepted Jackson's invitation. She's an old friend, Baker told it, and it said; Yes, but everyone is your friend and that's why I give you advice you'd do best to listen to.

But Jackson *was* an old friend, a very special friend. A war comrade, maybe even a lover. Although Baker didn't remember anything specific, sitting next to her he definitely felt that they had once had something special, and she certainly seemed to think so. For all the edge she tried to put into her voice and body-language, her trust was quite wonderfully naïve.

The cart rolled over neatly-trimmed green grass at a leisurely walking pace and circled around a big stand of bamboos and yellow-flowered mimosa, and there was one of the cabins, a dome turfed over with grass, little round windows like rabbit holes glinting here and there. A door dilated as the cart approached, and then they were inside a big room with carpet all over the walls and pits for places to sit or sleep. When Baker remarked on the size of the place,

Jackson said that it didn't matter how big a cell it was, it was still a cell.

"I though this was cool at first," she said, "but I'd just upgraded is all. I'm still stuck here, but I think now I know a way out."

The sidekick had started to complain again. Baker winced and, something he hardly ever did, switched it to stand-by mode. The silence was a relief; he gave Jackson a goofy smile which obviously puzzled her.

She said, "You'll see who I work for, then you'll get an idea of what I mean."

They put on sticky shoes and shuffled down a long curved ramp into a lower level, coming out in a room that was all white tiles and bright light, with a circular pool of polystyrene balls rippling back and forth, something big and pink half-buried in them. Some kind of animal Baker thought, and then it spoke and he realized that it was a man, the fattest man he'd ever seen, masked with artificial-reality goggles and twiddling his hands this way and that.

"Time to wake up," Jackson said loudly. "I'm back, Berry, and I've brought a friend."

The fat man cut the air with a hand; his goggles unfilmed. "Where have you been?" he said, his voice childish and petulant.

"I was out on an errand," Jackson said, her voice echoing off the tiles, "but I'm back now. Do you need anything?"

"Didn't know where you were," the man said.

"Well, here I am now. You been lying there all this time? You'll lose the use of your legs."

"Help me to the surface if you want," the man said, "but not right now. I'm deep in the Ten Thousand Flower Rift. I think I might get through to the Beasts's chateau this time."

He rose and fell with the big, slow waves that rolled from one side of the pool of polystyrene balls to the other and back again. There was a little machine floating in the air close by his head, holding a bulb of thick white liquid, and he lifted his face now and sucked at a straw noisily.

Jackson said quietly to Baker, "So now you see who I work for."

"He's got to be the fattest man I've ever seen. Massing, golly, it must be 200 kilos at least."

"One hundred sixty. He tends to spread out a bit lying down."

"What does he do?"

"Mostly he just lies right there and runs these antique 200-year-old sagas and drinks, or lies around on grass and runs his sagas and drinks. That's margarita mix he's working on there, he gets through a couple of liters of that a day. And he uses other stuff, too. He does his drugs, lying buck naked there or out on the grass under the sunlamps. They have some UV in their spectrum, so I have to rub cream on him to stop him burning. He can get about if he has to, but it hurts him even in microgravity, so he mostly stays on his back. There're air jets under the balls, help him stay afloat."

"I mean, who is he? How can he afford all this?"

"Berry Malachite Hong-Owen; his mother is Sri Hong-Owen. That doesn't mean anything to you? She invented one of the two important vacuum organism photosynthetic systems, made her rich as all hell. Berry is her son by her first and only marriage, a reject with a trust fund, doesn't have to do anything but let the money roll in." Jackson raised her voice and said, "You all right there, Berry? I got a bit of business with my friend here. You shout if you want anything."

Back up in the dome, Baker and Jackson sipped bulbs of a smoky brandy. Jackson lit a marijuana cigarette, too—Berry could afford the tax, she said.

Baker said, "How did you get the job? It looks like fun."

Jackson didn't answer for a moment, holding a volume of smoke before blowing it out and saying in a small, tight voice, "Fun? The one other thing Berry likes to do is fuck. He can manage it in microgravity, just about, although it takes some care." She fixed Baker with her bright blue eyes, daring him to say something. When he didn't, she took another drag and said through the smoke, "That's part of what I was doing before I met him—the fucking Redeemers sell you a prostitute's licence and you pay tax on every bit of business. I may be old, but some of the tweaks do like the exotic. The rest of the time I was part of the gardening crew, moving bushes and trees here and there, replanting flower beds. I didn't have much choice—I lost my ticket off through a piece of foolishness. I got to hear of Berry and did some research, and made myself indispensable to him. He likes older women—I think he misses his mother. But the fucker's crafty. His trust fund pays for room and service, but he doesn't have anything much in the way of transferable credit. Doesn't need it, he says, because he never leaves the hotel."

"Doesn't he pay you?"

"He did at first, but then I was living here and I told him to save his credit. It wasn't that much anyway, not enough to parlay up for any kind of good ticket and I don't fancy leaving here as a corpsicle in steerage."

Baker began to see where this was going, and felt a twinge of pleasurable excitement. He had been right to think that there might be something in this, and it could well fall within the very wide parameters which allowed him to operate without consulting the collective. He said cautiously, "The thing is, the ship isn't exactly mine."

"I'm not looking for a lift," Jackson said leaning forward through her cloud of smoke. "I'm looking for a partner in a deal so sweet it could rot your teeth just thinking about it. Let me tell you about Berry."

Berry's mother, Sri Hong-Owen, was a gene wizard with a shadowy, mysterious history. The system of artificial photosynthesis she had invented had made her as rich and famous as her rival, Avernus, but she had also done a lot of covert work before and after the Quiet War. Before the war, she was rumoured to have set up an illegal experiment in accelerated evolution of vacuum organisms somewhere in the Kuiper Belt for the Democratic Union of China; during the war, she had helped design the biowar organisms which had taken Europa, and she was said to have been involved in a covert program of human engineering. And after the war, she had announced that she was retiring (which no one believed), and had taken advantage of the resettlement scheme to take up residence at the edge of the ring system of Saturn.

"Potato One and Two," Jackson said. "Remember?"

"Sure, but they're just a couple of rocks, something to do with the military, I think. Anyway, no one lives there."

"That's what they want everyone to think," Jackson said.

Potato One and Two were the nicknames of a pair of co-orbital satellites, tiny chunks of rock which had probably been shattered off a larger body by some ancient impact. Their orbits were within 50 kilometres of each other, beyond the edge of the F Ring. Sri Hong-Owen lived in absolute seclusion on the larger moon, Janus; she had registered the smaller, Epimetheus, as an experimental area. Berry had left—or had been thrown out—ten years ago; the other son by her failed marriage, Alder Topaz Hong-Owen, was working somewhere on Earth, perhaps as liasion with whichever government or *corporado* was sponsoring his mother's current work. She had good and influential connections in the Three Powers Occupation Force; Jackson said that it was likely she was working on some covert military engineering program. The two moons were off-limits, protected by fierce automatic defence systems, but Berry had the right to return there.

Jackson told Baker, "Berry misses her badly. He talks about her a lot, but there's something which stops him returning. I think he was kinked, given some sort of conditioning. He has the codes which will get us through her defence system, and I know what they are—it didn't take anything more than withholding his margarita ration for a couple of days. We can say that he paid us to bring him back, ask for money to take him away again. It's like kidnaping, but in reverse."

"Suppose she doesn't pay up?"

Baker didn't need the prompting of his sidekick to know that Jackson wasn't telling him the whole story, not that it really mattered if his own scheme worked out, but he found that he liked the illicit thrill of becoming involved in her shady plot. Perhaps this was the way he had felt in the brief moments of combat, all those years ago before the accident had changed his life for ever.

Jackson shrugged. "She doesn't pay, then we say we'll kill him, or we'll think of doing some damage to her experiments. But really, why wouldn't she pay? Who'd want Berry around all the time?"

Baker and Jackson got Berry out of the pool of polystyrene balls and helped him totter on shaky legs up the ramp to the outside. He flopped down on the grass like a pink barrage balloon and demanded that Jackson rub cream into his skin. That took a while, Berry grunting and sometimes giggling as Jackson rubbed coconut-scented cream into the hectares of his pink flesh. Baker was pretty sure it would end in some kind of sex and wandered off, taking big floating steps, and found some shade under a stand of umbrella trees. A herd of miniature red-haired mammoths was grazing off in the distance, moving in tentative tip-toe slow motion. A vine twisted around one of the umbrella trees and Baker picked at its grapes, each a slightly different flavour bursting on his tongue, wondering if he should reactivate his sidekick. The truth was, he didn't want to hear what it would say; it wasn't programmed to take risks. He used his net to dial into Phoebe's infoweb, and did a little research of his own. At last Jackson floated down beside him and told him that Berry was asleep.

"So," she said, "will you do it?"

"Remind me of the percentages again."

"Twenty per cent goes to you, less any costs. But that's still a lot of credit."

"Sure. I mean, yes, count me in."

He realized that he'd been thinking about it while seeming not to think about anything at all. His net was very sophisticated. It was risky, but the potential—not the silly scheme of Jackson's—was huge.

Jackson leaned over and kissed him; he kissed her back.

"He's sleeping now," she said, after a while. "All that drinking and floating and floating and drinking does tire him out."

"He hasn't asked why I'm here?"

"I said you were my brother. He accepted that. Berry doesn't like to think too hard about things. He's like a kid. When he wakes up he'll want a drink, and I'll put something in it that'll keep him quiet so we can get him aboard."

"We have to take him?"

"I don't like it either. But it's the only way we can file a flight plan, and we'll need to prove that we really do have him when we get there."

Once they were aboard the scow and had everything squared away Jackson stripped off her jumper and trousers and they fucked. Baker couldn't think of it as making love; it was as much a business transaction as his wedding night with the youngest wife of the collective. Jackson wanted to interface systems during sex, the way they used to, or so she claimed, but Baker held back. She fell straight asleep afterwards, and Baker thought about it all over again, looking for loose threads and unexpected angles.

They had gone aboard late at night. Jackson had slipped a tranquilizer into Berry's nightcap and he had fallen asleep almost immediately. They had used a luggage cart to get him to the docks, no problem there; the Redeemers didn't care what was loaded onto ships as long as they got their tax. That was another reason why Phoebe was so successful.

There hadn't been a problem stowing Berry away, either; Jackson had already thought of that.

As for the rest, the run itself was fairly simple, and Baker had already filed a flight plan, getting clearance with Berry's identity code just as Jackson had said he would. If Sri Hong-Owen had an agent in the intelligence network of the pan-Saturn flight control system, she'd already know someone was on the way; she might already be taking counter-measures. Baker would have to think of what she might do, and how to get around it.

He was scared but also elated. After going over every-thing in his head, he could at last fall asleep.

But when he woke up, things had gone badly wrong.

He woke up because Jackson was slapping him, slapping his face, slapping him hard in a back-and-forth rhythm with the same angry intensity with which she had attacked the servi-tor, saying over and over, "You fucker. Come on out of it, you fucker. Come on. Don't die on me."

He tried to get away but he was trussed like a food an-imal in the web hammock in the centre of the scow's com-pact lifesystem. Jackson's left hand gripped his right wrist tightly. His head hurt badly and behind the pain there was a terrible absence. Stuff hung in front of Jackson's angry, intent, face—columns, indices, a couple of thumbnails. She had jacked her net into his, broken into it using some kind of Trojan horse, and was using it to run the ship. Hand-hold-ing, the pilots had called it, a kind of piggy-backing that had been used in training.

The soundscape of the scow had changed. Beneath the ususal whir of fans, the steady chug of the humidifier and the nearly subliminal hum of the lights was the intermittent thump of attitude thrusters and a chorus of pings and pop-ping noises.

Barker jerked his head back so that Jackson's next blow missed; she swung halfway around with the momentum. "What," he said, so full of fear that he thought for a mo-ment he would start to cry. He swallowed something salty and said, "What have you done?"

"You work it out," she said, and let go of his wrist and turned her back on him.

It took him less than a second to call up the data. The scow was in orbit around Phoebe, docked with its chain of cargo pods and slowly rotating in barbecue mode.

A thumbnail picture showed the patchwork of the little moon's tightly curving globe. Only 200 kilometres in diameter, it was a captured unmodified primitive object, mostly carbonaceous material mixed with water ice, almost entirely grown over with vacuum organisms which used the energy of sunlight to turn methane ice and carbonaceous tars formed five billion years ago, when the Solar System had first condensed, into useful carbon compounds. The patches were of all shapes but only four muted colours; orange-brown, reddish-brown, sooty black, mottled grey. Phoebe was like a dented and battered patchwork ball or a gigantic version of the four-colour map problem, curving away sharply in every direction.

Another thumbnail showed Berry floating in faint red light, half-filling the scow's water tank. An air mask was clamped over his face. Baker had objected to Jackson's idea on hygiene grounds, but she had pointed out that the water was recycled anyway, and the filter system could easily be rerouted to clean the water coming out of the tank as well as that going in. Berry seemed to be asleep, curled up like a huge late-term embryo, the umbilical cord of airline and nutrient feed connected to his face rather than his belly, hands clasped piously under his chins, a continuous chain of bubbles trickling from the vent of his air mask.

Baker clicked everything off. Jackson was hunched up at the far end of the cramped lifesystem, an arm's length away. She had livid marks on her throat and deep scratches on her arms were still oozing blood into the air. She said, "You almost died. Your net shut down your vagus reflexes when I hacked it. And when I tried to revive you, you tried to kill me. Don't you know what they did to you?"

"You shouldn't have messed with it," Baker said.

"I did it to free you!"

Jackson's face was pinched white, harsh and old-looking;

only her bright blue eyes seemed alive. She shuddered all over and said more quietly, "They made you into a slave. A *thing*."

They had both had military neural nets installed when they had been inducted, but Baker's net had been considerably upgraded after his accident; it was now more like a symbiont than a machine enhancement of his nervous system. When Jackson had jacked into it, she had been able to access only a few of its functions. She had got the ship up into orbit, and docked manually with the train of cargo pods, but she hadn't been able to activate the flight plan he'd filed. And when she had tried to hack into its root directory, his net had easily repelled her efforts and had triggered a number of defence routines.

Baker said, "Why are you doing this? Aren't we friends?"

"Because I'm tired of giving blow-jobs to Berry. Because I can't bear to see an old comrade turned into a zombie so dumb he doesn't even know what he is. Because I was in prison in Angola for ten years and I'd sooner die than go back."

Half of the Redeemers' business was running the port. The other half was running the correctional facilities for the Saturn system—the vacuum farms. Angola was the worst of them; eight out of ten prisoners died before completing their sentence.

Baker said, "Well, I did wonder about the tattoos. What were you in for?"

"Just load and run the flight plan," Jackson said, and smiled bloodlessly. "Okay, maybe I got greedy and fucked up. I need you, and I won't let you back out."

Baker said, "I wasn't your first choice of pilot, was I? You had an agreement with someone else, and I bet that's why you were in the pilots' canteen. But then you saw me, and thought you could make a better deal."

"I still rescued you," she said.

"How much were you going to get? From the first deal."

"It was the same as the one we made, except I was to

get the 20-percent cut. But that's blown away. We're in this together or we're both dead, and Berry too. Your call."

It might be a bluff, but Jackson didn't look like the kind of person who would start something she couldn't finish. Baker pulled down the flight plan, checked it over out of habit, and activated it.

The rumble of the scow's motor filled the lifesystem. Acceleration gripped Baker; he drifted gently onto the padding at the rear of the cabin. Jackson hooked an arm around a staple and stared at him from what was now definitely the ceiling. And in the tank, Berry woke up amidst clashing pressure waves which distorted the red light into clashing lines and sheets and plaintively asked what was going on.

Neither Baker nor Jackson slept during the 65 hours of the flight. Their military nets could keep them awake for more than a week, switching consciousness back and forth between the right and left hemispheres of their brains. Sometimes Baker would feel a little sluggish and his saliva would taste strange, but there were no other side effects.

Jackson didn't stay mad at him, but she remained wary. It wasn't his fault that she had activated the defence routines. They were there to protect the collective's investment. He told her this, and that he was happy and liked the life he had been given, but it only provoked a torrent of abuse. He wished that he had his sidekick to explain things, to help sort out the muddle, but Jackson had suppressed it—he had the horrible feeling that she had in fact erased it. When he asked her about this, she said that it was time that he started thinking for himself. He could never be the man he'd been when she had known him, but he could be his own man now.

She did unbend enough to tell him a little of her life. While he had been drifting in the crippled singleship, neither alive nor dead, she had used her sign-off pay to start up a haulage company. When that had failed, outcompeted by rail guns, she had joined a collective long enough to know that it wasn't for her, and then had become a smuggler, intercepting packages of forbidden technologies in the rings while on apparently innocent cargo runs. An industrial spy had broken up the cartel she had mostly worked for, and someone in the cartel had given her up to protect himself, and that was how she had ended up in the vacuum farms of Phoebe.

She was still bitter about it. During the Quiet War, the Outer System colonists, split into more than a dozen rival enclaves, had hardly been able to fight back at all. In only three months, their infrastructures had been so devastated that they had been forced to surrender their hegemony. But what had happened since made you wonder who had really won after all, Jackson said. The tweaks had the upper hand in the Outer System, even if their various assemblies, moots, councils, conclaves and congresses were now in principle subservient to the Three Powers Occupying Force. Despite incentives and tax breaks, the various emigration schemes sponsored by the victors of the Quiet War had mostly failed; new settlers couldn't compete with established co-operatives and collectives, and unless they signed away their right to return to Earth in exchange for engineering they were not allowed to have children and tended to die young of problems associated with living in microgravity. Meanwhile, the central administration of the Outer System was falling apart as adapted colonists began to spread through the thousands of dirty snowballs and rocks of the Kuiper Belt. There was talk of another war, one in which Jackson wouldn't be able to fight. She was too old and slow for combat now; she had been sidelined by history.

Baker listened patiently to her rants. He tried to talk with Berry, too, but Jackson had set up a feed of lemon-flavored alcohol and the man was only partly coherent. In one of his more lucid moments, he said, "You shouldn't go near my mother. She's dangerous. All of her are dangerous."

"You mean she has other children?"

"You could call them that," Berry said. "They're crazy

bad." His voice, muffled by the airmask, sounded as if it was coming from the bottom of a well.

"How many brothers and sisters do you have?"

"It isn't like that. Alder would know, I guess . . . They look after me, always have, so maybe they're not so bad. Not to me. They saved me other times . . ."

Baker felt a faint stirring, as if his sidekick was about to waken. He wished it would, if only to say that it told him so. When nothing happened, he said, "Other times? What happened, Berry?"

Berry was silent for a while. Then he said, "I should get out of here now. My skin is all puffy."

Baker tried to imagine what the lifesystem would be like with 160 kilos of dripping wet Berry crammed into it. He said, "You hang in there. Play your sagas."

"It isn't the same," Berry said. "The emulation in this system is horrible. When can you get me back to the hotel?"

"Well, I'm not sure. Soon."

"I'd like margarita. That always goes down smooth."

"Maybe you should stop drinking."

"What's the point of stopping? Get me some margarita and I might help you out."

Jackson was amused by Baker's attempts to talk with Berry. She said that you couldn't get any sense out of the man. His brain had been fried in alcohol, most of the switches jammed open or jammed closed, whole areas dead and blasted. Like a low-grade robot, he could follow his routines, but had trouble with anything outside them.

"You want to know anything, you ask me," she said.

Baker thought that he had already learnt something useful from Berry. He said, "What will happen after we insert into orbit?"

"I'll tell you on a need-to-know basis, just like the old times."

But the old times were gone for ever. His original self must have loved her fiercely for a residue of that love to have survived death, and Baker, who was vicariously fascinated by other peoples' lives, and watched a lot of the old psychodramas when he wasn't working, thought wistfully that once upon a time they must have been like Romeo and Juliet. But whatever they'd once been, that was then and this was now.

The scow accelerated for more than 40 hours. The idea was to come in on a fast, short trajectory, decelerating hard at the last moment. Baker spent much of that time watching the view, a thumbnail of the lifesystem in one corner to let him keep a eye on Jackson—he was worried that she might suddenly try something stupid.

Phoebe's orbit was not only retrograde, but inclined to the equatorial plane of Saturn. As the scow drove inwards, the entire system was spread out ahead and below, nine major moons and more than a hundred smaller bodies, Saturn a pale half-disc at the centre, circled by his rings like an exquisite bit of jewellery.

Baker never tired of this privileged view. He spent a lot of time watching it while working through his options. He wasn't as brain-damaged as Jackson thought, and the enhancements to his net gave him a lot of computational power. He worked up several scenarios and played the simulations over and over, finally choosing the simplest one with a sense of doors closing irrecoverably behind him. He wondered if Jackson had inserted a parasitic eavesdropper into his net; if she had, she gave no sign that she knew what he was planning.

As Saturn grew closer, the ring system began to resolve details in the sunlit arc that swept out beyond the planet; two unequal halves separated by the gap of the Cassini division, each half further divided into fine parallel bands, with dark irregular spokes in the bright B ring that could be seen to rotate if watched long enough.

Then the motor cut out and they were in freefall again. There were only a couple of hours in turnover. Jackson spent much of them supervising the decoupling of the scow from the cargo train. Normally it would recouple on the other end of the train, thrusters pointing ahead for deceleration. But Jackson's manual link closed down halfway through the manoeuvre and scow fired off several orientation bursts, turned end-for-end and immediately lit its main engines in a brief burn. At the same time, the thrusters of the cargo train started to fire.

Berry started complaining over the link; Jackson snarled at him to shut up and was suddenly right in Baker's face, swarming down the lifesystem cabin against the pull of the thrust and grabbing his right wrist. A Trojan horse smashed its way into his net, spilling voracious subroutines. For a panicky minute he was deaf and dumb and blind—it was like being raped from the inside out.

Light and sound came back. Baker discovered that he was in freefall again. Jackson had shoved away from him and was studying him intently, her blue eyes cold behind the tendrils of red hair that drifted loose over her face.

Baker closed up all the indices and files she'd pulled open and said shakily, "You shouldn't have done that."

"Christ, they really did a number on you, Baker. You're not a man any more. You're a bundle of routines. You're a lapdog. This is your chance to get free of the leash, and you're fucking it up."

Baker's net was suppressing adrenalin production; otherwise he would have been trembling with flight reaction and stinking up the lifesystem with sweat. He said. "We're in this together. I've accepted that. I thought it would be a good idea to dump the cargo in a high orbit. Makes us more manoeuvrable and saves reaction mass. We'll get there earlier than the flight plan allows, so we can surprise Berry's mother."

It was the best lie he had been able to come up with. He sipped at a bulb of orange-flavored glucose solution and watched her work it through. At last, she said. "I know you're trying to fuck me over, but I can't figure out how, not yet. But I will, and then I'll know what to do with you. Meanwhile, climb into your pressure suit. There's a chance that Berry's mother might have changed her defence systems since he left."

"I thought you got the codes from him. And she knows we're bringing him here."

"The codes are 20 years old, and she might not believe us. We've got 15 minutes before the main burn, so get moving."

They only just made it.

The scow, decelerating, fell behind the cargo train. The string of half-silvered beads dwindled against the sweep of the rings, vanishing into the planet's shadow as the scow swung in around the nightside. Vast lightning storms illuminated sluggish bands of storm systems that could have swallowed Earth without a ripple. Then the rings appeared, a silver arc ahead of the dawning diamond point of the sun. The scow's motor rumbled continuously, decelerating at just over one gravity. Baker was heavier than he had been for years. Lying flat on the padding of the lifesystem, he tried to find a comfortable position within his pressure suit to wait it out, but there always seemed to be some seam or wrinkle digging into him. Jackson lay beside him, her unloved right hand holding his unloved left so that she could access the ship through his net. They lay there like spent lovers.

"Seems hard to remember how we stood this on Earth," Baker said at one point. "I almost envy Berry, floating in that tank."

"Just keep quiet," Jackson said. "I'm watching everything. If something goes wrong, you're toast."

She didn't say it with much conviction, Baker thought. For the first time, he felt that he might have a chance to win back from this. It was clear that she hadn't been able to work out what he'd done. He felt pity for her—she was out-of-date, left behind by the accelerating changes that were sweeping through the Outer System. She should have returned to Earth; out here, the aggression which had helped win the Quiet War was not a survival trait. Individualism counted for nothing in the Outer System. To survive, you had to commit yourself to helping others, who in turn would help you.

Baker said, "What's wrong? You said you remembered how good I was. I'm even better now."

"I remember you always thought you were a hotshot, but didn't have much to back it up. You were a company man, Baker, even when you were in the service. You were always happiest following orders. You had no initiative. That's one thing about you that hasn't changed."

"Nothing you can say can hurt me more than what you tried to do to me," Baker said, with a fair imitation of wounded pride, thinking that *her* initiative had got her into prison, and now into this. He pulled down the view to shut her out.

The rings spanned the curve of the planet in a thousand shades of grey and brown and white, casting a shadow across the bulge of its equator. The scow was coming in at a narrow angle above the plane of the rings, and they spread to port like a highway a million lanes wide. Zooming in with the scow's telescope, Baker could see the seemingly solid plane break apart in lanes of flecks that grew into rocks and bergs flashing in the sunlight as they tumbled, a storm of motes forever falling around the planet.

The scow plunged stern-first towards the gap beyond the outer edge of the narrow F ring. Jackson started a looped broadcast of the code she had dug out of Berry. Their target was still around the curve of the planet, coming towards them out of night; they'd rendezvous with it just at its dawn. Baker wanted to look for the cargo train, but wasn't sure that he could do it without Jackson catching on.

"I was wondering," he said, after a while, "what you'll do if this works out."

"That's none of your fucking business."

"We might not survive it."

"I intend to. You could have set yourself free, Baker."

"Things have changed."

"This is the frontier, Baker. It's far from the antfarms of Earth. It's where people can walk tall and make their fortunes if they have the intelligence and the backbone."

"Or end in the vacuum farms."

"I had some bad luck. I'm going to turn that around. You might be content to give up your free will to a bunch of farmers who sit inside rocks like bugs in a bad apple. Well, I'm not."

She said more, but Baker tuned it out. The scow was just about to begin its final course correction. He patched telescope scans into a 360-degree perspective. The rings stretched away ahead and behind, flattened into a narrow line that bisected the sky. A single speck was bracketed ahead: their target.

Janus was roughly the same size as Phoebe, an irregular body like the profile of a fist. It was pockmarked with craters, most eroded by billions of years of micrometeorite sleet and further softened by patches of vacuum organism growth. One small circular crater had been tented over, and shone greenly with internal lights. There was a ring of silver around it. The scow spotted one of the defence drones a hundred kilometres out and presented Baker with a grainy image of the tiny, deadly thing: a slim body less than two metres long, with a flat radar dish at one end and the swollen bowl of an oversized motor at the other. No radar probed the scow; nothing moved to intercept it. The broadcast code must be working.

The scow shuddered, spinning this way and that, making a series of short burns before finally shutting down its motor. Now it was falling in the same orbit as the little moon, barely 20 kilometres away.

Jackson started what seemed to be a one-sided conversation—she had made contact with someone on Janus, it seemed, but she wouldn't allow Baker to switch into the channel.

"I have him right here," she said, "just like I told you.

You must know he's aboard—that's why I could shut down your defence drones. Don't try and target me manually, the ship will blow up if radar locks on it. Because he asked me to, don't let's go into all that again. Well, I expect that he misses you all. Yes, I can bring evidence, but it might be easier if you came up here, or I landed the ship. Well, okay, that's fine by me too. Creepy little fucker," she added, turning to Baker.

"Can you really blow up the ship?"

"Only if it's absolutely necessary."

"That was Berry's mother you were talking with?"

"Some kind of agent, I think. It wants me to go down there with evidence I brought Berry back."

Jackson sealed up her pressure suit but did not go out through the airlock; instead, she opened an internal access hatch and plunged into the water tank. Berry was supine. She had added a relaxant to his alcohol mix. Baker watched as she snipped off the little finger from Berry's right hand and came back out.

"It has to be fresh," she said, grinning at Baker through her helmet's visor. She was pumped up with excitement. "That way she'll know we're not kidding. You're not going to give me any trouble, are you?"

"Maybe you had better tell me what you've thought of."

"We're going down together. And if I see any sign that the ship is moving out of orbit, I'll blow it."

"I should stay here with Berry."

"And have you swing the ship around and torch me?"

"I wouldn't do that. I'm in this with you."

"You'd better be, because you're going to be my backup. They're expecting one person. You'll be a surprise. They won't know who you are or what you'll be doing while I walk in there."

They used a little jet unit to pull them across, touching down two kilometres from the tented crater, which was somewhere beyond the close, sharply-curved horizon. Except for his annual safety certification exercises, Baker had hardly ever done any vacuum work. His p-suit was intelligent and responsive, but a residual stiffness blunted his reflexes; he let go a moment too soon and tumbled end for end when he touched down on the little moon's surface.

He tumbled a fair way—in Janus's microgravity, he could bounce a couple of hundred metres off the surface with the gentlest of kicks. At last the suit fired a grapple and he slewed to a halt with a cloud of dust raining straight down all around. He was at the edge of a dense field of tall black blades that sloped away to the close horizon. Some reached up to four metres; all grew from thick rhizomes that snaked half-buried through the dusty regolith; all had turned the flat surfaces of their blades towards the sun's yellow spark.

Jackson threw a camo cloth over the jet unit and crept towards Baker on her belly, supple as a snake in her yellow p-suit. She checked him over and began to assemble a hollow tube and a scaffold cradle from components she had strapped to her back-pack.

"What are you doing?"

"It's amazing what you can get in the way of surplus weaponry, if you have the credit. This is a missile launcher. The Europans made them to shoot down drones like the ones we operated, only they didn't have time to deploy them before the hydrogen bomb broke open the crust. I paid for this through Berry's room service. It fires up to ten smart micromissiles, but I only need two. One is aimed at the scow, the other at the dome over the horizon.

"Ah. I thought you were joking about blowing up the ship."

Jackson said flatly, "I don't joke about business."

She started to adjust the angle of the tube by minute increments, finally sitting back in a squat. "It's running, ready to go in three hours. Try and move it now and the charge will explode. Try and rip out the chip that controls it—same thing. The only way to stop it is to use a code. You think I'm a fuck-up, but I know what I'm doing here."

Baker couldn't see Jackson's face because the sun was

reflecting off the gold-tinted visor of her helmet, but he could imagine her tigerish grin. He said, "I don't doubt it."

"You stay right there. I'll be telling them that you'll fire the mortar at any sign of trouble, so don't stray. And remember that I'm linked to the ship just like you. Try anything—especially try and close down my link—and I'll blow her. Sit tight. Enjoy the view. I'll be back soon."

Baker sat tight, watching Saturn's crescent slowly wax above the sharp, irregular edge of the horizon. Like almost all of Saturn's moons, Janus was tidally locked, and kept one face permanently turned towards its primary. Sri Hong-Owen had sited her home at the edge of sub-Saturnian hemisphere; Saturn stood permanently at the horizon, his rings arching beyond his banded crescent like the string of a drawn bow—he dominated half the sky, shedding a bilious light over the pockmarked slope. Janus was so small that wherever you looked the ground appeared to slope away—Baker felt that he was hugging the top of a hill that was plunging towards Saturn's storms, a hill studded with half-buried boulders of all sizes which cast multicolored shadows. In the other direction, the outer ring system scratched a thin arch across the width of the sky, with several of the moons bright against a dusting of stars. There was Dione, which had its own satellite trailing at 60 degrees of arc in the same orbital path; there was the tiny crescent of Titan, lit not only by the Sun but by the terraforming fusion lamps hung in equatorial orbit.

Baker wondered what it would be like when Janus was overtaken by its co-orbital moon, Epimetheus. Passing only 50 kilometres away, Epimetheus would eclipse Saturn and exchange a fraction of its momentum with Janus; the two moons would swap orbits and Janus would slowly accelerate away in the lower orbit. The orbital exchange happened every four years, and was not a stable configuration; in slightly under ten million years the two moons would collide, and it was thought that the fragments would eventually coalesce into a single body.

He thought his plan through again. With the insurance of the cargo train, he was pretty sure that he could get out of this alive. The rest was as imponderable as ever, but he was confident that he could make some friends here. That was what he was good at, after all. Of course, he'd underestimated Jackson, and it was only pure dumb luck that she hadn't upgraded her net—otherwise he was pretty sure that she would have disposed of him as soon as she had control of the scow. But Jackson wasn't the problem now. He was pretty sure that she would be killed as soon as she walked into the habitat. Although it certainly increased his chance of survival, part of him—the fragmented bits of his old self—wished that he'd warned her.

The p-suit's lifesystem made comforting hums and soft hisses; it was like being inside a tent exactly his size.

Baker broke radio silence to try and talk with Berry, but the man was gurgling inside his mask, drunk or asleep, and wouldn't answer.

He tried that counting trick: *one potato, two potato, three potato, four.* Tested it against the system clock of his net, tried different intonations, couldn't get it to come out right. Maybe it was just a story Jackson had spun to draw him in. It didn't matter. He didn't need dumb tricks like that, not any more.

Time passed. Baker had always been calm in the squeeze of danger—to his way of thinking, there was no sense in getting caught up in useless speculation, it was best to face any situation with an uncluttered mind. In any case, there was nothing he could do until either Jackson came back or Berry's mother came for him. He set up a couple of alarms on his p-suit's system and fell asleep.

And woke an hour later to find four pressure-suited figures kneeling by him, visors blankly reflecting the grey-brown moonscape. They were as small as children. A fifth figure was examining Jackson's missile launcher.

Baker tried to sit up, and discovered that his suit was bound by a thousand tough, tightly-wrapped fibres. He squashed the first tremors of alarm and said as calmly as he could, "There's a couple of things you should know."

The ring of silver around the tented crater was a plantation of things like flowers, tough wiry stalks five metres tall rising straight out of dusty ice, each bearing a single big white dish-shaped bloom with a black cylinder protruding from its centre. The dishes were all turned in one direction, towards the setting sun. It was pitch black beneath the packed dishes, but Baker's captors carried him at the same fast gliding gait with which they'd crossed the open ground.

Just as he was carried out of the far side of the plantation, Baker thought he saw a flash at the horizon, and wondered if that had been the missile launcher. Then he and his captors plunged down a steep terraced slope, following a path sketched in dabs of green fox-fire. Baker didn't ask where they were taking him. He was just grateful that so far he had not been killed.

The slope became a tunnel, hung from floor to ceiling with a thousand stiff black curtains that must have formed a pressure lock, because the tunnel suddenly opened up at the lip of a huge bowl of greenery under a thousand brilliant lamps, with flocks of what looked like birds floating lazily at different layers in the air, Saturn a blank-faced giant peering in at the construction diamond tent which capped the vast space.

Baker's pressure-suited captors dropped him at the edge of the bowl and threw themselves over the drop, bouncing like balls from terrace to terrace and finally vanishing into a stand of tree ferns. Baker's bonds slowly dissolved, snapping apart like brittle elastic as he picked himself up.

A woman was moving towards him through the air above the green gulf, sitting on a throne borne up by what looked like cherubs. She was not Sri Hong-Owen but one of her daughters. She was young, golden-skinned and unselfconsciously naked. She had a tweak's etiolated build, her long arms and legs skinny but supple, her breasts no more than enlarged nipples on her prominent rib cage. A cloud of black hair floated around her narrow face.

When Baker asked her name, she smiled and said that no names were needed here, where all were one mind, one flesh. He asked then where her mother was, and the golden-skinned woman told him that she had moved on, which at first Baker took to mean *died.*

"Alder descended to the Earth to continue our mother's work there," the woman said, "and Berry went his own way. He is only our half-brother, and is weak-minded, but we love him anyway. Our mother would have killed him, we think, but she no longer needs to make small decisions like that, and we decided to show mercy."

"How many are you?"

Baker had unlatched the helmet of his p-suit and stood with it tucked under his arm, like an old-fashioned knight in front of his enthroned queen. The cherubs had flown away—they had little patience, the woman had said when they left, being full of the joy of life lived moment to moment.

"There are more than enough of us to deal with you or anyone else who tries to invade our kingdom," she told Baker now. "We have killed many in the last 20 years—spies, pirates, adventurers, the merely curious. But you are the first to think of kidnaping Berry, and you are the first to threaten our mother. How did you know?"

"Luck, I guess," Baker said, wondering what he was supposed to have guessed.

The woman leaned forward, gazing intently at him through her floating tangle of black hair. "Berry is not dead."

Her gaze compelled. Baker said, "No. No, not when I left him."

"Then you are luckier than you know," the woman said.

"What about Jackson?"

"Was that her name?"

"You killed her, didn't you? You should know she aimed a missile at this place."

"We dealt with it."

"Ah. I thought I saw an explosion."

"The one who tried to disarm it was killed."

"So you killed Jackson in return."

"No, we killed the woman because she threatened us. Any of us would sacrifice our lives for the good of the clade, but all of us would die to save our mother. We love her more than life itself. You should know that we are tracking the cargo train and have calculated its trajectory."

When Baker had briefly wrested control of the scow from Jackson, he had sent the cargo train on a trajectory that would end in a collision with Epimetheus after three orbits of Saturn, less than 20 hours now. He said, "I was going to tell you about that. I don't mean any harm by it. I want to be friends. The cargo train—it's just insurance, that's all."

The woman made no gesture, but children appeared at various levels of the burgeoning greenery. No, not children: they were naked creatures the same size as his pressure-suited captors, so pale and skinny that they seemed partly transparent, like certain deep-sea creatures. They were quite sexless. Their heads were small and wedge-shaped, sloping straight back from skin-covered dimples where their eyes should have been; their ears flared out like bat's wings; their hands had only three fingers, spaced like a crane's grab. Four of them gripped the arms of Baker's p-suit with implacable strength.

"We will kill you slowly for your presumption," the woman said, "and our defence drones will destroy the cargo train."

Baker said. "I don't think you want to do that. If it's destroyed, the debris will still hit and do just as much harm, but if you leave it be, I can change its orbit once we've made a deal."

The woman shrugged. "It is unlikely that the impact will hurt our mother, for most of her is far underground. But it will damage her enegry-gathering systems, and we cannot allow even that. You will change its orbit now."

Baker said stubbornly, "We can make a deal. That's why I'm here."

"No," the golden-skinned woman said serenely. "No bargains. Change the orbit of the cargo train and we may let you leave. Otherwise we will keep you here, alive and in great pain."

"You didn't kill me," Baker said. "Of course you want to bargain. I want to set up a trading agreement between your clade and my collective. You must have plenty of biological novelties, for instance. In exchange, we can supply you with trace elements, or anything else you might need. I did a little research and I know you deal exclusively with the private citizens who bankrolled this experiment. I bet my collective can offer you better supply contracts. And we can guarantee confidentiality."

"There will be no trade," the woman said. "We need nothing. Our mother made this garden. It is all we need. You will do as we ask."

"I have to be on the scow to do it," Baker said, "so you'll have to let me go anyway. There's plenty of time. I can show you the figures on the trade my collective does with the Titan terraforming project. Think it over. I mean no harm to your mother. I didn't know she was on Epimetheus. I thought she was here."

"She is not *on* Epimetheus," the woman said, "she is *becoming* Epimetheus. Think what you will do. I will return soon."

Cherubs whirled down and lifted the chair and the woman into the air. As she dwindled away, the workers released Baker and vanished into the greenery with unnerving swift silence.

The golden-skinned woman did not return for many hours. Baker wasn't worried; he was sure that she was discussing the offer with her mother, and the longer it took the more likely it was that he could hook them. He found the airlock, but the black sheets had stiffened and would not let him pass. A little way beyond, at the foot of a steep vine-covered cliff, a flash of bright yellow caught his attention. It was Jackson's p-suit helmet. The visor was cracked around a burn hole; the padding inside was crusted with drying blood.

Baker cradled it, tears pricking at his eyes; although he had not loved her, he had loved the idea of remembering that he had once loved her, and what he was mourning now was that lost part of his life. She had not understood that when she had tried to manipulate him; she had not really understood much of what she had done. The only thing she had been right about was that ordinary humans had no place in the Outer System: here was the proof.

He dropped the helmet and turned back to explore the rim of the freefall jungle bowl. The lush green thickets were full of strange creatures: things like snakes, but with narrow human heads and pale human skin: little black-furred tarsiers with microcephalic human faces; white worms working like mobile fingers through the crumbling soil. The things Baker had thought were birds were more like black-furred bats, with leathery wings as wide as his outstretched arms; when he climbed out along the smooth limb of a tree above the bowl of the jungle a flock of them wheeled and dive-bombed him, spattering him with their dung.

Baker laughed and retreated, crashing unhandily through thick foliage in his p-suit. He was not afraid of anything here. He controlled the cargo train: he had the upper hand. He had thought to threaten Sri Hong-Owen with the destruction of her experimental sites, and although he didn't understand what the woman had told him, he was certain that his bargaining position was even stronger than he had hoped. His sidekick had been wrong after all. Everything was going to work out. Except for Jackson, of course. It was a pity about Jackson, but after she tried to cut him out of the deal he really had had no choice but to let her walk unknowingly to her own death.

At last, the golden-skinned woman returned, borne as before through the air on a chair sustained by cherubs. Workers stepped out of the greenery and stood on either side of her chair as the cherubs set her down and whirled away.

"I hope we can talk," Baker said.

"We have agreed to tell you about us," the woman said. "Listen."

Sri Hong-Owen wanted to become truly immortal, the woman said. She had used cloning as a first step, although she knew that it would not be enough. Clones are exact genetic copies, but personality is determined by a combination of genes, environment and experience. A clone would have to have been subjected to every single one of her own experiences to become a perfect copy. Even so, she experimented with the effects of various types of memory downloads and artificial-reality scenarios on the personalities of female clones, and then she had created the clade and its habitat, and given it over to the charge of her daughter clones. The clade valued knowledge, not things. Its treasure store was in its self-regulating ecosystem and the genetic diversity it had fashioned from a genome library derived from a few plants and microorganisms and from Sri Hong-Owen herself; every animal in the habitat was derived from her by gengineering and forced evolution. Given the right conditions, the clade could persist forever.

Meanwhile, Sri Hong-Owen reshaped herself.

She developed vacuum organisms which turned sunlight into electrical energy with almost one-hundred-per-cent efficiency—the ring of dish flowers around the habitat were an early prototype. They were forming a blanket across the surface of Epimetheus, and Sri Hong-Owen's modified body was growing through the moon's icy crust like blue mould through cheese. It was already the largest organism in the Solar System, larger even than the mycelial mats which underlay Earth's temperate forests, and which she now somewhat resembled. Copies of her original body were cached here and there in that mass, and there were more than a hundred copies of her brain, all sharing the same sensory inputs, the same thoughts. They were as alike as possible. Eventually the mycelium would completely embrace the moon. It would grow thrusters which would subtly alter the moon's orbit, slingshotting it repeatedly through Saturn's gravity well until it gained enough velocity to escape to the stars.

"Probably Vega," the golden-skinned woman told Baker. "There's a ring of debris around Vega twice the size of our Solar System, millions of comets and planetoids and asteroids. She will fill it with clades like ours, and then move on to other systems where planets failed to form. She is the first real transhuman, but there will be others—those who sponsored her work, to begin with."

Baker smiled. He did not believe half of what he had been told. He said, "If she is truly immortal then she must value her life immensely."

"What are you to her? She could fill the galaxy. In time, she could fill a million galaxies. Planets are unnecessary. We have evolved beyond planets. We have evolved beyond the human form. We can make ourselves over into a thousand kinds of organism, all fitter for life in space than mere humans. The tweaks are a first step, lungfish on the shore of space. We will go much further."

"My collective has already made over a tented crater on Rhea, much as this one has been transformed. Other collectives are making homes in planetoids, mining comet heads . . . There are many different ways of making a living, and no need at all to depend on trade with anyone on Earth. Trade with us instead. If you had time to look at those figures—"

"All of you are still human," the woman said. "We have evolved beyond that."

"She's right," someone else said, and a second golden-skinned woman came into the clearing with an elegant motion that was half-walking, half-swimming. She held something between her small breasts with both hands.

"You've decided," Baker said. "That's good."

"We've decided," the woman said, and released what she held.

It flew straight at Baker on a blur of membranous wings, a tiny bat with a wasp's long abdomen. He tried to knock it out of the air but it was too fast and his pressure suit slowed him. It dodged his clumsy blow and caught at his hair with claws. Something sank into his scalp, pushing between the sutures of his skull, and black pain swept the world away.

When it came back, the two golden-skinned women were looking down at him. Baker pushed up and gingerly touched the top of his head; hundreds of hair-thin wires with sticky-tagged ends came loose, slowly falling to the ground around him. He said, "What did you do?"

"Evolution is cruel," the first woman said. "Those forms which are less successful will die. Perhaps we will keep some of you, out of sentiment. And Baker, while he lives, needs help, of course."

"I'm not sure I understand," Baker said. He felt quite calm, as if he had entered an artificial reality and could leave any time he wanted. "I thought evolution was all about change, but you do not want to change."

Suddenly he felt his sidekick at his back and a warning twinge in his head like a cold needle in his core. Ordinarily he would have welcomed its return, but there seemed to be something wrong with it; it was fierce and strong and silent.

He said, "You did something to me, didn't you? Something with those wires, something to my net."

The second woman said, "We are a new kind of evolution. The body changes at will, and the mind lives on."

"Tell me what you did!"

"After a little while," the first woman said, "you won't ever worry about it."

Baker said, "You want me to think like you? Is that it?

Listen, you can't last forever in isolation. People need other people."

"That is why we will send you back," the first woman said. "You can only think in the old way. Although we love him dearly, that was always Berry's trouble."

Then the sidekick seized Baker. He couldn't move. His body felt bloated, unmanageable, fiery hot, a pupa melting and changing inside the carapace of the p-suit.

The wires had downloaded new programs into his net and reactivated his sidekick: now his sidekick was changing him. Part of his personality fell away, falling from his mind into darkness as icebergs calve from a glacier.

At last the work was done and the world came back to him. His sidekick was at his back, stronger than ever, his mentor and his friend.

They all gathered to watch him go, workers, cherubs, human-skinned snakes and crabs, naked monkey-things which tended the gardens, all one family, one flesh, one thought, one clade.

"You are one of us now," they said. "A different flesh but one of us. Our faithful servant. You will divert the cargo train because you know that no harm must come to our mother. You will guard our brother now and forever."

He did what they wanted.

He was one of them.

His collective finally found him on Dione. He and Berry were staying in the only hotel in a raw construction town, the first stage of an ambitious plan to tent the Latium Chasma, the fissure which cut a deep groove across the northern half of the sub-Saturnian hemisphere. The hotel could not supply the kind of luxury that Berry was used to; after only a few days he told Baker that he wanted to move on.

Baker was returning from the port. He always transacted business in person; even deeply encrypted phone lines were not to be trusted. He had arranged transport to one of the garden habitats that orbited Titan, a tourist place where people went to use telepresence to explore the storms which were resurfacing the giant moon. He was sure that Berry would like it; gardens reminded him of the happy days of his childhood, in the garden of his mother.

They jumped into Baker's capsule just before it pulled out of the station, a young woman and an older man. The young woman wanted to know if he recognized her. "We slept together to seal the contract," she said, her eyes searching his face. "You were always my favourite. You must remember."

Baker tried to be polite. "I do not know you," he lied. "I am sorry."

The young woman touched the man's arm.

"Ralf is a lawyer. We filed a bond here. If you need privacy to talk we can provide it. We know you logged a flight with two passengers. One was an old friend of yours. Vera Flamillion Jackson. We know where you went, but we don't know what happened. Please tell me. Whatever happened to you can be reversed, I'm sure of it."

"I don't think so. You want your slave back. Don't deny that you think of him as your property. Well, he isn't. He is one of us, now."

And so on, a tide of anger rolling over Baker, submerging him so completely that he no longer knew if he or the sidekick was speaking. He came to himself in the atrium of Berry's hotel suite. The entry phone was flashing but he ignored it.

"Well, it's time we moved anyway," he said to the air, as he moved through the rooms to the private pool where Berry floated.

The sidekick was fading at his back, as beneficent as the warmth of the sun; before it vanished it told him with approval that he had done well. And then he saw Berry, floating pink and naked in steaming water amongst palmettoes and bamboos, a tray of food on his hairless chest, sucking on a drink bulb, and the unfortunate incident didn't matter any more.

Berry spat the straw from his mouth and said, "You've been away. I don't like it when you're away."

"I've arranged a new place for us."

"Oh, that. Good. Can't stay in one place too long. That's the secret."

"Do you think she might need us one day? Do you think we might be allowed to return?"

Berry bent his head and sucked up the last of the margarita mix with a rattling noise. When he looked up, there were tears swelling in his eyes. He said, "We're nothing to her now. We're too human. You're here to serve me. By serving me you serve the clade. That's all you need to know. Now help me out. My skin's wrinkling."

"Of course," Baker said, and went to get the oils and unguents, filled with boundless unqualified love for his master.

SOLDIERS HOME

William Barton

William Barton was born in Boston in 1950 and currently resides in Durham, North Carolina. For most of his life, he has been an engineering technician, specializing in military and industrial technology. He was at one time employed by the Department of Defense, working on the nation's nuclear submarine fleet, and is currently a freelance writer and computer consultant. His stories have appeared in Aboriginal SF, Asimov's Science Fiction, Amazing, Interzone, Tomorrow, Full Spectrum, *and other markets. His books include the novels* Hunting On Kunderer, A Plague of All Cowards, Dark Sky Legion, When Heaven Fell, The Transmigration of Souls *(which was a finalist for the Philip K. Dick Award), and* Acts of Conscience, *and, in collaboration with Michael Capobianco,* Iris, Fellow Traveler, *and* Alpha Centauri. *His most recent novels are* White Light, *in collaboration with Michael Capobianco, and the new solo novel,* When We Were Real.

In the vivid story that follows, he tells the compelling story of a heartsick and battle-weary veteran of an unimaginably strange high-tech future war who returns to an abandoned space colony, one that has been drifting lost and deserted among the stars for generations, to face again some old and implacable enemies, and to reaffirm the truth of that old saying about how You Can't Go Home again . . . or perhaps to learn that maybe you can*—but only if you're willing to pay the price.*

The stars belong to no one.

They lie against the empty black in drifted clots and jagged heaps of meaningless white light. Nothing to pin your hopes on, just brilliant dots strewn at random across the void, an empty stage where we live and die, and nothing more.

I stood on the lip of a gaped-open docking platform, toes of my boots hanging over the abyss, watching the taxi back away from the ruined habitat I'd chosen, hard vacuum freezing cold in my eyes, crisp nothingness on my skin. The taxi was already no more than a black splotch against the stars visible only by the intermittent red twinkle of thrusters and the pale, tenuous blue exhaust of its field modules device.

It grew small against the sky before turning away, ghostlight covering its outline, hesitated for an instant, then vacated its place among the stars, though I could still hear the pilot superimposed over the datawarren chatter in my head. I dropped his channel, then pushed away the rest, dropping it outside my shield, standing still, in utter silence.

With the taxi gone, the stars seemed remote. Unreal.

They used to mean so much to me, those faraway stars. What happened to the boy who would stand alone on a midnight hillside, warm wind curling round him, looking up at this same clutter of stars, imagining himself out among them? Gone, I suppose. Erased along with the hillside, with the world on which it sat, gone with all the people who lived there, ground away to ashes and dust. Gone to nothing along with so much else, until I sometimes imagine only I remain.

Foolishness.

The taxi pilot, a Spinfellow who'd looked to me like nothing so much as an old brass bed frame collapsed against the ship's control nexus in a shambles of broken coil springs, had been some kind of a soldier in the war, though clearly not the same kind as me. A pilot, I guess, killing clean and cold.

Hard to tell with something so utterly alien as a Spinfellow, agrammatical voice chattering in my head like the screeching bedsprings of a remote, manic fuck, but he'd seemed almost sorry about the way his people had used mine to break the age-old deadlock of a war that went on and on. Sorry, but it's what you get, showing up at just the right moment, humanity at the bloated endstage of an expanding-shell culture, just when cannon fodder was needed most.

Not so many of us now, hm?

I'd tried to accommodate his wish to talk, telling about all the wonderful battles I'd seen, all the Starfish I'd killed, but kept falling silent, going away. Finally he gave up, glad to abandon me here on the edge of the void with my pitiful pile of junk.

It's funny how what I remember most now is just waking up at a repair station, glitter-eyed unmod nurse bending over me, seeing me awake. "Welcome back, Mr. Ashe."

Welcome the hell back.

Your Squadmates? No, sorry, you were the only one who made it.

I didn't find out 'til much later that the Starfish had found our little corner of space, had come in and cleaned out humanity's clustered homeworlds, hoping to stem the tide of cannon fodder and turn back a sudden, improbable Spinfellow victory.

Remembered battles? No. They all smear together now, as if there were only one, full of fire and pain, very little of it my own.

As I stood still, looking at nothing, I could see the stars turn, counter to the habitat's slow spin, rising up from below my feet, crossing straight up, disappearing somewhere behind me. No sun. No other light. This had been an interstellar depot out on the edge of what'd once been human space, seven light-years from the nearest star system, abandoned now for centuries, its running lights gone dark.

I'd seen these sorts of things before. Knew what I'd find inside.

Knew what I hoped to find.

Finally, stars grown stale as everything else, I picked up my gear and turned away, facing the dark habitat, letting my eyes see infrared so I could locate the door.

There.

Might as well go on in.

• • •

From the heights of the endcap mountains of an old-style cylindrical habitat, even under the bright midday glare of full stemshine illumination, you can see details almost five hundred kilometers away, tall structures like mountains peeking out of the haze, floating like dull purple ghosts behind Rayleigh-scattering sky.

This had been a big residential-industrial complex, one of the biggest they made in the old days, out on the expanding frontier, when humanity was mighty and young, giant freighters pushing lightspeed as they plied the void between the suns, bold explorers plumbing the remotest deep, in our thousand years as a starfaring species pushing hundreds of light-years in all directions away from old Earth.

I could feel the stemshine's light prickling on my skin, turning me green wherever it touched. I pulled off my tunic and dropped it on top of the backpack, pack sucking it in, tucking it away, and watched the fuzz of downy hair on my chest turn from coal black to spun gold, pallid skin underneath suffusing briefly pink, then pale spring green slowly darkening.

Organelles. Cellular well-being. As if God were in his Heaven and everything was right with this world, any world, even with my world.

I can picture what the habitat must have been like before the war, back when I was a boy. It was in this sector of the frontier that First Contact came, and how excited they must have been, receiving news that one of our explorer fleets had stumbled on the wreck of an alien starship.

Imagine the scene. That ruined ship, complete with survivors, sprawled on the surface of an inhospitable world. And those lovely, grateful aliens, little beings like turquoise wolves, with spindly arms where their ears should be and great, golden, many-faceted eyes, bursting through a tissue-thin communication barrier with their superior data-processing capability, then carefully explaining that their ship, once repaired, could go faster than light, and would we be interested in the technology?

I remember how excited my father was when the news came through the datawarren. Yes, we'd fix their ship, help them go home, and then the stars would be ours, more stars than ever populated any of our dreams.

Down in the lowlands, landscape curving up to right and left, stretching out straightaway into the mist ahead as far as the eye could see, disappearing in blue, there were clouds, white and gray, and green jungle, blotched with the shadows of those clouds, patches of fog, the twisted lightning bolts of artistically laid-out rivers, sandhills, dune fields, red rock canyons, and the dark, misty crags of faraway mountains.

At the end of the world, so remote its foothills were lost in the mist, one mountain seemed to have a pennon of snow blowing from its peak.

When I was a boy, living on the skin of a eutropic habitat, with its down-curving horizon like a natural world cast in miniature, we had mountains like that. Exactly like that, modeled, I'm sure, on the same original.

That was the world where I lived, still growing up, when the first Spinfellow scoutship nosed into human space, long before we managed to fix the refugees' ship, before we even understood they *were* refugees, or what they were running from.

Straight down, looking down the sheer crags of the endcap mountains, a tiny dot circled, rising and falling on the thermals. Probably as high as it can go, air thinning out after only a few dozen kilometers. And big, whatever it was, visible without magnification from so far away. Do I want to see it? No, though it might be just what I'm looking for.

I shouldered my pack, picked up the rest of my gear in one hand, turned and started walking, clockwise, in the direction of spin, looking for the elevator down. It would be broken, most likely, but I knew I could jump down the shaft, slowing myself as necessary by squeezing the railguide.

Sooner or later, I'll get where I'm going.
No hurry.
No God-damned hurry at all.

From down on one of its floor panels, a cylinder habitat's not that different from a natural world. To be sure, the world rises around you like an English saddle, but you might be in a big valley, after all, and . . . well. A human being's like a bug in the grass, more concerned with his own little space than the grandeur beyond.

I got out my gun and assembled it, rearranged my pack, tucking other gear in to take its place, took a long look up into brilliant blue heaven, shimmery stemshine hanging like a bar of molten gold trying to hide behind the sky, then set off down the game trail.

There were patches of forest separated by broad, grassy fields, fields dotted by thousands of little yellow flowers. Here and there were odd piles of ruin, things that looked a little bit like collapsed buildings and broken-down bulldozers, crawled all over by red strangler vine.

I wonder how long it took to get like this?

How long did it take for the trees in the parks to realize they were free, free to seed the winds, be fruitful, multiply, and cover their world? How long before the grassy walkways jumped their fences or tunneled underneath the way *gramineae* will, taking over every space in sight? What job did the strangler vines have, back when they were slaves?

I wonder how long it took this world to grow so beautiful.

Something tiny and black arrowed toward me, arrowing out of the misty blue sky, circling my head, round and round, fluttering like a bat lost in daylight.

It screamed something, wordlike, shrill, laughing, hysterical, laughing at me, cartoon creature imposed on an Impressionist's overwrought landscape, then banked away, soaring between two copses of tall, thin, swaying brown trees, up, up, gone.

From far away, far in the same direction, there came a brief *rat-a-tat-tat*, like someone imitating machine-gun fire on a child's tin drum.

I stood still, not really waiting for it to come back and talk to me, breathing in the scent of a broken-down world. Here was the turpentine smell of old pine trees. There the fresh stink of new-mown hay. Behind both, almost hidden, a soft, alluring tang of half-burnt silicone lubricant.

Used to smell that a lot, when we worked with the tank companies. A reassuring smell. Infantrymen and tanks. The smell of history. I can see them now, down all the centuries, marching together into the guns.

Beyond the trees there was a boulder field, uptilted rock hiding the forward horizon. Not that you'd call it that, landscape just going on and on until it faded away, fading into the sky. I found a way up, hopping from stone to stone, and . . .

The thing reared in front of me just as I crested the highest rock, casting a giant's shadow. Thing like a dinosaur, I guess you'd say. Red eyes and scaly skin, blotched and freckled with a thousand metallic tints. Clutching hands and broad, toothy jaws.

Silver teeth like so many triangles, one just like the next, shining in the stemlight, dripping pale yellow oil like saliva.

Red eyes looking down at me.

Seeing me.

Knowing me for what I am?

I'd heard this place had been used for a military hardware dump, not long before the end of the war, just for throwing things away, useless things that were too hard to destroy.

Things you wouldn't want to bring home with you.

Especially if you still imagined you had a home.

So what would this be, with its red eyes rolling, hungry jaws opening and closing like that?

I remembered a construction battalion I'd run across once.

Yeah. Maybe one of those things.

I thumbed the charge button on my gun and listened to the condenser whine.

There! That caught its attention.

Put the gun to my shoulder and looked through the sight.

The green light winked once. *Ready*.

We stood still, two old war machines, locked in one last tableau.

Red eyes looking at me, waiting.

Oh, God.

Red eyes full of fear.

I lowered the gun and looked up at the thing, smelling its hot oil breath, breath like summer sunshine.

I thumbed the détente button, feeling the gun's charge dissipate.

Go ahead then.

Red eyes staring down at me.

For Christ's sake.

Just a digging machine, that's all.

It turned and scrambled away, claws crackling in the dirt, kicking up a sandstorm that obscured half the sky, kicking up boulders the size of cars as it fled, boulders bounding around, crashing down on my pile of rocks, boulders exploding, splinters flying.

None of them managed to crash down on me.

Not that it would have done any good.

After a while, I shouldered the gun, hanging it from the strap, and walked on, emptying myself of useless feeling.

Toward the end of a long afternoon, twilight's first glimmer signaled by the stemshine's gold taking on a sullen, brassy hue, I found the valley of my dreams, gentle vale dropping down from the endless plains, slim indigo rivers winding across a hilly lowland, dotted with clusters of trees in the lesser vales between, valley opening on a northward vista, landscape fading out in blue as always.

I picked a campsite at the crest of a low hill, close by the side of the river, hill caught in a little oxbow bend, dropped my pack, and watched the tent erect itself, supports walking like insect limbs, shell slithering into place, stakes screwing themselves deep in the dirt.

There was a soft breeze blowing down the valley, taking me from behind, warm on my bare skin, skin made a rich, blackening green by the long day's ultraviolet blaze, gust of wind tossing my hair, then running away down the valley and away, marking its passage through waves of grass.

Distant buzzing.

I turned toward the sound, and there was a tiny biplane dipping over the landscape, up and down, back up again, wings painted white, flashing in stemlight, a red stripe here, another one there, swooping low over pale splotches in clustered bits of forest, dusting them with a transparent gray nutrient cloud.

Like a living thing.

Living and wise.

Soft buzzing like a faraway insect.

I opened my scanner array and listened for him over the sudden roar of the datawarren. There. Discordant robot chatter, no one talking to no one listening, remarks addressed to the ghosts of long-erased controllers.

Snap.

Silence again.

Fading buzz of a toylike engine.

Nearby chitter of something small. A clatter of little tin gears.

I went down to the riverside, knelt on crunchy gravel, thrust my head into the deep blue water and drank. A hint of metallic salt. The strong flavor of gasoline, gasoline cooked up from old cometary CHON, leaking from something dead, way upstream.

I opened my eyes underwater, shifting my visual peak away from green, on toward blue, and watched shadows materialize out of the murk. There, there, and there. Sleek shapes, not so much like fish, but close enough.

Who knows what they might originally have been for?

Holding position against the sluggish current with their lazily turning propellers.

I stood, cold water streaming down my chest and back, soaking into the waist of my pants, walked back up onto the hill, and rummaged in the pack. Cookstove? Well, maybe later. Get it out, anyway. I found the case with my fishing gear, tucked it under my arm and walked down to the river, started walking upstream aways, water bubbling softly on my right, looking out at the rocks and eddies.

Cluster of roots over there. Lots of shadows under water.

Some flat land there where the soil had washed away, covered up with water now, forming something like a swamp in among the trees. Farther in, some of the trees had been gnawed around the base by something that must imagine it could play at being a beaver. Maybe if I looked long enough, I might find a dam and pond, pond on its way to becoming a meadow.

That'd be nice.

There was a cloud of . . . I don't know, call them midges, little black dots rising and falling over the swamp. Microscopic vision, quickly tuned, showed me a glint of chromium steel, little blue glass eyes, the transparent blur of tiny silver wings.

It's so God-damned pretty here.

After a while, as the sky slowly turned from brass to lustrous red-gold, I found a big, flat black rock sticking out into the river, rock warm as a dying griddle from daylong stemlight. Water was flowing around the rock, humped up into a long, arcing bowshock, curve broken farther out by a string of rounded boulders.

I put the case down and opened it up, pulling out rod and reel, unfolding it, snapping everything into place, stood again and played its preylight out over the river. There. Things clustered beyond the rocks, floating in quiet lee water. Some bigger fish, if that's what you want to call them, deep down, over by the far bank.

I put my thumb on the bait button and slid one finger

through the flycaster's trigger guard. Made my fisherman's stance and stood still, not quite taking aim.

Overhead the sky was turning to muddy orange, stemshine a broad, hazy band of crimson, sky around it stained pale brown. Nothing else. No clouds. No . . .

High, high up, a silent vee of black dots, drifting along.

My eyes zoomed in, uninvited, showing me the shape of each black dot.

Balloonsailers, half black shark, half dirigible, half jet engine, soaring through the sky, each one twenty meters from stem to stern. See their gaping mouths, the dark serrated shapes of matte-gray berylloceramic teeth? See the glimmer of their silver eyes?

If I listened carefully, I could hear the intermittent mutter of their engines, driving them against the wind.

Their fins twisted and the vee arced, turning away, sinking deep in the dull mist of nightfall.

What if they'd seen me?

Was I ready?

Don't know.

I looked back down, at the flycasting rod in my hands, line unfired, baits unmounted, looked out across the now black water, water picking orange-and-red highlights from the sky.

In there somewhere, the first surrogates were waiting, undead.

I sat down, laying the rod gently by my side, lay back on the warm surface of the rock, warm stone like blood against my skin, cradled the back of my head in one palm, and looked up into the sky, watching it darken.

Soon, I thought, the stars will come out.

Surely they made this place have a night full of stars.

I remember once, on leave, how some of us went spearfishing in a zero-gee habitat we'd found. Not a human habitat. Not human at all. No, this was far from the homes we knew, deep in what had once been Starfish territory, now in Spinfellow hands, thanks in no small measure to us.

It was a wonderful place, a great big bag of a world, full of thick, sweet air, floating globule ponds, seas made entirely of mist.

We swam among them, jetting stretches of air with our backpacks, exploring airy tangles of seaweed jungle. Diving deep in great, clear, undulating amoebas of water.

I don't know where we found the spearguns.

I remember we had fun, shooting those silvery things, things that screamed as they died, even under water. Killing them, cutting them up, cooking them, eating them.

Someone said they heard these things were the inhabitants of this sector, beings who'd once had a star-spanning empire of their own, but by then it didn't matter. Sentient or not, they tasted damned good, though our Spinfellow-supplied systemic symbionts insisted we could get no nutrition from them at all.

Something about levorotation.

I remember floating with my friends in a misty blue-green sky, eating long, thin, silvery people, smacking my lips over their flavor, joking with my friends, and remembering how my father and I used to fish together, when I was a boy.

It wasn't like that at all.

More like this, with gear just like this, he and I standing hip-deep in swift, oily brown water, holding our fancy fly-casters . . . I remember how serious my father's eyes would get, as we fished away one long morning after another, one of my mother's silvergirl servants standing on the shore, watching us, shanghaied from household chores to carry our gear and cook whatever lunch we caught.

At some point, while I lay on my stone, remembering these things, the sky grew black overhead and the stars came out, stars shining between broad, featureless panels of black, light streaming in from the galaxy beyond.

They were the same stars after all, refusing to change for me.

Finally, I went to bed, crawling into the empty blackness of the tent.

• • •

In the morning, I stood on my hilltop beneath a cold cobalt dawn, blue sky striated with a barely visible herringbone pattern, streamers of dusty light from a dark, golden stemshine.

That way, the light seemed to say.

It's over there.

I stretched, feeling wonderful in some insensate way. splendid animal health, a sense of meaningless being.

Down below, the stream was a sinuous rille of molten metal, reflecting a perfect mixture of sky light, chuckle of moving water blending promiscuously with the soft, whispering wind.

They write poems about this stuff.

When I turned away from the river, there in the distance, hanging in blue space, rising out of the mist, was the faraway mountain, streamer of snow blowing from its peak, stilled by distance, like a motionless white flag.

After a while, I knelt and opened my pack, rummaging around until I found the ballonet gun in its compact case. I opened it up on the hillside by the tent and began going through an assembly routine I could do not only with my eyes shut, not only in my sleep, but perhaps even if I were dead.

Barrel. Condenser. Stock. Arming mechanism. Power source.

I twisted it together, one part following another in magically perfect succession, made the last connection, everything together just so, and felt it grow ever so slightly warm to the touch.

Hefted it.

Looked through the sight.

Armed my weapon and switched off the safeties, listening to the condenser whine.

The ready light blinked green.

Yes. Yes, I remember

I remember how we used to worry about how warm it got, giving us away in combat, compromising our stealth.

But this wasn't a sniper gun. No. More like a portable artillery piece.

I thumbed the détente button and felt it grow still in my hands, engaged the safeties and slung it over my shoulder, hanging by an indestructible gray strap, not quite a mass of insensible plastic, still warm to the touch. Still alive as I stood looking at my faraway mountain with its beckoning white flag.

Time to go.

It was cold on the mountain.

I could sense the cold, though I can never *be* cold. Ice and snow? Nothing. Not when you've had vacuum on your skin, when you've stood in the void between the stars, on some forgotten chunk of ice, stood on the brink of absolute zero, waiting for the fire.

But I could know the cold.

This cold now.

Could remember what cold had been.

It took me the better part of a day and a night to walk to the mountain, human exhaustion and hunger discarded as luxuries, feeling like a strong mechanical man, walking and walking, over the plains, up the foothills to steeper slopes, then climbing, ballonet gun slung across my back.

After a while, the slopes turned to bare, gray, vertical rock, my fingers digging in like pitons. *Crack.* Stone giving way to flesh.

Once, I slipped, sliding on my back across a scree-slick slope, shooting over a knife's edge, out into space, twisting in the air, reaching out, catching myself in a spalled-open crevice, hand wedging in with just the tiniest flicker of pain, body flailing above the void, slapping hard against the cliff-face with a sound like a wet rag, hanging on, dangling, feet down over some howling abyss, listening to the wind, wondering what it would be like.

Maybe a thousand meters to the snowfield below, this one handhold the last one I could possibly have reached.

I could see myself tumbling, end over end, all the long way down, eyes closed so I wouldn't see the ground reach out for me.

Would that have been enough?

No way to know.

Just a fantasy, compounded of remembered fears.

In a more real world, this one perhaps, I would've picked myself up from a man-shaped hole in the snow, grimacing at my carelessness, checked to make sure the gun was all right, would've begun the long climb all over again.

After a while, I lifted myself back over the ledge, unwedged my hand, shook out its little cramp, and went on, climbing a bit more carefully. Only a bit. No hurry. No hurry at all.

You'll get there soon enough, Mr. Ashe.

High up, up above the clouds, the mountain leveled out, and I walked along a knife-edged ridge of tight-packed snow toward the final peak. The sky was a remote, brilliant blue here, silver-blue, like cold steel, the world spread out below like the inside of a pipe, stemshine stretching out this way and that to infinity above, painful white light hiding the world beyond.

I stopped, looking at nothing, my breath like a plume of frost, each breath ending in a cloud of tiny snowflakes.

Wasteful, that.

I set a timer on the heat exchangers in my nose and throat, starting and stopping bloodflow as I inhaled and exhaled. There. Better. I could do without the oxygen, of course, but wanted it nonetheless.

World like a painting.

Like some cheap, mass-produced art.

How many worlds like this did we make before that old human universe came to an end? Millions, perhaps?

How many of them now remain?

Only a few.

Junk art resting on the rubbish heap, waiting for the bulldozer to come.

That old world seemed so limitless. Limitless, and I could hardly wait to grow up, to get out *into* it, get away from my circumscribed childhood, out into the infinite black deep between the stars.

Do I remember when it ended?

Maybe so.

I remember a day long ago, a day floating isolated in my past, so separated from the rest I have no way of knowing who or what I was back then. My sister and I had one of the household silvergirls up in a seldom-visited part of the attic that day, so I suppose we'd gotten old enough to be a little on the naughty side, making it practice kissing with us.

I remember my sister giggling as I carefully pushed my tongue between its cold lips, trying to look like a character in a drama, silent silvergirl snatched from household chores, trying its best to give me what I wanted.

Maybe we had a datanode up there with us, calling in music from the household net, making the silvergirl dance with us. I remember there was a party coming up, that we'd wanted to look oh-so-sophisticated for our friends.

Nodes are real smart, are supposed to figure out what's important, tell you what you need to know, not just what you want. This one suddenly dropped the music, projected imagery into the attic's air, my sister going, "*Huh* . . ." Surprise in her voice

The silvergirl pulled away from me, hand on my chest, turning to look just as I did.

There was a mountain, just like this one, under a stark violet sky with two pale blue suns, a snowy ridge just like this one, alien starship strewn in pieces down a long, white slope.

Human ships hovering overhead.

Then a tight close-up, showing us those alien crewmen standing in the snow, watching us come in for a landing.

I looked at the silvergirl first. Nothing in its empty silver eyes, but . . . the silvergirl was looking at me. Waiting. As if it knew something I didn't. We sent it down the service chute, back on duty, then went on down ourselves, knowing Dad would be digging for data.

Looking back, I feel that I knew what was coming, impossible foreknowledge implanted in memory because I lived through everything that came afterward.

So I remember fear as well as breathless excitement.

And when we found out about the great war, I remember how proud we were at being invited to take part.

Not far from the top of the peak, up above the source of the snowy plume, I found a little hollow where I could rest, scanning the sky, sheltered from the wind, looking round at the world's brilliant vistas. From here, the snow was no more than mist, a transparent mist stretching away into the sky, hiding nothing.

I stood still, looking upward, my frequency sensitivities roving however they would. The sky grew bright, then dark, shadows emerging from beyond the blue. Faraway places, faraway things.

Beyond the stemshine, I knew, lay only more world, world beyond the sky just exactly like this, going round and round without end or beginning. Not really a world at all. Merely an artifact, like a silvergirl, or a gun.

Hanging strung between crags nearby was something like an orb spider's web, frost glistening on its strands, something like a spider hanging there, stemlight glinting from shiny metal limbs, picking out colored metal eyes.

Every now and again, it would whisper to itself, or perhaps to me, whispering in something that sounded like an unknown language, a soft, suggestive voice, utterly without meaning.

The stuff of myth, I know.

Raven. Pallas. Nevermore.

Bullshit.

Ominous whispering, ghostly creatures watching you from

the dark, knowing something you don't, creatures who would warn you if only you had the wit to understand.

But you don't, because you're not a creature in a myth, nor an artifact in a story.

Just a human being, frail and small, for all the changes wrought upon you by artificers beyond imagining.

Sometime . . . sometime, long ago, I stopped being a man and started being . . . what? I don't know.

An instrument.

Superhuman.

Unafraid.

Almost indestructible.

We knew we could die, but it didn't seem to matter.

We were supermen, together, and nothing more.

Overhead, kilometers away, I could see a score of bird-like things circling. Not what I'm waiting for, of course.

I remembered standing on a mountain not so very different from this one, not quite so high, but craggy, gray, cold. It was a natural world, not much like a human world, with cold nitrogen air, frigid nitrogen contaminated by gaseous ammonia, with icy liquid ethane that would sometimes condense and fall like rain.

The sun, not our sun, nor any sun we'd ever known, shone like a tiny, brilliant silver dot in a dull blue-purple sky. There were clouds, very high up, like tissue stratus, colored paler blue-white.

Spinfellows dropped us here one day, armed to the teeth, as they say, and told us to kill whoever was lurking about; the people of this world were enemies, they said, in league with the terrible Starfish foe.

I remember they ran like buffalo across the plain below, the people of this world, armed only with spears and bows.

I remember going down among them afterward, walking among their hulked and steaming carcasses, dead bodies covered with stiff, icy chrome-steel fur, like thin, silvery metal strands.

Walking among them, I remembered decorating the Yuletide tree with my family, a very little boy then, doing the tree with my laughing mother, my smiling father holding my sister up to watch as we draped it all over with thin, silvery metal strands.

Our guns had melted holes in the plain, leaving craters behind, coagulating craters full of chemical icewater.

I remember standing, quiet for a while, looking at a dead soldier, a soldier lying half-submerged in molten ground, slowly freezing into its grave. Its eyes were open and seemed to look at me, but utterly expressionless, without sight, life, meaning.

Another piece of myth, the eyes of the dead regarding the living, full of accusation.

All I had to do now was wait.

Finally they came, as the stemlight began to fade and the sky turned magenta.

Maybe a dozen of them, balloonsailers in a long line, far away, no more than black dots, strung out across the darkening sky. Impossibly remote overhead, the stemshine was no more than a smear of brilliant rust, fading into the ruddy afterglow.

I made my eyes behave, suppressing telescopic vision, making them remain no more than specks, like disciplined gnats in the long autumnal twilight.

That was how they looked before, though it wasn't on a world like this.

It must be horrible for them, discarded as worthless junk, cast away in an abandoned pipe, an inside-out world, a miniature world, adrift between the stars.

I remember that other world.

Immense.

Cold.

Like blue Neptune, with vast islands of fluffy aerogel ice floating in an empty blue sky, remote triple suns clustering together, tiny on the horizon, achingly brilliant for all their distance, streaking the sky with sunset, red, gold, green smeared together, yet still distinct.

We didn't know when the Spinfellows would come for us, or if they would, although the battle was long over.

We'd killed their surrogates, hoped the Spinfellows would pick us up, take us away to fight another day—and knew what would happen if the Starfish caught us here.

They'll come.

Sure they will.

Spinfellows need us to win their war.

Win the war at last.

Balance of power broken.

Starfish on the run.

I remember that it was Santos who suddenly pointed off into that reddening sky. *There.*

It was somebody else muttered, *Damn. Balloonsailers.*

Probably left behind, just like us, waiting for the Starfish to come, hoping the Spinfellows didn't get here first, knowing what would happen to them if they did.

Maybe there were seventy of us left out of the thousand who'd been combat-dropped a few days before. You could look around and see bad luck written across haggard faces.

Tired.

Even supermen get tired.

Half of us unarmed.

Most of the rest with nothing more than torches, a few grenades. We'd been rooting Beetles from the tunnels in the aerogel clouds, burning them, blasting tunnel mouths shut . . . watching those dots in the sky, I wondered if we could reopen a tunnel in the little time left.

No.

I'd looked down at the ballonet gun in my hands, knowing I was one of the few artillerymen left, knowing the others, with their useless torches and pitiful grenades, would be looking at me now.

I remember I tried to grin.

God knows what it must have looked like.

I remember I thumbed the arming button, listening to the condenser's whine, just like now.

I remember the balloonsailers came at us out of the sunset, just like now, as those nameless triple suns fell through the clouds, spreading a momentarily brilliant fan, a cascade of colors against the sky, Bifrost beckoning us homeward bound.

I wonder why they came?

Why not simply go away, hide in the shadows, pray for their Starfish to come?

Just doing their jobs, that's all.

Just like us.

They came, maybe forty or fifty of them in all, stooping on us out of a blackening sky, while frosty white stars popped out up above.

I remember I fired once, just as they came in range, hit one, watching him flare, bumbling out of formation, falling away into the infinite darkness below our little white island.

Maybe I would've liked watching him fall, fire sputtering sullen red, falling away to nothing, then gone.

No time.

The condenser whined, the ready light blinked, I fired again, someone else fired, other balloonsailers blazed and fell, one of them dropping onto the soft ice nearby, blazing up as oxygen got to it, making a sudden plume of blue smoke as it burned into the fragile ground.

People began firing their torches as they made the first pass, yellow-white fire splashing harmlessly.

There were screams.

When the balloonsailers arced away, there weren't so many of us anymore. I got another one as it receded, balloonsailer exploding in a burst of beautiful silver light, sky suddenly freckled with lovely vermilion sparks. The shadow of a man fell from the explosion, arms and legs flailing as he dropped into black nowhere.

He'd fall for a long time before atmospheric pressure and growing heat killed him.

Supermen are tough.

Not too tough for these other soldiers, though.

I wonder where the Starfish found them?

Maybe they just made them.

I remember wedging myself into a little crack in the ice, I remember that I kept on shooting, while friends of mine screamed and died.

At some point, I watched the last balloonsailer catch fire, twist against the starry, starry night, arc off on its back, turn nose-down, and crash, exploding brilliant red, not far away.

When I pulled myself from the crevice, there were three other men standing, that's all, men with guns just like mine.

Spinfellows came for us the next morning and took us away into yellow sunrise, not commenting on what they'd found.

I sat now, watching the red sky turn deep indigo, watching the balloonsailers come. Out of the fading backdrop, three broad panels of stars began to form, still pale, still far away, nighttime hardly begun.

Wait.

Wait for it.

Wait 'til they're close enough.

I thumbed the condenser, feeling the gun arm itself in my hands. There, that's got their attention. They turned hard against the sky, arcing toward me, forming up for a combat run.

The spider muttered something and, when I looked, it was scurrying from its web.

They came, slowing, become like graceful ice dancers, circling the mountain peak, spiraling in close, round and round, watching me, waiting.

Will I have to shoot one to get it started?

Or can I just stand and wait. Wait for them to . . .

I sighted in, looking through the scope, watching the ready light blink.

Now?

I imagined the detonation.

Imagined the first balloonsailer falling, on fire, down to the earth below.

After a while, I lowered the gun, thumbed the détente button, and felt it grow still in my hands.

I laid it aside and stood, looking up at the balloonsailers, watching them circle about.

After a while, the circle broke and they began to stream away, receding into the night.

The last one called out to me, some high, incomprehensible wail, sounding so utterly lost.

When it was gone, when I was alone again, I wondered.

Maybe they miss their comrades.

Maybe, as they circled, round and round, they were only waiting for the same thing as I was.

Why is this so God-damned *hard?*

Somehow the night was dark, cold wind whipping around me, making a low moan that seemed to come from all directions, from nowhere close by.

The spider got back in his web, chanting softly to himself, vaguely distracting, like theme music put in a drama by some incompetent producer who thought it might have something to do with atmosphere, with the ambiance of his tale.

I sat, clutching the gun between my thighs, hugging its warmth to my chest. In the dark and cold, I must be blazing infrared, making the crag a lighthouse beacon to sensitive eyes below. How many ersatz animals, how many abandoned machines, seeing my light, would grow nervous, wondering what it might mean? Or, worse yet, knowing.

All of them, perhaps.

I couldn't do it.

And neither could they.

Too complex a plan?

Well, the gun's in your hands, warm and suggestive, beckoning, waiting, as deadly as any balloonsailer who ever lived.

Not so hard to do what has to be done.

So just . . . but I continued to sit, emptied of imagery, unable to conjure the necessary scene.

Harder then I ever imagined it'd be, that's all.

Suddenly, I saw what it would look like to the creatures below, lost machines all, when I tripped the arming button, listened to the condenser whine, watched the ready light blink, a tiny spark of welcoming green, positioned the emission point and pulled the trigger.

It'd look, for just a moment, like someone had punched a hole through the walls of creation, out into whatever lies beyond.

Then it'd be done.

Over with.

As fast and unmomentous as anything in this universe could ever be.

I realized the spider had fallen silent.

When I looked up, there were two shadows, humanoid shapes on the ridgeline, flat black against the lesser darkness beyond.

I let my eyes get up to their tricks, making the night go steely gray and fill up with countless details.

Two silvergirls, sleek and slim, starlight glinting here and there, standing still, were looking down on me. One of them was obviously maimed, its left arm gone, socket exposed, a tatter of hanging shreds, like muscle and bone made of twisted, blackened metal. The other . . . face torn away, eyes and all, ragged hole covered over by a clumsily shaped, riveted-on patch. It had a radarset strapped to its head, grid nodding slowly, back and forth, up and down, cable running in under one side of the patch.

Nothing, just the two of them standing there, the blind one holding on to the cripple's lone hand.

After a while, the blind one said, "Well. And I thought they were no more." Soft silvergirl voice without emotion, just like my mother's silvergirls, all those long years ago, cold, remote, doing as they were told.

I could still taste their lips on mine; hear my sister's laughter.

They turned away, slipped below the ridgeline, down into the night, and were gone.

After a while, I stood, tucking the ballonet gun under my arm, and went to stand on the ridgeline where they'd been, while the spider chattered senselessly away. You could see their footsteps in the snow, a trail of pale blotches leading away down the slope, no creature so cold that it leaves no trace.

I started walking slowly after them, not thinking of what I might want, or why.

In time, the darkness and cold were banished by orange morning light, stemshine flaring to life, coloring the sky, flooding fields of ruins and runaway garden forest, picking out patches of shadowy haze, bits of fog gathered in the hollows, burning them away.

Something like a free-flying kite, complete with child-made, knotted-rag white tail, floated overhead, dark shadow against a sky turning from orange to yellow, on its way to cornflower blue.

I'd walked down off the mountain, following the glow of my damaged silvergirls' trail. The splotches of light grew more widely spaced. Running now, putting distance between us. Eventually, they began to stumble and fall, pick themselves up and go on.

I kept on walking, slow, steady, one foot after another after another, untiring, unable to fall or falter. Machines can't do this. Machines wear out. Machines grow old. Life renews itself, going on whether you want it to or not.

In full daylight, the trail of footsteps faded away, hidden. I let my eyes do what they needed to, finding the disturbances for me, showing me the way the silvergirls had gone.

I walked through a cool yellow-green forest of towering zinnias, immense flat flowers of orange and red nodding in the breeze a dozen meters overhead, came out in a clearing and saw where the silvergirls had lived.

Gone now.

They'd left things behind, artifacts, tools . . .

I kneeled in the entrance to a hut, looking at a strewn-out rubble of clothing. Abandoned human clothing, patched and repaired, lovingly maintained.

Pretty things.

Feminine things.

Silvergirls went naked in the household where I was a boy, on the world where I grew up, on all the worlds where humans lived, and live no more.

Silvergirls were things.

Things we made to serve us.

Things without souls.

Things without need for pretty things of their own.

I remember playing by myself, all alone in a sandbox, somewhere on the palace grounds. I had my little cars and trucks, aircraft and spaceships arrayed in the sand, arrayed on roads I'd graded with my little bulldozer toys.

I remember the silvergirl silent by my side, silvergirl detailed to watch me, silvergirl helping me pack sand in a plastic bucket, helping me upend it, lift it away, leaving a fat truncated cone behind, standing free, smooth and brown. A building maybe, or a mountain around which my roads could wind.

I remember looking up, seeing it look back at me with empty silvergirl eyes. I remember how it reached out to touch my hair, smooth it down ever so gently, hair lifted by a warm wind I hadn't noticed before.

Standing in the empty silvergirl village, village of remains, spoils from a worldwide refuse heap, I imagined them here, broken silvergirls, tossed away with all the rest of the junk, dressing up in their salvaged finery.

My mother's silvergirls . . .

I remembered suddenly being on a starship, orbiting in the sky, looking down at my homeworld.

Someone standing beside me had said, "It's like those pictures of Luna you sometimes see in old books."

Yes, like any terrestrial moon, or world, in the era of planetary formation, at the time of maximum bombardment, glowing pink under a haze of pale silica vapor, craters shining brilliant yellow-white amid red seas of flowing magma.

I turned away from the village and walked on, following them still.

I found her where the silvergirls left her staked out for me, naked, supine, spread-eagled, blindfolded, wrists bound to stakes driven into the damp, mossy ground, in a cool, dim green tunnel of a trail, cut through a forest of dry, long-dead trees under a canopy of pale, weeping vines.

I stood looking down at her, not a woman, not a child, not a human thing at all, with her short, feathery silver hair, long, slim, motionless limbs, bare, dry vulva sprung open by the position in which she'd been bound.

I remember once overhearing two women discuss that special moment when a man sees them naked for the first time.

The first one swore she could see the light of love dawning in his eyes.

The other nodded, smiling, looking ever so wise.

I remember wondering how it was they didn't know the truth.

Wondering why none of them seem to know, why they think men are something else entirely.

Maybe they don't want to know.

Maybe I wouldn't want to know, myself, about that terrible spasm of desire, nothing at all like love.

A moment like nothing so much as an inexplicable urge to strangle a kitten in your bare hands, kitten struggling as it dies, tongue protruding, eyes popping from its head, until there's nothing left in your hands but a sodden lump of empty, matted fur.

The allomorph's nostrils flared slightly, sampling for pheromones. The skin on her chest seemed to thicken imperceptibly, tiny pink nipples growing, perhaps, just a bit, vulval flesh darkening ever so slightly.

I stood still, waiting, watching a tool do its work.

She lifted her head, blindfold facing me, knowing where I was, tipping her face back and forth, as if trying to see.

My combat shield tickled, warning me I'd been probed by a short-range nerve-induction scanner.

I hadn't seen one of these in a long time, already had my protective implants before I met the first one. No way of knowing what it must be like to be worked over by a psychiatric allomorph, as naked as a human being possibly can be.

She licked her lips, a careful human gesture, part of an artfully programmed charade, and, voice hoarse, betraying some faux emotion that passed me by, whispered, "Are you really human? That . . . shield. I can't tell."

As I knelt on the forest floor, untying her bonds, her nostrils flared again, driving change, fuzz of silver hair blooming across her escutcheon, breasts beginning to form.

When the last rope was released, she sat quietly on the mossy ground and waited for me to take the blindfold away, exposing fathomless eyes of glass.

As we walked through dim green forest, over bright, stemlit plains dotted with tumbledown mechanical ruins, walking away from the silvergirls' trail, all the long way back to my no-longer abandoned camp, she said, "Call me Deseret."

"Desirée?"

She spelled it out for me.

Ah. Got it. "Ashe," I said.

At first, she tried to walk in front of me, naked and pretty, letting me watch her change from thing to girl to woman stage by stage. Tried to stop me from walking, getting in my path, slowing down, walking backward, facing me, smiling just so, getting upwind and flooding the air between us with desperate chemical signals.

I felt myself tighten up inside, just before the filters in

my lungs kicked in, cutting it off, exhaling her own coded provocation back at her.

She stood still in my path, looking up at me, a face so serious, head tipped back, hands clasped behind her waist, heels apart, toes pointing slightly away from the centerline of her body, shine of desire visible on her inner thighs.

I'd stood still, looking down at her for just a moment, then stepped to one side, stepped around her, and walked on.

She stayed behind me for a while after that, walking softly, footfalls almost inaudible, keeping up, nonetheless. When she came abreast of me, walking head down, as if pensive, she was a girl again, woman-parts mostly reabsorbed.

Somewhere, some time, in some long-ago factory, they made her to be a tool, useful to a human world in which she had no nonfunctional role.

I wonder if her designers, men and women long vanished, ever imagined she'd walk down this trail, lost and useless, full of unimaginable longings.

She's the only child of those dead souls, left behind in the noösphere to mark their passing. A pencil vanishes utterly, used up, thrown away, but its dust persists in drawings made, words written down.

Overhead, a vee of shiny birdlike things flew, crossing our path not far ahead, low enough I could hear the soft buss of their shiny metal wings, one red, one green, one blue, stemlight glinting as they passed from left to right. Deseret's head tipped as she watched them, tracking quickly, some unknown hunger filling her pretty face, not reaching into the depths of her clear, featureless eyes.

Eyes like tiny, optically perfect windows into an unlit room.

She glanced at me and I wondered how her face could be pretty. So many human cultures, races new and old, formed across time and space. No one thing for the word *pretty* to mean.

If I'd been looking, I would've seen the pretty face form, using my own face as a template, an appropriate pretty girl for a standard pretty superman. Now that I was watching, she became distinctly more female again.

I said, "Why'd they put you out like that?" Not that I couldn't guess.

She smiled, making my heart falter, no filter ever made that can stop a pretty girl's smile. Not without erasing the man within from the mannequin without. "Get you off their trail. Give them a little more time to get away."

Maybe the silvergirls imagined me on top of her, not even undoing those bonds, blindfold in place, allomorph spread out for me just so. He's human, male, this is all he really needs, they might whisper among themselves, remembering a time when they lived among humans, male and female alike.

"Did you live with them?" Imagining panicky silvergirls betraying a friend? Humans made them. Maybe we made them with all our flaws.

She shook her head, looking up at the sky, empty blue now, not a cloud in sight. The stemshine was brightening, burning white, burning the sky dark azure, making it seem impossibly far away. When she turned and looked at me, we stopped walking. Not a girl anymore.

She said, "I try to stay away from them. Let them get on with their business. Hope they'll let me get on with mine."

Their business. What business is there for abandoned tools? I walked on, waiting, stemlight coloring my skin emerald.

After a while, Deseret said, "It's their world now, Green Man. They're afraid you've come to take it away."

"And you?"

"No world for me."

The tent was just where I left it, sturdy and stiff atop its little hill, clasped in a crook of a slow-running river. Overhead, the stemshine was darkening, turning red against the dark blue sky, some tawny light beginning to form, emerging everywhere across the sky at once.

No horizon here.

I knelt and opened the pack, marveling that I'd remembered to put the cookstove away before setting out on my final errand, taking my gun on its long, pointless walk to the mountain, the gun now lying flat on the ground beside me, unfired.

Something in the gun might have longings too. . . .

Deseret stood a little distance away, back toward me, looking out across the landscape, hair ruffling in the wind. It seemed a little longer now then it'd been before, and from this angle, she was more woman than girl. Subtle effects, tried and true, tried and tried again.

Overhead, vermilion began spilling through the sky.

I pulled the cookstove out of the pack and sat cross-legged on the ground, looking at its shiny metallic resistance elements, a technology older, by just the tiniest bit, than starships. Older than what made me as well.

I released the first and simplest of my locks, feeling hunger bloom in my gut.

Softly, Deseret said, "In the olden days, I used to come here with a friend."

I pulled a ration card from the pack and set it on the stove, not bothering to read the label, trying not to remember what those olden days were like, trying not to picture what Deseret might have been like, picturing who her friend might have been.

A man like me? A client for whatever health-maintenance compact had owned her, had thrown her away, or merely forgotten her?

Or just some other tool?

Friend is such a complicated word.

I got out another pack and put it beside the first, ordering the stove to do its job. Deseret turned, probably picking up my command with her scanners. That's *her* job, left over from the olden days.

I saw she'd turned woman again, but subdued, barely defined.

Just enough.

She said, "Is one of those for me?"

I nodded.

She said, "I'm glad you remembered we can eat."

Something hooted from a patch of dark forest over where the valley floor began to slope upward toward the plain. Beyond the forest, towering out of the mist of distance, the end-cap cliffs were colored blood-red, etched with shadows by the fading stemlight.

Somewhere far overhead, unseeable by mortal eyes, an indistinct blotch of gray to me, lay the backside of the docking portal. When I arrived, I hadn't given any thought to how I might get out again.

I turned away and found Deseret standing before me, fully fleshed out once more, face shadowed and reddened by the fading light, body swollen, prepared, ready.

Nothing in her empty eyes, of course.

Beyond her, the ration cards were expanding on the stovetop, opening like flowers, rich steam rising, bringing us the flavor of the meal. One pack held a steak, baked potato, sour cream, butter, onions. The other one was a sausage pizza.

She touched me, making me look down. Breasts against me now, flattening out just so. Hand on my chest, fingers splayed. Face . . . *ineffable*. Isn't that what we say when we see . . . well. Still nothing in her eyes.

I shook my head slowly, trying to turn away, to reach for the meals that neither of us needed.

Familiar.

That's all.

Familiar comfort.

She said, "Please."

The utter desperation.

I know what it is to be a broken tool, thrown away, discarded as useless.

So you do what you have to do then, like any good soldier.

The filters and locks released and went down in proper sequence.

• • •

The most beautiful thing in the world is a woman's face while you make love to her.

Your hands do what they do, like robot hands belonging to another, working a body glimpsed from the corner of one eye, all dark shadow and faraway depth. Some other world. Some other place. Some other time.

All you can see is eyes full of fire, a face made taut and wonderful by the familiar tides of desire.

Sunrise.

But no sun.

Stemshine blossoming overhead, familiar golden bar melting out of the black depths of interstellar night, filling the world with light.

The valley outside the tent was the same, come morning. Same warm wind, same winding stream, same ersatz mechanical man looking out at it through indestructible eyes.

Except some part of him knows he's not a machine, not *made* to be anything in particular, not made at all.

"Come home with me."

That's all she said as we stood together, watching stemlight wash over the nameless world. Come home with me, soldier.

I wonder who thought up those lines for her to say?

Imagination conjured a programmer for me, some small fat man with greasy skin, a tangle of filthy gray hair, hunched over an antique keyboard, typing away with sweaty palms.

How could a man like that imagine such a woman's face, tell it how to look, what to reflect, back into the eyes of the watcher?

Some historical drama no doubt, seen as a child and forgotten into the depths of subconscious memory, becoming its own archetype.

A silent nod.

Tent folding itself up with a word, crawling into the backpack.

Then we were away, walking through the ruin of the world.

As if it were the only world, and we the only ones in it.

Walking by the glittery stream with its rush of dark water.

Listening to the soft howl of wind, bending through the tops of swaying old trees.

Loblolly pines. I remember that's what they're called.

In time I realized Deseret was skipping by my side, laughing, looking at me.

Not quite singing.

Maybe just in her heart.

Or whatever you want to call the thing that rests inside a living machine.

We rested together on a beach beside a depthless blue ocean beneath a colorless noonday sky, though neither of us needed rest, would ever need to rest.

Tireless, like the machines of myth.

In time, we walked on, skirting a dank, dark green forest, tall, gaunt trees that seemed to exude a pale gray mist, gray mist filling the spaces between, hiding the depths of the forest. Walked across the foothills of some nameless, blocky mountains, broken blue stone veined with bright silver, mountains perhaps no more than some industrial residue, waiting for a recycling crew that would never come again.

Stood together on a hillside, holding hands like children, looking down on another small valley, more secluded than the other, holding just the tiniest of streams. There was a lot of messy-looking shrubbery, thorn bushes, clearings here and there, a little sandy beach, a few tents in the shadow of a scrubby old apple tree, green apples hanging from its branches like Christmas-tree ornaments.

And beside the tree, buried in regolith to its axles, treads broken and gone . . .

I whispered, "Main battle tank. Standard ARM Corporation Model 56, body-style IIa." As I watched, its turret seemed to shift in my direction. Seemed to, but there was only a soft, stuttering whine of broken gears, a distant, chattery whir. The turret settled, stuck in place, but the periscope sensor lifted and slowly turned to look.

Deseret whispered, "His name is Thomas."

Sunset sky, deep indigo overhead, striated with the barest hint of lilac . . . the stemshine hung far beyond the blue, like a dim cloud of slag, on the edge of fiery oblivion. In two great, arching bands to either side, stars were appearing as the darkness deepened.

Strange, strange new world for such a tired old universe.

Empires beyond the stars that destroyed us all, yet survived themselves.

Nothing of the old, gray widow-maker.

No widows left behind.

No lost children.

Nothing left but their broken old toys.

Deseret and her two friends, Holly and Melina were their names, lived together in a little valley, in the shadow of Thomas the Main Battle Tank, living on because they had nothing better to do, keeping, they said, out of the silvergirls' way.

Someday, they said, the world will be made whole again by the silvergirls' labor.

What place in it for us, then? they whispered, one by one. Maybe none, was the chorused answer.

I made them dinner on my little campstove, scanning their joy, freely given, like memories of sunlight, long ago fled, sat by the open flap of the tent with Deseret at my side . . .

The other two were watching, I could see, holding themselves rigid, in neutral state, holding their pheromones in. Honor among machines, not striving for each other's position? What humans were ever so honest, ever so honorable as that?

Behind us in the gathering darkness, Thomas stirred in his grave, a rustle of mostly dead engine parts, a whisper of jammed gears rubbing softly together, a pattering shower of corrosion.

Overhead, a pattern of lights sailed the sky, coming between us and the stars. Balloonsailers. No running lights, of course, just the pale fire of engine exhaust. If I listened, I could hear the rumble of combustion.

I pictured myself firing on them again, from the summit of my cold, snowy mountain, and found I could no longer remember why I came. Oh, I know the reason. Remember it all too well. But the reason's gone, along with that cold ache . . . too many old machines, too many broken tools with that same old ache inside.

Deseret leaned close, rubbing her soft head against my shoulder, rubbing on skin proof against any degree of vacuum and cold, flesh that could withstand . . .

She whispered, "Drop your shields?"

Take off that too-human flesh. Expose that warm, soft underbelly . . . When I did, she let me sample what was inside Holly and Melina, flooding me with their need.

Too human

No. A human wouldn't care.

They're just machines, after all.

Things made for us, not we for them.

"Ashe?"

I took a deep breath, held it for a long moment, let it go. Felt something flood out of me, some unknown fear.

"All right."

You do what you have to do, if you are who you are.

Midnight, and the stars arced overhead in two dense bands, striping the sky between swathes of black. Somewhere up there, the stemshine hung, visible light output suspended. If I wanted to look, I could see the infrared, night-warmth radiated to the grounds below. If I wanted to look, I could see other lands, faraway lands, hanging overhead beyond the sky. If I wanted to look, there would be my tall, cold mountain, pennon of snow still trailing in the wind like a motionless flag. If I wanted to.

Wind whispering endlessly in the trees.

As if this were a natural world, wind driven by the chaotic heat engines of climate, by the rolling twist of coriolis force.

Fans. Somewhere here, underground, there are fans.

I could picture them, great blades turning, slowly, slowly, casting long shadows down the ductwork.

Maybe once there were children here. Bold children who would sneak into the ductwork, walk deep underground, come to see the slow fans turn, filling their world with wind. Maybe they took silvergirls along for company.

A whisper from the darkness.

I walked toward it.

"Hello, soldier," it said, voice sounding as though called forth from the dust.

"Hello, Thomas, old comrade."

"Have we met?"

"Does it matter?"

Brief pause, then, "No. Of course not."

We know each other well, battle tank and infantryman. I could remember marching in his shadow, time and time again. He could remember me swarming round him in countless, stickman shadows, daring the fire.

We've been together forever.

He said, "Why'd you come, soldier?"

I shrugged, knowing he'd see. "It . . . seemed like the place for me to . . ." What? What do I want to say?

Thomas, voice so very warm then, whispered, "I understand."

Do you? Of course you do. I reached out and put my hand on one crumpled fender, feeling the way whiskers had sprung from the composite, breaking, popping up out of half-melted osmiridium matrix. Once upon a time, there'd been coherent light reflex armor mounted here. Taken away, some long time ago.

I pictured the armorers walking away, carrying their salvage, leaving him here to die. Did they understand it would take so long? Did they care?

Evidently not.

He said, "I'd leave, if I could."

There was a cold hand on my heart. "I understand."

He said, "I knew you would, soldier. I knew I could count on you."

I laid my head on his fender, breathing in the scent of old machine.

He said, "I saw you on the mountain, soldier. I was afraid you wouldn't wait for me."

"Sorry. I . . ." I remembered myself upon the cold mountain, alone with the whispering spider and my poor paralyzed hands. One little tug, that's all it would've taken, but I . . . I said, "The balloonsailers knew."

He said, "They always do. They've been waiting as long as any one of us."

Any one of us.

Then, he said, "I was hoping the silvergirls would wait, but they haven't. I'm sorry, soldier."

When I turned my senses on and looked skyward, there they were, circling round and round like witches on their broomsticks, coming for me, I suppose. Coming for us.

It was the moment in which they would secure their future.

I wish I knew what was in their minds. Wish I had known. A brief moment of explanation, that's all. This is so unnecessary.

As are all such moments.

Too late.

Thomas's turret groaned and his guns tilted skyward. "Get the allomorphs away, soldier. I'll hold them off."

His guns went *pom-pom*, stuttering so loud, brilliant streaks of violet leaping skyward.

My tent exploded in a gout of orange flame, a compact mushroom cloud.

I got to the backpack, surrounded by molten fragments, small red flames guttering on the ground, got it open, felt myself grow suddenly vast and terrible, summoning all-too-human fire in the service of my all-too-human name.

Looked skyward, reaching out for them.

When it ended, there was nothing left but smoke, bits of

dying flame. And the voice of Thomas the Main Battle Tank, punched into pieces by the silvergirls' fire, whispering, "Soldier . . ." Ever so softly, "Please, soldier. I've been such a good machine. Please don't let me down. . . ."

I looked at him for just a moment, featureless in the darkness, molten metal sizzling in pools on the red-hot ground. Nodded slowly, knowing he might still be able to see.

You do what you have to do then.

If you're a good soldier.

I buried what little of Holly I could find, buried her among the smoldering fragments of Thomas the Main Battle Tank, pushing his parts together in the crater my gun left behind. No need for a marker. Not here.

Maybe the silvergirls will come someday, clean up this mess, dispose of what's useless, recycle the rest into shiny new machines. No matter that they'll be gone then. I'll remember who they were.

There was enough left of Melina I knew she could be saved, given the resources of any decent machine shop, so I bundled up the pieces and put them away in my backpack, rolling them up in magic canvas one by one, imagining each bit stirred, ever so slightly, at my touch.

Deseret?

Evidently, she'd managed to get out of the tent just before the silvergirls struck, had been running away from the blast. From some angles, she looked like a sleeping child, eyes closed, face quiet and sweet. I found her foot quite easily, lodged at the base of a broken tree. Looked for her arm a little while before giving it up.

I know a man can make her a new arm she'll never know is not the same.

I dropped my shields and awoke her with a scan, watched her eyes of glass open and look at me.

Strange how, with no armor between us, they don't seem empty anymore.

Whispered: "Soldier . . ."

"I'm here."

She said, "My friends . . . all my friends . . ."

I said, "Sleep now, Deseret. Sleep and dream. When you awaken, I'll still be here."

The eyes closed.

Face in repose.

Something almost like a smile there.

Smile of a child who trusts you'll keep your given word.

When she was put away, I shouldered the backpack and went on my way, back across broken old landscape, all the way to the endcap mountains.

I climbed the red cliffs as the stemshine blossomed to life, throwing my shadow before me on meaningless crags, no more than the artifice of some maker's hand, infinitely less than the splendor of a wild world, made by no hand at all, the imagining of some insensate mind.

Stood for a long time, then looking out into the blue mist of the silvergirls' world, at broad, rolling, ruin-filled plains, rivers, seas, ranges of dark-shadowed hills, my own special mountain with its white spray of snow.

Broke the gun between my hands and threw it away, down into the world for the silvergirls to find. Turned away and went out the lock, out to where the faraway stars rolled and rolled, unaffected by foolish deeds, senseless pride, useless fear.

Stood for a while, watching them turn, marveling at how little it's taken to bring me here. What did I think I was going to accomplish? Nothing, I suppose. And nothing left now but to open the datawarren connector and summon a ride.

You do what you have to do.

Because, sometimes, all that's left is life.

LEGACIES

Tom Purdom

Tom Purdom made his first sale in 1957, to Fantastic Universe, *and has subsequently sold to* Analog, The Magazine of Fantasy and Science Fiction, Star, *and most of the major magazines and anthologies. In recent years, he's become a frequent contributor to* Asimov's Science Fiction. *He is the author of one of the most unfairly forgotten SF novels of the sixties, the powerful and still-timely* Reduction in Arms, *about the difficulties of disarmament in the face of the mad proliferation of nuclear weapons, as well as such novels as* I Want the Stars, Tree Lord of Imeten, Five Against Arlane, *and* The Barons of Behavior. *Purdom lives with his family in Philadelphia, where he reviews classical music concerts for a local newspaper, and is at work on several new novels.*

In the fascinating story that follows, he gives us a subtle, bittersweet, and moving examination of the special problems and challenges that growing up in a career military family can bestow—even in a high-tech future, where wars are fought in deep space.

Deni Wei-Kolin was asleep in the childcare center at Hammarskjold Station when the fifteen assault vehicles began their kamikaze run into Rinaswandi Base. Rinaswandi was in the asteroid belt, about a third of the way around the sun from the Earth-Moon system, so it would be a good twenty-five minutes before a signal carrying news of the attack reached Hammarskjold and the other man-made satellites that orbited Earth and Luna. The signal would actually reach

Hammarskjold a full second later than it reached some of the other habitats, in fact. Hammarskjold was the off-Earth military headquarters of the UN Secretariat and it had been placed in a lunar orbit, for the kind of accidental political reasons that usually decide such matters. Given the positions of the Earth and the Moon at the time the signal started its journey, the message from Rinaswandi actually had to zap past Earth before a big antenna sucked it into Hammarskjold's electronic systems.

Deni's mother, Gunnery Sergeant Wei, got the news a bit earlier than most of the fifteen billion people who currently inhabited the solar system. The military personnel stationed in Rinaswandi Base had been under siege for seventeen days when the attack began. For twelve hours out of every twenty-four, Deni's mother had been plugged into the Rinaswandi defense system, ready to respond the moment the alert signal pinged into her ear and the injector built into her combat suit shot a personalized dose of stimulant/tranquilizer into her thigh.

All around Sergeant Wei people were beginning to stir. There were twenty of them crammed into the command module—a place that was only supposed to provide working space for six—and you couldn't shift your weight without disturbing someone. Half of them were merely observers—support people and administrative wallahs. Gunnery Sergeant Wei could hear little whispers and murmurs as they caught glimpses of the symbols moving across the screens in front of the combat specialists.

The stimulant/tranquilizer started spreading its chemical blessings through Sergeant Wei's nervous system. The long, carefully groomed fingers of her left hand slipped into position just below the keypad she would use to direct the missiles, guns, and electronic devices under her control.

The acting commander of Rinaswandi Base, Logistics Captain Tai, was a slender young man who tended to relate to his subordinates with a lot of handclapping and mock-enthusiastic banter. Even now, when the arrows and icons on his screens represented real vehicles armed with real ammunition, the voice in Sergeant Wei's earphones sounded like it was sending some kind of sports team into a tournament.

"Allll right, people. As you can see, ladies and gentlemen, they're all bunched up on one side of our happy little home, in Quadrants III and IV. Apparently they're hoping they can overwhelm whatever we've got on that side. Gunner Three—take the eight targets on the left in your quadrant. Gunner Four—take everything in your quadrant plus the four on the right in Quadrant Three. Gunner One, Gunner Two—be prepared to switch your attentions to the other two quadrants. But I would appreciate it—to say the least—if you would keep an eye out for anybody trying to slip in on your side while we're looking the other way. Let's not assume they're as dumb as we think they are."

In the childcare center, twenty-five light-minutes away, Sergeant Wei's son was sleeping with his right arm draped across the stuffed animal he had been given when he was two—a hippopotamus, about half as long as he was tall, that Deni had named Ibar. Two of the children sleeping near him had parents on Rinaswandi. Six had parents on the four hydrogen-fusion torch ships that had accelerated away from Hammarskjold Station, crammed with troops and equipment, two days after Rinaswandi had come under siege.

Every day all the children in the childcare center stretched out on the big shaggy rug in the playroom and listened to a briefing. Every day, the younger ones focused their best I'm-a-good-student stares on an orbital diagram that showed the current positions of Hammarskjold Station, Rinaswandi, the four torch ships, and a place in the asteroid belt called Akara City. They all knew, as well as their young minds could grasp it, that Akara City had been ruled for five decades by a strong-willed mayor who had turned it into a bustling commercial center in which half a million people took full advantage of the raw materials available in the asteroid belt. The mayor had died, her successor had been caught in a financial scandal, and the turmoil had somehow led to a classic breakdown of social order—a breakdown that had been manipulated by an obscure married couple who had emigrated to Akara City after they had been chased out of a Zen-Random communal colony. In the last six months, according to the teachers who gave the briefing, Mr. and Mrs. Chen had done some "very bad things." One of the bad things they had done had been killing people—about three hundred, according to the most believable news reports. They had also engaged in approximately two thousand involuntary personality modifications—but that was a crime young children sometimes had trouble understanding.

Six weeks ago, a hundred troops could have torched into Rinaswandi Base, picked up the weapons and fighting vehicles stockpiled in its vaults, and deposed Mr. and Mrs. Chen in a few hours. As usual, however, the international politicians had dithered about "sovereignty" and the exact border that defined the line between "internal" and "external" affairs. And while they dithered, Mr. and Mrs. Chen had managed to establish communications with an officer at Rinaswandi who had been greedier than his psychological profiles had indicated. The equipment stockpiled in Rinaswandi had become part of the Chens' arsenal and the personnel stationed in Rinaswandi had crammed themselves into their command module and started watching their screens.

The teachers at the childcare center would never have told their charges the politicians had "dithered," of course. They were officers in the Fourth International Brigade. Proper military people never say bitter things about politicians during official, approved briefings.

Nobody on Hammarskjold told Deni they felt sorry for him, either. That was another thing military people didn't do. If anyone *had* given Deni a pat and a sympathetic word, however, he would have thanked them very politely and even looked a little thoughtful. For a moment, in fact, he would have thought he really did feel sad.

Deni's mother had been stationed on Rinaswandi for two

months before the siege had broken out. For most of the second month, his father, Assault Sergeant Kolin, had been trying to convince him a boy of his age shouldn't sleep with a stuffed hippopotamus. It hadn't been as bad as the time his father had made him stop wetting the bed. That time Deni had been forced to endure almost six weeks of hand slappings, sarcastic baby talk, and "confinement to quarters" in a sopping bed.

Deni was seven years old. For four of those years—over half his lifetime—one of his parents had been away on some kind of military assignment. When his mother was gone, he lived with an easygoing, enjoy-it-while-you-can father whose basic indolence was punctuated by periods in which Assault Sergeant Kolin became obsessed by the belief his son needed "discipline." When his father was away, Deni's days were dominated by a goal-oriented mother who believed every moment of a child's life should be as productive as she could make it. When they were both home, he frequently found himself pressing against a wall, knees doubled against his chest, while they engaged in "domestic disputes" that sometimes ended in bruised faces and even broken bones.

Deni's day-to-day life in the childcare center had its flaws. He still had to sit through the daily message Sergeant Wei videoed from Rinaswandi, in spite of the siege. He still had to send his mother a return message in which he assured her he was practicing his flute two hours and fifteen minutes every day—the minimum a boy as talented as her son should practice, in Sergeant Wei's opinion. He still had to spend three hours a week talking to an officer named Medical Captain Min, who kept pestering him with questions about the way he felt about different things. All in all, however, the last fifteen days of Deni's life had been a lot pleasanter than most of the other two-week periods he could remember. Somewhere in the center of his personality, sleeping with his hippopotamus, there was a little boy who would have been quite happy if neither of his parents ever came home again.

And that, of course, was the problem.

• • •

Medical Captain Dorothy Min was a tall young woman with a round, pleasant face and a manner that correlated with her appearance. Deni Wei-Kolin might have liked her very much, in fact, if she had been a teacher or a childcare specialist. At 23:07 Hammarskjold time—forty-two minutes after the Rinaswandi defense system had decided it was under attack—Captain Min was sitting in front of the communications screen in her personal quarters. She was revising a statement in which she requested, for the fourth time, that she be allowed to communicate with Deni's parents. She was staring at a paragraph in which she explained—once again—the major reason she wanted to apply a procedure that she and her colleagues usually referred to as an "esem."

I can only repeat what I've already said before, the paragraph under consideration read. *The death of one of Deni's parents—especially in combat—could result in permanent, lifelong psychological damage if we do not apply the appropriate preventive measure before that happens. Fantasies about his parents' deaths have become an important component of Deni's emotional structure. The death of one of his parents could trigger guilt reactions no seven-year-old personality can possibly handle. It has now been fourteen days since I originally asked for permission to discuss this matter with Gunnery Sergeant Wei and Assault Sergeant Kolin. If either of his parents is killed in combat before we can provide him with the benefits of at least one session with an ego-strengthening emotional modification procedure, the prognosis for Deni's future emotional development is about as hopeless as it can get.*

Half the space on Captain Min's screen was cluttered with paragraphs and charts she had included in the three memos she had already addressed to the commander of the Akara Assault Force. She should keep her memo short, her contact on the torch ships had told her, but she shouldn't assume General Lundstrom had read her previous communications.

This time, her contact had assured her, the message would bypass the general's overprotective staff.

She touched the screen with her finger and drew an X over the now in It has now been fourteen days. The now added a little emphasis, in her opinion, but her contact had made it clear every word counted.

A light glowed over a loudspeaker. "Captain Dorothy Min has a call from Dr. Bedakar Barian," the communications system murmured. "Emergency Priority."

Captain Min tapped the accept button on her keyboard. A plump, bearded face replaced the text on her screen.

"There's a report on Trans-Solar, Dorothy—and attack on Rinaswandi. Have you seen it yet?"

Captain Min grabbed her stylus and scratched a command on the notebook lying beside her right hand. Dr. Barian's face receded to the upper left quarter of her communications screen. A printed news bulletin started scrolling across the right half.

"I told my system to monitor the Akara crisis and alert me if it picked up any major developments," Dr. Barian said. "Trans-Solar may not be as trustworthy as the stuff you people get through channels, but it looks like it's a lot faster."

Captain Min had been wearing her working uniform while she dictated. Now her hands reached down and automatically tightened the belt on her tunic. One of the purposes of military training, her father had always claimed, was the development of a military alter ego—a limited personality that could take control of your responses whenever you were confronted with realities that would have overwhelmed any normal human. The surge of emotion reached a danger point, a circuit kicked in, and the hard, clear responses of the professional officer or NCO replaced the messy turbulence of the human being cringing inside the uniform.

There were no pictures yet. All Trans-Solar had was a few messages from Rinaswandi and a statement from Mr. and Mrs. Chen claiming that the "center of international militarism" on Rinaswandi had been "effectively terminated."

"That's crazy," Captain Min said. "Even for them it's crazy."

"It's what they've been telling us they were going to do for the last seventeen days."

"It's still crazy. They could have pulled a quarter of our assault force away from the attack on Akara City just by maintaining a low-level threat against Rinaswandi. Now they don't even have the threat."

"Apparently their assessment of the situation doesn't conform to standard military logic."

Dr. Barian lived in Nous Avon, the smallest of the Five Cities that housed most of the human beings who inhabited the space between Earth and Luna. Captain Min had never met him in person but his face had dominated her communication screens—and her dreams—from the day he had become her mentor for her training in family therapy. She was especially familiar with the look he got on his face when he was contemplating the follies of people who wore uniforms.

Dr. Barian was, in her opinion, one of the best teachers she had ever worked with. The lectures, reading materials and learning programs he had chosen for her had always been first rate. His criticisms of her work had almost always made sense. He just happened to believe the human brain turned into sludge the moment you put a blue hat on top of it.

"You'd better call the childcare center," Dr. Barian said. "Right away. Tell them you want Deni kept away from any contact that may give him the news—video, other children. Make it clear you're the one who's going to tell him—no one else."

He lowered his head, as if he were examining some notes, then looked up again. "Then I think it's time you and I stopped playing games, young woman. We're both well aware that everything you've been saying in all your memos only proves that Deni should have been put through the complete modification procedure the day his father went riding off to war. You're supposed to be a therapist, Dorothy—a healer.

The people who wrote the laws can't make your decisions for you."

Captain Min stared at him. This was the first time Dr. Barian had made it absolutely clear he thought she should have applied the esem without waiting for the parents' consent. He had been dropping hints ever since the Akara crisis had started developing, but he had never put it quite so bluntly.

"We still don't even know Sergeant Wei is dead, Dr. Barian. Don't you think we should verify that before we start asking ourselves if we've got a right to start ignoring the law?"

"From what you're saying, it sounds like most of the control module has been blown up. If she isn't dead, then we've had a scare that should convince you we're risking that child's welfare—unnecessarily—every day we sit around trying to avoid the inevitable. There's no way anyone can determine a child has received the benefits of an esem, Dorothy. If you can arrange things so you give him the news in your office, you can apply the procedure in complete privacy—without the slightest possibility anyone will know you've done it. If his parents give you a nice legal, properly authorized permission statement later on, you can pretend you executed the esem then."

"I'm well aware no one will be able to prove I administered the esem without a legal authorization, Dr. Barian. You've pointed that out to me at least four times in the last two weeks."

"I understand your feelings, Dorothy. You aren't the first therapist who's been put in a position like this. All I can tell you is that if he were my patient I would have resolved the whole issue two weeks ago. The whole idea of requiring parental consent in a situation like this is absurd. Deni's parents are the last people in the universe who could possibly understand why he needs that kind of help."

"Sergeant Wei would have agreed to the esem sooner or later. Every report I've given you for the last ten weeks contains some indication she would have given me her consent sometime in the next few months. We both know her husband would have given in sooner or later just to keep the peace, once she started working on him."

"But she didn't. And now she's never going to."

Captain Min's screen blinked. The face of her commanding officer, Medical Colonel Pao, popped onto the lower left-hand corner.

"I have a message for you from General Lundstrom, Dorothy. Can I assume you've already been advised of the news regarding Rinaswandi?"

"I've just been looking at the report on Trans-Solar, sir. My mentor, Dr. Barian, is on the line with me now—listening in."

"General Lundstrom apparently recorded this message only five minutes after she got the news herself. She wants to know if you still want to discuss the esem procedure with Sergeant Kolin."

Captain Min swallowed. "Does that mean Sergeant Wei is definitely considered a casualty?"

"Are you serious?" Dr. Barian murmured. "I can't believe you could still think anything else, Dorothy."

"I'm afraid that has to be the assumption," Colonel Pao said. "We're still listening for messages from Rinaswandi, but I don't think anybody's very optimistic."

"Can you advise General Lundstrom I said yes, sir? Tell them I'll need about an hour to prepare a statement for Sergeant Kolin. The communications time lag between here and the ships is almost eleven minutes now. There's no way I can engage in a real discussion with him."

"Let me talk to your colonel," Dr. Barian said.

Captain Min stared at him. She started to turn him down and reluctantly decided the combative glint in his eye was a good indication he would respond with an embarrassing flurry of argument. "Dr. Barian would like to discuss something with you, Colonel Pao."

"Can you ask him if it's absolutely necessary?"

Captain Min stopped for a moment and switched to the section of her brain cells that contained her ability to speak in Techno Mandarin. She had been talking to Colonel Pao in Ghurkali—the official working language of the Fourth International Brigade. Dr. Barian had picked up a good listening knowledge of Ghurkali, but she knew he would be more comfortable speaking one of the three international languages.

"Colonel Pao wants to know if it's absolutely necessary, Dr. Barian."

"At this point I would say it's about as necessary as anything I've ever done."

She raised her eyebrows a fraction of a centimeter, to let Colonel Pao know she was having problems, and the colonel gave her a nod and answered in the language she had chosen. "Go ahead, Dorothy."

She tapped the buttons that would turn the situation into a full conference call and Dr. Barian started talking as soon as Colonel Pao's face appeared on the screen.

"Dr. Min has made three attempts to communicate with Deni Wei-Kolin's parents, Colonel Pao. I assume you've read the reports she's submitted to General Lundstrom."

"I read every word in them before I forwarded them with my approval, Dr. Barian."

"Then I assume you recognize the gravity of the present situation. The ego-strengthening personality modification is the treatment of choice in situations in which a child is being subjected to the strains Deni has been absorbing. It's an absolute necessity when one of the parents who has been responsible for those strains dies prematurely. We are discussing one of the best-documented phenomena in the literature. No child Deni's age can deal with the guilt that is going to begin eating at his sense of self-worth the moment he hears his mother is dead. His primary reaction to his mother's death will be the creation of a cluster of unconscious guilt feelings that will distort his entire personality."

Colonel Pao nodded politely. "I'm well aware of that, sir. Captain Min included all that information in her reports."

"Under normal circumstances," Dr. Barian said, "we could continue with the standard procedure Dr. Min has been following. Dr. Min would continue counseling the parents three times a week for another year. Eventually they would acquire some insight into Deni's needs and give her permission to proceed with the modification procedure. Dr. Min asked for permission to continue the counseling sessions when the Akara crisis broke out and it was denied her on the ground that it would subject Deni's parents to too much stress at a time when they might be forced to carry out the more violent aspects of their military duties. She then asked for permission to discuss the situation with them just once, to see if they might agree to the modification as an emergency procedure. We've now spent *two weeks* waiting for a reply. All our efforts to contact Deni's parents have met with bureaucratic delaying tactics. And now that we're in an emergency situation—now that the very thing we feared has happened—your general has finally seen some sense and agreed to let us ask a man who's under extreme stress for permission to do something we should have done days ago."

Colonel Pao frowned. "Are you telling me you don't believe Captain Min should accept General Lundstrom's offer, Dr. Barian?"

"I think it's time someone pointed out that Captain Min hasn't been *permitted* to talk to Deni's parents. We're going to be talking to Deni's father under the worst possible conditions. If our efforts fail—the primary reason will be the fact that we've been forced into this position because your general and her staff have spent the last two weeks doing everything they could to evade their responsibilities."

Colonel Pao belonged to a subgroup that the sociologists who studied the military community sometimes referred to as the "military aristocracy." Members of his family had been serving in United Nations military units since the years in which the first international brigades had been formed on

Earth. From his earliest days in the army, when he had been a young intern, people had been impressed by the way he always conducted himself with the controlled graciousness of the classic Confucian gentleman.

Two weeks ago, just before the torch ships had left Hammarskjold, Captain Min had spent a few hours with a young surgical captain who had been responsible for loading the hospital equipment. The captain had let his mind wander at a critical moment and the entire loading process had been snarled into a tangle that could have delayed departure by ten hours if Colonel Pao hadn't suddenly started offering courteously phrased "suggestions." The captain was one of the most self-absorbed young men Captain Min had ever known, but even he had been forced to admit that he would have disemboweled a subordinate who had created the kind of mess he had manufactured.

"I realize General Lundstrom may have behaved somewhat cautiously," Colonel Pao said. "I must tell you, however, that I might have tried to postpone a decision on this matter myself, if I were in her position. General Lundstrom is responsible for the lives of four hundred beings. If Sergeant Kolin does go into combat—and we've been given every reason to think combat is unavoidable—the lives of all the people around him could depend on his reactions. General Lundstrom wouldn't have been doing her duty if she hadn't worried about something that could have a significant effect on his emotional state."

"Your bureaucratic maneuvering may have destroyed the future of a defenseless child. If—"

Captain Min's hand leaped to the keyboard. She jabbed at the appropriate buttons and cut the link between Colonel Pao and Dr. Barian.

"Dr. Barian and I will get to work on our statement for Sergeant Kolin right away, sir. Please thank General Lundstrom for me."

"Please give Dr. Barian my regards, Dorothy."

A neutral background color replaced Colonel Pao's face

in the lower left quarter of the screen. In the upper left quarter, Dr. Barian was looking at her defiantly.

"We needed to get that on the record," Dr. Barian said. "I made a recording of my side of the conversation, with a record of who else was on the line."

"Colonel Pao is one of the most respected men I've ever known," Captain Min said. "He always treats everybody around him with respect—and they normally respond by treating him the way he treats them."

"He's a military bureaucrat just like everybody else you're dealing with, young woman. You should have put a statement like that in your files the day he and the rest of your military *colleagues* started giving you the runaround."

The director of the childcare center looked relieved when he realized he wouldn't have to break the news to Deni himself. Two of his full-time charges had parents on Rinaswandi. Eleven of the kids who had parents on the torch ships were old enough to realize Mr. and Mrs. Chen had just demonstrated their parents really were charging into danger.

"I'm sorry we didn't call you right away," the director said. "I'm afraid we've really been in a turmoil here."

Dorothy nodded. "How long can you keep Deni quarantined?"

"He should be all right until just before breakfast—until 0730. We've made it a point not to make any mention of the news when they first wake up, just in case something like this happened, but there's no way we can keep it quiet once the day kids come in."

"He's going to know there's something odd going on as soon as he sees me showing up that early. I'm not exactly one of his favorite people."

"We'll make a private room available. I'll tell the night counselor you need to take Deni into her room as soon as you get there."

Dr. Barian's precise high-speed Techno Mandarin broke into the conversation. "Dr. Min needs to take her patient directly to her office. This situation has important therapeutic ramifications. She needs to see him in a place where she can spend as much time with him as she needs."

"Have somebody tell Deni I've got some extra questions I need to ask him," Dorothy said. "Don't tell him any more than that—make it sound like one of those things grown-ups do and kids have to put up with. Tell him I'm sorry—tell him I've promised you I'm having strawberry muffins with real butter brought into the office just to make up for it. He claims that's the best thing he and his father eat for breakfast when they're alone together."

Given the communications lag, there was only one way to handle the situation. An autonomous discussion program had to be transmitted to the torch ship. The program would be outfitted with a general strategy and equipped with critical information and prerecorded discussions of the treatment. Then they would sit back and watch as their screens told them how Sergeant Kolin had reacted eleven minutes ago.

Dr. Barian had reviewed almost every session Dorothy had spent with Sergeant Kolin. He quibbled with her over some of the numerical estimates she plugged into the program, but no one could argue with her overall evaluation of the sergeant's personality structure.

Deni's father had grown up in an "extended family network" that had been created by a complicated series of divorces and regrouping. He had spent his formative years in a complex web of relationships in which no one and everyone was responsible for the children. His emotional development had been shaped by a situation in which he and nine other children were involved in a ceaseless competition for the love and praise of thirty adults who were heavily involved in their own competitions and interactions. He had never experienced the love of someone who considered him the absolute dead center of the universe. He had covered up his own lack of self-esteem by convincing himself he had enough self-esteem for twenty people. Then he had buried his insecurities a couple of meters deeper by telling himself other people were just as bouncy and assertive as he thought he was. His son, he had told Dorothy on several occasions, was about as stuck on himself as a boy could be. Deni would have been a lot easier to handle, Sergeant Kolin believed, if his mother hadn't succumbed to the delusion she had given birth to a genius.

Sergeant Wei and Sergeant Kolin belonged to the class that created some of the worst problems military family therapists had to live with. They were both people who responded to the enticements of the recruiting commercials precisely because their own childhoods had been developmental disasters. Deni's mother had pushed and punished because she herself had grown up in a family that had lived on the edge of chaos. His father had hammered at him because it was the only way Sergeant Kolin could deny the existence of the hungry boy inside himself.

If someone had put Deni's parents inside an esem treatment chamber at some point in *their* childhoods, their son might not be facing a psychological catastrophe. Essentially, the esem was supposed to endow Deni with a powerful, totally unsmashable feeling that he was a worthwhile person. In families where everything was working the way it was supposed to, the child developed that feeling from parents who communicated—day after day, year after year—a normal amount of love and a general sense that the child was valued. Deni would get it in two hours, with the help of half a dozen drugs and an interactive, multisensory program. The drugs would throw him into a semiconscious state, immerse him in an ocean of calm, and dissolve his defenses against persuasion. The program would monitor all the standard physiological reactions while it bombarded him with feelings, ideas, and experiences that "rectified the deficits in his domestic environment." The intervention was usually applied three times, over the period of a month, but even one application could be helpful.

In the midst of winter, a twentieth-century philosopher

named Albert Camus had once said, *I found that there was in me an invincible summer.* For the rest of his life, no matter how he was treated, Deni would be held erect by the summer the esem would plant in the center of his personality.

So how should they convince an exceptionally un-esem'd adult male that he should let them transform his son into the kind of person he thought he was? Dorothy had originally assumed Deni's mother would be the one who accepted the need for the esem. Once Sergeant Wei had acquired some insight into the realities of her family life, Dorothy had believed, there was a good chance she would buy the esem for the same reasons she bought expensive learning programs and other products that could help her son "achieve his full potential." And once Deni's mother had made up her mind, the relevant analyses all indicated Sergeant Kolin would eventually let her have her way.

Their best hope, in Dorothy's view, was an appeal to some of the most powerful emotions nurtured by the military culture. Normally Sergeant Kolin would have rooted himself behind an armored wall as soon as anyone claimed his son needed special treatment. Now they could get around his defenses by claiming Deni was a combat casualty. The program should play on the idea that Deni had been wounded, Dorothy argued. It should portray the esem as a kind of emotional antibiotic.

Dr. Barian wanted to work with the emotional dynamics that coupled guilt with idealization. The Kolin-Wei marriage, in Dr. Barian's opinion, had been one of the worst mixtures of dependency and hostility he had ever examined. It had been so bad he felt confident they could assume Sergeant Kolin had already started idealizing his wife's memory. Their best approach, therefore, would be an appeal that treated the esem as if it were primarily supposed to help Deni deal with the loss of his mother. Dorothy was correct when she objected that the idealization process usually didn't acquire any real force for several days—but Dr. Barian wouldn't be surprised, in this case, if it had kicked into action the moment Sergeant Kolin had been advised his wife might be dead.

"We're talking about one of the fundamental correlations in the literature, Dorothy. The worse the relationship, the stronger the tendency to idealize."

Dorothy started to argue with him, then glanced at the clock and compromised. The program would open with the combat casualty approach and follow it with a couple of tentative comments on the special problems of boys who had lost their mothers. If Sergeant Kolin made a response that indicated he was already locked into the idealization process, the program would shift tracks and start developing the idea that the boy needed special help because he had lost the support of a special person.

The really divisive issue was the description of the therapy. Dr. Barian wanted her to prepare a description that talked about the procedure as if they were merely going to bathe Deni in love. They *might* include a hint that they were trying to replace the love Deni had lost when his mother had died. But there would be no reference whatsoever to the effect on the patient's self-image.

That was a little like describing an antibiotic without mentioning it killed germs, of course. Dr. Barian apparently had his own ideas about the meaning of the term "informed consent." In his case, the important word was obviously "consent."

Deni would have been surprised to hear it, but he and his parents were only the second family Captain Min had ever worked with. Her original doctorate had been a Ph.D. in educational psychology, not family therapy. The Secretariat had paid for it and she had assumed she would pay off the debt by spending six years in uniform working with military training systems. Instead, the military personnel experts had looked at the data on their screens and discovered the Fourth International Brigade had a pressing need for family therapists. A crash program had been set up and she had spent her first eighteen months as an officer working on a second doctorate—under the guidance of a civilian mentor who apparently believed there was an inverse relationship between intelligence and the number of years someone had spent in the military. In her case, in addition, Dr. Barian had seemed to feel her childhood had subtracted an additional twenty points from her IQ.

It was the first time she had encountered someone with Dr. Barian's attitude. She had spent two years in a lunar "socialization academy" when she had been a teenager, but 80 percent of the children in her cohort had been the offspring of military people and international bureaucrats. At first she had thought Dr. Barian was trying to probe her responses to the kind of stresses she might receive from her patients. Then she had decided she would just have to ignore his comments on her "contaminated upbringing."

Dr. Barian had hammered at her resolution as if he thought his career depended on it. Much of her training involved long sessions with simulations of patient-therapist relationships. Most of the simulated people who appeared on her screens were trapped in simulated messes that were so foolish—and unbelievable—that she frequently found herself wondering how the human race had made it to the twenty-second century. In the critiques that followed the simulations, Dr. Barian loved to remind her that her reactions to her imaginary patients had probably been distorted by the "inadequacies" in her own "formative environment."

"My upbringing was about as good as it could be, Dr. Barian," she had told him once. "I may have more sympathy for the way military people look at things than you do, but it isn't because anybody indoctrinated me. My father may not have been the most loving man who ever lived, but he was so responsible he must have scanned half the research that's been done on military families in the last fifty years. He must have interviewed half a dozen foster care candidates every time he had to leave me alone, just to make sure they really would give me a consistent environment, just like all the literature said they should."

Naturally, Dr. Barian had then started questioning her feelings about her father.

Nineteen years ago, when Dorothy had been six, she had sat on a rug that had looked exactly like the shaggy rug Deni and his schoolmates sat on when they received their daily briefing. In her case, the orbital diagram on the screen had only contained two symbols—a circle that represented a single torch ship and an oval that represented a Lumina Industries mining asteroid.

The 150 men and women who had taken over the asteroid had belonged to a group that had somehow convinced themselves the city of Rome, on Earth, was the center of all evil and the sole reason mankind could not achieve political perfection. They had killed fifty people in a surprise attack that had put them in control of the torch that was supposed to shove the asteroid and its load of minerals into orbit about the Earth. Then they had set up their defensive weaponry and placed the asteroid on a course that would bring it down somewhere on the southern Italian peninsula. Her father, Pilot Sergeant Min, had made eight ferry trips to the surface of the asteroid, carrying assault troops and heavy weapons.

Her father had been her only parent for most of her childhood, but there had been no danger she would ever succumb to guilt feelings if he had happened to die in combat. After her mother had left them, her father had shouldered full responsibility for her upbringing—and carried out his parental duties in the same way he had fulfilled every other obligation life had loaded on him.

It hadn't been a natural thing, either. Her father was currently living in retirement in Eratosthenes Crater, on the Moon, and she knew he was perfectly content with a relationship that was limited to biweekly phone calls. He was, at heart, the kind of man who was happiest when he was hanging around with other adults like himself. As far as she could tell, he now spent most of his waking hours with a group of cronies whose idea of Heaven was an NCO club that never closed.

The last time she had talked to him, she had been looking for advice on the best way to speed up consideration of her request to speak to Deni's parents. It had been a serious matter, but they had both enjoyed the way he had folded his arms over his chest and pondered the subject with all the exaggerated, slightly elephantine dignity of a senior NCO who had been asked to give a junior officer his best advice.

"Are you asking me, Captain, if I'm still connected with the sergeant's network?"

"I did have something like that in mind, Sergeant."

"As it turns out, I do have a friend who has a certain position on General Lundstrom's staff. I'd rather not mention her name, but I suspect she might be willing to give me some useful advice on the best way to slip your next report past the general's aides. She might even give it a little judicious help if I gave her some good reasons to do it."

"That would be most helpful, Sergeant."

"Then I shall attend to it with the utmost dispatch, Captain."

Military parents like Deni's father and mother had a well-documented tendency to think of the family as a military unit, with the parents as the officers, and the children, inevitably, as members of the lower ranks. *Her* father had called her "Lieutenant" from the time she was two years old. For most of her childhood, she had been herself as a younger person who was being guided and supported by an experienced, gently ironic senior who respected her potential.

It was 02:04 by the time they got the program ready for transmission. At 02:15 the transmission began to arrive at the ship. At 02:20 Sergeant Kolin sat down in front of a screen and started watching Dorothy's presentation. At 02:31 his face appeared on Dorothy's communication screen and she got her first look at his response to her efforts.

The program opened with a recording in which Dorothy discussed the effects of combat deaths on children. The presentation was calm, statistical, and scrupulously accurate. On the auxiliary screen on her right, she could watch her neat, fully uniformed image and correlate the statements it was making with the reactions flickering across Sergeant Kolin's face.

"Do you have any questions about anything I've said so far?" the recording asked.

Sergeant Kolin shook his head. He had always kept his guard up during their counseling sessions and he was falling into the same pattern now. Most of her information about his personality came from his responses to interactive video dramas. The dramas that had worked had usually been designed so they practically forced the subject to make a response.

Dorothy's hands tightened on her desktop. She hated watching herself make presentations. Every flaw in her delivery jumped out at her. She saw her head dip just a fraction of a centimeter—a brief, tiny lapse in concentration—and she winced at the way she had telegraphed the fact that she was about to say something significant.

"In this case," the Dorothy on the screen said, "there's the added factor that the parent who's become a casualty is the child's mother. The relationship between a young boy and his mother frequently includes emotional overtones that can't be replaced by any other kind of relationship."

Her image paused for a carefully timed instant—a break that was supposed to give Sergeant Kolin the chance to start a response. He leaned forward with the beginning of a frown on his face and a subtitle lit up on the auxiliary screen. *Light positive response detected. Continuing probe.*

The program's visual interpretation capabilities were limited to relatively large-scale body movements, but Dorothy had been able to list three actions that should be given extra weight—and the first item on the list had been that tendency to lean forward. Sometimes, if you waited just a moment longer, Sergeant Kolin would lean a little further and say something that could lead to three minutes of real discussion.

This time he just settled back again. If he had started idealizing his wife's memory, he apparently didn't feel like expressing the feelings the idealization had aroused.

"I'm afraid there's a good possibility he's just angry," Dorothy said. "This isn't the first time I've seen that kind of tight-lipped expression."

"Angry at us?" Dr. Barian said.

"He really hates the whole idea of people examining his feelings. He looks like he's in one of those moods where he'd like to pick up his chair and throw it at the screen."

The program had apparently reached a similar conclusion. Her image had already slipped into a sentence that treated the mother-son relationship as if it was merely a side issue. The sound system let out a blip, to remind Sergeant Kolin he was looking at a recording, and the program switched to her description of the therapy.

Dorothy had drastically revised her standard description. She had included a shot of the treatment chamber, but the shot only showed part of the cover and it only lasted a couple of seconds.

She had done everything she could to make it clear they weren't "rewiring" Deni. "To a large extent," the video Dorothy said, "we're just giving Deni in advance the effects of all the love he's going to be missing during the next few years." She had touched on the danger of guilt feelings, but she had skipped over the relationship between guilt and the anger evoked by demanding parents.

The program reached a checkpoint. "Do you have any comments you would like to make, Sergeant Kolin? Please feel free to speak as freely as you want to. This program can answer almost any question you can ask."

Sergeant Kolin leaped out of his chair. His head disappeared from the screen for a moment. The camera readjusted its field of vision and focused on a face that was contorted with rage.

Deni's father had been trained in the same NCO schools every sergeant in the Fourth International Brigade had attended. Sergeants never bellowed. Their voices dropped to tight, controlled murmurs that made the anger on their faces look a hundred times more intense.

"My son doesn't need people poking into his brain," Sergeant Kolin said. "My son will get all the attention he needs from the person who's supposed to give it to him."

Dorothy's image stared at him while the program raced through alternative responses. The screen dissolved into an abstract pattern that was supposed to be emotionally neutral. An avuncular synthetic voice took over the conversation.

"We're sorry if we've angered you, Sergeant Kolin," the voice said. "We're trying to explain this procedure under difficult circumstances. Captain Min has prepared answers to most of the questions people raise when they're asked to approve this type of emotional intervention."

Dorothy bit her lip. Her right hand hovered over her notebook with the stylus poised to start writing—as if some part of her nervous system still didn't believe her orders had to cross eleven light-minutes before they evoked a response from the program.

She had prepared a statement the program could jump to if Sergeant Kolin expressed his basic hostility to the very idea of psychological "tempering." The program should have switched to the statement, but it had responded to his display of anger instead.

"This isn't working," Dr. Barian murmured.

Sergeant Kolin dropped into his armchair. He rested his hands on his knees and stared at the screen.

"Tell Captain Min to continue," Sergeant Kolin said.

Dorothy's hand started inscribing instructions on her notebook. "He knows he's been recorded," she said. "He knows he has to give us a minimum amount of cooperation. He may be ready to explode but he's still thinking about his career, too."

"So he'll sit there. And listen. And say no."

Her image had returned to the screen. The program had switched to her review of the psychological dangers faced by children who had lost a parent—a review she had included in the program so it could be used in situations in which they needed to mark time. The program was still reacting to his anger. There was no indication it was going to deal with his feelings about psychological intervention.

She drew a *transmit* symbol at the bottom of her last instruction and her orders began creeping across the Solar System. Eleven minutes ago the program had made a misjudgment. Eleven minutes from now—twenty-two minutes after the original mistake—it would receive a message ordering it to deal with Sergeant Kolin's hostility to psychological tampering.

"You've done about as well as anyone could have, Dorothy," Dr. Barian said. "I couldn't have done it any better myself. It isn't your fault they made you wait so long you had to work through a program."

"It should have understood," Dorothy said. "It should have switched to the psychological tampering track as soon as he made that remark about people poking holes in his son's brain. It shouldn't have let that slip past it."

"The anger response was too strong. It picked up the anger and it didn't hear the content. You aren't the first person who's seen a program make a mistake she would have avoided."

Sergeant Kolin had sat like that for a big part of half the sessions she'd had with him. His eyes were fixed on the screen. His face looked attentive and interested. And she knew, from experience, that he wasn't hearing one word in three.

"It isn't your fault, Dorothy. You might have had a chance if they'd let you talk to him when the time lag was only a couple of minutes. The fiddled around with your request and how you've got a hopeless situation."

She wrote another set of commands on her notebook and bent over the dense, black-on-yellow format she had chosen the last time she had felt like fooling around with her displays. Somewhere in the mass of information she had collected on Sergeant Kolin there had to be a magic fact that would drill a hole through his resistance.

"Your patient is in exactly the same position as a child who'dying of a disease," Dr. Barian said. "Would you wait for his father's permission—or some general's permission—if he needed a new lung or a new spinal cord? Your first responsibility is to that child—not some set of rules thought up by people who are still living in the Dark Ages."

The last useless paragraphs in Sergeant Kolin's file scrolled across her notebook. She raised her head and discovered Dr. Barian was regarding her with an expression that actually looked understanding.

"There's another consideration you might want to factor into your decision making process," Dr. Barian said. "It may be your friend Colonel Pao is right—maybe General Lundstrom's staff did do the right thing when they decided her mental state is so delicate they might be endangering four hundred combat troops if they bothered her with a difficult matter like this. It's also true that the military personnel on those ships are all volunteers. They *agreed* to take the risk they're taking. Deni didn't volunteer for anything."

She had dispatched her new set of instructions at 02:58. At 03:09 it arrived at the torch ship. At 03:20 she saw the program switch to the path it should have taken in the first place. At 03:40, she ordered it to switch to the termination routing and started waiting for the images that would tell her Sergeant Kolin had refused permission. Dr. Barian started talking the moment she took her eyes off her notebook.

• • •

She picked up Deni at the door of the childcare center, in a cart she had requested from Special Services when it had finally occurred to her they would probably provide her with anything she asked for "under the circumstances." She had even been given a route that had been specially—and unobtrusively—cleared of any traffic that might cause her problems. A few of the pedestrians stared when they saw a cart with a child sitting in the passenger seat, but they all looked away as soon as their brains caught up with their reflexes.

Hammarskjold Station was a military base, so its public spaces looked something like the public spaces of a civilian space city and something like the decks of a torch ship. The corridors had been landscaped with trees, fountains, and little gardens, just like the corridors in lunar cities, but it had all been done in the hyper-manicured style that characterized most military attempts at decorating. The doors that lined the walls came in four sizes and three colors. The gardens were spaced every hundred meters and they all contained one tree, a carpet of flowers that was as trim as a major's mustache, and two (2), three (3), or four (4) shrubs selected from a list of twenty (20).

"I thought I wasn't supposed to see you until after lunch," Deni said.

"I had to make some changes in my schedule," Dorothy said, with deliberate vagueness.

"Am I going to have to see you during breakfast from now on?"

"It's just this once."

The big, utilitarian elevator near the childcare center opened as soon as the cart approached it. It went directly to the fourth level without stopping, and she turned left as she cleared the door and started working her way around the curve of the giant wheel that had been her home since the day she had been born.

The strawberry muffins had big chunks of real strawberries embedded in them. The butter had been synthesized in a

Food Services vat, but to everyone who lived off-Earth, it was the "real thing"—an expensive, luxurious alternative of the cheaper look-alikes. The milk in the big pitcher was flavored with real strawberries, too—and laced with a carefully measured dose of the tranquilizer that had given her the best results when she had slipped it to him in the past.

"Did I get the muffins the same temperature your father gets them?" Dorothy said.

Deni stopped chewing for a moment and nodded politely. He never talked with his mouth full. His mother had dealt with that issue before he was three.

"Are we talking about my feelings some more?"

"Maybe later. Right now—why don't we just relax and have breakfast? I'm kind of fond of real butter myself."

"How many can I have?"

"Well, I bought six. And I'll probably only be able to eat two myself. I'd say you can count on eating at least three."

She glanced at the notebook sitting beside her coffee cup. The chair Deni was sitting in looked like a normal dining chair, but it was packed with the same array of noninvasive sensors that had been crammed into the therapeutic chair he normally used. His heartbeat, blood pressure, muscle tension, and movement-count all agreed with the conclusion a reasonably sensitive human being would have drawn from the enthusiasm with which he was biting into his muffin.

Deni had finished the last bite of his second muffin and given her a quick glance before he reached for the third. The numbers on the notebook were all advancing by the appropriate amount as the tranquilizer took hold.

She stood up and strolled toward her desk with her coffee cup in her hand. "Take your time, Deni. Don't worry about it if you decide you can't finish it."

She called up a status report on her desk screen and stared the same numbers she had gone over only two hours ago. The drugs she needed for the esem were all sitting in the appropriate places on her shelves. The devices that were supposed to deliver the drugs were all functional. The components that would deliver the appropriate images, sounds, and sensations all presented her with green lights when she asked for an equipment check.

She had thought about putting Deni under and checking the current state of his feelings but she had known it was a stupid idea as soon as it had popped into her head. She knew what his real feelings were. Every test she had run on him in the last three months had confirmed he was still in the grip of the emotions she had observed when she had begun working with him.

She had begun her sessions with Deni with a two-hour diagnostic unit in which he had been drugged semiconscious. Deni didn't remember any of it, but she had stored every second of the session in her confidential databanks. Any time she wanted to, she could watch Deni's hands curl—as if he was strangling someone—as he relived an evening in which his parents might have killed each other if they hadn't both been experts in the art of falling. She knew exactly what he really thought about the time his father had taken his flute away from him for two weeks. She had observed his childish rage at the cage of work and study his mother had erected around his life.

She scrawled another code number on her notebook and the results of the work she had done last night appeared on her desk screen. She had been ready to crawl into bed as soon as she had made Deni's travel arrangements but Dr. Barian had insisted they should prepare a complete quantified prognosis. They had spent over fifty minutes haggling over a twenty-two-item checklist. Dr. Barian had insisted nineteen of her estimates were wildly out of line and tried to replace every one of them with the most pessimistic numbers he could produce.

In the end, it hadn't really mattered which set of numbers you used. The most optimistic prognosis the program could come up with merely offered *some* hope that *someday* the boy *might* voluntarily seek out a therapist. *Someday*, just possibly, he *might* ask for the treatment that would pull him out of the emotional swamp that was going to start sucking at his psyche the moment he learned his mother had died.

And that's your best prognosis, Captain. Based on numbers most experienced therapists would consider hopelessly optimistic.

"How are you coming, Deni?"

"I think I'm starting to feel a little burpy, ma'am."

She waved the numbers off the screen and turned around. His glass still held about three fingers of milk.

"I've got a pill I'd like you to take. Can your tummy hold enough milk to help you get a pill down?"

On the main communications screen, Mr. and Mrs. Chen were holding a press conference. The "reporters" were all "volunteers" from their own Zen-Random congregation, but that was a minor matter. The questions would have been a little different if the Chens had been facing real media types, but the answers would have been the same.

A bona fide journalist, for example, might have asked them how they would answer all the military analysts who thought they had made a tactical mistake when they destroyed Rinaswandi. The phony reporter on the screen had merely asked his leaders if they could tell the people how the attack had improved their military position.

"I think the answer to that is obvious," Mrs. Chen said. "The forces that were guarding Rinaswandi Base can now join the force defending our city. The Secretariat mercenaries will be faced with a force of overwhelming size, with every weapon and vehicle controlled by a volunteer who is prepared to make any sacrifice to preserve the state of moral liberation we have created in our city. . . ."

Every two or three minutes—for reasons Dorothy couldn't quite grasp—the Chens let the camera pick up a bald, slump-shouldered man who seemed to shrink against the wall as soon as he realized a lens was pointed his way. If there was one person in this situation who wasn't going to come out of it alive, Dorothy knew, it was Major Jen Raden—the officer who had betrayed the equipment stashed on Rinaswandi.

Her father was only one-eighth Gurkhali, but no one had ever had to remind him—or any other member of the Fourth International Brigade—that he belonged to an institution which could trace its origins to the Fourth Gurkha Rifles, the ancient, battle-scarred infantry regiment the Indian government had donated to the United Nations in the years when the Secretariat had acquired its first permanent forces. I will keep faith, the Gurkha motto had run—and they had proved it in battle after battle, first in the service of the British Empire, then in the service of the Republic of India, and finally under the flag that was supposed to represent humanity's best response to its own capacity for violence.

A light glowed on Dorothy's communications board. A line of type appeared at the bottom of the screen. *Call from Pilot Sergeant Min. Nonpriority.*

On the couch, Deni was still sleeping peacefully. The monitor she had clipped to his wrist was still transmitting readings that indicated he would sleep for the full two hours the deep-sleep pill was supposed to deliver. There were two messages from Dr. Barian in her communications system, but she hadn't looked at either of them.

She tapped the appropriate button on her keyboard. Her father stared at her out of the screen with a blurred, puffy-eyed look that immediately triggered off a memory of beery odors—a memory that was so strong it was hard to believe the communications system could only transmit sounds and images. She wasn't the only member of her family who had been up most of the night.

"Good morning, daughter. I hope I'm not disturbing anything."

"I was just sitting here watching the news. I've got something I'm supposed to do, but I'm giving myself a little break."

"I've been thinking about the family you've been concerned about. It seems to me you indicated one of the parents was stationed on Rinaswandi. . . ."

She nodded. "It was the mother. The son's sleeping on the couch in my office."

Her father leaned back and folded his arms across his chest—but this time neither of them smiled. She had realized, at some point in her teens, that it was a body posture that frequently indicated he was trying to keep his reactions under control. He arranged his arms like that, she had decided, so he wouldn't run his hands across his face or do something else that might affect the image a good sergeant tried to maintain.

"I was afraid something like that might have happened. Have they told him yet?"

"I told them I'd do it."

"That's not the easiest job you can volunteer for."

"I still haven't told him. I'm letting him sleep while I think about . . . the best way to approach it."

"I only did that twice all the time I was on active duty. If you don't mind me giving you some advice—I never talked to anybody who thought they'd found a good way to do it. Whatever you do, you're not going to be happy with it."

"There's some special problems in this case—some reactions he'll probably have because of the family problems I was trying to deal with."

Sergeant Min frowned. "You were trying to get permission for some special procedure . . . for something that would help him with the possibility his parents might become casualties. . . ."

"We tried to get permission from his father last night and we couldn't do it. Dr. Barian thinks we failed because they stalled us for so long we had to communicate across a big communications lag. I'm inclined to think we might have failed anyway."

"And what does that mean?"

"It means basically that we end up with a human being

who's permanently crippled psychologically. I could show you the numbers and explain them but that's what they all add up to. He'll be just as much of a casualty as anybody who'd been physically wounded."

"And nobody ever asked him if he wanted to enlist. . . ."

"That's essentially what Dr. Barian said."

"I'm sorry, Dorothy. It sounds to me like you've done everything anyone could have."

"I'm not blaming myself, Papa. I'm just sorry it's happening."

"There isn't anything else you can do? There isn't some possibility he'll get some kind of therapy later? When he's old enough to make his own decision?"

"It's possible, but the odds are against it. We're talking about something that will eventually affect almost every aspect of his personality. When a child has certain kinds of problems with his parents, the death of one of his parents can create unconscious feelings . . . guilt feelings . . . that are so powerful they influence everything he does. People tend to protect the personalities they've acquired. Somebody who's rebellious, unruly, and angry usually isn't going to feel he needs a treatment that will give him a different outlook—even when he isn't satisfied with the kind of life his emotions have led him into."

"Major Raden has a lot to answer for."

"Dr. Barian seems to feel it's mostly General Lundstrom's fault."

"Or some of those babus on her staff."

She shrugged. "They were trying to protect her—to shield her from distractions."

"She's a general. She's supposed to look after her troops. If she can't put up with a little pestering from a medical captain without going into convulsions, she shouldn't be wearing the pips."

When Dorothy had been fourteen, one of her best friends had been plagued with a father who had "confined her to quarters" almost every other weekend—usually for some trivial matter like a dusty piece of furniture or a piece of clothing that didn't look "inspection presentable." Her first boyfriend had been a wary thirteen-year-old whose father seemed to watch everything his children did for signs of "weakness."

There were people in Dorothy's opinion, for whom military life was a kind of moral exoskeleton. Their upbringing had left them with no useful values or goals. The ideals imposed on them by their military indoctrination were the only guidelines they had.

She never experienced the kind of problems Deni had lived with, but she had no trouble relating her records of his case to the things she had observed during her own childhood. Press one set of buttons and the database presented you with a recording of a counseling session in which Sergeant Kolin justified a punishment by arguing that people would behave "like animals" if no one imposed any "discipline" on them. Press another set, and you got to watch Sergeant Wei, in a message she had transmitted from Rinaswandi, telling Deni she hoped he was practicing his flute and spending enough time with his learning programs—and never once suggesting she loved him or hoped he was having a little fun.

Press a third combination, and the database gave you a look at the hour she had spent with Deni on the day he had received his tenth message from his mother. They had sat on the couch, side by side, and she had spent most of the session stubbornly trying to evoke some kind of comment on his reactions to his mother's exhortations.

"How did you feel about the length of the message?" the Insistent, Patient Therapist had prodded. "Was it too short? Would you like it better if she sent you a longer message every two or three days?"

Deni shrugged. "It was all right."

The therapist stifled the natural response of a normal adult and produced an attempt at a conciliatory smile. "Try again,

Deni. Is there anything else you wish your mother had talked about? Besides school? And music practice? We're not here to play, soldier."

She had been dealing with the great problem that confronted every therapist who tried to get military children to talk about their emotions—the trait that had been observed by almost every researcher who had ever explored the child-rearing customs of this odd little subculture. The one thing that seemed to be true about all military children was their tendency to pick up, almost at birth, the two great commandments of military life: don't complain, don't talk about your feelings. Her solution had been to tell him it was a task—a duty the officer in command of the situation expected him to fulfill to the best of his ability.

It had helped some, but only some. The resistance she was dealing with couldn't be eliminated by direct orders and nagging persistence. Talk therapy was only a second-best stopgap—a procedure that she kept up mostly so she could convince herself she was doing something while she waited for the day his mother finally agreed he needed the only help that could do him any good.

He won't have the slightest idea you did it, Dr. Barian had said. *His father won't know you did it. No one. Somebody may wonder, fifteen years from now, why a kid with his prognosis has turned out so well, but they'll probably assume he just happened to beat the odds. He'll just have the kind of life he should have—the kind of life you've got.*

Deni looked up at her from the couch. His right hand made a little twitching movement.

"You fell asleep," Dorothy said. "I thought I'd let you rest."

He frowned. He was old enough to know she gave him medicines that affected his feelings, but she wasn't sure he realized she would do it without telling him first.

His eyes shifted toward the time strip on her desk. "Can I go home now? Are we finished?"

He pulled up his legs and sat up. "They start play time in ten minutes, Captain Min. It isn't my fault I fell asleep."

"Deni—"

"Yes, ma'am?"

"I'd like you to go sit in the chair you usually sit in. I'd like you to do it now, if you don't mind. There's something I have to talk about with you—something that happened last night."

The ceremony for the people who had died at Rinaswandi took place in the biggest theater in Hammarskjold, two days after the attack. Deni sat in the front row, with the other children whose parents had been killed. Dorothy could watch him, from her place in the ranks of the medical personnel, and note how he was still maintaining the same poise he had adopted in the cart when she had driven him back to the childcare center.

It was the same ceremony she had attended with her father, nineteen years ago, in memory of the people who had died in the assault on the Lumina mining asteroid. The names of the dead would be read one by one. (Twenty this time, thirty-three then.) A lone trumpeter would play "The Last Post." The minute of silence—timed precisely to the second—would end with the bagpipes roaring into one of the big, whirling, totally affirmative marches the Gurkha regiments had inherited, three hundred years in the past, from the British officers who had introduced them to European military music.

That was how you always did it at a military ceremony. First, you remembered the dead. Then—the moment over, the tribute paid—you returned to the clamor and bustle of life. She lived in a world in which people sometimes died, her father had said when he had explained it to her. You never forgot they had died, but you didn't let it keep you from living.

Her father hadn't asked her if she wanted to go to the Lumina ceremony. And she had known, without being told, that it wasn't something they could discuss. There were some things that had to be left unsaid, even with the kind of father she had. She had never told him, for example, about the nights, the whole year after he had returned from the Lumina "incident," when she had stared at the ceiling of her bedroom and tried to ignore the pictures that kept floating into her head.

She had given Colonel Pao a recommendation for a week of deep-sleep therapy, to be implemented sometime in the next month, and he had indicated he would probably approve it. Colonel Pao didn't think there would be any problems, either, with her recommendation for a long-term follow-up, from now until Deni's legal maturity, that would include any legal procedures that might reduce the damage. If there was one thing everyone in the chain of command understood, it was the plight of a child who had lost a parent in combat.

"... It's the same basic idea you always come back to," she had told Colonel Pao. "The point they always emphasize in all those courses on military ethics they make you take in baby officer's school. My father even explained it to me when I was a child—when I asked him how he could be sure he was doing the right thing when he helped kill people. If you're a soldier ... then for you morality is defined by the law. A soldier is someone who engages in legally authorized acts of violence. If you take away the law, then there's no difference between us and a bunch of thugs. If we can't obey the law, too ... at least the important laws ..."

Dr. Barian hadn't been particularly impressed with her attempts to explain herself, of course. He had stared at her as if she had just suggested they should deal with the Akara situation by poisoning half the people in the asteroid belt.

"The only difference between an army and a bunch of thugs," Dr. Barian had told her, "is that armies work for governments and thugs don't. You turned your back on a helpless child because you felt you had to stick to the letter of some rule a pack of politicians set up so they could appease a mob of voters who can't tell the difference between an esem and a flogging."

Behind his desk, to the left, Colonel Pao had set up a serenity corner with a compositon composed of green plants and dark, unevenly glazed pottery. He had arranged two chairs so they faced it from slightly different angles, and he had insisted they should sit in the chairs and drink tea while they talked. On the sound system a wooden flute had been tracing a long meditative line.

"I take it," Colonel Pao had said, "that you feel you might have proceeded with the esem if you had been a civilian."

Dorothy shrugged. "My father always used to claim that a good sergeant took care of the people under him. I have a feeling that if you took it to a vote half the people on this base might have felt I should have thrown the rules out the airlock and given a casualty whatever he needed."

"And how do you feel about that?"

She shrugged again. "When I think about it that way—I feel like Dr. Barian's absolutely right and I've acted like a priggish junior officer who thinks rules are more important than human beings."

The left side of the serenity corner was dominated by a thin, long-necked jar that would have thrown the entire composition out of balance if it had been one centimeter taller. She focused her eyes on the line of the neck and tried to concentrate on the way it intersected a thin, leafless branch. Then she lost control and snapped her head toward the trim, carefully positioned figure in the other chair.

"He was sitting right in front of me, sir! I had to look him in the face when I told him his mother was dead. I could be watching what this has done to him for the next ten years if I decide to stay in. If I had my way we'd have a law that let us set up some kind of committee—without giving the parents an absolute veto—whenever we got into this kind of emergency. If all the people like Dr. Barian had their way, there wouldn't be any rules at all and we could spend our lives arbitrarily altering people's personalities just because we felt it was good for them. My father, the people on Rinaswandi—they spent their lives trying to build a wall around chaos. There has to be a law regulating personality modification! Even when it's as benign as this one. Just like there have to be laws that tell you when it's all right to engage in violence."

Colonel Pao folded his arms over his chest. He tipped his head to one side—as if he were concentrating on the long arc the flute was describing—and Dorothy settled back in her chair and waited while he collected his thoughts.

He had shifted his thought processes to the formal, somewhat bureaucratic phrases he tended to adopt when he communicated in Techno Mandarin. "It is my personal opinion," he said, "that any responsible observer would have to agree that you did everything anyone could resonably expect you to do. You took everything into account—including a point many civilians have trouble understanding. You did everything you could to get a favorable response from Sergeant Kolin. You made a real decision, furthermore, when you arrived at the moment when a decision couldn't be postponed. You didn't just stand there and let the situation drift into a decision by default."

Colonel Pao raised his bowl of tea to his lips. He stared at the center of the serenity composition over the top of the bowl and Dorothy waited again.

"I could tell you that I think you made the right choice and try to ease your feelings by providing you with whatever authority I may possess. I could even tell you that you did the wrong thing and try to give you the comforting illusion someone knows what's right and wrong in these situations. The truth is I can't tell you any more than I've already said. If I understood the principles of ethical philosophy as well as I would like to, I think I would conclude that you applied the Confucian principle of reciprocity, even if I couldn't guarantee you made the most ethical choice. You treated Deni the way you probably would want to be treated yourself. If you or I were in Deni's position . . . if someone had to make a decision that might affect us the way this one affects him . . . then I think we would want it to be someone who's been as thoughtful and conscientious as you've been."

He rested his bowl on the tray beside his chair and switched back to Ghurkali—the language of her infancy. "Does that help you, Captain? Does it give you any comfort?"

"I think so, sir. Yes, sir."

"The other thing I think I should say is related to something you and I have in common, so perhaps I'm biased. Still, there have been moments—during the less illustrious interludes in my career—when it's been the only thought that's kept me functioning."

He reached across the space between the chairs and rested his hand on her shoulder. It would have been a perfectly unremarkable gesture if anyone else had done it; in his case it was the first time he had touched her since she had been six years old and the duty officer at the post clinic, young Surgical Captain Pao, had held her hand while the first aid equipment had repaired a greenstick fracture in her left arm. Colonel Pao frequently touched his patients who needed encouragement or reassurance, but he tended to be physically reserved with everyone else.

"Just remember, Dorothy—Deni isn't the only person who didn't volunteer."

MOON DUEL

Fritz Leiber

With a fifty-year career that stretched from the "Golden Age" Astounding *of the 1940s to the beginning of the nineties, the late Fritz Leiber was an indispensable figure in the development of modern science fiction, fantasy, and horror. It is impossible to imagine what those genres would be like today without him, except to say that they would be the poorer for it. Probably no other figure of his generation (with the possible exception of L. Sprague de Camp) wrote in as many different genres as Leiber, or was as important as he was to the development of each. Leiber can be considered to be one of the fathers of modern "heroic fantasy," and his long sequence of stories about Fafhrd and the Gray Mouser remains one of the most complex and intelligent bodies of work in the entire subgenre of "Sword & Sorcery" (which term Leiber himself is usually credited with coining). He may also be one of the best—if not the best—writers of the supernatural horror tale since Lovecraft and Poe, and was writing updated "modern" or "urban" horror stories like "Smoke Ghost" and the classic* Conjure Wife *long before the work of Stephen King engendered the Big Horror Boom of the middle 1970s and brought that form to wide popular attention.*

Leiber was also a towering Ancestral Figure in science fiction as well, having been one of the major writers of both Campbell's "Golden Age" Astounding *of the forties—with works like* Gather, Darkness*—and H.L. Gold's* Galaxy *in the fifties—with works like the classic "Coming Attraction" and the superb novel* The Big Time, *which still holds up as one of the best SF novels ever written—and then going on to contribute a steady stream of superior fiction to the magazines and anthologies of the sixties, the sev-*

enties, and the eighties, as well as powerful novels such as The Wanderer *and* Our Lady of Darkness. The Big Time *won a well-deserved Hugo in 1959, and Leiber also won a slew of other awards: all told, six Hugos and four Nebulas, plus three World Fantasy Awards—one of them the prestigious Life Achievement Award—and a Grandmaster of Fantasy Award.*

Here he takes us to the bleak, airless surface of the Moon for a battle of wits and weapons among strange antagonists—one that proves that, in combat, even the smallest and most seemingly inconsequential of actions can have very large (and unforeseen) consequences . . .

Fritz Leiber's other books include The Green Millennium, A Spectre Is Haunting Texas, The Big Engine, *and* The Silver Eggheads, *the collections* The Best of Fritz Leiber, The Book of Fritz Leiber, The Change War, Night's Dark Agents, Heroes and Horrors, The Mind Spider, *and* The Ghost Light, *and the seven volumes of Fafhrd-Gray Mouser stories, now being reissued in massive omnibus trade-paperback editions; the most recent such volume is* Farewell to Lankhmar.

First hint I had we'd been spotted by a crusoe was a little *tick* coming to my moonsuit from the miniradar Pete and I were gaily heaving into position near the east end of Gioja crater to scan for wrecks, trash, and nodules of raw metal.

Then came a *whish* which cut off the instant Pete's hand lost contact with the squat instrument. His gauntlet, silvery in the raw low polar sunlight, drew away very slowly, as if he'd grown faintly disgusted with our activity. My gaze kept on turning to see the whole shimmering back of his helmet blown off in a gorgeous sickening brain-fog and blood-mist that was already falling in the vacuum as fine red snow.

A loud *tock* then and glove-sting as the crusoe's second

slug hit the miniradar, but my gaze had gone back to the direction Pete had been facing when he bought it—in time to see the green needle-flash of the crusoe's gun in a notch in Gioja's low wall, where the black of the shadowed rock met the gem-like starfields along a jagged border. I unslung my Swift* as I dodged a long step to the side and squeezed off three shots. The first two shells must have traveled a touch too high, but the third made a beautiful fleeting violet globe at the base of the notch. It didn't show me a figure, whole or shattered, silvery or otherwise, on the wall or atop it, but then some crusoes are camouflaged like chameleons and most of them move very fast.

Pete's suit was still falling slowly and stiffly forward. Three dozen yards beyond was a wide black fissure, though exactly how wide I couldn't tell because much of the opposite lip merged into the shadow of the wall. I scooted toward it like a rat toward a hole. On my third step, I caught up Pete by his tool belt and oxy tube while his falling front was still inches away from the powdered pumice, and I heaved him along with me. Some slow or overdrilled part of my brain hadn't yet accepted he was dead.

Then I began to skim forward, inches above the ground myself, kicking back against rocky outcrops thrusting up through the dust—it was like fin-swimming. The crusoe couldn't have been expecting this nut stunt, by which I at least avoided the dreamy sitting-duck slowness of safer, higher-bounding moon-running, for there was a green flash behind me and hurtled dust faintly pittered my soles and seat. He hadn't been leading his target enough. Also, I knew now he had shells as well as slugs.

I was diving over the lip three seconds after skoot-off when Pete's boot caught solidly against a last hooky out-

---

*All-purpose vacuum rifle named for the .22 cartridge which as early as 1940 was being produced by Winchester, Remington, and Norma with factory loads giving it a muzzle velocity of 4,140 feet, almost a mile, a second.

crop. The something in my brain was still stubborn, for I clutched him like clamps, which made me swing around with a jerk. But even that was lucky, for a bright globe two yards through winked on five yards ahead like a mammoth firefly's flash, but not quite as gentle, for the invisible rarified explosion-front hit me hard enough to *boom* my suit and make the air inside slap me. Now I knew he had metal-proximity fuses on some of his shells too—they must be very good at mini-stuff on his home planet.

The tail of the pale green flash showed me the fissure's bottom a hundred yards straight below and all dust, as ninety percent of them are—pray God the dust was deep. I had time to thumb Extreme Emergency to the ship for it to relay automatically to Circumluna. Then the lip had cut me off from the ship and I had lazily fallen out of the glare into the blessed blackness, the dial lights in my helmet already snapped off—even they might make enough glow for the crusoe to aim by. The slug had switched off Pete's.

Ten, twelve seconds to fall and the opposite lip wasn't cutting off the notched crater wall. I could feel the crusoe's gun trailing me down—he'd know moon-G, sticky old five-foot. I could feel his tentacle or finger or claw or ameboid bump tightening on the trigger or button or what. I shoved Pete away from me, parallel to the fissure wall, as hard as I could. Three more seconds, four, and my suit *boomed* again and I was walloped as another green flash showed me the smooth-sifted floor moving up and beginning to hurry a little. This flash was a hemisphere, not a globe—it had burst against the wall—but if there were any rock fragments they missed me. And it exactly bisected the straight line between me and Pete's silvery coffin. The crusoe knew his gun and his Luna—I really admired him, even if my shove had pushed Pete and me, action and reaction, just enough out of the target path. Then the fissure lip had cut the notch and I was readying to land like a three-legged crab, my Swift reslung, my free hand on my belted dust-shoes.

• • •

Eleven seconds' fall on Luna is not much more than two on earth, but either are enough to build up a velocity of over fifty feet a second. The dust jarred me hard, but thank God there were no reefs in it. It covered at least all the limbs and front of me, including my helmet-front—my dial lights, snapped on again, showed a grayness fine-grained as flour.

The stuff resisted like flour, too, as I unbelted my dust-shoes. Using them for a purchase, I pulled my other arm and helmet-front free. The stars looked good, even gray-dusted. With a hand on each shoe, I dragged out my legs and, balancing gingerly on the slithery stuff, got each of my feet snapped to a shoe. Then I raised up and switched on my headlight. I hated that. I no more wanted to do it than a hunted animal wants to break twigs or show itself on the skyline, but I knew I had exactly as long to find cover as it would take the crusoe to lope from the notch to the opposite lip of the fissure. Most of them lope very fast, they're that keen on killing.

Well, we started the killing, I reminded myself. *This time I'm the quarry.*

My searchlight made a perverse point of hitting Pete's shimmering casket, spread-eagled, seven-eighths submerged, like a man floating on his back. I swung the beam steadily. The opposite wall was smooth except for a few ledges and cracks and there wasn't any overhang to give a man below cover from someone on top.

But a section of the wall on my side, not fifty yards away, was hugely pocked with holes and half-bubbles where the primeval lava had foamed high and big against the feeble plucking of lunar gravity. I aimed myself at the center of that section and started out. I switched off my headlight and guided myself by the wide band of starfields.

You walk dust-shoes with much the same vertical lift and low methodical forward swing as snowshoes. It was nostalgic, but hunted animals have no time for memory-delicatessen.

Suddenly there was more and redder brightness overhead

than the stars. A narrow ribbon of rock along the top of the opposite wall was glaringly bathed in orange, while the rim peaks beyond glowed faintly, like smoldering volcanoes. Light from the orange ribbon bounced down into my fissure, caroming back and forth between the walls until I could dimly see again the holes I was headed for.

The crusoe had popped our ship—both tanks, close together, so that the sun-warmed gasses, exploding out into each other, burned like a hundred torches. The oxyaniline lasted until I reached the holes. I crawled through the biggest. The fading glow dimly and fleetingly showed a rock-bubble twelve feet across with another hole at the back of it. The stuff looked black, felt rough yet diamond-hard. I risked a look behind me.

The ribbon glow was darkest red—the skeleton of our ship still aglow. The ribbon flashed green in the middle—a tiny venomous dagger—and then a huge pale green firefly winked where Pete lay. He'd saved me a fourth time.

I had barely pushed sideways back when there was another of those winks just outside my hole, this one glaringly bright, its front walloping me. I heard through the rock faint *tings* of fragments of Pete's suit hitting the wall, but they may have been only residual ringings, from the nearer blast, in my suit or ears.

I scrambled through the back door in the bubble into a space which I made out by crawling to be a second bubble, resembling the first even to having a back door. I went through that third hole and turned around and rested my Swift's muzzle on the rough-scooped threshold. Since the crusoe lived around here, he'd know the territory better wherever I went. Why retreat farther and get lost? My dial lights showed that about a minute and a half had gone by since Pete bought it. Also, I wasn't losing pressure and I had oxy and heat for four hours—Circumluna would be able to deliver a rescue force in half that time, if my message had got through and if the crusoe didn't scupper them too. Then I got goosy again about the glow of the dial lights and snapped them off. I started to change position and was suddenly afraid the crusoe might already be trailing me by my transmitted sounds through the rock, and right away I held stock still and started to listen for *him.*

No light, no sound, a ghost-fingered gravity—it was like being tested for sanity-span in an anechoic chamber. Almost at once dizziness and the sensory mirages started to come, swimming in blue and burned and moaning from the peripheries of my senses—even waiting in ambush for a crusoe wouldn't stop them; I guess I wanted them to come. So though straining every sense against the crusoe's approach, I had at last to start thinking about him.

It's strange that men should have looked at the moon for millennia and never guessed it was exactly what it looked like: a pale marble graveyard for living dead men, a Dry Tortuga of space where the silver ships from a million worlds marooned their mutineers, their recalcitrants, their criminals, their lunatics. Not on fertile warm-blanketed earth with its quaint adolescent race, which such beings might harm, but on the great silver rock of earth's satellite, to drag out their solitary furious lives, each with his suit and gun and lonely hut or hole, living by recycling his wastes; recycling, too, the bitter angers and hates and delusions which had brought him there. As many as a thousand of them, enough to mine the moon for meals and fuel-gases and to reconquer space and perhaps become masters of earth—had they chosen to cooperate. But their refusal to cooperate was the very thing for which they'd been marooned, and besides that they were of a half thousand different galactic breeds. And so although they had some sort of electronic or psionic or what-not grapevine—at least what happened to one maroon became swiftly known to the others—each of them remained a solitary Friday-less Robinson Crusoe, hence the name.

I risked flashing my time dial. Only another thirty seconds gone. At this rate it would take an eternity for the two hours to pass before I could expect aid *if* my call had got through, while the crusoe— As my senses screwed themselves tighter to their task, my thoughts went whirling off again.

Earthmen shot down the first crusoe they met—in a moment of fumbling panic and against all their training. Ever since then the crusoes have shot first, or tried to, ignoring our belated efforts to communicate.

I brooded for what I thought was a very short while about the age-old problem of a universal galactic code, yet when I flashed my time dial again, seventy minutes had gone somewhere.

That really froze me. He'd had time to stalk and kill me a dozen times—he'd had time to go home and fetch his dogs!—my senses couldn't be *that* good protection with my mind away. Why even now, straining them in my fear, all I got was my own personal static: I heard my heart pounding, my blood roaring, I think for a bit I heard the Brownian movement of the air molecules against my eardrums.

What I hadn't been doing, I told myself, was thinking about the crusoe in a systematic way.

He had a gun like mine and at least three sorts of ammo.

He'd made it from notch to fissure-lip in forty seconds or less—he must be a fast loper, whatever number feet; he might well have a jet unit.

And he'd shot at the miniradar ahead of me. Had he thought it a communicator?—a weapon?—*or some sort of robot as dangerous as a man . . . ?*

My heart had quieted, my ears had stopped roaring, and in that instant I heard through the rock the faintest *scratching.*

Scratch-scratch, scratch-scratch, scratch, scratch, scratch it went, each time a little louder.

I flipped on my searchlight and there coming toward me across the floor of the bubble outside mine was a silver spider as wide as a platter with four opalescent eyes and a green-banded body. Its hanging jaws were like inward-curving notched scissor blades.

I fired by automatism as I fell back. The spider's bubble was filled with violet glare instantly followed by green. I was twice walloped by explosion-fronts and knocked down.

That hardly slowed me a second. The same flashes had shown me a hole in the top of my bubble and as soon as I'd scrambled to my feet I leaped toward it.

I did remember to leap gently. My right hand caught the black rim of the hole and it didn't break off and I drew myself up into the black bubble above. It had no hole in the top, but two high ones in the sides, and I went through the higher one.

I kept on that way. The great igneous bubbles were almost uniform. I always took the highest exit. Once I got inside a bubble with no exit and had to backtrack. After that I scanned first. I kept my searchlight on.

I'd gone through seven or seventeen bubbles before I could start to think about what had happened.

That spider had almost certainly not been my crusoe—or else there was a troop of them dragging a rifle like an artillery piece. And it hadn't likely been an hitherto-unknown, theoretically impossible, live vacuum-arthropod—or else the exotic biologists were in for a great surprise and I'd been right to wet my pants. No, it had most likely been a tracking or tracking-and-attack robot of some sort. Eight legs are a useful number, likewise eight hands. Were the jaws for cutting through suit armor? Maybe it was a robot pet for a lonely being. Here, Spid!

The second explosion? Either the crusoe had fired into the chamber from the other side, or else the spider had carried a bomb to explode when it touched me. Fine use to make of a pet! I giggled. I was relieved, I guess, to think it likely that the spider had been "only" a robot.

Just then—I was in the ninth or nineteenth bubble—the inside of my helmet misted over everywhere. I was panting and sweating and my dehumidifier had overloaded. It was as if I were in a real peasouper of a fog. I could barely make out the black loom of the wall behind me. I switched out my headlight. My time dial showed seventy-two minutes gone. I switched it off and then I did a queer thing.

I leaned back very carefully until as much of my suit as possible touched rock. Then I measuredly thumped the rock ten times with the butt of my Swift and held very still.

Starting with ten would mean we were using the decimal system. Of course there were other possibilities, but . . .

Very faintly, coming at the same rate as mine, I heard six thuds.

What constant started with six? If he'd started with three, I'd have given him one, and so on through a few more places of pi. Or if with one, I'd have given him four—and then started to worry about the third and fourth places in the square root of two. I might take his signal for the beginning of a series with the interval of minus four and rap him back two, but then how could he rap me minus two? Oh why hadn't I simply started rapping out primes? Of course all the integers, in fact all the real numbers, from thirty-seven through forty-one had square roots beginning with six, but which one . . . ?

Suddenly I heard a *scratching* . . .

My searchbeam was on again, my helmet had unmisted, my present bubble was empty.

Just the same I scuttled out of it, still trending upward where I could. But now the holes wouldn't trend that way. They kept going two down for one up and the lines of bubbles zigzagged. I wanted to go back, but then I might hear the scratching. Once the bubbles started getting smaller. It was like being in solid black suds. I lost any sense of direction. I began to lose the sense of up-down. What's moon-gravity to the numbness of psychosis? I kept my searchlight on although I was sure the glow it made must reach ten bubbles away. I looked all around every bubble before I entered it, especially the overhang just above the entry hole.

Every once in a while I would hear somebody saying Six! Six? Six! like that and then very rapidly seven-eight-nine-five-four-three-two-one-naught. How would you rap naught in the decimal system? That one I finally solved: you'd rap ten.

Finally I came into a bubble that had a side-hole four feet across and edged at the top with diamonds. Very fancy. Was this the Spider Princess' boudoir? There was also a top hole but I didn't bother with that—it had no decor. I switched off my searchlight and looked out the window without exposing my head. The diamonds were stars. After a bit I made out what I took to be the opposite lip of the fissure I'd first dove in, only about one hundred feet above me. The rim-wall beyond looked vaguely familiar, though I wasn't sure about the notch. My time dial said one hundred eighteen minutes gone as I switched it off. Almost time to start hoping for rescue. Oh great!—with their ship a sitting duck for the crusoe they wouldn't be expecting. I hadn't signaled a word besides Extreme Emergency.

I moved forward and sat in the window, one leg outside, my Swift under my left arm. I plucked a flash grenade set for five seconds from my belt, pulled the fuse and tossed it across the fissure, almost hard enough to reach the opposite wall.

I looked down, my Swift swinging like my gaze.

The fissure lit up like a boulevard. Across from me I knew the flare was dropping dreamily, but I wasn't looking that way. Right below me, two hundred feet down, I saw a transparent helmet with something green and round and crested inside and with shoulders under it.

Just then I heard the *scratching* again, quite close.

I fired at once. My shell made a violet burst and raised a fountain of dust twenty feet from the crusoe. I scrambled back into my bubble, switching on my searchlight. Another spider was coming in on the opposite side, its legs moving fast. I jumped for the top-hole and grabbed its rim with my free hand. I'd have dropped my Swift if I'd needed my other hand, but I didn't. As I pulled myself up and through, I looked down and saw the spider straight below me eyeing me with its uptilted opalescent eyes and doubling its silver legs. Then it straightened its legs and sprang up toward me, not very fast but enough against Luna's feeble gravitational tug to put it into this upper room with me. I knew it mustn't touch me and I mustn't touch it by batting at it. I had started to shift the explosive shell in my gun for a slug, and its green-banded body was growing larger, when there was a green blast in the window below and its explosion-front, *booming* my suit a little, knocked the spider aside and out of sight before it made it through the trap door of my new bubble. Yet the spider didn't explode, if that was what had happened to the first one; at any rate there was no second green flash.

My new bubble had a top hole too and I went through it the same way I had the last. The next five bubbles were just the same too. I told myself that my routine was getting to be like that of a circus acrobat—except who stages shows inside black solidity?—except the gods maybe with the dreams they send us. The lava should be transparent, so the rim-wall peaks could admire.

At the same time I was thinking how if the biped humanoid shape is a good one for medium-size creatures on any planet, why so the spider shape is a good one for tiny creatures and apt to turn up anywhere and be copied in robots too.

The top hole in the sixth bubble showed me the stars, while one half of its rim shone white with sunlight.

Panting, I lay back against the rock. I switched off my searchlight. I didn't hear any scratching.

The stars. The stars were energy. They filled the universe with light, except for hidey holes and shadows here and there.

Then the number came to me. With the butt of my Swift I rapped out five. No answer. No scratching either. I rapped out five again.

Then the answer came, ever so faintly. Five knocked back at me.

Six five five—Planck's Constant, the invariant quantum of energy. Oh, it should be to the minus 29th power, of course, but I couldn't think how to rap that and, besides, the basic integers were all that mattered.

I heard the *scratching* . . .

I sprang and caught the rim and lifted myself into the glaring sunlight . . . and stopped with my body midway.

Facing me a hundred feet away, midway through another top-hole—he must have come very swiftly by another branch of the bubble ladder—he'd know the swiftest ones—was my green-crested crusoe. His face had a third eye where a man's nose would be, which with his crest made him look like a creature of mythology. We were holding our guns vertically.

We looked like two of the damned, half out of their holes in the floor of Dante's hell.

I climbed very slowly out of my hole, still pointing my gun toward the zenith. So did he.

We held very still for a moment. Then with his gun butt he rapped out ten. I could both see and also hear it through the rock.

I rapped out three. Then, as if the black bubble-world were one level of existence and this another, I wondered why we were going through this rigamarole. We each knew the other had a suit and a gun (and a lonely hole?) and so we knew we were both intelligent and knew math. So why was our rapping so precious?

He raised his gun—I think to rap out one, to start off pi.

But I'll never be sure, for just then there were two violet bursts, close together, against the fissure wall, quite close to him.

He started to swing the muzzle of his gun toward me. At least I think he did. He must know violet was the color of my explosions. I know I thought someone on my side was shooting. And I must have thought he was going to shoot me—because a violet dagger leaped from my Swift's muzzle and I felt its sharp recoil and then there was a violet globe where he was standing and moments later some fragment *twinged* lightly against my chest—a playful ironic tap.

He was blown apart pretty thoroughly, all his constants scattered, including—I'm sure—Planck's.

It was another half hour before the rescue ship from Circumluna landed. I spent it looking at earth low on the horizon and watching around for the spider, but I never saw it. The rescue party never found it either, though they made quite a hunt—with me helping after I'd rested a bit and had my batteries and oxy replenished. Either its power went off when its master died, or it was set to "freeze" then, or most likely go into a "hide" behavior pattern. Likely it's still out there waiting for an incautious earthman, like a rattlesnake in the desert or an old, forgotten land mine.

I also figured out, while waiting in Gioja crater, there near the north pole on the edge of Shackleton crater, the only explanation I've ever been able to make, though it's something of a whopper, of the two violet flashes which ended my little mathematical friendship-chant with the crusoe. They were the first two shells I squeezed off at him—the ones that skimmed the notch. They had the velocity to orbit Luna, and the time they took—two hours and five minutes—was right enough.

Oh, the consequences of our past actions!

SAVIOR

Robert Reed

Robert Reed sold his first story in 1986, and quickly established himself as a frequent contributor to The Magazine of Fantasy and Science Fiction *and* Asimov's Science Fiction, *as well as selling many stories to* Science Fiction Age, Universe, New Destinies, Tomorrow, Synergy, Starlight, *and elsewhere. Reed is almost as prolific as a novelist as he is as a short story writer, having produced eight novels to date, including* The Lee Shore, The Hormone Jungle, Black Milk, The Remarkables, Down the Bright Way, Beyond the Veil of Stars, An Exaltation of Larks, *and* Beneath the Gated Sky. *His most recent book is his long-overdue first collection,* The Dragons of Springplace. *He lives in Lincoln, Nebraska, where he's at work on a novel-length version of his 1997 novella, "Marrow."*

Here he gives us a powerful and poignant look at some of the things a soldier might have to do if he wants to be a savior of his people—and at the bitter personal cost of doing *them.*

Grandpa showed up early. I was still in bed, still hard asleep. And Mom pulled at my arm, telling me, "Get up, darling." But I couldn't make myself. I was too tired. Grandpa was standing in the door. I'm pretty sure of that. Mom asked if this was a good thing, considering. Mom said, "Considering," more than once. But Grandpa didn't say one word. Then I was sitting up, halfway awake, and she told me, "Your clothes are laid out. Go on, honey." And they let me dress alone in the dark.

My shirts and pants were new and warm and comfortably scratchy. But my boots were left over from last year. Even though they'd grown out as far as they could, and even though my toes felt cramped up inside them, I liked them. And I liked my hunting vest, even though it was too big and heavy. It was Grandpa's once. I liked its dirty orange color and its old smells. And whenever I put it on, before it got too heavy for me, I liked how it felt. With all those shells stuck into its little elastic pockets, I felt like a soldier. I felt dangerous and safe wrapped up inside all that ammunition.

Both of them were waiting in the kitchen. Grandpa was talking until he heard me. He looked up and smiled and said, "Ready?"

Mom was crying. Not like last night, but she was wiping at her face and smiling at me, her eyes red and ugly. "You two have fun today," she said. As if it was an order. Then she gave Grandpa a big hug and me a wet kiss, then tried to kiss me again. But I slipped outside before she could.

Grandpa always bought himself a new truck for Opening Day.

That year's truck was parked between our houses, already running and every light burning. We climbed in, and I said, "Hi, Solomon."

Solomon was standing on the back seat, watching everything with happy yellow eyes. "Hello, Sammy," he said. "Bird day, bird day, bird day—!"

Grandpa said, "Quiet."

Solomon was a retriever-techie mix. His dog brain had a chip add-on, and there was a voice box stuck in his neck. The box made him sound like a little kid. Except he was an old dog. And I liked him, sort of. Even if we weren't friends, exactly. Dogs can be awfully jealous, and we never liked sharing Grandpa with one another.

We rolled down the long drive and past Grandpa's house, then through the first tall black gate. I waved at the night guards. There were a dozen of them, maybe more. The main road went past all those cameras and reporters. Grandpa took us out the back road to the slickway, then let the truck drive. I started to feel the warm seat under me, and I sat back and shut my eyes, and it wasn't until the dog said, "Birds," that I was awake again.

"I smell birds," said that kid's voice. "I smell birds!"

We had turned off the slickway. Grandpa was driving again, steering us down a road that looked like two paths running through the tall brown grass. I heard the grass slipping under us. The sun wasn't up. Except for a little glow past a line of trees, there wasn't anything that looked like a sunrise. I pulled myself up and coughed, then asked, "How soon?"

"Soon," said the dog. "Soon, soon."

The television was on. The news was playing with the sound turned down low. When Grandpa's face appeared on the little screen, Grandpa turned it off. Then he let the truck roll to a stop, and there was nothing to hear but warm air blowing from the vents. I felt the heat on my bare face and in my crammed-together toes. Looking out the window, I knew it was cold. Even for November. And I knew that I was comfortable here, and happy enough, and did we have to walk through these cold dark fields?

I asked the question in my head. Nowhere else.

Grandpa hadn't said one word. He usually liked to tell me our plans and ask how I was feeling, and he'd remind me how I needed to be careful all the time. Hunting wasn't a game. But when he wouldn't talk, I asked, "When does it get light?"

He said nothing.

I looked at him and saw him looking at me. Only he wasn't. Mom always told me that he had a kindly face, and maybe I knew what she meant. But something about those old eyes made me squirm. Just for that moment.

Then he patted me on the knee, saying, "Soon."

It's what the dog had said, only Grandpa's voice was old and tired and he didn't sound as if he meant it.

• • •

My gun was my grandfather's when he was a boy. He gave it to me, even though we kept it at his house where he could keep it clean for me. I always liked its weight when I first picked it up, and I loved the slick sharp sounds it made when I loaded it. The black barrel was always cold to touch. The wood parts were decorated with checkerboards where your hands held tight, and the butt was padded with thick pink rubber. Where Grandpa's guns were fancy and new, mine was simple. It didn't have any videocam or adjustable shells. I shot old-fashioned shells. Plastic and brass and nickel-iron shot. The only new trick was the strapped on safety that kept me from accidentally shooting at people or myself.

The safety told me, "I am on the job."

Solomon whispered, "This way, hurry. This way."

"Wait," Grandpa told him.

But the dog kept going, his old hips fighting to keep up.

"He didn't hear you," I ventured.

"No, he hears," he said. "He just pretends to be deaf."

The sun was coming up, finally. But the sky in front of us was still dark, full of stars and the low stations and the big geosynchronous cities. I looked up, and maybe I was watching for the starship. And maybe Grandpa saw me looking. Because he took me by the shoulder, saying nothing. Just sort of steering me toward the field.

All sorts of crops had been growing on that ground. The harvesters had left their marks, tilling up the black ground as they passed. Here and there were masses of green leaves. Some cold-happy tailored vegetable was mixed in with the dead stalks and empty steak pods and the dried up melon vines. Just walking in that field was work. My gun and vest and boots were getting heavy. Even if I was bigger than last year, and stronger, I'd forgotten, like I always forgot, how much it hurt to pull your feet through those tangled vines.

"Slow," said Grandpa. To the dog.

The sun eased its way over the horizon. I turned and looked back at it and at the new truck, squinting hard.

Grandpa said, "Pay attention."

To me.

The dog had stopped in front of a mound of brown stalks. Sniffing hard. Was it pheasants? Or quail? Or one of the tailored species? I was hoping for something big and fancy. A screamer, or even a flashbird. Stepping closer, I lifted my gun up to my shoulder, and that's when Solomon started to growl, the black fur on his neck standing up straight, and his old body leaping inside the mound.

"Get back here!" Grandpa yelled.

Suddenly there was this wild growling.

"Come!" Grandpa screamed. "Come here!"

And the growling turned to squealing. Solomon practically flew out of there, his head down and his eyes almost shut. He went straight toward the first person that he saw. Which was me. And I smelled him exactly when Grandpa said, "Shit!"

Said, "Skunk!"

It wasn't just a smell. The stink that you smell on the slickway, that hangs around a dead skunk, is nothing compared to the juices that come out of a living animal. It's like getting hit in the nose with a hockey stick. You feel it as much as you smell it, and it makes you sick. That's why I turned and tried to run.

Grandpa was shouting, "Stop!"

He said, "Heel!"

He said, "Son-of-a-bitch!" and began firing. *Boom, Boom.* And I turned, watching him aiming square at the mound. At the skunk. *Boom. Boom.* And *boom.*

I'd never seen Grandpa that way. In the low bright light, he looked almost young, his face full of color and his eyes big and his gloved hands shoving in another five shells, every move slick and smooth. Then he aimed again, this time at the sky, and he fired off all five shots before he felt done.

Solomon was rolling in the stalks and vines, fighting to get rid of the stink.

I just stood there, feeling useless and sad.

Grandpa lowered his gun, then said, "Back to the truck, boys. Now."

Solomon was saying, "Shit, shit, shit, shit!"

I looked at the sky, up where Grandpa had been shooting, and that's when I saw the starship hanging there. Big as a big coin held at arm's length, and the same color as a coin, but square-looking, with shadows filling up the nozzles of its huge, dead engines.

The farmhouse was an old house.

The farmer was an old man who didn't have any hair on his head, or anywhere. He looked at us through his storm door, then said, "Oh," with a quiet little voice. His eyes couldn't have been any bigger.

Grandpa said, "Mr. Teeson? My people talked to you this summer. About giving me permission to go hunting on your land?"

"I remember that, sir. Absolutely."

Solomon was in the yard, panting. Grandpa had gotten here by driving slowly, letting the dog chase us all the way.

Mr. Teeson opened his door and stepped out, and he said, "Colonel Sattis." He said, "I can't believe this . . . Jesus . . . !"

Grandpa said, "Damned skunks."

"May I?" The farmer stuck out his hand, saying, "It's an honor."

Grandpa seemed surprised, maybe even bothered. But he managed to say, "The honor's mine." He always said those words, and he always wiped both hands against his shirt before offering one of them. Then he sort of smiled and shook the farmer's hand, asking, "Is there any way you might help? My stupid old dog ran into a skunk."

Mr. Teeson wrinkled up his nose and said, "I kind of figured that."

Then both men laughed. And Grandpa seemed more relaxed, saying, "This is my grandson. Sam, this is Mr. Teeson."

The farmer looked at me and said, "Hello, son."

I said, "Sir."

Then he winked at me, saying, "You know, I've admired your grandfather forever. I want you to know that."

Grandpa said, "Thank you."

"I had a cousin who was in the Service with you, sir."

"Perhaps I know him." Grandpa was being polite, or interested. I couldn't tell which. "In Alpha Division, perhaps?"

"No. He was a lieutenant in Beta Division."

Alpha was my grandfather's unit. Most of them lived, and all of the Betas died.

But the farmer didn't seem too sad, hunching over to explain, "Your grandpa's a great man. Did you know that?"

The man had awful breath. I swallowed and said, "I know, sir."

"I bet you do." He looked at Grandpa again. "A fine boy."

"The best."

Solomon gave a big complaining howl.

The farmer shook his head and started back into his house. "I don't have any of that new skunk-gunk, Colonel. But I keep something almost as good."

Grandpa said, "Thank you. So much."

We waited on the porch. I could hear a television. I couldn't make out what was being said, but it sounded like the news. It sounded important and angry, and I looked at Grandpa for a moment, then realized that he was deafer than his dog.

The farmer came back smiling, carrying a couple of tall cans of tomato juice. When he saw my look, he winked and said, "This is the best cure we had for a lot of years, son."

"I hate that stuff," I told him. "Do we have to drink it?"

That made both men laugh. But Grandpa's laugh was louder than normal, and the sound of it was wrong somehow.

I kept my distance, watching. Grandpa got the dog by his neck. Solomon was moaning, saying, "Shit," over and over again until Grandpa said, "That's enough!" Then the farmer led us around back, and he actually held the dog while Grandpa peeled off his shirts and boots and finally his pants. It was still very cold outside, and just seeing him made me shiver. Grandpa took the dog back and said, "Okay." The farmer opened the first can, and Grandpa poured it on the thick black fur, working it in as if it was soap. He was holding the dog by the loose skin of the neck, and Solomon twisted and kicked, and Grandpa was soon covered with the juice, and Solomon howled and complained and shook himself half-dry, little splashes of tomato juice sprinkled over both men.

I was glad not to be helping.

But I began to feel guilty, not having anything important to do.

The farmer opened the second can, laughing hard about something. Out of guilt, I asked if there was anything I should do, and he wiped his dirty face with a dirtier arm, telling me, "I don't think so, Sam." Then he said, "Colonel Sattis," with a big, crisp voice. "The boy looks sort of cold."

Just in my toes and fingers, I thought.

But I didn't say a word.

I'd never seen Grandpa look that messy. He was the kind of person who wants his hair just so, even if there wasn't much of it. He liked nice clothes, and he always tried to look younger than he was. But there he was, wearing nothing except underwear and the sticky juice. I could see his pale belly hanging forward, his arms smooth and soft. And the smooth skin of his body made his face look more wrinkly than ever, and tired, even when he tried very hard to smile.

He said, "Sam. Why don't you go sit in the car then."

"No, you don't." The farmer waved at me, saying, "We won't be much longer. Wait inside my house, if you want."

"He smells," Grandpa promised.

"Who doesn't?" Mr. Teeson was the only one laughing, telling me, "Just stay off the furniture. All right, Sam?"

I felt like a coward, and I felt relieved.

I walked back around and through the front door, sitting on the floor, Indian-style. They were showing the same digital on the old-fashioned TV. Again. And since nobody was there to tell me not to watch, I decided not to change networks.

I decided to see it through. For once.

The humongous king was wearing nothing but a thin web

of black wires, and it was hanging in the air, facedown. Its body was pink and hairless, and I don't care what some people say, it looked gross. It was huge and ugly, its thick legs kicking and its hands trying to grab one another, fingers big as my forearm curling and uncurling, the thin pink blood flowing from where the wires bit tight, then dripping fast to the glass floor.

Soldiers were walking under the alien.

Someone asked, "What next?" and another person—a woman—shouted, "Delta team's still trying to dock! And Beta isn't reporting!"

"Earth status?" said a nearby voice. A voice I knew.

The woman said, "Status unchanged, sir."

Someone else said, "Colonel." Then, "Nantucket's underwater now, sir."

The Colonel stepped into view. Not knowing that an alien camera was buried in the thick glass wall, he said, "Fuck," with that strong voice. He looked mostly the same, except the hair was thick and brown, and the face was smoother. He was a handsome man, and that's not me saying it. My history book called him, "The handsome colonel from the nation's heartland."

He said, "Fuck," a second time, his breath hanging in the cold air. "What about Beta?"

"No news. Sir."

Beta Division had tried to attack the weapons arrays, which was suicide. I read that in my history books, too. Most of them were cooked by the radiation before they even got to their targets. Which was probably what happened to Mr. Teeson's poor cousin.

I felt a good little dose of anger.

"Okay," said Colonel Sattis. "Thank you."

Then he picked up a fat alien microphone, using both hands where the king would hold it with one. "No more patience," he said. "I'm too fucking tired."

What he said went into a gray box, and the box spoke to the humongous in its own rumbling language.

The humongous answered, and the box translated it as, "It is not we! We are blameless, friend!"

"Quiet," said the Colonel. He sighed and said, "We've already been here. You *claim* that some faction's responsible. Some cult—"

The humongous said several words.

"Fanatics!" the box shouted. Over and over.

The Colonel carried the microphone with him, walking up underneath the alien. "But there's got to be some way," he said. "Assuming that you're telling the truth. These fanatics have control of your engines and your weapons, and you really can't take those systems back. But you know things. Your ancestors built this damned ship! And you're *not* going to be stupid. Not while your people are melting our ice caps . . . !"

The Colonel stopped screaming, catching his breath.

The humongous's face was straight above. As big as an elephant's face, it opened its black, black eyes, and the rubbery mouth said something.

The translation box said, "Move your people. Flee the ocean. That is the best solution."

"No!" the Colonel roared.

"They only want your cold landmass. A tiny part of your world—"

"Bullshit." The Colonel threw down the microphone and screamed, "Someone get me tools. And that map!"

"Which map?" asked the woman soldier.

He said, "Of their bodies. Their physiology. I want to know what I'm dealing with!" Then he started to pull off his uniform—this was where Mom sent me to bed last night—and that's when I got up off the floor and turned the television off. It wasn't that I couldn't take it. It wasn't that I wasn't curious. It's just that someone new was walking up on the front porch.

The stranger said, "Hello."

I said, "Hi," through the storm door.

He was very tall and dark. All I remember about his face

was that he looked as if he wanted to be somewhere else. Dressed in a suit, he looked strange. Maybe he was going to a wedding, I was guessing.

Staring in at me, he asked, "Is your father home?"

I said, "No."

Dad hasn't lived with us since I was three.

The stranger looked past me, squinting. Thinking to himself. He seemed halfway confused until he looked back, noticing what I was wearing. "Christ," he said. "You're the grandson, aren't you?"

I didn't say one word.

"Where is he?" the stranger asked.

Suddenly I felt sick, staring out at Grandpa's truck and the brown car parked behind it. I wanted to say something. I meant to lie, if only I could have thought of a good one.

But before I had one, a second man shouted, "I hear him! He's around back somewhere."

The tall man gave me another look, something sorry in his face.

Then he was gone.

I ran through the house, finding my way out the back door. I caught Grandpa washing his arms and bare chest with a garden hose and a lump of yellow soap. He was smiling, almost. The farmer was standing with him. Saying something. The dog was rolling himself dry in the grass. I could barely smell the skunk, and it was probably what was still sticking to me.

Grandpa said, "What is it, Sam?"

"Some men," I muttered.

Then the tall man was with us. All at once he was there, talking as if he'd done nothing all morning but practice what he was going to say now.

He said, "Sir."

With a hurried voice, he said, "I've been asked by Senator Lee to come here and warn you. In an hour, the UN issues a warrant for your arrest. And it would be best for everyone if you'll surrender yourself as soon as possible—"

"Just a minute," someone snapped.

It was Mr. Teeson. Where I thought my grandfather would cut the man off, it was the bald farmer who said, "You bastards. You stupid, stupid bastards . . . !"

The strangers in suits blinked and straightened their backs.

"This man," said the farmer. "He's a great man! Don't you children understand that simple fact? If it wasn't for Colonel Sattis, none of you pissy little ungratefuls would have ever been born . . . !"

The tall man said, "Mr. Sattis."

Grandpa was shaking. From the cold, maybe. He turned and picked up his shirts and his pants off the ground, and with a weak hand, he tried brushing away bits of dried grass. But it was too much work, and he gave up trying. He put on his pants and shirts, one after another, and after a minute, the tall man repeated himself.

"Mr. Sattis."

"Colonel Sattis," the farmer told them.

"Colonel," said the tall man. "Your old friend's doing you a considerable favor here. If it wasn't for his personal intervention, a brigade of marshals would be coming for you . . . instead of us. . . ."

I remembered the Senator. I remembered him laughing, drinking beer, and eating catfish on my grandfather's patio.

"Naturally," said the tall man, "you'll be free to retain legal counsel."

The farmer said, "Jesus!"

The second man growled, "This isn't your concern, sir."

Grandpa held up a hand, asking everyone to be quiet. Then he said, "I'm enjoying the day with my grandson. My grandson. And you come here under these circumstances . . . and what am I supposed to do . . . ? Go quietly . . . ?"

"We're warning you," said the second man. "We aren't here to arrest you!"

Grandpa looked at him, saying nothing. Then he looked upward as he finished buttoning his last shirt, asking, "What's going to happen? A trial?"

"Yes, sir," said the tall man. "There's got to be one now."

Grandpa said something under his breath. Then he looked in my direction, his face soft and white and very old. "So who finally filed charges against me?" he asked. "One of the humongoustarian groups?"

"Actually," said the tall man, "our own government is the plaintiff."

Again, the farmer said," Jesus."

Grandpa just nodded, saying in a sour way, "Of course they would."

Mr. Teeson took a few steps, screaming, "If you don't get off my land, boys . . . !"

"Stop," said Grandpa. To everyone. Then to the farmer, he said, "Thanks, Jim. For all your help, that you very much."

"This is bullshit," the farmer told him.

Grandpa didn't argue. He just turned to the others, asking, "May we finish our hunt? I promised this boy a pheasant, and we haven't seen even one bird yet."

The tall man looked at his partner, then down at his shiny shoes. "We aren't here to arrest anyone, Mr. Sattis. Like we told you."

"But we could escort you home again," said the other man.

Grandpa opened his pants and stuffed in his shirttails. He didn't move quickly, but he knew what he was doing. He told them, "Thank you for the generous offer. But I don't think so."

Then he looked at me, something in his eyes scaring me.

Nobody knew that there was a camera inside the wall.

The wall and camera were destroyed along with the rest of the king's room. Melted away by the nuclear blast. My grandfather set the nuke himself. He did it because his team needed time and confusion to get where they needed to be. To do what had to be done. And for setting the bomb and killing at least a few thousand of the king's followers, Grandpa won the first of three Medals of Honor.

Grandpa never knew that he was being watched.

He set off the bomb not to hide evidence, but to help.

Everything seen by that camera—not just that day, but for the last ten thousand years—ended up inside a different part of the ship. Sitting, and waiting. The humongous had a thing about the past. A fat chunk of their starship was left to shrines and cemeteries and digital warehouses full of everything that had ever happened on board. Every tunnel and big room, and even their toilets, had cameras. It took our best scientists ten hard years just to learn how to pipe power into those warehouses. Then it took ten more to learn how to get anything out of them but random goop. And it's still awfully tough working inside the starship. Without a breath of air in the place, every walk means space suits. And without one watt of power on board, every light and every machine needs its juice from human reactors strung clear out on the outermost hull.

I've read plenty, and I've seen even more on television and in the movies. But what I knew best was what Mom told me. Not Grandpa. Nobody was supposed to ask him about the humongous. Mom always told me, "He doesn't like to dwell on the war." Then she would do it for me, telling what little she knew, telling the same handful of stories over and over again.

Last night, after watching too much of the news, Mom told me her favorite one again. As if for the first time.

She told me how she'd seen the war.

"I was about your age," she began. Which is how she always began, even when I was only five years old. "And you can't imagine how scared I was," she told me, sitting in the middle of the television with me, holding my hand with one of hers.

"The world was being attacked," she said, "which was one of the reasons I was scared. It was a totally unprovoked attack. You know what unprovoked means?"

"Unfair," I volunteered.

She nodded, saying, "It was that, too. You're right."

Then she swallowed some of her cocktail, and wiped her eyes, and she said, "But I was more scared because it was my father who was up there. Who was leading the counter-attack."

I nodded, acting as if I didn't know anything.

"The aliens were talking to us with different voices," she said. "Everyone knew it. Some of the voices were halfway friendly, and others just told us to get back from the ocean. And meanwhile, the south pole was melting, and seas were rising, and Mom and I were hiding in the basement, knowing that it was just a matter of days or hours until those awful energy guns would be pointed at us."

She shook her head, saying, "You can't imagine how it was!"

I thought I could, but I didn't say it.

She took another swallow, then said, "I got tired of the basement." As if she was afraid that I might tell someone, she said, "Against Grandma's orders, I sneaked out into the yard, in the dark, when I knew that the starship would rise up in the south. If it fired at me, I was dead anyway. Outside or in the basement, or ten miles underground, I would die . . . and before that happened, I needed to see the starship for myself . . ."

"You saw the starship die instead," I said. I couldn't help myself.

She acted as if I'd done something wrong. Breaking a rule, maybe. But instead of saying so, she put her hands in her lap, saying, "I saw it happen. When every hatch and airlock and those . . . those dilation zones . . . when the reactors quit and they opened up, I saw all that air and cold water pouring out of the starship . . . !"

Mom swallowed, telling me, "That was the worst moment, Sam. I didn't know what was going on."

Then she squeezed my hand, telling me, "But I know better now. And now what I saw—what I remember so clearly—looks beautiful to me. What I remember . . . it was like some enormous comet was born right above me, milky and spreading all the way across the sky. Later I found out that the world was saved, and it was my own father who had done it. He did most of it himself. And I don't think that there's ever been a happier, prouder child than me."

She took another sip of her cocktail, and another.

Then she told me something new. Something that I never expected.

"When your grandfather came back to earth," she confessed, "and after all the parades and interviews and the medal ceremonies, he came home. Finally. It was the middle of the night, and he walked into my bedroom and sat on the edge of my bed, and he put his face down into his hands, and he cried. That's the only time that I've ever seen your grandfather cry. When Mom died last year, there weren't two tears from him. But he sat there and wept for almost an hour . . . !"

I had to ask, "Why?"

"Because." It was obvious to Mom, but she needed a sip before she said it. "Because he was so very glad to see me, Sammy. And that's all it means!"

The farmer felt awful. Felt sick.

He said so, and he looked so, his face twisted as if he was ready to bring up his breakfast. "The bastards," he kept saying, walking us back toward the truck after the men in suits had gone. "Of all the nerve! Tracking you down, just to harass you . . . !"

Grandpa didn't say one word.

Solomon was hunting again, following a scent out of the yard and into the trees. Grandpa looked at his dog, but he didn't say anything.

I shouted for him. "Come here, boy. Come!"

But the dog had gone deaf again.

"It's not fair," the farmer sputtered. "Trying to punish you like this. Now. They feel guilty, and this is how they try to make things right."

Grandpa gave a little half-nod.

"Christ," said old Mr. Teeson, "it isn't as if you *knew*. . . ."

We'd reached the truck, and Grandpa stopped at his door. Doing nothing.

"You didn't know," said the farmer.

Grandpa turned. "What do you mean?"

"About the humongous, and what the king was telling you . . . all of that . . ."

"What was the king telling me?"

The man licked his lips, then said, "The ship was split up into factions. With the worst group trying to make a home for itself."

Grandpa didn't make one sound.

The farmer pulled a hand over his scalp, then looked at me. Talking only to me, he asked, "So what if the king was telling the truth? Nobody understood those aliens, and your grandfather had to act. He had to do *something*—"

"Shut up." The same as he said it years ago, talking to the humongous, Grandpa told Mr. Teeson, "Shut up." Then he turned and shouted, "Come on, boy! We're leaving!"

As hard as his stiff legs could manage, Solomon came back across the yard.

"I'm sorry," the farmer whispered.

Then he said, "Colonel," one last time.

Grandpa opened the back door and grumbled, "Get in."

The dog tried, but he was too sore and too tired.

He whined when his jump fell short, and Grandpa grabbed him by the neck and threw him into the back, making him squeal even worse.

I had never, ever asked him about the humongous or the starship.

I knew better.

It was so much of a rule that I couldn't remember ever being told not to do it. Although I must have been. Mom or Grandma must have said, "Don't," in an important voice. "Don't ever," they would have told me. "He doesn't like talking about it, Sammy."

I didn't ask. Even then, I didn't.

Grandpa was driving again, following a good road between the fields and little ribbons of trees, and the dog was in the back, licking his sore spots. Grandpa was the one who said, "You know what they haven't found? Those three days before. The three days we spent talking to that king. Talking to his princes or his advisors, or whatever they were. Hearing things that sounded like promises. Only nothing ever changed.

" 'We are working,' they said. 'We are trying.' They kept chanting, 'Soon, soon, soon, soon, soon.' And all that time, people were dying, and cities in every part of the world were drowning."

I stared at my grandfather, saying nothing.

"That idiot Teeson was right," he told me. "There was plenty that I didn't know. Like why it smelled inside their ship. As bad as skunk, almost. I assumed that because they were aliens, they must have liked the stink. The king didn't tell me that their ship was on its last oars, and the stink and those enormous empty rooms and all the factions and all of the rest of the bullshit were measures of how bad things had gotten."

He said, "Sam." He said, "Do anything, and there is always something you don't know. Always. Even if it comes out for the very best, there were facts and figures that you didn't consider. And that's why it's the weakest, sickest, saddest apology to say that you did it wrong because you didn't have some perfect golden knowledge at your disposal."

He seemed to be talking to me, but thinking back, I know that he was talking more to himself. His voice was steady and dry and strong, and a little bit strange because of it. Grandpa couldn't have sounded more like his old self. And for reasons that I couldn't name, that made me feel scared and a little bit sick.

All at once, he said, "Here."

We turned off the paved road, following the edge of a wide field. And that's when I remembered the place. Last year, we'd come here to hunt, and this was where I shot my first pheasant. I could still see the shot in my mind, all those feathers knocked loose and the bird dropping and me racing the dog to get to it first.

At the top of a little hill, we stopped.

But instead of hunting, we sat. Saying nothing.

Grandpa turned on the television, jumping through the channels until he found what he wanted. Then with his steady voice starting to break, he said, "Your mother hasn't let you watch it clear through. Has she?"

I looked at him, and blinked, and I managed to say, "No, sir."

"Watch it now," he told me.

He ordered me.

Even on that little screen, it was sick to see. There was my grandfather, suddenly young, standing naked underneath the alien king. He was covered with pink blood, and he was holding a long knife, and dangling beside him were two of the king's dicks. The third dick was lying at his feet, long as a man is tall, and like a live fish, still flopping. And Grandpa was screaming, "Tell me! How do we stop them?! *How?!*"

"I die," the king answered, his voice huge and weak at the same time. "Please. I die. Please."

Grandpa shoved the knife up into the body itself, letting a river of blood pour over him. And he screamed, "The leads! Give 'em here!"

Someone came running, a black and a red cable in hand.

"Where is it?" Grandpa asked, looking down at some sort of biological map.

Someone said something. I couldn't hear what.

Neither could he. "That fat bunch of nerves . . . where *is* it . . . ?"

The woman came close enough to point—

And Grandpa shoved the wires up into that wide wet hole, then stepped back and said again, "How do we stop this?"

"I die," said the king.

Grandpa turned and said, "Do it!"

Someone said, "Sir—?"

"Shit!" he screamed. Then he moved over to a human-made box and hit a red button, and nothing happened for a half second. Maybe longer. Then the king gave out a wail,

big and deep, and he started to move, caught between those two strong nets and flopping like his own dick, only faster. Stronger. Flopping and flinging himself, and screaming right up until the nets broke free and he dropped onto the bloody floor. And he still kept moving, that whole long body arching up until Grandpa finally hit the red button again.

Again, Grandpa asked, "How can we stop this?"

The king said, "No."

Then he said, "I won't tell you."

And Grandpa, my grandpa turned off the television. He said, "Look at me." Then he took both of his thumbs, wiping the tears off my face. And after a little while, he said, "Wait here. Stay with the truck."

I didn't feel like hunting.

Not anymore.

I was numb and sick, and sadder than I thought I could ever be. I barely heard Grandpa opening the back end, then shutting it again. Then I didn't hear anything until this sobbing started, and I forced myself to turn and look into the back. The dog was in the back end of the truck. Tied up. He was saying, "I want to go," with his little-kid voice.

I climbed out and went around back. It took me a minute or two to figure out the latch, then lift the gate high enough to unlock it. Then I saw which gun was missing, and I picked up the empty case, not really thinking. Just feeling sicker all the time. And the dog begged. Not using words, but sounding like an old-fashioned dog. So I undid the leash, and he jumped down and started off down along a line of trees.

I followed him.

I found myself starting to run, my boots heavy and getting heavier. But I kept the dog in sight, right up till he slid down down into a draw. And I got to the draw and stopped, spotting my shotgun's safety lying at my feet.

"I am dismantled," the machine told me.

There was a little pond in the draw. And trees. Grandpa was sitting on a downed log with the gun barrel put up into his mouth. He didn't hear me. He was too busy working at the angle of gun, trying to get everything just so.

I tried to talk.

My voice quit working, but I managed to make a whimpering sound.

Then without pulling the barrel out of his mouth, he halfway turned and saw me, his eyes getting wider and brighter, and somehow farther away.

I stepped closer.

Talking around the barrel, he told me, "Go away."

I was thinking what he said about never knowing enough. About how a man can't just wait till he has perfect knowledge to act.

Grandpa was crying.

"Leave me alone," he said. Louder this time.

I don't know where I got the strength, but I told him, "No."

Then I told him, "They're going to find you innocent. If you explain things."

Then I sat down on the ground. Waiting.

After a little while, Grandpa managed to pull the barrel out of his mouth and put the gun at his feet, and acting more embarrassed than anything, he wiped at his tears and the rest of his face, and he pulled out a comb and ran it through his hair. Three times. I counted. Then with a tight little voice, he said, "Sam."

He said, "Do me a favor? Pick up this gun for me. Would you, please?"

GALACTIC NORTH

Alastair Reynolds

Persistence can be a virtue, especially in war . . . but perhaps—as in the breakneck, relentlessly paced, gorgeously colored story that follows, which sweeps us along on a cosmic chase across thousands of light-years of space and millions of years of time—it can sometimes be taken a bit too far . . .

New writer Alastair Reynolds is a frequent contributor to Interzone, *and has also sold to* Asimov's Science Fiction *and elsewhere. His first novel,* Revelation Space, *already being hailed as one of the major SF books of the year, has just appeared. A professional scientist with a Ph.D. in astronomy, he comes from Wales, but lives in the Netherlands.*

LUYTEN 726–8
COMETARY HALO—AD 2303

The two of them crouched in a tunnel of filthy ice, bulky in space suits. Fifty metres down the tunnel the servitor straddled the bore on skeletal legs, transmitting a thermal image onto their visors. Irravel jumped whenever the noise shifted into something human, cradling her gun nervously.

"Damn this thing," she said. "Hardly get my finger round the trigger."

"It can't read your blood, Captain." Markarian, next to her, managed not to sound as if he was stating the obvious. "You have to set the override to female."

Of course. Belatedly, remembering the training session on Fand where they'd been shown how to use the weapons—

months of subjective time ago; years of worldtime—Irravel told the gun to reshape itself. The memory-plastic casing squirmed in her gloves to something more manageable. It still felt wrong.

"How are we doing?"

"Last teams in position. That's all the tunnels covered. They'll have to fight their way in."

"I think that might well be on the agenda."

"Maybe so." Markarian sighted along his weapon like a sniper. "But they'll get a surprise when they reach the cargo."

True: the ship had sealed the sleeper chambers the instant the pirates had arrived near the comet. Counter-intrusion weaponry would seriously inconvenience anyone trying to break in, unless they had the right authorization. And there, Irravel knew, was the problem; the thing she would rather not have had to deal with.

"Markarian," Irravel said. "If we're taken prisoner, there's a chance they'll try and make us give up the codes."

"Don't think that hasn't crossed my mind already." Markarian rechecked some aspect of his gun. "I won't let you down, Irravel."

"It's not a question of letting me down," she said, carefully. "It's whether or not we betray the cargo."

"I know." For a moment they studied each other's faces through their visors, acknowledging what had once been more than professional friendship; the shared knowledge that they would kill each other rather than place the cargo in harm's way.

Their ship was the ramliner *Hirondelle*. She was damaged; lashed to the comet for repair. Improbably sleek for a creature of vacuum, her four-kilometre-long conic hull tapered to a needle-sharp prow and sprouted trumpet-shaped engines from two swept-back spars at the rear. It had been Irravel's first captaincy: a routine 17-year hop from Fand, in the Lacaille 9352 system, to Yellowstone, around Epsilon Eridani—with 20,000 reefersleep colonists. What had gone wrong should only have happened once in a thousand trips:

a speck of interstellar dust had slipped through the ship's screen of anticollision lasers and punched a cavernous hole in the ablative ice-shield, vaporizing a quarter of its mass. With a massively reduced likelihood of surviving another collision, the ship had automatically steered toward the nearest system capable of supplying repair materials.

Luyten 726-8 had been no one's idea of a welcoming destination. No human colonies had flourished there. All that remained were droves of scavenging machines sent out by various superpowers. The ship had locked into a scavenger's homing signal, eventually coming within visual range of the inert comet which the machine had made its home, and which ought to have been chequered with resupply materials. But when Irravel had been revived from reefersleep, what she'd found in place of the expected goods were only acres of barren comet.

"Dear god," she'd said. "Do we deserve this?"

Yet, after a few days, despair became steely resolve. The ship couldn't safely travel anywhere else, so they would have to process the supplies themselves, doing the work of the malfunctioning surveyor. It would mean stripping the ship just to make the machines to mine and shape the cometary ice—years of work by any estimate. That hardly mattered. The detour had already added years to the mission.

Irravel ordered the rest of her crew—all 90 of them—to be warmed, and then delegated tasks, mostly programming. Servitors were not particularly intelligent outside of their designated functions. She considered activating the other machines she carried as cargo—the greenfly terraformers—but that cut against all her instincts. Greenfly machines were Von Neumann breeders, unlike the sterile servitors. They were a hundred times cleverer. She would only consider using them if the cargo was placed in immediate danger.

"If you won't unleash the greenflies," Markarian said, "At least think about waking the Conjoiners. There may only be four of them, but we could use their expertise."

"I don't trust them. I never liked the idea of carrying them in the first place. They unsettle me."

"I don't like them either, but I'm willing to bury my prejudices if it means fixing the ship faster."

"Well, that's where we differ. I'm not, so don't raise the subject again."

"Yes," Markarian said, and only when its omission was insolently clear did he bother adding: "Captain."

Eventually the Conjoiners ceased to be an issue, when the work was clearly under way and proceeding normally. Most of the crew were able to return to refeersleep. Irravel and Markarian stayed awake a little longer, and even after they'd gone under, they woke every seven months to review the status of the works. It began to look as if they would succeed without assistance.

Until the day they were woken out of schedule, and a dark, grapple-shaped ship was almost upon the comet. Not an interstellar ship, it must have come from somewhere nearby—probably within the same halo of comets around Luyten 726-8. Its silence was not encouraging.

"I think they're pirates," Irravel said. "I've heard of one or two other ships going missing near here, and it was always put down to accident."

"Why did they wait so long?"

"They had no choice. There are billions of comets out here, but they're never less than light-years apart. That's a long way if you only have in-system engines. They must have a base somewhere else to keep watch, maybe light-weeks from here, like a spider with a very wide web."

"What do we do now?"

Irravel gritted her teeth. "Do what anything does when it gets stuck in the middle of a web. Fight back."

But the *Hirondelle*'s minimal defences only scratched against the enemy ship. Oblivious, it fired penetrators and winched closer. Dozens of crab-shaped machines swarmed out and dropped below the comet's horizon, impacting with seismic thuds. After a few minutes, sensors in the furthest tunnels registered intruders. Only a handful of crew had been woken. They broke guns out of the armoury—small arms designed for pacification in the unlikely event of a shipboard riot—and then established defensive positions in all the cometary tunnels.

Nervously now, Irravel and Markarian advanced round the tunnel's bend, cleated shoes whispering through ice barely more substantial than smoke. They had to keep their suit exhausts from touching the walls if they didn't want to get blown back by superheated steam. Irravel jumped again at the pattern of photons on her visor and then forced calm, telling herself it was another mirage.

Except this time it stayed.

Markarian opened fire, squeezing rounds past the servitor. It lurched aside, a gaping hole in its carapace. Black crabs came round the bend, encrusted with sensors and guns. The first reached the ruined servitor and dismembered it with ease. If only there'd been time to activate and program the greenfly machines they'd have ripped through the pirates like a host of furies, treating them as terraformable matter.

And maybe us too, Irravel thought.

Something flashed through the clouds of steam; an electromagnetic pulse that turned Irravel's suit sluggish, as if every joint had corroded. The whine of the circulator died to silence, leaving only her frenzied breathing. Something pressed against her backpack. She turned slowly around, wary of falling against the walls. There were crabs everywhere. The chamber in which they'd been cornered was littered with the bodies of the other crew members; pink trails of blood or ice reaching from other tunnels. They'd been killed and dragged here.

Two words jumped to mind: kill yourself. But first she had to kill Markarian, in case he lacked the nerve himself. She couldn't see his face through his visor. That was good. Painfully, she pointed the gun toward him and squeezed the trigger. But instead of firing, the gun shivered in her hands, stowing itself into a quarter of its operational volume. "Thank you for using this weapon system," it said cheerfully.

Irravel let it drift to the ground.

A new voice rasped in her helmet. "If you're thinking of surrendering, now might not be a bad time."

"Bastard," Irravel said softly.

"Really the best you can manage?" The language was Canasian—what Irravel and Markarian had spoken on Fand—but heavily accented, as if the native tongue was Norte or Russish, or spoken with an impediment. "Bastard's quite a compliment compared to some of the things my clients come up with."

"Give me time; I'll work on it."

"Positive attitude—that's good." The lid of a crab hinged up, revealing the prone form of a man in a mesh of motion-sensors. He crawled from the mesh and stepped onto the ice, wearing a space suit formed from segmented metal plates. Totems had been welded to the armour, around holographic starscapes infested with serpentine monsters and scantily clad maidens.

"Who are you?"

"Captain Run Seven." He stepped closer, examining her suit nameplate. "But you can call me Seven, Irravel Veda."

"I hope you burn in hell, Seven."

Seven smiled—she could see the curve of his grin through his visor; the oddly upturned nostrils of his nose above it. "I'm sensing some negativity here, Irravel. I think we need to put that behind us, don't you?"

Irravel looked at her murdered adjutants. "Maybe if you tell me which one was the traitor."

"Traitor?"

"You seemed to have no difficulty finding us."

"Actually, you found us." It was a woman's voice this time. "We use lures—tampering with commercial beacons, like the scavenger's." She emerged from one of the other attack machines, wearing a suit similar to Seven's, except that it displayed the testosterone-saturated male analogues of his space-maidens; all rippling torsos and chromed codpieces.

"Wreckers," Irravel breathed.

"Yeah. Ships home in on the beacons, then find they ain't going anywhere in a hurry. We move in from the halo."

"Disclose all our confidential practices while you're at it, Mirsky," Seven said.

She glared at him through her visor. "Veda would have figured it out."

"We'll never know now, will we?"

"What does it matter?" she said. "Gonna kill them anyway, aren't you?"

Seven flashed an arc of teeth filed to points and waved a hand toward the female pirate. "Allow me to introduce Mirsky, our loose-tongued but efficient information retrieval specialist. She's going to take you on a little trip down memory lane; see if we can't remember those access codes."

"What codes?"

"It'll come back to you," Seven said.

They were taken through the tunnels, past half-assembled mining machines, onto the surface and then into the pirate ship. The ship was huge: most of it living space. Cramped corridors snaked through hydroponics galleries of spring wheat and dwarf papaya, strung with xenon lights. The ship hummed constantly with carbon dioxide scrubbers, the fetid air making Irravel sneeze. There were children everywhere, frowning at the captives. The pirates obviously had no reefersleep technology: they stayed warm the whole time, and some of the children Irravel saw had probably been born after the *Hirondelle* had arrived here.

They arrived at a pair of interrogation rooms where they were separated. Irravel's room held a couch converted from an old command seat, still carrying warning decals. A console stood in one corner. Painted torture scenes fought for wallspace with racks of surgical equipment; drills, blades and ratcheted contraptions speckled with rust.

Irravel breathed deeply. Hyperventilation could have an

anaesthetic effect. Her conditioning would in any case create a state of detachment: the pain would be no less intense, but she would feel it at one remove.

She hoped.

The pirates fiddled with her suit, confused by the modern design, until they stripped her down to her shipboard uniform. Mirsky leant over her. She was small-boned and dark-skinned, dirty hair rising in a topknot, eyes mismatched shades of azure. Something clung to the side of her head above the left ear; a silver box with winking status lights. She fixed a crown to Irravel's head then made adjustments on the console.

"Decided yet?" Captain Run Seven said, sauntering into the room. He was unlatching his helmet.

"What?"

"Which of our portfolio of interrogation packages you're going to opt for."

She was looking at his face now. It wasn't really human. Seven had a man's bulk and shape, but there was at least as much of the pig in his face. His nose was a snout, his ears two tapered flaps framing a hairless pink skull. Pale eyes evinced animal cunning.

"What the hell are you?"

"Excellent question," Seven said, clicking a finger in her direction. His bare hand was dark-skinned and feminine. "To be honest, I don't really know. A genetics experiment, perhaps? Was I the seventh failure, or the first success?"

"Are you sure you want an honest answer on that?"

He ignored her. "All I know is that I've been here in the halo around Luyten 726-8—for as long as I can remember."

"Someone sent you here?"

"In a tiny automated spacecraft; perhaps an old lifepod. The ship's governing personality raised me as well as it could; attempted to make of me a well-rounded individual." Seven trailed off momentarily. "Eventually I was found by a passing ship. I staged what might be termed a hostile takeover bid. From then on I've had an organization largely recruited from my client base."

"You're insane. It might have worked once, but it won't work with us."

"Why should you be any different?"

"Neural conditioning. I treat the cargo as my offspring—all 20,000 of them. I can't betray them in any way."

Seven smiled his piggy smile. "Funny; the last client thought that too."

Sometime later Irravel woke alone in a reefersleep casket. She remembered only dislocated episodes of interrogation. There was the memory of a kind of sacrifice, and, later, of the worst terror she could imagine—so intense that she could not bring its cause to mind. Underpinning everything was the certainty that she had not given up the codes.

So why was she still alive?

Everything was quiet and cold. Once she was able to move, she found a suit and wandered the *Hirondelle* until she reached a porthole. They were still lashed to the comet. The other craft was gone; presumably en route back to the base in the halo where the pirates must have had a larger ship.

She looked for Markarian, but there was no sign of him.

Then she checked the 20-sleeper chambers; the thousand-berth dormitories. The chamber doors were all open. Most of the sleepers were still there. They'd been butchered, carved open for implants, minds pulped by destructive memory-trawling devices. The horror was too great for any recognizable emotional response. The conditioning made each death feel like a stolen part of her.

Yet something kept her on the edge of sanity: the discovery that 200 sleepers were missing. There was no sign that they'd been butchered like the others, which left the possibility that they'd been abducted by the pig. It was madness; it would not begin to compensate for the loss of the others—but her psychology allowed no other line of thought.

She could find them again.

• • •

Her plan was disarmingly simple. It crystallized in her mind with the clarity of a divine vision. It would be done.

She would repair the ship. She would hunt down Seven. She would recover the sleepers from him. And enact whatever retribution she deemed fit.

She found the chamber where the four Conjoiners had slept, well away from the main dormitories, in part of the ship where the pirates were not likely to have wandered. She was hoping she could revive them and seek their assistance. There seemed no way they could make things worse for her. But her hopes faded when she saw the scorch marks of weapon blasts around the bulkhead; the door forced.

She stepped inside anyway.

They'd been a sect on Mars, originally; a clique of cyberneticists with a particular fondness for self-experimentation. In 2190 their final experiment had involved distributed processing—allowing their enhanced minds to merge into one massively parallel neural net. The resultant event—a permanent, irrevocable escalation to a new mode of consciousness—was known as the Transenlightenment.

There'd been a war, of course.

Demarchists had long seen both sides. They used neural augmentation themselves, policed so that they never approached the Conjoiner threshold. They'd brokered the peace, defusing the suspicion around the Conjoiners. Conjoiners had fuelled Demarchist expansion from Europa with their technologies, fused in the white-heat of Transenlightenment. Four of them were along as observers because the *Hirondelle* used their ramscoop drives.

Irravel still didn't trust them.

And maybe it didn't matter. The reefersleep units—fluted caskets like streamlined coffins—were riddled with blast holes. Grimacing against the smell, Irravel examined the remains inside. They'd been cut open, but the pirates seemed to have abandoned the job halfway through, not finding the kinds of implants they were expecting. And maybe not even recognizing that they were dealing with anything other than normal humans, Irravel thought—especially if the pirates who'd done this hadn't been among Seven's more experienced crewmembers; just trigger-happy thugs.

She examined the final casket; the one furthest from the door. It was damaged, but not so badly as the others. The display cartouches were still alive, a patina of frost still adhering to the casket's lid. The Conjoiner inside looked intact: the pirates had never reached him. She read his nameplate: Remontoire.

"Yeah, he's a live one," said a voice behind Irravel. "Now back off real slow."

Heart racing, Irravel did as she was told. Slowly, she turned around, facing the woman whose voice she recognized.

"Mirsky?" she said.

"Yeah, it's your lucky day." Mirsky was wearing her suit, but without the helmet, making her head seem shrunken in the moat of her neck-ring. She had a gun on Irravel, but the way she pointed it was halfhearted, as if this was a stage in their relationship she wanted to get over as quickly as possible.

"What the hell are you doing here?"

"Same as you, Veda. Trying to figure out how much shit we're in; how hard it'll be to get this ship moving again. Guess we had the same idea about the Conjoiners. Seven went berserk when he heard they'd been killed, but I figured it was worth checking how thorough the job had been."

"Stop; slow down. Start at the beginning. Why aren't you with Seven?"

Mirsky pushed past her and consulted the reefersleep indicators. "Seven and me had a falling-out. Fill in the rest yourself." With quick jabs of her free hand she called up different display modes, frowning at each. "Shit, this ain't gonna be easy. If we wake this guy without his three friends, he's gonna be psychotic; no use to us at all."

"What kind of falling-out?"

"Seven reckoned I was holding back too much in the interrogation; not putting you through enough hell." She scratched at the silver box on the side of her head. "Maybe we can wake him, then fake the cybernetic presence of his friends—what do you think?"

"Why am I still alive, if Seven broke into the sleeping chambers? Why are you still alive?"

"Seven's a sadist. Abandonment's more his style than a quick and clean execution. As for you, the pig cut a deal with your second-in-command."

The implication of that sunk in. "Markarian gave him the codes?"

"It wasn't you, Veda."

Strange relief flooded Irravel. She could never be absolved of the crime of losing the cargo, but at least her degree of complicity had lessened.

"But that was only half the deal," Mirsky continued. "The rest was Seven promising not to kill you: Markarian agreed to join the *Hideyoshi*; our main ship." She told Irravel that there'd been a transmitter rigged to her reefersleep unit, so that Markarian would know she was still alive.

"Seven must have known he was taking a risk leaving both of us alive."

"A pretty small one. The ship's in pieces and Seven will assume neither of us has the brains to patch it back together." Mirsky slipped the gun into a holster. "But Seven assumed the Conjoiners were dead. Big mistake. Once we figure a way to wake Remontoir safely, he can help us fix the ship; make it faster too."

"You've got this all worked out, haven't you?"

"More or less. Something tells me you aren't absolutely ready to start trusting me, though."

"Sorry, Mirsky, but you don't make the world's most convincing turncoat."

She reached up with her free hand, gripping the box on the side of her head. "Know what this is? A loyalty-shunt. Makes simian stem cells; pumps them into the internal carotid artery, just above the cavernous sinus. They jump the blood-brain barrier and build a whole bunch of transient structures tied to primate dominance hierarchies; alpha-male shit. That's how Seven had us under his command—he was King Monkey. But I've turned it off now."

"That's supposed to reassure me?"

"No, but maybe this will."

Mirsky tugged at the box, ripping it away from the side of her head in curds of blood.

LUYTEN 726-8
COMETARY HALO—AD 2309

Irravel felt the *Hirondelle* turn like a compass needle. The ramscoops gasped at interstellar gas, sucking lone atoms of cosmic hydrogen from cubic metres of vacuum. The engines spat twin beams of thrust, pressing Irravel into her seat with two gees of acceleration. Hardly moving now, still in the local frame of the cometary halo, but in only six months she would be nudging lightspeed.

Her seat floated on a boom in the middle of the dodecahedral bridge. "Map," Irravel said, and was suddenly drowning in stars; an immense 30-light-year-wide projection of human-settled space, centred on the First System.

"There's the bastard," Mirsky said, pointing from her own hovering seat, her voice only slightly strained under the gee-load. "Map; give us projection of the *Hideyoshi*'s vector, and plot our intercept."

The pirate ship's icon was still very close to Luyten 726-8; less than a tenth of a light-year out. They had not seen Seven until now. The thrust from his ship was so tightly focused that it had taken until now for the widening beams of the exhaust to sweep over *Hirondelle*'s sensors. But now they knew where he was headed. A dashed line indicated the likely course, arrowing right through the map's heart and out toward the system Lalande 21185. Now came the intercept vector, a near-tangent which sliced Seven's course beyond Sol.

"When does it happen?" Irravel said.

"Depends on how much attention Seven's paying to what's coming up behind him, for a start, and what kind of evasive stunts he can pull."

"Most of my simulations predict an intercept between 2325 and 2330," Remontoire said.

Irravel savoured the dates. Even for someone trained to fly a starship between systems, they sounded uncomfortably like the future.

"Are you sure it's him—not just some other ship that happened to be waiting in the halo?"

"Trust me," Mirsky said. "I can smell the swine from here."

"She's right," Remontoire said. "The destination makes perfect sense. Seven was prohibited from staying here much longer, once the number of missing ships became too large to be explained away as accidents. Now he must seek a well-settled system to profit from what he has stolen."

The Conjoiner looked completely normal at first glance—a bald man wearing a ship's uniform, his expression placid—but then one noticed the unnatural bulge of his skull, covered only in a fuzz of baby hair. Most of his glial cells had been supplanted by machines which served the same structural functions but which also performed specialized cybernetic duties, like interfacing with other commune partners or external machinery. Even the organic neurones in his brain were now webbed together by artificial connections which allowed transmission speeds of kilometres per second; factors of ten faster than in normal brains. Only the problem of dispersing waste heat denied the Conjoiners even faster modes of thought.

It was seven years since they'd woken him. Remontoire had not dealt well with the murder of his three compatriots, but Irravel and Mirsky had managed to keep him sane by feeding input into the glial machines, crudely simulating rapport with other commune members. "It provides the kind of comfort to me that a ghost limb offers an amputee," Remontoire had said. "An illusion of wholeness—but no substitute for the real thing."

"What more can we do?" Irravel said.

"Return me to another commune with all speed."

Irravel had agreed, provided Remontoire helped with the ship.

He hadn't let her down. Under his supervision, half the ship's mass had been sacrificed, permitting twice the acceleration. They had dug a vault in the comet, lined it with support systems, and entombed what remained of the cargo. The sleepers were nominally dead—there was no real expectation of reviving them again, even if medicine improved in the future—but Irravel had nonetheless set servitors to tend the dead for however long it took, and programmed the beacon to lure another ship, this time to pick up the dead. All that had taken years, of course—but it had also taken Seven as much time to cross the halo to his base; time again to show himself.

"Be so much easier if you didn't want the others back," Mirsky said. "Then we could just slam past the pig at relativistic speed and hit him with seven kinds of shit." She was very proud of the weapons she'd built into the ship, copied from pirate designs with Remontoire's help.

"I want the sleepers back," Irravel said.

"And Markarian?"

"He's mine," she said, after due consideration. "You get the pig."

NEAR LALANDE 21185—AD 2328

Relativity squeezed stars until they bled colour. Half a kilometre ahead, the side of Seven's ship raced toward Irravel like a tsunami.

The *Hideyoshi* was the same shape as the *Hirondelle;* honed less by human whim than the edicts of physics. But the *Hideyoshi* was heavier, with a wider cross section, incapable of matching the *Hirondelle*'s acceleration or of pushing so close to C. It had taken years, but they'd caught up with Seven, and now the attack was in progress.

Irravel, Mirsky and Remontoire wore thruster-pack equipped suits, of the type used for inspections outside the ship, with added armour and weapons. Painted for effect, they looked like mechanized Samurai. Another 47 suits were slaved to theirs, acting as decoys. They'd crossed 50,000 kilometres of space between the ships.

"You're sure Seven doesn't have any defences?" Irravel had asked, not long after waking from reefersleep.

"Only the in-system ship had any firepower," Mirsky said. She looked older now; new lines engraved under her eyes. "That's because no one's ever been insane enough to contemplate storming another ship in interstellar space."

"Until now."

But it wasn't so stupid, and Mirsky knew it. Matching velocities with another ship was only a question of being faster; squeezing fractionally closer to lightspeed. It might take time, but sooner or later the distance would be closed. And it had taken time, none of which Mirsky had spent in reefersleep. Partly it was because she lacked the right implants—ripped out in infancy when she was captured by Seven. Partly it was a distaste for the very idea of being frozen, instilled by years of pirate upbringing. But also because she wanted time to refine her weapons. They had fired a salvo against the enemy before crossing space in the suits, softening up any weapons buried in his ice and opening holes into the *Hideyoshi*'s interior.

Now Irravel's vision blurred, her suit slowing itself before slamming into the ice.

Whiteness swallowed her.

For a moment she couldn't remember what she was doing here. Then awareness came and she slithered back up the tunnel excavated on her fall, until she reached the surface of the *Hideyoshi*'s ice-shield.

"Veda—you intact?"

Her armour's shoulder-mounted comm laser found a line-of-sight to Mirsky. Mirsky was 20 or 30 metres away, around the ship's lazy circumference, balancing on a ledge of ice. Walls of it stretched above and below like a rockface, lit by the glare from the engines. Decoys were arriving by the second.

"I'm alive," Irravel said. "Where's the entry point?"

"Couple of hundred metres upship."

"Damn. I wanted to come in closer. Remontoire's out of line-of-sight. How much fuel do you have left?"

"Scarcely enough to take the chill off a penguin's dick."

Mirsky raised her arms above her head and fired lines into the ice, rocketing out from her sleeves. Belly sliding against the shield, she retracted the lines and hauled herself upship.

Irravel followed. They'd burned all their fuel crossing between the two ships, but that was part of the plan. If they didn't have a chance to raid Seven's reserves, they'd just kick themselves into space and let the *Hirondelle* home in on them.

"You think Seven saw us cross over?"

"Definitely. And you can bet he's doing something about it, too."

"Don't you do anything that might endanger the cargo, Mirsky—no matter how tempting Seven makes it."

"Would you sacrifice half the sleepers to get the other half back?"

"That's not remotely an option."

Above their heads crevasses opened like eyes. Pirate crabs erupted out, black as night against the ice. Irravel opened fire on the machines. This time, with better weapons and real armour, she began to inflict damage. Behind the crabs, pirates emerged, bulbous in customized armour. Lasers scuffed the ice; bright through gouts of steam. Irravel saw Remontoire now: he was unharmed, and doing his best to shoot the pirates into space.

Above, one of Irravel's shots dislodged a pirate.

The *Hideyoshi*'s acceleration dropped him toward her. When the impact came she hardly felt it, her suit's guylines staying firm. The pirate folded around her like a broken toy then bounced back against the ship, pinned there by her suit. He was too close to shoot unless Irravel wanted to blow herself into space. Distorted behind glass, his face shaped a word. She got in closer until their visors were touching. Through the glass she saw the asymmetric bulge of a loyalty-shunt.

The face was Markarian's. At first it seemed like absurd coincidence. Then it occurred to her that Seven might have sent his newest recruit out to show his mettle. Maybe Seven wouldn't be far behind. Confronting adversaries was part of the alpha-male inheritance.

"Irravel," Markarian said, voice laced with static. "I'm glad you're alive."

"Don't flatter yourself you're the reason I'm here, Markarian. I came for the cargo. You're just next on the list."

"What are you going to do—kill me?"

"Do you think you deserve any better than that?" Irravel adjusted her position. "Or are you going to try and justify betraying the cargo?"

He pulled his aged features into a smile. "We made a deal, Irravel; the same way you made a deal about greenfly. But you don't remember that, do you?"

"Maybe I sold the greenfly machines to the pig," she said. "If I did that, it was a calculated move to buy the safety of the cargo. You, on the other hand, cut a deal with Seven to save your neck."

The other pirates were holding fire, nervously marking them. "I did it to save yours, actually. Does that make any sense?" There was wonder in his eyes now. "Did you ever see Mirsky's hand? That was never her own. The pirates swap limbs as badges of rank. They're very good at connective surgery."

"You're not making much sense, Markarian."

Dislodged ice rained on them. Irravel looked around in time to see another pirate emerging from a crevasse. She recognized the suit artwork: it was Seven. He wore things, strung around his utility belt in transparent bags like obscene fruit. She stared at them for a few seconds before their nature clicked into horrific focus: frozen human heads.

Irravel stifled a reaction to vomit.

"Yes," Run Seven said. "Ten of your compatriots, recently unburdened of their bodies. But don't worry—they're not harmed in any fundamental sense. Their brains are intact—provided you don't warm them with an ill-aimed shot."

"I've got a clear line of fire," Mirsky said. "Just say the word and the bastard's an instant anatomy lesson."

"Wait," Irravel said. "Don't shoot."

"Sound business sense, Captain Veda. I see you appreciate the value of these heads."

"What's he talking about?" Mirsky said.

"Their neural patterns can be retrieved." It was Remontoire speaking now. "We Conjoiners have had the ability to copy minds onto machine substrates for some time now, though we haven't advertised it. But that doesn't matter—there have been experiments on Yellowstone which approach our early successes. And these heads aren't even thinking: only topologies need to be mapped, not electrochemical processes."

The pig took one of the heads from his belt and held it to eye level, for inspection. "The Conjoiner's right. They're not really dead. And they can be yours if you wish to do business."

"What do you want for them?"

"Markarian, for a start. All that Demarchy expertise makes for a very efficient second-in-command."

Irravel glanced down at her prisoner. "You can't buy loyalty with a box and a few neural connections."

"No? In what way do our loyalty-shunts differ from the psychosurgery which your world inflicted on you, Irravel, yoking your motherhood instinct to 20,000 sleepers you don't even know by name?"

"We have a deal or not?"

"Only if you throw in the Conjoiner as well."

Irravel looked at Remontoire; some snake part of her mind weighing options with reptilian detachment.

"No!" he said. "You promised!"

"Shut up," Seven said. "Or when you do get to rejoin your friends, it'll be in installments."

"I'm sorry," Irravel said. "I can't lose even ten of the cargo."

Seven tossed the first head down to her. "Now let Markarian go and we'll see about the rest."

Irravel looked down at him. "It's not over between you and me."

Then she released him, and he scrambled back up the ice toward Seven.

"Excellent. Here's another head. Now the Conjoiner."

Irravel issued a subvocal command; watched Remontoire stiffen. "His suit's paralysed. Take him."

Two pirates worked down to him, checked him over and nodded toward Seven. Between them they hauled him back up the ice, vanishing into a crevasse and back into the *Hideyoshi.*

"The other eight heads," Irravel said.

"I'm going to throw them away from the ship. You'll be able to locate them easily enough. While I'm doing that, I'm going to retreat, and you're going to leave."

"We could end this now," Mirsky said.

"I need those heads."

"They really fucked with your psychology big-time, didn't they?" She raised her weapon and began shooting Seven and the other pirates. Irravel watched her carve up the remaining heads; splintering frozen bone into the vacuum.

"No!"

"Sorry," Mirsky said. "Had to do it, Veda."

Seven clutched at his chest, fingers mashing the pulp of

the heads, still tethered to his belt. She'd punctured his suit. As he tried to stem the damburst, his face was carved with the intolerable knowledge that his reign had just ended.

But something had hit Irravel too.

SYLVESTE INSTITUTE, YELLOWSTONE ORBIT, EPSILON ERIDANI—AD 2415

"Where am I?" Irravel asked. "How am I thinking this?"

The woman's voice was the colour of mahogany. "Somewhere safe. You died on the ice, but we got you back in time."

"For what?"

Mirsky sighed, as though this was something she would rather not have had to explain this soon.

"To scan you, just like we did with the frozen heads. Copy you into the ship."

Maybe she should have felt horror, or indignation, or even relief that some part of her had been spared.

Instead, she just felt impatience.

"What now?"

"We're working on it," Mirsky said.

TRANS-ALDEBARAN SPACE—AD 2673

"We saved her body after she died," Mirsky said, wheezing slightly. She found it hard to move around under what to Irravel was the ship's normal two and a half gees of thrust. "After the battle we brought her back on board."

Irravel thought of her mother dying on the other ship, the one they were chasing. For years they had deliberately not narrowed the distance, holding back but not allowing the *Hideyoshi* to slip from view.

Until now, it hadn't even occurred to Irravel to ask why.

She looked through the casket's window, trying to match her own features against what she saw in the woman's face, trying to project her own 15 years into Mother Irravel's adulthood.

"Why did you keep her so cold?"

"We had to extract what we could from her brain," Mirsky said. "Memories and neural patterns. We trawled them and stored them in the ship."

"What good was that?"

"We knew they'd come in useful again."

She'd been cloned from Mother Irravel. They were not identical—no Mixmaster expertise could duplicate the precise biochemical environment of Mother Irravel's womb, or the shaping experiences of early infancy, and their personalities had been sculpted centuries apart, in totally different worlds. But they were still close copies. They even shared memories: scripted into Irravel's mind by medichines, so that she barely noticed each addition to her own experiences.

"Why did you do this?" she asked.

"Because Irravel began something," Mirsky said. "Something I promised I'd help her finish."

STORMWATCH STATION, AETHRA, HYADES TRADE ENVELOPE—AD 2931

"Why are you interested in our weapons?" the Nestbuilder asked. "We are not aware of any wars within the *chordate phylum* at this epoch."

"It's a personal matter," Irravel said.

The Nestbuilder hovered a metre above the trade floor, suspended in a column of microgravity. They were oxygen-breathing arthropods who'd once ascended to spacefaring capability. No longer intelligent, yet supported by their self-renewing machinery, they migrated from system to system, constructing elaborate, space-filling structures from solid diamond. Other Nestbuilder swarms would arrive and occasionally occupy the new nests. There seemed no purpose to this activity, but for tens of thousands of years they had been host to a smaller, cleverer species known as the

Slugs. Small communities of Slugs—anything up to a dozen—lived in warm, damp niches in a Nestbuilder's intricately folded shell. They had long since learned how to control the host's behavior and exploit its subservient technology.

Irravel studied a Slug now, crawling out from under a lip of shell material.

The thing was a multicellular invertebrate not much larger than her fist; a bag of soft blue protoplasm, sprouting appendages only when they were needed. A slightly bipolar shadow near one end might have been its central nervous system, but there hardly seemed enough of it to trap sentience. There were no obvious sense or communicational organs, but a pulsing filament of blue slime reached back into the Nestbuilder's fold. When the Slug spoke, it did so through the Nestbuilder; a rattle of chitin from the host's mouthparts which approximated human language. A hovering jewel connected to the station's lexical database did the rest, rendering the voice calmly feminine.

"A personal matter? A vendetta? Then it's true." The mouthparts clicked together in what humans presumed was the symbiotic creature's laughter response. "You *are* who we suspected."

"She did tell you her name was Irravel, guy," Mirsky said, sipping black coffee with delicate movements of the exoskeletal frame she always wore in high gravity.

"Among you *chordates,* the name is not so unusual now," the Slug reminded them. "But you do fit the description, Irravel."

They were near one of the station's vast picture windows, overlooking Aethra's mighty, roiling cloud decks, 50 kilometres below. It was getting dark now and the stormplayers were preparing to start a show. Irravel saw two of their seeders descending into the clouds; robot craft tethered by a nearly invisible filament. The seeders would position the filament so that it bridged cloud layers with different static potentials; they'd then detach and return to Stormwatch, while the filament held itself in position by rippling along its length. For hundreds of kilometres around, other filaments would have been placed in carefully selected positions. They were electrically isolating now, but at the stormplayer's discretion each filament would flick over into a conductive state a massive, choreographed lightning flash.

"I never set out to become a legend," Irravel said. "Or a myth, for that matter."

"Yes. There are so many stories about you, Veda, that it might be simpler to assume you never existed."

"What makes you think otherwise?"

"The fact that a *chordate* who could have been Markarian also passed this way, only a year or so ago." The Nestbuilder's shell pigmentation flickered briefly revealing a picture of Markarian's ship.

"So you sold weapons to him?"

"That would be telling, wouldn't it?" The mouthparts clattered again. "You would have to answer a question of ours first."

Outside, the opening flashes of the night's performance gilded the horizon; like the first stirrings of a symphony. Aethra's rings echoed the flashes, pale ghosts momentarily cleaving the sky.

"What is it you want to know?"

"We Slugs are among the few intelligent, starfaring cultures in this part of the Galaxy. During the War against Intelligence we avoided the Inhibitors by hiding ourselves among the mindless Nestbuilders."

Irravel nodded. Slugs were one of the few alien species known to humanity who would even acknowledge the existence of the feared Inhibitors. Like humanity, they'd fought and beaten the revenants at least for now.

"It is the weaponry you seek which enabled us to triumph—but even then only at colossal cost to our phylum. Now we are watchful for new threats."

"I don't see where this is leading."

"We have heard rumors. Since you have come from the

direction of those rumours—the local stellar neighbourhood around your phylum's birth star—we imagined you might have information of value."

Irravel exchanged a sideways glance with Mirsky. The old woman's wizened, age-spotted skull looked as fragile as paper, but she remained an unrivalled tactician. They knew each other so well now that Mirsky could impart advice with the subtlest of movements; expression barely troubling the lined mask of her face.

"What kind of information were you seeking?"

"Information about something that frightens us." The Nestbuilder's pigmentation flickered again, forming an image of—something. It was a splinter of grey-brown against speckled blackness—perhaps the Nestbuilder's attempt at visualizing a planetoid. And then something erupted across the surface of the world, racing from end to end like a film of verdigris. Where it had passed, fissures opened up, deepening until they were black fractures, as if the world were a calving iceberg. And then it blew apart, shattering into a thousand green-tinged fragments.

"What was that?" Irravel said.

"We were rather hoping you could tell us." The Nestbuilder's pigmentation refreshed again, and this time what they were seeing was clearly a star, veiled in a toroidal belt of golden dust. "Machines have dismantled every rocky object in the system where these images were captured; Ross 128, which lies within eleven light-years of your birth star. They have engendered a swarm of trillions of rocks on independent orbits. Each rock is sheathed in a pressurized bubble membrane, within which an artificial plant-based ecosystem has been created. The same machines have fashioned other sources of raw material into mirrors, larger than worlds themselves, which trap sunlight above and below the ecliptic and focus it onto the swarm."

"And why does this frighten you?"

The Nestbuilder leant closer in its column of microgravity. "Because we saw it being resisted. As if these machines had never been intended to wreak such transformations. As if your phylum had created something it could not control."

"And—these attempts at resistance?"

"Failed."

"But if one system was accidentally transformed, it doesn't mean . . ." Irravel trailed off. "You're worried about them crossing interstellar space, to other systems. Even if that happened—couldn't you resist the spread? This can only be human technology—nothing that would pose any threat to yourselves."

"Perhaps it was once human technology, with programmed limitations to prevent it replicating uncontrollably. But those shackles have been broken. Worse, the machines have hybridized, gaining resilience and adaptability with each encounter with something external. First the Melding Plague, infection with which may have been a deliberate ploy to bypass the replication limits."

Irravel nodded. The Melding Plague had swept human space 400 years earlier, terminating the Demarchist *Belle Epoque.* Like the Black Death of the previous millennium, it evoked terror generations after it had passed.

"Later," the Nestbuilder continued, "it may have encountered and assimilated Inhibitor technology, or worse. Now it will be very hard to stop, even with the weapons at our disposal."

An image of one of the machines flickered onto the Nestbuilder's shell, like a peculiar tattoo. Irravel shivered. The Slug was right: waves of hybridization had transformed the initial architecture into something queasily alien. But enough of the original plan remained for there to be no doubt in her mind. She was looking at an evolved greenfly; one of the self-replicating breeders she had given Captain Run Seven. How it had broken loose was anyone's guess. She speculated that Seven's crew had sold the technology on to a third party, decades or centuries after gaining it from her. Perhaps that third party had reclusively experimented in the Ross 128 system, until the day when greenfly tore out of their control."

"I don't know why you think I can help," she said.

"Perhaps we were mistaken, then, to credit a 500-year-old rumour which said that you had been the original source of these machines."

She had insulted it by daring to bluff. The Slugs were easily insulted. They read human beings far better than humans read Slugs.

"Like you say," she answered. "You can't believe everything."

The Slug made the Nestbuilder fold its armoured, spindly limbs across its mouthparts, a gesture of displeased huffiness.

"You *chordates,*" it said. "You're all the same."

INTERSTELLAR SPACE—AD 3354

Mirsky was dead. She had died of old age.

Irravel placed her body in an armoured coffin and ejected her into space when the *Hirondelle*'s speed was only a hairsbreadth under light. "Do it for me, Irravel," Mirsky had told her, toward the end. "Keep my body aboard until we're almost touching light, and then fire me ahead of the ship."

"Is that what you want?"

"It's an old pirate tradition. Burial at C." She forced a smile which must have sapped what little energy she had left. "That's a joke, Irravel, but it only makes sense in a language neither of us have heard for a while."

Irravel pretended that she understood. "Mirsky? There's something I have to tell you. Do you remember the Nestbuilder?"

"That was centuries ago, Veda."

"I know. I just keep worrying that maybe it was right."

"About what?"

"Those machines. About how I started it all. They say it's

spread now; to other systems. It doesn't look like anyone knows how to stop it."

"And you think all that was your fault?"

"It's crossed my mind."

Mirsky convulsed, or shrugged—Irravel wasn't sure. "Even if it was your fault, Veda, you did it with the best of intentions. So you fucked up slightly. We all make mistakes."

"Destroying whole solar systems is just a fuck-up?"

"Hey, accidents happen."

"You always did have a sense of humour, Mirsky."

"Yeah; guess I did." She managed a smile. "One of us needed one, Veda."

Thinking of that, Irravel watched the coffin fall ahead, dwindling until it was only a tiny mote of steel-gray, and then nothing.

SUBARU COMMONWEALTH—PLEIADES PLUSTER—AD 4161

The starbridge had long ago attained sentience.

Dense with machinery, it sung an endless hymn to its own immensity, throbbing like the lowest string on a guitar. Vacuum-breathing acolytes had voluntarily rewired their minds to view the bridge as an actual deity, translating the humming into their sensoria and passing decades in contemplative ecstasy.

Clasped in a cushioning field, an elevator ferried Irravel down the bridge from the orbital hub to the surface in a few minutes, accompanied by an entourage of children from the ship, many of whom bore in youth the hurting imprint of Mirsky's genes. The bridge rose like the stem of a goblet from a ground terminal which was itself a scalloped shell of hyperdiamond, filled with tiered perfume gardens and cascading pools, anchored to the largest island in an equatorial archipelago. The senior children walked Irravel down to a beach of silver sand on the terminal's edge, where jewelled crabs moved like toys. She bid the children farewell, then waited, warm breezes fingering the hem of her sari.

Minutes later, the children's elevator flashed heavenward.

Irravel looked out at the ocean, thinking of the Pattern Jugglers. Here, as on dozens of other ocean worlds, there was a colony of the alien intelligences. Transformed to aquatic bodyplans themselves, the Subaruns had established close rapport with the aliens. In the morning, she would be taken out to meet the Jugglers, drowned, dissolved on the cellular level, every atom in her body swapped for one in the ocean, remade into something not quite human.

She was terrified.

Islanders came toward the shore, skimming water on penanted trimarans, attended by oceanforms, sleek gloss-grey hybrids of porpoise and ray, whistlespeed downshifted into the human spectrum. The Subarun epidermal scales shimmered like imbricated armour, biological photocells drinking scorching blue Pleiadean sunlight. Sentient veils hung in the sky, rippling gentle like aurorae, shading the archipelago from the fiercest wavelengths. As the actinic eye of Taygeta sank towards the horizon, the veils moved with it like living clouds. Flocks of phantasmagoric birds migrated with the veils.

The purple-skinned elder's scales flashed green and opal as he approached Irravel along the coral jetty, stick in one webbed hand, supported by two aides, third shading his aged crown with a delicately watercoloured parasol. The aides were all descended from late-model Conjoiners; they had the translucent cranial crest through which bloodflow had once been channelled to cool their supercharged minds. Seeing them gave Irravel a dual-edged pang of nostalgia and guilt. She had not seen Conjoiners for nearly a thousand years, ever since they had fragmented into a dozen factions and vanished from human affairs. Neither had she entirely forgotten her betrayal of Remontoire.

But that had been so long ago.

A Communicant made up the party, gowned in brocade, hazed by a blur of entoptic projections. Communicants were small and elfin, with a phenomenal talent for natural languages, augmented by Juggler transforms. Irravel sensed that this one was old and revered, despite the fact that Communicant genes did not express for great longevity.

The elder halted before her.

The head of his walking stick was a tiny lemur skull inside an egg-sized space helmet. He spoke something clearly ceremonial, but Irravel understood none of the sounds he made. She groped for something to say, recalling the oldest language in her memory, and therefore the one most likely to be recognized in any far-flung human culture.

"Thank you for letting us stop here," she said.

The Communicant hobbled forward, already shaping words experimentally with his wide, protruding lips. For a moment his sounds were like an infant's first attempts at vocalization. But then they resolved into something Irravel understood.

"Am I—um—making the slightest sense to you?"

"Yes," Irravel said. "Yes, thank you."

"Canasian," the Communicant diagnosed. "Twenty-third, twenty-fourth centuries, Lacaille 9352 dialect, Fand subdialect?"

Irravel nodded.

"Your kind are very rare now," he said, studying her as if she was some kind of exotic butterfly. "But not unwelcome." His features cracked into an elfin smile.

"What about Markarian?" Irravel said. "I know his ship passed through this system less than 50 years ago—I still have a fix on it as it moves out of the cluster."

"Other lighthuggers do come, yes. Not many—one or two a century."

"And what happened when the last one came through?"

"The usual tribute was given."

"Tribute?"

"Something ceremonial." The Communicant's smile was wider than ever. "To the glory of Irravel. With many actors, beautiful words, love, death, laughter, tears."

She understood, slowly, dumbfoundedly.

"You're putting on a play?"

The elder must have understood something of that. Nodding proudly, he extended a hand across the darkening bay, oceanforms cutting the water like scythes. A distant raft carried lanterns and the glimmerings of richly painted backdrops. Boats converged from across the bay. A dirigible loomed over the archipelago's edge, pregnant with gondolas.

"We want you to play Irravel," the Communicant said, beckoning her forward. "This is our greatest honour."

When they reached the raft, the Communicant taught Irravel her lines and the actions she would be required to make. It was all simple enough—even the fact that she had to deliver her parts in Subarun. By the end of evening she was fluent in their language. There was nothing she couldn't learn in an instant these days, by sheer force of will. But it was not enough. To catch Markarian, she would have to break out of the narrow labyrinth of human thought entirely. That was why she had come to Jugglers.

That night they performed the play, while boats congregated around them, top-heavy with lolling islanders. The sun sank and the sky glared with a thousand blue gems studding blue velvet. Night in the heart of the Pleiades was the most beautiful thing Irravel had dared imagine. But in the direction of Sol, when she amplified her vision, there was a green thumbprint on the sky. Every century, the green wave was larger, as neighbouring solar systems were infected and transformed by the rogue terraforming machines. Given time, it would even reach the Pleiades.

Irravel got drunk on islander wine and learnt the tributes' history.

The plots varied immensely, but the protagonists always resembled Markarian and Irravel; mythic figures entwined by destiny, remembered across 2,000 years. Sometimes one or the other was the clear villain, but as often as not they were both heroic, misunderstanding each other's motives in true tragic fashion. Sometimes they ended with both parties dying. They rarely ended happily. But there was always some kind of redemption when the pursuit was done.

In the interlude, she felt she had to tell the Communicant the truth, so that he could tell the elder.

"Listen, there's something you need to know." Irravel didn't wait for his answer. "I'm really her; really the person I'm playing."

For a long time he didn't seem to understand, before shaking his head slowly and sadly.

"No; I thought you'd be different. You seemed different. But many say that."

She shrugged. There seemed little point arguing, and anything she said now could always be ascribed to wine. In the morning, the remark had been quietly forgotten. She was taken out to sea and drowned.

GALACTIC NORTH—AD 9730

"Markarian? Answer me."

She watched the *Hideyoshi*'s magnified image, looming just out of weapons range. Like the *Hirondelle,* it had changed almost beyond recognition. The hull glistened within a skein of armouring force. The engines, no longer physically coupled to the rest of the ship, flew alongside like dolphins. They were anchored in fields which only became visible when some tiny stress afflicted them.

For centuries of worldtime she had made no attempt to communicate with him. But now her mind had changed. The green wave had continued for millennia, an iridescent cataract spreading across the eye of the Galaxy. It had assimilated the blue suns of the Subaran Commonwealth in mere centuries—although by then Irravel and Markarian were a thousand light-years closer to the core, beginning to turn away from the plane of the Galaxy, and the death screams of those gentle islanders never reached them. Nothing stopped it, and once the green wave had swallowed them, systems fell silent.

The Juggler transformation allowed Irravel to grasp the enormity of it; allowed her to stare unflinchingly into the horror of a million poisoned stars and apprehend each individually.

She knew more of what it was, now.

It was impossible for stars to shine green, any more than an ingot of metal could become green-hot if it was raised to a certain temperature. Instead, something was veiling them—staining their light, like coloured glass. Whatever it was stole energy from the stellar spectra at the frequencies of chlorophyll. Stars were shining through curtains of vegetation, like lanterns in a forest. The greenfly machines were turning the Galaxy into a jungle.

It was time to talk. Time—as in the old plays of the dead islanders—to initiate the final act, before the two of them fell into the cold of intergalactic space. She searched her repertoire of communication systems, until she found something which was as ancient as ceremony demanded.

She aimed the message laser at him, cutting through his armour. The beam was too ineffectual to be mistaken as anything other than an attempt to talk. No answer came, so she repeated the message in a variety of formats and languages. Days of shiptime passed—decades of worldtime.

Talk, you bastard.

Growing impatient, she examined her weapons options. Armaments from the Nestbuilders were among the most advanced: theoretically they could mole through the loam of spacetime and inflict precise harm anywhere in Markarian's ship. But to use them she had to convince herself that she knew the interior layout of the *Hideyoshi.* Her mass-sensor sweeps were too blurred to be much help. She might as easily harm the sleepers as take out his field nodes. Until now, it was too much risk to contemplate.

But all games needed an end.

Willing her qualms from mind, she enabled the Nestbuilder armaments, feeling them stress spacetime in the *Hirondelle*'s belly, ready to short-circuit it entirely. She selected attack loci in Markarian's ship; best guesses that would cripple him rather than blow him out of the sky.

Then something happened.

He replied, modulating his engine thrust in staccato stabs. The frequency was audio. Quickly Irravel translated the modulation.

"I don't understand," Markarian said. "Why you took so long to answer me, and why you ignored me so long when I replied?"

"You never replied until now," she said. "I'd have known if you had."

"Would you?"

There was something in his tone which convinced her that he wasn't lying. Which left only one possibility: that he had tried speaking to her before, and that in some way her own ship had kept this knowledge from her.

"Mirsky must have done it," Irravel said. "She must have installed filters to block any communications from your ship."

"Mirsky?"

"She would have done it as a favour to me; maybe as an order from my former self." She didn't bother elaborating: Markarian was sure to know she had died and then been reborn as a clone of the original Irravel. "My former self had the neural conditioning which kept her on the trail of the sleepers. The clone never had it, which meant that my instinct to pursue the sleepers had to be reinforced.

"By lies?"

"Mirsky would have done it out of friendship," Irravel said. And for a moment she believed herself, while wondering how friendship could seem so like betrayal.

Markarian's image smiled. They faced each other across an absurdly long banquet table, with the Galaxy projected above it, flickering in the light of candelabra.

"Well?" he said, of the green stain spreading across the spiral. "What do you think?"

Irravel had long ago stopped counting time and distance, but she knew it had been at least 15,000 years and that many light-years since they had turned from the plane. Part of her knew, of course: although the wave swallowed suns, it had no use for pulsars, and their metronomic ticking and slow decay allowed positional triangulation in space and time with chilling precision. But she elected to bury that knowledge beneath her conscious thought processes: one of the simpler Juggler tricks.

"What do I think? I think it terrifies me."

"Our emotional responses haven't diverged as much as I'd feared."

They didn't have to use language. They could have swapped pure mental concepts between ships: concatenated strings of qualia, some of which could only be grasped in minds rewired by Pattern Jugglers. But Irravel considered it sufficient that they could look each other in the eye without flinching.

The Galaxy falling below had been frozen in time: light waves struggling to overtake Irravel and Markarian. The wave had seemed to slow, and then halt its advance. But then Markarian had turned, diving back toward the plane. The Galaxy quickened to life, rushing to finish 30,000 years of history before the two ships returned. The wave surged on. Above the banquet table, one arm of the star-clotted spiral was shot through with green, like a mote of ink spreading into blotting paper. The edge of the green wave was feathered, fractal, extending verdant tendrils.

"Do you have any observations?" Irravel asked.

"A few." Markarian sipped from his chalice. "I've studied the patterns of starlight among the suns already swallowed by the wave. They're not uniformly green—it's correlated with rotational angle. The green matter must be concentrated near the ecliptic, extending above and below it, but not encircling the stars completely."

Irravel thought back to what the Nestbuilder had shown her.

"Meaning what?" she asked, testing Markarian.

"Swarms of absorbing bodies, on orbits resembling comets, or asteroids. I think the greenfly machines must have dismantled everything smaller than a Jovian, then enveloped the rubble in transparent membranes which they filled with air, water and greenery—self-sustaining biospheres. Then they were cast adrift. Trillions of tiny worlds, around each star. No rocky planets any more."

Irravel retrieved a name from the deep past. "Like Dyson spheres?"

"Dyson clouds, perhaps."

"Do you think anyone survived? Are there niches in the wave where humans can live? That was the point of greenfly, after all: to create living space."

"Maybe," Markarian said, with no great conviction. "Perhaps some survivors found ways inside, as their own worlds were smashed and reassembled into the cloud . . ."

"But you don't think it's very likely?"

"I've been listening, Irravel—scanning the assimilated regions for any hint of an extant technological culture. If anyone did survive, they're either keeping deliberately quiet or they don't even know how to make a radio signal by accident."

"It was my fault, Markarian."

His tone was rueful. "Yes . . . I couldn't help but arrive at that conclusion."

"I never intended this."

"I think that goes without saying, wouldn't you? No one could have guessed the consequences of that one action."

"Would you?"

He shook his head. "In all likelihood, I'd have done exactly what you did."

"I did it out of love, Markarian. For the cargo."

"I know."

She believed him.

"What happened back there, Markarian? Why did you give up the codes when I didn't?"

"Because of what they did to you, Irravel."

He told her. How neither Markarian nor Irravel had shown any signs of revealing the codes under Mirsky's interrogation, until something new was tried.

"They were good at surgery," Markarian said. "Seven's crew swapped limbs and body parts as badges of status. They knew how to sever and splice nerves." The image didn't allow her to interrupt. "They cut your head off. Kept it alive in a state of borderline consciousness, and then showed it to me. That's when I gave them the codes."

For a long while Irravel said nothing. Then it occurred to her to check her old body, still frozen in the same casket where Mirsky had once revealed it to her. She ordered some children to prepare the body for a detailed examination, then looked through their eyes. The microscopic evidence of reconnective surgery around the neck was too slight to have ever shown up unless one was looking for it. But now there was no mistaking it.

I did it to save your neck, Markarian had said, when she had held him pinned to the ice of Seven's ship.

"You seem to be telling the truth," she said, when she had released the children. "The nature of your betrayal was . . ." And then she paused, searching for the words, while Markarian watched her across the table. "Different than I assumed. Possibly less of a crime. But still a betrayal, Markarian."

"One I've lived with the 300 years of subjective time."

"You could have returned the sleepers alive at any time. I wouldn't have attacked you." But she didn't even sound convincing to herself.

"What now?" Markarian said. "Do we keep this distance, arguing until one of us has the nerve to strike against the other? I've Nestbuilder weapons as well, Irravel. I think I could rip you apart before you could launch a reprisal."

"You've had the opportunity to do so before. Perhaps you never had the nerve, though. What's changed now?"

Markarian's gaze flicked to the map. "Everything. I think

we should see what happens before making any rash decisions, don't you?"

Irravel agreed.

She willed herself into stasis; medichines arresting all biological activity in every cell in her body. The 'chines would only revive her when something—anything—happened, on a Galactic timescale. Markarian would retreat into whatever mode of suspension he favoured, until woken by the same stimulus.

He was still sitting there when time resumed, as if only a moment had interrupted their conversation.

The wave had spread further now. It had eaten into the Galaxy for 10,000 light-years around Sol—a third of the way to the core. There was no sign that it had encountered resistance—at least nothing that had done more than hinder it. There had never been many intelligent, starfaring cultures to begin with, the Nestbuilder had told her. Perhaps the few that existed were even now making plans to retard the wave. Or perhaps it had swallowed them, as it swallowed humanity.

"Why did we wake?" Irravel said. "Nothing's changed, except that it's become larger."

"Maybe not," Markarian said. "I had to be sure, but now I don't think there's any doubt. I've just detected a radio message from within the plane of the Galaxy; from within the wave."

"Yes?"

"Looks like someone survived after all."

The radio message was faint, but nothing else was transmitting on that or any adjacent frequency, except for the senseless mush of cosmic background sources. It was also in a language they recognized.

"It's Canasian," Markarian said.

"Fand subdialect," Irravel added, marvellingly.

It was also beamed in their direction, from somewhere deep in the swathe of green, almost coincident with the position of a pulsar. The message was a simple one, frequency modulated around one and a half megahertz, repeated for a few minutes every day of Galactic time. Whoever was sending it clearly lacked the resources to transmit continuously. It was also coherent: amplified and beamed.

Someone wanted to speak to them.

The man's disembodied head appeared above the banquet table, chiselled from pixels. He was immeasurably old; a skull draped in parchment; something that should have been embalmed rather than talking.

Irravel recognized the face.

"It's him," she said, in Markarian's direction. "Remontoire. Somehow he made it across all this time."

Markarian nodded slowly. "He must have remembered us, and known where to look. Even across thousands of light-years, we can still be seen. There can't be many objects still moving relativistically."

Remontoire told his story. His people had fled to the pulsar system 20,000 years ago—more so now, since his message had taken thousand of years to climb out of the Galaxy. They had seen the wave coming, as had thousands of other human factions, and like many they had observed that the wave shunned pulsars; burnt-out stellar corpses rarely accompanied by planets. Some intelligence governing the wave must have recognized that pulsars were valueless; that even if a Dyson cloud could be created around them, there would be no sunlight to focus.

For thousands of years they had waited around the pulsar, growing ever more silent and cautious, seeing other cultures make errors which drew the wave upon them, for by now it interpreted any other intelligence as a threat to its progress, assimilating the weapons used against it.

Then—over many more thousands of years—Remontoire's people saw the wave learn, adapting like a vast neural net, becoming curious about those few pulsars which harboured planets. Soon their place of refuge would become nothing of the sort.

"Help us," Remontoire said. "Please."

• • •

It took 3,000 years to reach them.

For most of that time, Remontoire's people acted on faith, not knowing that help was on its way. During the first thousand years they abandoned their system, compressing their population down to a sustaining core of only a few hundred thousand. Together with the cultural data they'd preserved during the long centuries of their struggle against the wave, they packed their survivors into a single hollowed-out rock and flung themselves out of the ecliptic using a mass-driver which fuelled itself from the rock's own bulk. They called it Hope. A million decoys had to be launched, just to ensure that Hope got through the surrounding hordes of assimilating machines.

Inside, most of the Conjoiners slept out the 2,000 years of solitude before Irravel and Markarian reached them.

"Hope would make an excellent shield," Markarian mused, as they approached it. "If one of us considered a pre-emptive strike against the other."

"Don't think I wouldn't."

They moved their ships to either side of the dark shard of rock, extended field grapples, then hauled it in.

"Then why don't you?" Markarian said.

For a moment Irravel didn't have a good answer. When she found one, she wondered why it hadn't been more obvious before. "Because they need us more than I need revenge."

"A higher cause?"

"Redemption," she said.

HOPE; GALACTIC PLANE—AD CIRCA 40,000

They didn't have long. Their approach, diving down from Galactic North, had drawn the attention of the wave's machines, directing them toward the one rock which mattered. A wall of annihilation was moving toward them at half the speed of light. When it reached Hope, it would turn it into the darkest of nebulae.

Conjoiners boarded the *Hirondelle* and invited Irravel into the Hope. The hollowed-out chambers of the rock were Edenic to her children, after all the decades of subjective time they'd spent aboard since last planetfall. But it was a doomed paradise, the biomes grey with neglect, as if the Conjoiners had given up long ago.

Remontoire welcomed Irravel next to a rockpool filmed in grey dust. Half the sun-panels set into the distant honeycombed ceiling were black.

"You came," he said. He wore a simple smock and trousers. His anatomy was early-model Conjoiner almost fully human.

"You're not him, are you. You look like him—sound like him—but the image you sent us was of someone much older."

"I'm sorry. His name was chosen for its familiarity my likeness shaped to his. We searched our collective memories and found the experiences of the one you knew as Remontoire . . . but that was a long time ago and he was never known by that name to us."

"What was his name?"

"Even your Juggler cortex could not accommodate it, Irravel."

She had to ask. "Did he make it back to a commune?"

"Yes, of course," the man said, as if her question was foolish. "How else could we have absorbed his experiences back into the Transenlightenment?"

"And did he forgive me?"

"I forgive you now," he said. "It amounts to the same thing."

She willed herself to think of him as Remontoire.

The Conjoiners hadn't allowed themselves to progress in all the thousands of years they waited around the pulsar, fearing that any social change—no matter how slight—would eventually bring the wave upon them. They had studied it, contemplated weapons they might use against it—but other than that, all they had done was wait.

They were very good at waiting.

"How many refugees did you bring?"

"One hundred thousand." Before Irravel could answer, Remontoire shook his head. "I know; too many. Perhaps half that number can be carried away on your ships. But half is better than nothing."

She thought back to her own sleepers. "I know. Still, we might be able to take more . . . I don't know about Markarian's ship, but—"

He cut her off, gently. "I think you'd better come with me," said Remontoire, and then led her aboard the *Hideyoshi.*

"How much of it did you explore?"

"Enough to know there's no one alive anywhere in this ship," Remontoire said. "If there are 200 cryogenically frozen sleepers, we didn't find them."

"No sleepers?"

"Just this one."

What they'd arrived at was a plinth, supporting a reefersleep casket, encrusted with gold statuary; space-suited figures with hands folded across their chests like resting saints. The glass lid of the casket was veined with fractures; the withered figure inside older than time. Markarian's skeletal frame was swaddled in layers of machines, all of archaic provenance. His skull had split open, a fused mass spilling out like lava.

"Is he dead?" Irravel asked.

"Depends what you mean by dead." The Conjoiner's hand sketched across the neural mass. "His organic mind must have been completely swamped by machines centuries ago. His linkage to the *Hideyoshi* would have been total. There would have been very little point discriminating between the two."

"Why didn't he tell me what had become of him?"

"No guarantee he knew. Once he was in this state, with

his personality running entirely on machine substrates, he could have edited his own memories and perceptual inputs—deceiving himself that he was still corporeal."

Irravel looked away from the casket, forcing troubling questions from her mind. "Is his personality still running the ship?"

"We detected only caretaker programs; capable of imitating him when the need arose, but lacking sentience."

"Is that all there was?"

"No." Remontoire reached through one of the casket's larger fractures, prising something from Markarian's fingers. It was a sliver of computer memory. "We examined this already, though not in great detail. It's partitioned into 190 areas, each large enough to hold complete neural and genetic maps for one human being, encoded into superposed electron states on Rydberg atoms."

She took the sliver from him. It didn't feel like much. "He burned the sleepers onto this?"

"Three hundred years is much longer than any of them expected to sleep. By scanning them he lost nothing."

"Can you retrieve them?"

"It would not be trivial," the Conjoiner said. "But given time, we could do it. Assuming any of them would welcome being born again, so far from home."

She thought of the infected Galaxy hanging below them, humming with the chill sentience of machines. "Maybe the kindest thing would be to simulate the past," she said. "Recreate Yellowstone, and revive them on it, as if nothing had ever gone wrong."

"Is that what you're advocating?"

"No," she said, after toying with the idea in all seriousness. "We need all the genetic diversity we can get, if we're going to establish a new branch of humanity outside the Galaxy."

She thought about it. Soon they would witness Hope's destruction, as the wave of machines tore through it with the mindlessness of stampeding animals. Some of them might try and follow the *Hirondelle,* but so far the machines moved too slowly to catch the ship, even if they forced it back toward Galactic North.

Where was there to go?

There were globular clusters high above the Galaxy—tightly packed shoals of old stars where the wave hadn't reached, but where fragments of humanity might have already sought refuge. If the clusters proved unwelcoming, there were high-latitude stars, flung from the Galaxy a billion years ago, and some might have dragged their planetary systems with them. If those failed—and it would be tens of thousands of years before the possibilities were exhausted—the *Hirondelle* could always loop around toward Galactic South and search there, striking out for the Clouds of Magellan. Ultimately, of course—if any part or fragment of Irravel's children still clung to humanity, and remembered where they'd come from, and what had become of it, they would want to return to the Galaxy, even if that meant confronting the wave.

But they would return.

"That's the plan then?" Remontoire said.

Irravel shrugged, turning away from the plinth where Markarian lay. "Unless you've got a better one."

MASQUE OF THE RED SHIFT

Fred Saberhagen

Fred Saberhagen is best known in the genre for the creation of the "Berserker" series, one of the most famous series in science fiction history, which by now, after its creation in the early sixties, has expanded to include dozens of short stories (gathered in collections such as Berserker, The Ultimate Enemy, The Berserker Wars, *and* Berserker Lies*), as well as novels (such as* Brother Assassin, Berserker Planet, Berserker Man, The Berserker Throne, *and* Berserker: Blue Death*), and even a shared-world anthology,* Berserker Base, *where other writers tried their hands at playing with Saberhagen's intricate Berserker universe. In addition to the Berserker books, Saberhagen is also the author of four other important series, the multivolume "Book of Swords" series (collected in an omnibus volume as* The Complete Book of Swords*), the multivolume "Book of Lost Swords" series (collected as* The Lost Swords: The First Triad *and* The Lost Swords: The Second Triad*), the three-volume "Empire of the East" series (collected in an omnibus volume as* Empire of the East*), and the "Dracula" series, which includes* The Dracula Tapes, The Holmes-Dracula File, An Old Friend of the Family, Thorn, Dominion, *and* A Matter of Taste. *His many other books include* The Golden People, Pyramids, The Veils of Azlaroc, Octagon, A Century of Progress, *and two novels written in collaboration with the late Roger Zelazny,* Coils *and* The Black Throne.

Here, in one of the most elegant and suspenseful of all Berserker stories, he shows us that even in the high-tech world of space warfare, one man can still make a difference—sometimes he can make all *the difference.*

I

Finding himself alone and unoccupied, Felipe Nogara chose to spend a free moment in looking at the thing that had brought him out here beyond the last fringe of the galaxy. From the luxury of his quarters he stepped up into his private observation bubble. These, in a raised dome of invisible glass, he seemed to be standing outside the hull of his flagship *Nirvana.*

Under that hull, "below" the *Nirvana*'s artificial gravity, there slanted the bright disk of the galaxy, including in one of its arms all the star-systems that Earth-descended man had yet explored. But in whatever direction Nogara looked, bright spots and points of light were plentiful. They were other galaxies, marching away at their recessional velocities of tens of thousands of miles per second, marching on out to the optical horizon of the universe.

Nogara had not come here to look at galaxies, however; he had come to look at something new, at a phenomenon never before seen by men at such close range.

It was made visible to him by the apparent pinching-together of the galaxies beyond it, and by the clouds and streamers of dust cascading into it. The star that formed the center of the phenomenon was itself held beyond human sight by the strength of its own gravity. Its mass, perhaps a billion times that of Sol, so bent spacetime around itself that not a photon of light could escape it with a visible wavelength.

The dusty debris of deep space tumbled and churned, falling into the grip of the hypermass. The falling dust built up static charges until lightning turned it into luminescent thunderclouds, and the flicker of the vast lightning shifted into the red before it vanished, near the bottom of the gravitational hill. Probably not even a neutrino could escape this sun. And no ship would dare approach much closer than *Nirvana* now rode.

Nogara had come out here to judge for himself if the recently discovered phenomenon might soon present any danger to inhabited planets; ordinary suns would go down like chips of wood into a whirlpool if the hypermass found them in its path. But it seemed that another thousand years would pass before any planets had to be evacuated; and before then the hypermass might have gorged itself on dust until its core imploded, whereupon most of its substance could be expected to reenter the universe in a most spectacular but less dangerous form.

Anyway, in another thousand years it would be someone else's problem. Right now it might be said to be Nogara's—for men said that he ran the galaxy, if they said it of anyone.

A communicator sounded, calling him back to the enclosed luxury of his quarters, and he walked down quickly, glad of a reason to get out from under the galaxies.

He touched a plate with one strong and hairy hand. "What is it?"

"My lord, a courier ship has arrived. From the Flamland system. They are bringing . . ."

"Speak plainly. They are bringing my brother's body?"

"Yes, my lord. The launch bearing the coffin is already approaching *Nirvana*."

"I will meet the courier captain, alone, in the Great Hall. I want no ceremony. Have the robots at the airlock test the escort and the outside of the coffin for infection."

"Yes, my lord."

The mention of disease was a bit of misdirection. It was not the Flamland plague that had put Nogara's half-brother Johann Karlsen into a box, though that was the official story. The doctors were supposed to have frozen the hero of the Stone Place as a last resort, to prevent his irreversible death.

An official lie was necessary because not even High Lord Nogara could lightly put out of the way the one man who had made the difference at the Stone Place nebula. In that battle seven years ago the berserker machines had been beaten; if they had not been, intelligent life might already be extinct in the known galaxy. The berserkers were huge automated warships, built for some conflict between long-vanished races and now the enemies of everything that lived. The fighting against them was still bitter, but since the Stone Place it seemed that life in the galaxy would survive.

The Great Hall was where Nogara met daily for feasting and pleasure with the forty or fifty people who were with him on *Nirvana,* as aides or crewmen or entertainers. But when he entered the Hall now he found it empty, save for one man who stood at attention beside a coffin.

Johann Karlsen's body and whatever remained of his life were sealed under the glass top of the heavy casket, which contained its own refrigeration and revival systems, controlled by a fiber-optic key theoretically impossible to duplicate. This key Nogara now demanded, with a gesture, from the courier captain.

The captain had the key hung around his neck, and it took him a moment to pull the golden chain over his head and hand it to Nogara. It was another moment before he remembered to bow; he was a spaceman and not a courtier. Nogara ignored the lapse of courtesy. It was his governors and admirals who were reinstituting ceremonies of rank; he himself cared nothing about how subordinates gestured and postured, so long as they obeyed intelligently.

Only now, with the key in his own hand, did Nogara look down at his frozen half-brother. The plotting doctors had shaved away Johann's short beard, and his hair. His lips were marble pale, and his sightless open eyes were ice. But still the face above the folds of the draped and frozen sheet was undoubtedly Johann's. There was something that would not freeze.

"Leave me for a time," Nogara said. He turned to face the end of the Great Hall and waited, looking out through the wide viewport to where the hypermass blurred space like a bad lens.

When he heard the door ease shut behind the courier captain he turned back—and found himself facing the short figure of Oliver Mical, the man he had selected to replace Johann as governor on Flamland. Mical must have entered as the spaceman left, which Nogara thought might be taken as symbolic of something. Resting his hands familiarly on the coffin, Mical raised one graying eyebrow in his habitual expression of weary amusement. His rather puffy face twitched in an overcivilized smile.

"How does Browning's line go?" Mical mused, glancing down at Karlsen. "'Doing the king's work all the dim day long'—and now, this reward of virtue."

"Leave me," said Nogara.

Mical was in on the plot, as was hardly anyone else except the Flamland doctors. "I thought it best to appear to share your grief," he said. Then he looked at Nogara and ceased to argue. He made a bow that was mild mockery when the two of them were alone, and walked briskly to the door. Again it closed.

So, Johann. If you had plotted against me, I would have had you killed outright. But you were never a plotter; it was just that you served me too successfully; my enemies and friends alike began to love you too well. So here you are, my frozen conscience, the last conscience I'll ever have. Sooner or later you would have become ambitious, so it was either do this to you or kill you.

Now I'll put you away safely, and maybe someday you'll have another chance at life. It's a strange thought that someday you may stand musing over my coffin as I now stand over yours. No doubt you'll pray for what you think is my soul. . . . I can't do that for you, but I wish you sweet dreams. Dream of your Believers' heaven, not of your hell.

Nogara imagined a brain at absolute zero, its neurons superconducting, repeating one dream on and on and on. But that was nonsense.

"I cannot risk my power, Johann." This time he whispered the words aloud. "It was either this or have you killed." He turned again to the wide viewport.

II

"I suppose Thirty-three's gotten the body to Nogara already," said the Second Officer of Esteeler Courier Thirty-four, looking at the bridge chronometer. "It must be nice to declare yourself an emperor or whatever, and have people hurl themselves all over the galaxy to do everything for you."

"Can't be nice to have someone bring you your brother's corpse," said Captain Thurman Holt, studying his astrogational sphere. His ship's C-plus drive was rapidly stretching a lot of timelike interval between itself and the Flamland system. Even if Holt was not enthusiastic about his mission he was glad to be away from Flamland, where Mical's political police were taking over.

"I wonder," said the Second, and chuckled.

"What's that mean?"

The Second looked over both shoulders, out of habit formed on Flamland. "Have you heard this one?" he asked. "Nogara is God—but half of his spacemen are atheists."

Holt smiled, but only faintly. "He's no mad tyrant, you know. Esteel's not the worst-run government in the galaxy. Nice guys don't put down rebellions."

"Karlsen did all right."

"That's right, he did."

The Second grimaced. "Oh sure, Nogara could be worse, if you want to be serious about it. He's a politician. But I just can't stand that crew that's accumulated around him the last few years. We've got an example on board now of what they do. If you want to know the truth, I'm a little scared now that Karlsen's dead."

"Well, we'll soon see them." Holt sighed, and stretched. "I'm going to look in on the prisoners. The bridge is yours, Second."

"I relieve you, sir. Do the man a favor and kill him, Thurm."

A minute later, looking through the spy-plate into the courier's small brig, Holt could wish with honest compassion that his male prisoner were dead.

He was an outlaw chieftain named Janda, and his capture had been the last success of Karlsen's Flamland service, putting a virtual end to the rebellion. Janda had been a tall man, a brave rebel, and a brutal bandit. He had raided and fought against Nogara's Esteeler empire until there had been no hope left, and then he had surrendered to Karlsen.

"My pride commands me to conquer my enemy," Karlsen had written once, in what he had thought was to be a private letter. "My honor forbids me to humble or hate my enemy." But Mical's political police operated with a different philosophy.

The outlaw might still be long-boned, but Holt had never seen him stand tall. The manacles still binding his wrists and ankles were of plastic and supposedly would not abrade human skin, but they served no sane purpose now and Holt would have removed them if he could.

A stranger, seeing the girl Lucinda who sat now at Janda's side to feed him, might have supposed her to be his daughter. She was his sister, five years younger than he. She was also a girl of rare beauty, and perhaps Mical's police had motives other than mercy in sending her to Nogara's court unmarked and un-brainwashed. It was rumored that the demand for certain kinds of entertainment was strong among the courtiers, and the turnover among the entertainers high.

Holt had so far kept himself from believing such stories. He opened the brig now—he kept it locked only to prevent Janda's straying out and falling childlike into an accident—and went in.

When the girl Lucinda had first come aboard his ship her eyes had shown helpless hatred of every Esteeler. Holt had been gentle and as helpful as possible to her in the days since then, and there was not even dislike in the face she raised to him now—there was a hope which it seemed she had to share with someone.

She said, "I think he spoke my name, a few minutes ago."

"Oh?" Holt bent to look more closely at Janda, and could see no change. The outlaw's eyes still stared glassily, the right eye now and then dripping a tear that seemed to have no connection with any kind of emotion. Janda's jaw was as slack as ever, and his whole body as awkwardly slumped.

"Maybe—" Holt didn't finish.

"What?" She was almost eager.

Gods of Space, he couldn't let himself get involved with this girl. He almost wished to see hatred in her eyes again.

"Maybe," he said gently, "it will be better for your brother if he doesn't make any recovery now. You know where he's going."

Lucinda's hope, such as it was, was shocked away by his words. She was silent, staring at her brother as if she saw something new.

Holt's wrist-intercom sounded.

"Captain here," he acknowledged.

"Sir, reporting a ship detected and calling us. Bearing five o'clock level to our course. Small and normal."

The last three words were the customary reassurance that a sighted ship was not possibly a berserker's giant hull. Berserkers all looked much alike, and what Flamland outlaws were left had no deep space ships, so Holt had no reason to be cautious.

He went casually back to the bridge and looked at the small shape on the detector screen. It was unfamiliar to him, but that was hardly surprising, as there were many shipyards orbiting many planets. Why, though, should any ship approach and hail him in deep space?

Plague?

"No, no plague," answered a radio voice, through bursts of static, when he put the question to the stranger. The video signal from the other ship was also jumpy, making it hard to see the speaker's face. "Caught a speck of dust on my last jump, and my fields are shaky. Will you take a few passengers aboard?"

"Certainly." For a ship on the brink of a C-plus jump to collide with the gravitation field of a sizable dust-speck was a rare accident, but not unheard-of; and it would explain the noisy communications. There was still nothing to alarm Holt.

The stranger sent over a launch which clamped to the courier's airlock. Wearing a smile of welcome for distressed passengers, Holt opened the lock. In the next moment he and the half dozen men who made up his crew were caught helpless by an inrush of man-sized machines—they were a berserker's boarding party, cold and ancient, merciless as nightmare.

The machines seized the courier so swiftly and efficiently that no one could offer real resistance, but they did not immediately kill any of the humans. They tore the drive units from one of the lifeboats and herded Holt and his crew and his erstwhile prisoners into the boat.

"It wasn't a berserker on the screen, it wasn't," the Second Officer kept repeating to Holt. The humans sat side by side, jammed against one another in the small space. The machines were allowing them air and water and food, and had started to take them out one at a time for questioning.

"I know it didn't look like one," Holt answered. "The berserkers are probably forming themselves into new shapes, building themselves new weapons. That's only logical, after the Stone Place. The only odd thing is that no one fore saw it."

A hatch clanged open, and a pair of roughly man-shaped machines entered the boat, picking their way precisely among the nine cramped humans until they reached the one they wanted.

"No, he can't talk!" Lucinda shrieked. "Don't take him!"

But the machines could not or would not hear her. They pulled Janda to his feet and marched him out. The girl followed, dragging at them, trying to argue with them. Holt could only scramble uselessly after her in the narrow space, afraid that one of the machines would turn and kill her. But they only kept her from following them out of the lifeboat, pushing her back from the hatch with metal hands as gently resistless as time. They were gone with Janda, and the hatch was closed again. Lucinda stood gazing at it blankly. She did not move when Holt put his arm around her.

III

After a timeless period of waiting, the humans saw the hatch open again. The machines were back, but they did not return Janda. Instead they had come to take Holt.

Vibrations echoed through the courier's hull; the machines seemed to be rebuilding her. In a small chamber sealed off by a new bulkhead from the rest of the ship, the berserker computer-brain had set up electronic eyes and ears and a speaker for itself, and here Holt was taken to be interrogated.

Speaking with a collection of recorded human words, the berserker questioned Holt at great length. Almost every question concerned Johann Karlsen. It was known that the berserkers regarded Karlsen as their chief enemy, but this one seemed to be obsessed with him—and unwilling to believe that he was really dead.

"I have captured your charts and astrogational settings," the berserker reminded Holt. "I know your course is to *Nirvana,* where supposedly the non-functioning Karlsen has been taken. Describe this *Nirvana*-ship used by the life-unit Nogara."

So long as it had asked only about a dead man, Holt had given the berserker straight answers, not wanting to be tripped up in a useless lie. But a flagship was a different matter, and now he hesitated. Still, there was little he could say about *Nirvana* if he wanted to. And he and his fellow prisoners had had no chance to agree on any plan for deceiving the berserker; certainly it must be listening to everything they said in the lifeboat.

"I've never seen the *Nirvana,*" he answered truthfully. "But logic tells me it must be a strong ship, since the highest human leaders travel on it." There was no harm in telling the machine what it could certainly deduce for itself.

A door opened suddenly, and Holt stared in surprise as a strange man entered the interrogation chamber. Then he saw that it was not a man, but some creation of the berserker. Perhaps its flesh was plastic, perhaps some product of tissue-culture.

"Hi, are you Captain Holt?" asked the figure. There was no gross flaw in it, but a ship camouflaged with the greatest skill looks like nothing so much as a ship that has been camouflaged.

When Holt was silent, the figure asked, "What's wrong?" Its speech alone would have given it away, to an intelligent human who listened carefully.

"You're not a man," Holt told it.

The figure sat down and went limp.

The berserker explained: "You see I am not capable of making an imitation life-unit that will be accepted by real ones face to face. Therefore I require that you, a real life-unit, help me make certain of Karlsen's death."

Holt said nothing.

"I am a special device," the berserker said, "built by the berserkers with one prime goal: to bring about with certainty Karlsen's death. If you help me prove him dead, I will willingly free you and the other life-units I now hold. If you refuse to help, all of you will receive the most unpleasant stimuli until you change your mind."

Holt did not believe that it would ever willingly set them free. But he had nothing to lose by talking, and he might at least gain for himself and the others a death free of most unpleasant stimuli. Berserkers preferred to be efficient killers, not sadists, though during the long war they had become experts on the human nervous system.

"What sort of help do you want from me?" Holt asked.

"When I have finished building myself into this courier we are going on to *Nirvana,* where you will deliver your prisoners. I have read the orders. After being interviewed by the human leaders on *Nirvana*, the prisoners are to be taken on to Esteel for confinement. Is it not so?"

"It is."

The door opened again, and Janda shuffled in, bent and bemused.

"Can't you spare this man any more questioning?" Holt asked the berserker. "He can't help you in any way."

There was only silence. Holt waited uneasily. At last, looking at Janda, he realized that something about the outlaw had changed. The tears had stopped flowing from his right eye.

When Holt saw this he felt a mounting horror that he could not have explained, as if his subconscious already knew what the berserker was going to say next.

"What was bone in the life-unit is now metal," the berserker said. "Where blood flowed, now preservatives are pumped. Inside the skull I have placed a computer, and in the eyes are cameras to gather the evidence I must have on Karlsen. To match the behavior of a brainwashed man is within my capability."

"I do not hate you," Lucinda said to the berserker when it had her alone for interrogation. "You are an accident, like a planet-quake, like a pellet of dust hitting a ship near light-speed. Nogara and his people are the ones I hate. If his brother was not dead I would kill him with my hands and willingly bring you his body."

"Courier Captain? This is Governor Mical, speaking for the High Lord Nogara. Bring your two prisoners over to *Nirvana* at once," he ordered.

"At once, sir."

After coming out of C-plus travel within sight of *Nirvana*, the assassin-machine had taken Holt and Lucinda from the lifeboat; then it had let the boat, with Holt's crew still on it, drift out between the two ships, as if men were using it to check the courier's fields. The men on the boat were to be the berserker's hostages, and its shield if it were discovered.

And by leaving them there it doubtless wanted to make more credible the prospect of their eventual release.

Holt had not known how to tell Lucinda of her brother's fate, but at last he had managed somehow. She had wept for a minute, and then she had become very calm.

Now the berserker put Holt and Lucinda into the crystal globe that served it for a launch, for the trip to *Nirvana.* The machine that had been Lucinda's brother was aboard the launch already, waiting, slumped and broken-looking as the man had actually been in the last days of his life.

When she saw that figure, Lucinda stopped. Then in a clear voice she said, "Machine, I wish to thank you. You have done my brother a kindness no human would do for him. I think I would have found a way to kill him myself before his enemies could torture him anymore."

IV

The *Nirvana*'s airlock was strongly armored, and equipped with automated defenses that would have repelled a rush of boarding machines, just as *Nirvana*'s beams and missiles would have beaten off any heavy-weapons attack a courier, or a dozen couriers, could launch. The berserker had foreseen all this.

An officer welcomed Holt aboard. "This way, Captain; we're all waiting."

"All?"

The officer had the well-fed, comfortable look that came with safe and easy duty. His eyes were busy appraising Lucinda. "There's a celebration under way in the Great Hall. Your prisoners' arrival has been much anticipated."

Music throbbed in the Great Hall, and dancers writhed in costumes more obscene than any nakedness. From a table running almost the length of the Hall, serving machines were clearing the remnants of what had been a feast. In a throne-like chair behind the center of the table sat the High Lord Nogara, a rich cloak thrown over his shoulders, pale wine before him in a crystal goblet. Forty or fifty revelers flanked him at the long table, men and women and a few of whose sex Holt could not at once be sure. All were drinking and laughing, and some were donning masks and costumes, making ready for further celebration.

Heads turned at Holt's entrance, and a moment of silence was followed by a cheer. In all the eyes and faces turned now toward his prisoners, Holt could see nothing like pity.

"Welcome, Captain," said Nogara in a pleasant voice, when Holt had remembered to bow. "Is there news from Flamland?"

"None of great importance, sir."

A puffy-faced man who sat at Nogara's right hand leaned forward on the table. "No doubt there is great mourning for the late governor?"

"Of course, sir." Holt recognized Mical. "And much anticipation of the new."

Mical leaned back in his chair, smiling cynically. "I'm sure the rebellious population is eager for my arrival. Girl, were you eager to meet me? Come, pretty one, around the table, here to me." As Lucinda slowly obeyed, Mical gestured to the serving devices. "Robots, set a chair for the man—there, in the center of the floor. Captain you may return to your ship."

Felipe Nogara was steadily regarding the manacled figure of his old enemy Janda, and what Nogara might be thinking was hard to say. But he seemed content to let Mical give what orders pleased him.

"Sir," said Holt to Mical. "I would like to see—the remains of Johann Karlsen."

That drew the attention of Nogara, who nodded. A serving machine drew back sable draperies, revealing an alcove in one end of the Hall. In the alcove, before a huge viewport, rested the coffin.

Holt was not particularly surprised; on many planets it was the custom to feast in the presence of the dead. After bowing to Nogara he turned and saluted and walked toward the alcove. Behind him he heard the shuffle and clack of Janda's manacled movement, and held his breath. A muttering passed along the table, and then a sudden quieting in which even the throbbing music ceased. Probably Nogara had gestured permission for Janda's walk, wanting to see what the brainwashed man would do.

Holt reached the coffin and stood over it. He hardly saw the frozen face inside it, or the blur of the hypermass beyond the port. He hardly heard the whispers and giggles of the revelers. The only picture clear in his mind showed the faces of his crew as they waited helpless in the grip of the berserker.

The machine clothed in Janda's flesh came shuffling up beside him, and its eyes of glass stared down into those of ice. A photograph of retinal patterns taken back to the waiting berserker for comparison with old captured records would tell it that this man was really Karlsen.

A faint cry of anguish made Holt look back toward the long table, where he saw Lucinda pulling herself away from Mical's clutching arm. Mical and his friends were laughing.

"No, Captain, I am no Karlsen," Mical called down to him, seeing Holt's expression. "And do you think I regret the difference? Johann's prospects are not bright. He is rather bounded by a nutshell, and can no longer count himself king of infinite space!"

"Shakespeare!" cried a sycophant, showing appreciation of Mical's literary erudition.

"Sir." Holt took a step forward. "May I—may I now take the prisoners back to my ship?"

Mical misinterpreted Holt's anxiety. "Oh ho! I see you appreciate some of life's finer things, Captain. But as you know, rank has it privileges. The girl stays here."

He had expected them to hold on to Lucinda, and she was better here than with the berserker.

"Sir, then if—if the man alone can come with me. In a prison hospital on Esteel he may recover—"

"Captain." Nogara's voice was not loud, but it hushed the table. "Do not *argue* here."

"No sir."

Mical shook his head. "My thoughts are not yet of mercy to my enemies, Captain. Whether they may soon turn in that direction—well, that depends." He again reached out a leisurely arm to encircle Lucinda. "Do you know, Captain, that hatred is the true spice of love?"

Holt looked helplessly back at Nogara. Nogara's cold eye said: One more word, courier, and you find yourself in the brig. I do not give two warnings.

If Holt cried berserker now, the thing in Janda's shape might kill everyone in the Hall before it could be stopped. He knew it was listening to him, watching his movements.

"I—I am returning to my ship," he stuttered. Nogara looked away, and no one else paid him much attention. "I will—return here—in a few hours perhaps. Certainly before I drive for Esteel."

Holt's voice trailed off as he saw that a group of the revelers had surrounded Janda. They had removed the manacles from the outlaw's dead limbs, and they were putting a horned helmet on his head, giving him a shield and spear and a cloak of fur, equipage of an old Norse warrior of Earth—first to coin and bear the dread name of berserker.

"Observe, Captain," mocked Mical's voice. "At our masked ball we do not fear the fate of Prince Prospero. We willingly bring in the semblance of the terror outside!"

"Poe!" shouted the sycophant in glee.

Prospero and Poe meant nothing to Holt, and Mical looked disappointed.

"Leave us, Captain," said Nogara, making a direct order of it.

"Leave, Captain Holt," said Lucinda in a firm, clear voice. "We all know you wish to help those who stand in danger here. Lord Nogara, will Captain Holt be blamed in any way for what happens here when he has gone?"

There was a hint of puzzlement in Nogara's clear eyes. But he shook his head slightly, granting the asked-for absolution.

And there was nothing for Holt to do but go back to the berserker to argue and plead with it for his crew. If it was patient, the evidence it sought might be forthcoming. If only the revelers would have mercy on the thing they thought was Janda.

Holt went out. It had never entered his burdened mind that Karlsen was only frozen.

V

Mical's arm was about her hips as she stood beside his chair, and his voice purred up at her: "Why, how you tremble, pretty one . . . it moves me that such a pretty one as you should tremble at my touch, yes, it moves me deeply. Now, we are no longer enemies, are we? If we are, I should have to deal harshly with your brother."

She had given Holt time to get clear of the *Nirvana.* Now she swung her arm with all her strength. The blow turned Mical's head halfway around, and made his neat gray hair fly wildly.

There was a sudden hush in the Great Hall, and then a roar of laughter that reddened all of Mical's face to match the handprint on his cheek. A man behind Lucinda grabbed her arms and pinned them. She relaxed until she felt his grip loosen slightly, and then she grabbed up a table knife. There was another burst of laughter as Mical ducked away and the man behind Lucinda seized her again. Another man came to help him and the two of them, laughing, took away the knife and forced her to sit in a chair at Mical's side.

When the governor spoke at last his voice quavered slightly, but it was low and almost calm.

"Bring the man closer," he ordered. "Seat him there, just across the table from us."

While his order was being carried out, Mical spoke to Lucinda in conversational tones: "It *was* my intent, of course, that your brother should be treated and allowed to recover." He paused to see the effect of that statement on her.

"Lying piece of filth," she whispered, smiling.

Mical only smiled back. "Let us test the skill of my mind-control technicians," he suggested. "I'll wager that no bonds will be needed to hold your brother in his chair, once I have done this." He made a curious gesture over the table, toward the glassy eyes that looked out of Janda's face. "So. But he will still be aware, with every nerve, of all that happens to him. You may be sure of that."

She had planned and counted on something like this happening, but now she felt as if she were exhausted by breathing evil air. She was afraid of fainting, and at the same time wished that she could.

"Our guest is bored with his costume." Mical looked up and down the table. "Who will be first to take a turn at entertaining him?"

There was a spattering of applause as a giggling effeminate arose from a nearby chair.

"Jamy is known for his inventiveness," said Mical in pleasant tones to Lucinda. "I insist you watch closely, now. Chin up!"

On the other side of Mical, Felipe Nogara was losing his air of remoteness. As if reluctantly. he was being drawn to watch. In his bearing was a rising expectancy, winning out over disgust.

Jamy came giggling, holding a small jeweled knife.

"Not the eyes," Mical cautioned. "There'll be things I want him to see, later."

"Oh, certainly!" Jamy twittered. He set the horned helmet gingerly aside, and wiped the touch of it from his fingers. "We'll just start like this on one cheek, with a bit of skin—"

Jamy's touch with the blade was gentle, but still too much for the dead flesh. At the first peeling tug, the whole lifeless mask fell red and wet from around the staring eyes, and his steel berserker-skull grinned out.

Lucinda had just time to see Jamy's body flung across the Hall by a steel-boned arm before the men holding her let go and turned to flee for their lives, and she was able to duck under the table. Screaming bedlam broke loose, and in another moment the whole table went over with a crash before the berserker's strength. The machine, finding itself discovered thwarted in its primary function of getting away with evidence on Karlsen, took as its secondary goal the old berserker one of simple killing. It moved through the Hall, squatting and hopping grotesquely, mowing its way with scythelike arms, harvesting howling panic into bundles of bloody stillness.

At the main door, fleeing people jammed one another into immobility, and the assassin worked among them, methodically mangling and slaying. Then it turned and came down the Hall again. It came to Lucinda, still kneeling where the table-tipping had exposed her; but the machine hesitated, recognizing her as a semi-partner in its prime function. In a moment it had dashed on after another target.

It was Nogara, swaying on his feet, his right arm hanging broken. He had come up with a heavy handgun from somewhere, and now he fired left-handed as the machine charged down the other side of the overturned table toward him. The gun-blasts shattered Nogara's friends and furniture but only grazed his moving target.

At last one shot hit home. The machine was wrecked, but its impetus carried it on to knock Nogara down again.

There was a shaky quiet in the Great Hall, which was wrecked as if by a bomb. Lucinda got unsteadily to her feet. There were sobs and moans and gropings everywhere, but no one else was standing.

She picked her way dazedly over to the smashed assassin-machine. She felt only a numbness, looking at the rags of clothing and flesh that still clung to its metal frame. Now in her mind she could see her brother's face as it once had been, strong and smiling.

Now there was something that mattered more than the dead, if she could only recall what it was—of course, the berserker's hostages, the good kind spacemen. She could try to trade Karlsen's body for them.

The serving machines, built to face emergencies on the order of spilled wine, were dashing to and fro in the nearest thing to panic that mechanism could achieve. They impeded Lucinda's progress, but she had the heavy coffin wheeled halfway across the Hall when a weak voice stopped her. Nogara had dragged himself up to a sitting position against the overturned table.

He croaked again: "—alive."

"What?"

"Johann's alive. Healthy. See? It's a freezer."

"But we all told the berserker he was dead." She felt stupid with the impact of one shock after another. For the first time she looked down at Karlsen's face, and long seconds passed before she could tear her eyes away. "It has hostages. It wants his body."

"No." Nogara shook his head. "I see, now. But no. I won't give him to berserkers, alive." A brutal power of personality still emanated from his broken body. His gun was gone, but his power kept Lucinda from moving. There was no hatred in her now.

She protested, "But there are seven men out there."

"Berserker's like me." Nogara bared pain-clenched teeth. "It won't let prisoners go. Here. The key. . . ." He pulled it from inside his torn-open tunic.

Lucinda's eyes were drawn once again to the cold serenity of the face in the coffin. Then on impulse she ran to get the key. When she did so Nogara slumped over in relief, unconscious or nearly so.

The coffin lock was marked in several positions, and she

turned it to EMERGENCY REVIVAL. Lights sprang on around the figure inside, and there was a hum of power.

By now the automated systems of the ship were reacting to the emergency. The serving machines had begun a stretcher-bearer service, Nogara being one of the first victims they carried away. Presumably a robot medic was in action somewhere. From behind Nogara's throne chair a great voice was shouting.

"This is ship defense control, requesting human orders! What is nature of emergency?"

"Do not contact the courier ship!" Lucinda shouted back. "Watch it for an attack. But don't hit the lifeboat!"

The glass top of the coffin had become opaque.

Lucinda ran to the viewport, stumbling over the body of Mical and going on without a pause. By putting her face against the port and looking out at an angle she could just see the berserker-courier, pinkly visible in the wavering light of the hypermass, its lifeboat of hostages a small pink dot still in place before it.

How long would it wait, before it killed the hostages and fled?

When she turned away from the port, she saw that the coffin's lid was open and the man inside was sitting up. For just a moment, a moment that was to stay in Lucinda's mind, his eyes were like a child's, fixed helplessly on hers. Then power began to grow behind his eyes, a power somehow completely different from his brother's and perhaps even greater.

Karlsen looked away from her, taking in the rest of his surroundings, the devastated Great Hall and the coffin. "Felipe," he whispered, as if in pain, though his half-brother was no longer in sight.

Lucinda moved toward him and started to pour out her story, from the day in the Flamland prison when she had heard that Karlsen had fallen to the plague.

Once he interrupted her. "Help me out of this thing; get

me space armor." His arm was hard and strong when she grasped it, but when he stood beside her he was surprisingly short. "Go on, what then?"

She hurried on with her tale, while serving machines came to arm him. "But why were you frozen?" she ended, suddenly wondering at his health and strength.

He ignored the question. "Come along to Defense Control. We must save those men out there."

He went familiarly to the nerve center of the ship and hurled himself into the combat chair of the Defense Officer, who was probably dead. The panel before Karlsen came alight and he ordered at once, "Get me in contact with that courier."

Within a few moments a flat-sounding voice from the courier answered routinely. The face that appeared on the communication screen was badly lighted; someone viewing it without advance warning would not suspect that it was anything but human.

"This is High Commander Karlsen speaking, from the *Nirvana.*" He did not call himself governor or lord, but by his title of the great day of the Stone Place. "I'm coming over there. I want to talk to you men on the courier."

The shadowed face moved slightly on the screen. "Yes, sir."

Karlsen broke off the contact at once. "That'll keep its hopes up. Now I need a fast launch. You, robots, load my coffin aboard one. I'm on emergency revival drugs now and if I live I may have to refreeze for a while."

"You're not really going there?"

Up out of the chair again, he paused. "I know berserkers. If chasing me is that thing's prime function it won't waste a shot or a second of time on a few hostages while I'm in sight."

"You can't go," Lucinda heard herself saying. "You mean too much to all men—"

"I'm not committing suicide; I have a trick or two in

mind." Karlsen's voice changed suddenly. "You say Felipe's not dead?"

"I don't think so."

Karlsen's eyes closed while his lips moved briefly, silently. Then he looked at Lucinda and grabbed up paper and a stylus from the Defense Officer's console. "Give this to Felipe," he said, writing. "He'll set you and the captain free if I ask it. You're not dangerous to his power. Whereas I . . ."

VI

From the Defense Officer's position, Lucinda watched Karlsen's crystalline launch leave the *Nirvana* and take a long curve that brought it near the courier at a point some distance from the lifeboat.

"You on the courier," Lucinda heard him say. "You can tell it's really me here on the launch, can't you? You can DF my transmission? Can you photograph my retinas through the screen?"

And the launch darted away with a right-angle swerve, dodging and twisting at top acceleration, as the berserker's weapons blasted the space where it had been. Karlsen had been right. The berserker spent not a moment's delay or a single shot on the lifeboat, but hurled itself instantly after the launch.

"Hit that courier!" Lucinda screamed. "Destroy it!" A salvo of missiles left the *Nirvana*, but it was a shot at a receding target, and it missed. Perhaps it missed because the courier was already in the fringes of the distortion surrounding the hypermass.

Karlsen's launch had not been hit, but it could not get away. It was a glassy dot vanishing behind a screen of blasts from the berserker's weapons, a dot being forced into the maelstrom of the hypermass.

"Chase them!" cried Lucinda, and saw the stars tint blue ahead; but almost instantly the *Nirvana*'s auto pilot countermanded her order, barking mathematical assurance that to accelerate any further in that direction would be fatal to all aboard.

The launch was now going certainly into the hypermass, gripped by a gravity that could make any engines useless. And the berserker-ship was going headlong after the launch, caring for nothing but to make sure of Karlsen.

The two specks tinted red, and redder still, racing before an enormous falling cloud of dust as if flying into a planet's sunset sky. And then the red shift of the hypermass took them into invisibility, and the universe saw them no more.

Soon after the robots had brought the men from the lifeboat safely aboard *Nirvana,* Holt found Lucinda alone in the Great Hall, gazing out the viewport.

"He gave himself to save you," she said. "And he'd never even seen you."

"I know." After a pause Holt said, "I've just been talking to the Lord Nogara. I don't know why, but you're to be freed, and I'm not to be prosecuted for bringing the damned berserker aboard. Though Nogara seems to hate both of us. . . ."

She wasn't listening; she was still looking out the port.

"I want you to tell me all about him someday," Holt said, putting his arm around Lucinda. She moved slightly, ridding herself of a minor irritation that she had hardly noticed. It was Holt's arm, which dropped away.

"I see," Holt said, after a while. He went to look after his men.

TIME PIECE

Joe Haldeman

Born in Oklahoma City, Oklahoma, Joe Haldeman took a B.S. degree in physics and astronomy from the University of Maryland, and did postgraduate work in mathematics and computer science. But his plans for a career in science were cut short by the U.S. Army, which sent him to Vietnam in 1968 as a combat engineer. Seriously wounded in action, Haldeman returned home in 1969 and began to write. He sold his first story to Galaxy *in 1969, and by 1976 had garnered both the Nebula Award and the Hugo Award for his famous novel* The Forever War, *one of the landmark books of the seventies. He took another Hugo Award in 1977 for his story "Tricentennial," won the Rhysling Award in 1983 for the best science fiction poem of the year (although usually thought of primarily as a "hard-science" writer, Haldeman is, in fact, also an accomplished poet, and has sold poetry to most of the major professional markets in the genre), and won both the Nebula and the Hugo Award in 1991 for the novella version of "The Hemingway Hoax." His story "None So Blind" won the Hugo Award in 1995. His novel* Forever Peace *won the John W. Campbell Memorial Award. His other books include two mainstream novels,* War Year *and* 1969, *the SF novels* Mindbridge, All My Sins Remembered, There Is No Darkness *(written with his brother, SF writer Jack C. Haldeman II),* Worlds, Worlds Apart, Worlds Enough and Time, Buying Time, The Hemingway Hoax, *and* Forever Peace, *and the "techno-thriller"* Tools of the Trade, *the collections* Infinite Dreams, Dealing in Futures, Vietnam and Other Alien Worlds, *and* None So Blind, *and, as editor, the anthologies* Study War No More, Cosmic Laughter, *and* Nebula Award Stories Seventeen. *His most recent book is the novel* Forever Free, *Haldeman lives part of the year in Boston, where he teaches writing at the Massachusetts Institute of Technology, and the rest of the year in Florida, where he and his wife, Gay, make their home.*

In the taut and fast-paced story that follows, he shows us that sometimes it's possible to win the battle and lose the war. *Or maybe lose* both—*slowly and inexorably.*

They say you've got a fifty-fifty chance every time you go out. That makes it one chance in eight that you'll live to see your third furlough; the one I'm on now.

Somehow the odds don't keep people from trying to join. Even though not one in a thousand gets through the years of training and examination, there's no shortage of cannon fodder. And that's what we are. The most expensive, best trained cannon fodder in the history of warfare. Human history, anyhow; who can speak for the enemy?

I don't even call them snails anymore. And the thought of them doesn't trigger that instant flash of revulsion, hate, kill-fever—the psyconditioning wore off years ago, and they didn't renew it. They've stopped doing it to new recruits; no percentage in berserkers. I was a wild one the first couple of trips, though.

Strange world I've come back to. Gets stranger every time, of course. Even sitting here in a bogus twenty-first-century bar, where everyone speaks Basic and there's real wood on the walls and peaceful holograms instead of plug-ins, and music made by men . . .

But it leaks through. I don't pay by card, let alone by coin. The credit register monitors my alpha waves and communicates with the bank every time I order a drink. And, in case I've become addicted to more modern vices, there's a feelie matrix (modified to look like an old-fashioned visiphone booth) where I can have my brain stimulated directly.

Thanks but no, thanks—always get this picture of dirty hands inside my skull, kneading, rubbing. Like when you get too close to the enemy and they open a hole in your mind and you go spinning down and down and never reach the bottom till you die. I almost got too close last time.

We were on a three-man reconnaissance patrol, bound for a hellish little planet circling the red giant Antares. Now red giant stars don't form planets in the natural course of things, so we had ignored Antares; we control most of the space around it, so why waste time in idle exploration? But the enemy had detected this little planet—God knows how—and about ten years after they landed there, we monitored their presence (gravity waves from the ships' braking) and my team was assigned the reconnaissance. Three men against many, many of the enemy—but we weren't supposed to fight if we could help it; just take a look around, record what we saw, and leave a message beacon on our way back, about a light-year out from Antares. Theoretically, the troopship following us by a month will pick up the information and use it to put together a battle plan. Actually, three more recon patrols precede the troop ship at one-week intervals; insurance against the high probability that any one patrol will be caught and destroyed. As the first team in, we have a pretty good chance of success, but the ones to follow would be in trouble if we didn't get back out. We'd be past caring, of course, the enemy doesn't take prisoners.

We came out of lightspeed close to Antares, so the bulk of the star would mask our braking disturbance, and inserted the ship in a hyperbolic orbit that would get us to the planet—Anomaly, we were calling it—in about twenty hours.

"Anomaly must be tropical over most of its surface." Fred Sykes, nominally the navigator, was talking to himself and at the two of us while he analyzed the observational data rolling out of the ship's computer. "No axial tilt to speak of. Looks like they've got a big outpost near the equator, lots of electromagnetic noise there. Figures . . . the goddamn snails like it hot. We requisitioned hot-weather gear, didn't we, Pancho?"

Pancho, that's me. "No, Fred, all we got's parkas and snowshoes." My full name is Francisco Jesus Mario Juan-José Hugo de Naranja, and I outrank Fred, so he should at least call me Francisco. But I've never pressed the point. Pancho it is. Fred looked up from his figure and the rookie, Paul Spiegel, almost dropped the pistol he was cleaning.

"But why . . ." Paul was staring. "We knew the planet was probably Earthlike if the enemy wanted it. Are we gonna have to go tromping around in space suits?"

"No, Paul, our esteemed leader and supply clerk is being sarcastic again." He turned back to his computer. "Explain, Pancho."

"No, that's all right." Paul reddened a bit and also went back to his job. "I remember you complaining about having to take the standard survival issue."

"Well, I was right then and I'm doubly right now. We've *got* parkas back there, and snowshoes, and a complete terranorm environment recirculator, and everything else we could possibly need to walk around in comfort on every planet known to man—*Dios!* That issue masses over a metric ton, more than a gigawatt laser. A laser we could use, but crampons and pith helmets and elephant guns . . ."

Paul looked up again. "Elephant guns?" He was kind of a freak about weapons.

"Yeah."

"That's a gun that shoots elephants?"

"Right. An elephant gun shoots elephants."

"Is that some new kind of ammunition?"

I sighed, I really sighed. You'd think I'd get used to this after twelve years—or four hundred—in the service. "No, kid, elephants were animals, big gray wrinkled animals with horns. You used an elephant gun to shoot *at* them.

"When I was a kid in Rioplex, back in the twenty-first, we had an elephant in the zoo: used to go down in the summer and feed him synthos through the bars. He had a long nose like a fat tail, he ate with that."

"What planet were they from?"

It went on like that for a while. It was Paul's first trip out, and he hadn't yet gotten used to the idea that most of his compatriots were genuine antiques, preserved by the natural process of relativity. At lightspeed you age imperceptibly, while the universe's calendar adds a year for every light-year you travel. Seems like cheating. But it catches up with you eventually.

We hit the atmosphere of Anomaly at an oblique angle and came in passive, like a natural meteor, until we got to a position where we were reasonably safe from detection (just above the south polar sea), then blasted briefly to slow down and splash. Then we spent a few hours in slow flight at sea level, sneaking up on their settlement.

It appeared to be the only enemy camp on the whole planet, which was typical. Strange for a spacefaring, aggressive race to be so incurious about planetary environments, but they always seemed to settle in one place and simply expand radially. And they do expand; their reproduction rate makes rabbits look sick. Starting from one colony, they can fill a world in two hundred years. After that, they control their population by infantiphage and stellar migration.

We landed about a hundred kilometers from the edge of their colony, around local midnight. While we were outside setting up the espionage monitors, the ship camouflaged itself to match the surrounding jungle optically, thermally, magnetically, etc.—we were careful not to get too far from the ship; it can be a bit hard to find even when you know where to look.

The monitors were to be fed information from flea-sized flying robots, each with a special purpose, and it would take several hours for them to wing into the city. We posted a one-man guard, one-hour shifts; the other two inside the ship until the monitors started clicking. But they never started.

Being senior, I took the first watch. A spooky hour, the jungle making dark little noises all around, but nothing happened. Then Fred stood the next hour, while I put on the deepsleep helmet. Figured I'd need the sleep—once data started coming in, I'd have to be alert for about forty hours. We could all sleep for a week once we got off Anomaly and hit lightspeed.

Getting yanked out of deepsleep is like an ice-water douche to the brain. The black nothing dissolved and there was Fred a foot away from my face, yelling my name over and over. As soon as he saw my eyes open, he ran for the open lock, priming his laser on the way (definitely against regulations, could hole the hull that way; I started to say something but couldn't form the words). Anyhow, what were we doing in free fall? And how could Fred run across the deck like that while we were in free fall?

Then my mind started coming back into focus and I could analyze the sinking, spinning sensation—not free fall vertigo at all but what we used to call snail-fever. The enemy was very near. Crackling combat sounds drifted in from outdoors.

I sat up on the cot and tried to sort everything out and get going. After long seconds my arms and legs got the idea, I struggled up and staggered to the weapons cabinet. Both the lasers were gone, and the only heavy weapon left was a grenade launcher. I lifted it from the rack and made my way to the lock.

Had I been thinking straight, I would've just sealed the lock and blasted—the presence in my mind was so strong that I should have known there were too many of the enemy, too close, for us to stand and fight. But no one can think while their brain is being curdled that way. I fought the urge to just let go and fall down that hole in my mind, and slid along the wall to the airlock. By the time I got there my teeth were chattering uncontrollably and my face was wet with tears.

Looking out, I saw a smoldering gray lump that must

have been Paul, and Fred screaming like a madman, fanning the laser on full over a 180-degree arc. There couldn't have been anything alive in front of him; the jungle was a lurid curtain of fire, but a bolt lanced in from behind and Fred dissolved in a pink spray of blood and flesh.

I saw them then, moving fast for snails, shambling in over thick brush toward the ship. Through the swirling fog in my brain I realized that all they could see was the light pouring through the open lock, and me silhouetted in front. I tried to raise the launcher but couldn't—there were too many, less than a hundred meters away, and the inky whirlpool in my mind just got bigger and bigger and I could feel myself slipping into it.

The first bolt missed me; hit the ship and it shuddered, ringing like a huge cathedral bell. The second one didn't miss, taking off my left hand just above the wrist, roasting what remained of my left arm. In a spastic lurch I jerked up the launcher and yanked the trigger, holding it down while dozens of micro-ton grenades popped out and danced their blinding way up to and across the enemy's ragged line. Dazzled blind, I stepped back and stumbled over the med-robot, which had smelled blood and was eager to do its duty. On top of the machine was a switch that some clown had labeled EMERGENCY EXIT; I slapped it, and as the lock clanged shut the atomic engines muttered—growled—screamed into life and a ten-gravity hand slid me across the blood-slick deck and slammed me back against the real-wall padding. I felt ribs crack and something in my neck snapped. As the world squeezed away, I knew I was a dead man but it was better to die in a bed of pain than to just fall and fall. . . .

I woke up to the less-than-tender ministrations of the med-robot, who had bound the stump of my left arm and was wrapping my chest in plastiseal. My body from forehead to shins ached from radiation burns, earned by facing the grenades' bursts, and the nonexistent hand seemed to writhe in painful, impossible contortions. But numbing anesthetic kept the pain at a bearable distance, and there was an empty space in my mind where the snail-fever had been, and the gentle hum told me we were at lightspeed; things could have been one flaming hell of a lot worse. Fred and Paul were gone but that just moved them from the small roster of live friends to the long list of dead ones.

A warning light on the control panel was blinking stroboscopically. We were getting near the hole—excuse me, "relativistic discontinuity"—and the computer had to know where I wanted to go. You go in one hole at lightspeed and you'll come out of some other hole; *which* hole you pop out of depends on your angle of approach. Since they say that only about one per cent of the holes are charted, if you go in at any old angle you're liable to wine up in Podunk, on the other side of the galaxy, with no ticket back.

I just let the light blink, though. If it doesn't get any response from the crew, the ship programs itself automatically to go to Heaven, the hospital world, which was fine with me. They cure what ails you and then set you loose with a compatible soldier of the opposite sex, for an extended vacation on that beautiful world. Someone once told me there were over a hundred worlds named Hell, but there's only one Heaven. Clean and pretty from the tropical seas to the Northern pine forests. Like Earth used to be, before we strangled it.

A bell had been ringing all the time I'd been conscious, but I didn't notice it until it stopped. That meant that the information capsule had been jettisoned, for what little it was worth. Planetary information, very few espionage-type data; just a tape of the battle. Be rough for the next recon patrol.

I fell asleep knowing I'd wake up on the other side of the hole, bound for Heaven.

I pick up my drink—an old-fashioned old-fashioned—with my new left hand and the glass should feel right, slick but slightly tacky with the cold-water sweat, fine ridges molded into the plastic. But there's something missing, hard to describe, a memory stored in your fingertips that a new growth has to learn all over again. It's a strange feeling, but in a way seems to fit with this crazy Earth, where I sit in my alcoholic time capsule and, if I squint with my mind, can almost believe I'm back in the twenty-first.

I pay for the nostalgia—wood and natural food, human bartender and waitress who are also linguists, it all comes dear—but I can afford it, if anyone can. Compound interest, of course. Over four centuries have passed on Earth since I first went off to the war, and my salary's been deposited at the Chase Manhattan Credit Union ever since. They're glad to do it; when I die, they keep the interest and the principal reverts to the government. Heirs? I had one illegitimate son (conceived on my first furlough) and when I last saw his gravestone, the words on it had washed away to barely legible dimples.

But I'm still a young man (at lightspeed you age imperceptibly while the universe winds down outside) and the time you spend going from hole to hole is almost incalculably small. I've spent most of the past half millennium at lightspeed, the rest of the time usually convalescing from battle. My records show that I've logged a trifle under one year in actual combat. Not bad for 438 years' pay. Since I first lifted off I've aged twelve years by my biological calendar. Complicated, isn't it—next month I'll be thirty, 456 years after my date of birth.

But one week before my birthday I've got to decide whether to try my luck for the fourth trip out or just collect my money and retire. No choice, really. I've got to go back.

It's something they didn't emphasize when I joined up, back in 2088—maybe it wasn't so obvious back then, the war only decades old—but they can't hide it nowadays. To many old vets wandering around, like animated museum pieces.

I could cash in my chips and live in luxury for another hundred years. But it would get mighty lonely. Can't talk to anybody on Earth but other bets and people who've gone to the trouble to learn Basic.

Everyone in space speaks Basic. You can't lift off until you've become fluent. Otherwise, how could you take orders from a fellow who should have been food for worms centuries before your grandfather was born? Especially since language melted down into one Language.

I'm tone-deaf. Can't speak or understand Language, where one word has ten or fifteen different meanings, depending on pitch. To me it sounds like puppy dogs yapping. Same words over and over; no sense.

Of course, when I first lived on Earth there were all sorts of languages, not just one Language. I spoke Spanish (still do when I can find some other old codger who remembers) and learned English—that was before they called it Basic—in military training. Learned it damn well, too. If I weren't tone-deaf I'd crack Language and maybe I'd settle down.

Maybe not. The people are so strange, and it's not just the Language. Mindplugs and homosex and voluntary suicide. Walking around with nothing on but paint and powder. We had Fullerdomes when I was a kid; but you didn't *have* to live under one. Now if you take a walk out in the country for a breath of fresh air, you'll drop over dead before you can exhale.

My mind keeps dragging me back to Heaven. I'd retire in a minute if I could spend my remaining century there. Can't, of course; only soldiers allowed in space. And the only way a soldier gets to Heaven is the hard way.

I've been there three times; once more and I'll set a record. That's motivation of a sort, I suppose. Also, in the unlikely event that I should live another five years, I'll get a commission, and a desk job if I live through my term as a field officer. Doesn't happen too often—but there aren't too many desk jobs that people can handle better than cyborgs.

That's another alternative. If my body gets too garbaged for regeneration, and they can save enough of my brain, I could spend the rest of eternity hooked up to a computer, as a cyborg. The only one I've ever talked to seemed to be happy.

I once had an African partner named N'gai. He taught me how to play O'wari, a game older than Monopoly or even chess. We sat in this very bar (or the identical one that was in its place two hundred years ago) and he tried to impress on my non-Zen-oriented mind just how significant this game was to men in our position.

You start out with forty-eight smooth little pebbles, four in each one of the twelve depressions that make up the game board. Then you take turns, scooping the pebbles out of one hole and distributing them one at a time in holes to the left. If you dropped your last pebble in a hole where your opponent had only one or two, why, you got to take those pebbles off the board. Sounds exciting, doesn't it?

But N'gai sat there in a cloud of bhang-smoke and mumbled about the game and how it was just like the big game we were playing, and every time he took a pebble off the board, he called it by name. And some of the names I didn't know, but a lot of them were on my long list.

And he talked about how we were like the pieces in this simple game; how some went off the board after the first couple of moves, and some hopped from place to place all through the game and came out unscathed, and some just sat in one place all the time until they got zapped from out of nowhere. . . .

After a while I started hitting the bhang myself, and we abandoned the metaphor in a spirit of mutual intoxication.

And I've been thinking about that night for six years, or two hundred, and I think that N'gai—his soul find Buddha—was wrong. The game isn't all that complex.

Because in O'wari, either person can win.

The snails populate ten planets for every one we destroy.

Solitaire, anyone?

ON THE ORION LINE

Stephen Baxter

Here's a harrowing look at the proposition that a soldier's duty is to survive, especially when trapped behind enemy lines, especially when those "enemy lines" are in the depths of interstellar space, thousands of light-years from Earth, and you have no ship, no shelter, and only a quickly dwindling supply of air. In those circumstances, you do anything you have *to do to survive—if you're strong enough to actually* do *it, that is!*

British writer Stephen Baxter made his first sale to Interzone *in 1987, and since then has become one of that magazine's most frequent contributors, as well as making sales to* Asimov's Science Fiction, Science Fiction Age, Zenith, New Worlds, *and elsewhere. Like many of his colleagues who are also engaged in revitalizing the "hard-science" story here in the nineties, Baxter often works on the Cutting Edge of science, but he usually succeeds in balancing conceptualization with storytelling, and rarely loses sight of the human side of the equation. His first novel,* Raft, *was released in 1991 to wide and enthusiastic response, and was rapidly followed by other well-received novels such as* Timelike Infinity, Anti-Ice, Flux, *and the H.G. Wells pastiche—a sequel to* The Time Machine—The Time Ships. *His other books include the novels,* Voyage, Titan, *and* Moonseed, *and the collections* Vacuum Diagrams: Stories of the Xeelee Sequence *and* Traces. *He's won the Philip K. Dick Award twice. His most recent books are the novels* Mammoth, Book One: Silverhair *and* Manifold: Time.

The *Brief Life Burns Brightly* broke out of the fleet. We were chasing down a Ghost cruiser, and we were closing.

The lifedome of the *Brightly* was transparent, so it was as if Captain Teid in her big chair, and her officers and their equipment clusters—and a few low-grade tars like me—were just floating in space. The light was subtle, coming from a nearby cluster of hot young stars, and from the rivers of sparking lights that made up the fleet formation we had just left, and beyond *that* from the sparking of novae. This was the Orion Line—six thousand light-years from Earth and a thousand lights long, a front that spread right along the inner edge of the Orion Spiral Arm—and the stellar explosions marked battles which must have concluded years ago.

And, not a handful of klicks away, the Ghost cruiser slid across space, running for home. The cruiser was a rough egg-shape of silvered rope. Hundreds of Ghosts clung to the rope. You could see them slithering this way and that, not affected at all by the emptiness around them.

The Ghosts' destination was a small, old yellow star. Pael, our tame Academician, had identified it as a fortress star from some kind of strangeness in its light. But up close you don't need to be an Academician to spot a fortress. From the *Brightly* I could see with my unaided eyes that the star had a pale blue cage around it—an open lattice with struts half a million kilometres long—thrown there by the Ghosts, for their own purposes.

I had a lot of time to watch all this. I was just a tar. I was fifteen years old.

My duties at that moment were non-specific. I was supposed to stand to, and render assistance any way that was required—most likely with basic medical attention should we go into combat. Right now the only one of us tars actually working was Halle, who was chasing down a pool of vomit sicked up by Pael, the Academician, the only non-Navy personnel on the bridge.

The action on the *Brightly* wasn't like you see in Virtual shows. The atmosphere was calm, quiet, competent. All you could hear was the murmur of voices from the crew and the equipment, and the hiss of recycling air. No drama: it was like an operating theatre.

There was a soft warning chime.

The Captain raised an arm and called over Academician Pael, First Officer Till, and Jeru, the Commissary assigned to the ship. They huddled close, conferring—apparently arguing. I saw the way flickering nova light reflected from Jeru's shaven head.

I felt my heart beat harder.

Everybody knew what the chime meant: that we were approaching the fortress cordon. Either we would break off, or we would chase the Ghost cruiser inside its invisible fortress. And everybody knew that no Navy ship that had ever penetrated a fortress cordon, ten light-minutes from the central star, and come back out again.

One way or the other, it would all be resolved soon.

Captain Teid cut short the debate. She leaned forward and addressed the crew. Her voice, cast through the ship, was friendly, like a cadre leader whispering in your ear. "You can all see we can't catch that swarm of Ghosts this side of the cordon. And you all know the hazard of crossing a cordon. But if we're ever going to break this blockade of theirs we have to find a way to bust open those forts. So we're going in anyhow. Stand by your stations."

There was a half-hearted cheer.

I caught Halle's eye. She grinned at me. She pointed at the Captain, closed her fist and made a pumping movement. I admired her sentiment but she wasn't being too accurate, anatomically speaking, so I raised my middle finger and jiggled it back and forth.

It took a slap on the back of the head from Jeru, the Commissary, to put a stop to that. "Little morons," she growled.

"Sorry, sir—"

I got another slap for the apology. Jeru was a tall, stocky woman, dressed in the bland, monastic robes said to date from the time of the founding of the Commission for Historical Truth a thousand years ago. But rumour was she'd seen plenty of combat action of her own before joining the Commission, and such was her physical strength and speed of reflex I could well believe it.

As we neared the cordon the Academician, Pael, started a gloomy countdown. The slow geometry of Ghost cruiser and tinsel-wrapped fortress star swivelled across the crowded sky.

Everybody went quiet.

The darkest time is always just before the action starts. Even if you can see or hear what is going on, all you do is think. What was going to happen to us when we crossed that intangible border? Would a fleet of Ghost ships materialise all around us? Would some mysterious weapon simply blast us out of the sky?

I caught the eye of First Officer Till. He was a veteran of twenty years; his scalp had been burned away in some ancient close-run combat, long before I was born, and he wore a crown of scar tissue with pride.

"Let's do it, tar," he growled.

All the fear went away. I was overwhelmed by a feeling of togetherness, of us all being in this crap together. I had no thought of dying. Just: let's get through this.

"Yes, *sir*!"

Pael finished his countdown.

All the lights went out. Detonating stars wheeled.

And the ship exploded.

I was thrown into darkness. Air howled. Emergency bulkheads scythed past me, and I could hear people scream.

I slammed into the curving hull, nose pressed against the stars.

I bounced off and drifted. The inertial suspension was out, then. I thought I could smell blood—probably my own.

I could see the Ghost ship, a tangle of rope and silver baubles, tingling with highlights from the fortress star. We were still closing.

But I could also see shards of shattered lifedome, a sputtering drive unit. The shards were bits of the *Brightly.* It had gone, all gone, in a fraction of a second.

"Let's do it," I murmured.

Maybe I was out of it for a while.

Somebody grabbed my ankle and tugged me down. There was a competent slap on my cheek, enough to make me focus.

"Case. Can you hear me?"

It was First Officer Till. Even in the swimming starlight that burned-off scalp was unmistakable.

I glanced around. There were four of us here: Till, Commissary Jeru, Acamedician Pael, me. We were huddled up against what looked like the stump of the First Officer's console. I realised that the gale of venting air had stopped. I was back inside a hull with integrity, then—

"Case!"

"I—yes, sir."

"Report."

I touched my lip; my hand came away bloody. At a time like that it's your duty to report your injuries, honestly and fully. Nobody needs a hero who turns out not to be able to function. "I think I'm all right. I may have a concussion."

"Good enough. Strap down." Till handed me a length of rope.

I saw that the others had tied themselves to struts. I did the same.

Till, with practiced ease, swam away into the air, I guessed looking for other survivors.

Academician Pael was trying to curl into a ball. He couldn't even speak. The tears just rolled out of his eyes. I stared at the way big globules welled up and drifted away into the air, glimmering.

The action had been over in seconds. All a bit sudden for an earthworm, I guess.

Nearby, I saw, trapped under one of the emergency bulkheads, there was a pair of legs—just that. The rest of the body must have been chopped away, gone drifting off with the rest of the debris from *Brightly.* But I recognised those legs, from a garish pink stripe on the sole of the right boot. That had been Halle. She was the only girl I had ever screwed, I thought—and more than likely, given the situation, the only girl I ever would get to screw.

I couldn't figure out how I felt about that.

Jeru was watching me. "Tar—do you think we should all be frightened for ourselves, like the Academician?" Her accent was strong, unidentifiable.

"No, sir."

"No." Jeru studied Pael with contempt. "We are in a yacht, Academician. Something has happened to the *Brightly.* The dome was designed to break up into yachts like this." She sniffed. "We have air, and it isn't foul yet." She winked at me. "Maybe we can do a little damage to the Ghosts before we die, tar. What do you think?"

I grinned. "Yes, sir."

Pael lifted his head and stared at me with salt water eyes. "Lethe. You people are monsters." His accent was gentle, a lilt. "Even such a child as this. You embrace death—"

Jeru grabbed Pael's jaw in a massive hand, and pinched the joint until he squealed. "Captain Teid grabbed you, Academician; she threw you here, into the yacht, before the bulkhead came down. I saw it. If she hadn't taken the time to do that, she would have made it herself. Was *she* a monster? Did *she* embrace death?" And she pushed Pael's face away.

For some reason I hadn't thought about the rest of the crew until that moment. I guess I have a limited imagination. Now, I felt adrift. The Captain—dead?

I said, "Excuse me, Commissary. How many other yachts got out?"

"None," she said steadily, making sure I had no illusions. "Just this one. They died doing their duty, tar. Like the Captain."

Of course she was right, and I felt a little better. Whatever his character, Pael was too valuable not to save. As for me, I had survived through sheer blind chance, through being in the right place when the walls came down: if the Captain had been close, her duty would have been to pull me out of the way and take my place. It isn't a question of human values but of economics: a *lot* more is invested in the training and experience of a Captain Teid—or a Pael—than in *me*.

But Pael seemed more confused than I was.

First Officer Till came bustling back with a heap of equipment. "Put these on." He handed out pressure suits. They were what we called slime suits in training: lightweight skinsuits, running off a backpack of gen-enged algae. "Move it," said Till. "Impact with the Ghost cruiser in four minutes. We don't have any power; there's nothing we can do but ride it out."

I crammed my legs into my suit.

Jeru complied, stripping off her robe to reveal a hard, scarred body. But she was frowning. "Why not heavier armour?"

For answer, Till picked out a gravity-wave handgun from the gear he had retrieved. Without pausing he held it to Pael's head and pushed the fire button.

Pael twitched.

Till said, "See? Nothing is working. Nothing but bio systems, it seems." He threw the gun aside.

Pael closed his eyes, breathing hard.

Till said to me, "Test your comms."

I closed up my hood and faceplate and began intoning, "One, two, three . . ." I could hear nothing.

Till began tapping at our backpacks, resetting the systems. His hood started to glow with transient, pale blue symbols. And then, scratchily, his voice started to come through. ". . . Five, six, seven—can you hear me, tar?"

"Yes, sir."

The symbols were bioluminescent. There were receptors on all our suits—photoreceptors, simple eyes—which could "read" the messages scrawled on our companions" suits. It was a backup system meant for use in environments where anything higher-tech would be a liability. But obviously it would only work as long as we were in line of sight.

"That will make life harder," Jeru said. Oddly, mediated by software, she was easier to understand.

Till shrugged. "You take it as it comes." Briskly, he began to hand out more gear. "These are basic field belt kits. There's some medical stuff: a suture kit, scalpel blades, blood-giving sets. You wear these syrettes around your neck, Academician. They contain painkillers, various gen-enged med-viruses . . . No, you wear it *outside* your suit, Pael, so you can reach it. You'll find valve inlets here, on your sleeve, and here, on the leg." Now came weapons. "We should carry handguns, just in case they start working, but be ready with these." He handed out combat knives.

Pael shrank back.

"Take the knife, Academician. You can shave off that ugly beard, if nothing else."

I laughed out loud, and was rewarded with a wink from Till.

I took a knife. It was a heavy chunk of steel, solid and reassuring. I tucked it in my belt. I was starting to feel a whole lot better.

"Two minutes to impact," Jeru said. I didn't have a working chronometer; she must have been counting the seconds.

"Seal up." Till began to check the integrity of Pael's suit; Jeru and I helped each other. Face seal, glove seal, boot seal, pressure check. Water check, oh-two flow, cee-oh-two scrub . . .

When we were sealed I risked poking my head above Till's chair.

The Ghost ship filled space. The craft was kilometres across, big enough to have dwarfed the poor, doomed *Brief Life Burns Brightly.* It was a tangle of silvery rope of depthless complexity, occluding the stars and the warring fleets. Bulky equipment pods were suspended in the tangle.

And everywhere there were Silver Ghosts, sliding like beads of mercury. I could see how the yacht's emergency lights were returning crimson highlights from the featureless hides of Ghosts, so they looked like sprays of blood droplets across that shining perfection.

"Ten seconds," Till called. "Brace."

Suddenly silver ropes thick as tree trunks were all around us, looming out of the sky.

And we were thrown into chaos again.

I heard a grind of twisted metal, a scream of air. The hull popped open like an eggshell. The last of our air fled in a gush of ice crystals, and the only sound I could hear was my own breathing.

The crumpling hull soaked up some of our momentum.

But then the base of the yacht hit, and it hit hard.

The chair was wrenched out of my grasp, and I was hurled upwards. There was a sudden pain in my left arm. I couldn't help but cry out.

I reached the limit of my tether and rebounded. The jolt sent further waves of pain through my arm. From up there, I could see the others were clustered around the base of the First Officer's chair, which had collapsed.

I looked up. We had stuck like a dart in the outer layers of the Ghost ship. There were shining threads arcing all around us, as if a huge net had scooped us up.

Jeru grabbed me and pulled me down. She jarred my bad arm, and I winced. But she ignored me, and went back to working on Till. He was under the fallen chair.

Pael started to take a syrette of dope from the sachet around his neck.

Jeru knocked his hand away. "You always use the casualty's," she hissed. "Never your own."

Pael looked hurt, rebuffed. "Why?"

I could answer that. "Because the chances are you'll need your own in a minute."

Jeru stabbed a syrette into Till's arm.

Pael was staring at me through his faceplate with wide, frightened eyes. "You've broken your arm."

Looking closely at the arm for the first time, I saw that it was bent back at an impossible angle. I couldn't believe it, even through the pain. I'd never bust so much as a finger, all the way through training.

Now Till jerked, a kind of miniature convulsion, and a big bubble of spit and blood blew out of his lips. Then the bubble popped, and his limbs went loose.

Jeru sat back, breathing hard. She said, "Okay. Okay. How did he put it?—You take it as it comes." She looked around, at me, Pael. I could see she was trembling, which scared me. She said, "Now we move. We have to find a LUP. A lying-up point, Academician. A place to hole up."

I said, "The First Officer—"

"Is dead." She glanced at Pael. "Now it's just the three of us. We won't be able to avoid each other any more, Pael."

Pael stared back, eyes empty.

Jeru looked at me, and for a second her expression softened. "A broken neck. Till broke her neck, tar."

Another death, just like that: just for a heartbeat that was too much for me.

Jeru said briskly, "Do your duty, tar. Help the worm."

I snapped back. "Yes, sir." I grabbed Pael's unresisting arm.

Led by Jeru, we began to move, the three of us, away from the crumpled wreck of our yacht, deep into the alien tangle of a Silver Ghost cruiser.

We found our LUP.

It was just a hollow in a somewhat denser tangle of silvery ropes, but it afforded us some cover, and it seemed to be away from the main concentration of Ghosts. We were still open to the vacuum—as the whole cruiser seemed to be—and I realised then that I wouldn't be getting out of this suit for a while.

As soon as we picked the LUP, Jeru made us take up positions in an all-round defence, covering a 360-degree arc.

Then we did nothing, absolutely nothing, for ten minutes.

It was SOP, standard operating procedure, and I was impressed. You've just come out of all the chaos of the destruction of the *Brightly* and the crash of the yacht, a frenzy of activity. Now you have to give your body a chance to adjust to the new environment, to the sounds and smells and sights.

Only here, there was nothing to smell but my own sweat and piss, nothing to hear but my ragged breathing. And my arm was hurting like hell.

To occupy my mind I concentrated on getting my night vision working. Your eyes take a while to adjust to the darkness—forty-five minutes before they are fully effective—but you are already seeing better after five. I could see stars through the chinks in the wiry metallic brush around me, the flares of distant novae, and the reassuring lights of our fleet. But a Ghost ship is a dark place, a mess of shadows and smeared-out reflections. It was going to be easy to get spooked here.

When the ten minutes were done, Academician Pael started bleating, but Jeru ignored him and came straight over to me. She got hold of my busted arm and started to feel the bone. "So," she said briskly. "What's your name, tar?"

"Case, sir."

"What do you think of your new quarters?"

"Where do I eat?"

She grinned. "Turn off your comms," she said.

I complied.

Without warning she pulled my arm, hard. I was glad she couldn't hear how I howled.

She pulled a canister out of her belt and squirted gunk over my arm; it was semi-sentient and snuggled into place, setting as a hard cast around my injury. When I was healed the cast would fall away of its own accord.

She motioned me to turn on my comms again, and held up a syrette.

"I don't need that."

"Don't be brave, tar. It will help your bones knit."

"Sir, there's a rumour that stuff makes you impotent." I felt stupid even as I said it.

Jeru laughed out loud, and just grabbed my arm. "Anyhow it's the First Officer's, and he doesn't need it anymore, does he?"

I couldn't argue with that; I accepted the injection. The pain started egging almost immediately.

Jeru pulled a tactical beacon out of her belt kit. It was a thumb-sized orange cylinder. "I'm going to try to signal the fleet. I'll work my way out of this tangle; even if the beacon is working we might be shielded in here." Pael started to protest, but she shut him up. I sensed I had been thrown into the middle of an ongoing conflict between them. "Case, you're on stag. And show this worm what's in his kit. I'll come back the same way I go. All right?"

"Yes." More SOP.

She slid away through silvery threads.

I lodged myself in the tangle and started to go through the stuff in the belt kits Till had fetched for us. There was water, rehydration salts and compressed food, all to be delivered to spigots inside our sealed hoods. We had power packs the size of my thumb nail, but they were as dead as the rest of the kit. There was a lot of low-tech gear meant to prolong survival in a variety of situations, such as a magnetic compass, a heliograph, a thumb saw, a magnifying glass, pitons and spindles of rope, even fishing line.

I had to show Pael how his suit functioned as a lavatory. The trick is just to let go; a slime suit recycles most of what you give it, and compresses the rest. That's not to say it's comfortable. I've never yet worn a suit that was good at absorbing odours. I bet no suit designer spent more than an hour in one of her own creations.

I felt fine.

The wreck, the hammer-blow deaths one after the other—none of it was far beneath the surface of my mind. But that's where it stayed, for now; as long as I had the next task to focus on, and the next after that, I could keep moving forward. The time to let it all hit you is after the show.

I guess Pael had never been trained like that.

He was a thin, spindly man, his eyes sunk in black shadow, and his ridiculous red beard crammed up inside his faceplate. Now that the great crises were over, his energy seemed to have drained away, and his functioning was slowing to a crawl. He looked almost comical as he pawed at his useless bits of kit.

After a time he said, "Case, is it?"

"Yes, sir."

"Are you from Earth, child?"

"No. I—"

He ignored me. "The Academies are based on Earth. Did you know that, child? But they do admit a few off-worlders."

I glimpsed a lifetime of outsider resentment. But I could care less. Also I wasn't a child. I asked cautiously, "Where are you from, sir?"

He sighed. "51 Pegasi. I-B."

I'd never heard of it. "What kind of place is that? Is it near Earth?"

"Is everything measured relative to Earth? . . . Not very far. My home world was one of the first extra-solar planets to be discovered—or at least, the primary is. I grew up on a moon. The primary is a hot Jupiter."

I knew what *that* meant: a giant planet huddled close to its parent star.

He looked up at me. "Where you grew up, could you see the sky?"

"No—"

"I could. And the sky was full of sails. That close to the sun, solar sails work efficiently, you see. I used to watch them at night, schooners with sails hundreds of kilometres wide, tacking this way and that in the light. But you can't see the sky from Earth—not from the Academy bunkers anyhow."

"Then why did you go there?"

"I didn't have a choice." He laughed, hollowly. "I was doomed by being smart. That is why your precious Commissary despises me so much, you see. I have been taught to think—and we can't have that, can we? . . ."

I turned away from him and shut up. Jeru wasn't "my" Commissary, and this sure wasn't my argument. Besides, Pael gave me the creeps. I've always been wary of people who knew too much about science and technology. With a weapon, all you want to know is how it works, what kind of energy or ammunition it needs, and what to do when it goes wrong. People who know all the technical background and the statistics are usually covering up their own failings; it is experience of use that counts.

But this was no loudmouth weapons tech. This was an Academician: one of humanity's elite scientists. I felt I had no point of contact with him at all.

I looked out through the tangle, trying to see the fleet's sliding, glimmering lanes of light.

There was motion in the tangle. I turned that way, motioning Pael to keep still and silent, and go hold of my knife in my good hand.

Jeru came bustling back, exactly the way she had left. She nodded approvingly at my alertness. "Not a peep out of the beacon."

Pael said, "You realise our time here is limited."

I asked, "The suits?"

"He means the star," Jeru said heavily. "Case, fortress stars seem to be unstable. When the Ghosts throw up their cordon, the stars don't last long before going pop."

Pael shrugged. "We have hours, a few days at most."

Jeru said, "Well, we're going to have to get out, beyond the fortress cordon, so we can signal the fleet. That or find a way to collapse the cordon altogether."

Pael laughed hollowly. "And how do you propose we do that?"

Jeru glared. "Isn't it your role to tell me, Academician?"

Pael leaned back and closed his eyes. "Not for the first time, you're being ridiculous."

Jeru growled. She turned to me. "You. What do *you* know about the Ghosts?"

I said, "They come from someplace cold. That's why they are wrapped up in silvery shells. You can't bring a Ghost down with laser fire because of those shells. They're perfectly reflective."

Pael said, "Not perfectly. They are based on a Planck-zero effect . . . About one part in a billion of incident energy is absorbed."

I hesitated. "They say the Ghosts experiment on people."

Pael sneered. "Lies put about by your Commission for Historical Truth, Commissary. To demonise an opponent is a tactic as old as mankind."

Jeru wasn't perturbed. "Then why don't you put young Case right? How *do* the Ghosts go about their business?"

Pael said, "The Silver Ghosts tinker with the laws of physics."

I looked to Jeru; she shrugged.

Pael tried to explain. It was all to do with quagma.

Quagma is the state of matter which emerged from the Big Bang. Matter, when raised to sufficiently high temperatures, melts into a magma of quarks—a quagma. And at such temperatures the four fundamental forces of physics unify into a single superforce. When quagma is allowed to cool and expand its binding superforce decomposes into four sub-forces.

To my surprise, I understood some of this. The principle of the GUTdrive, which powers intrasystem ships like *Brief Life Burns Brightly*, is related.

Anyhow, by controlling the superforce decomposition, you can select the ratio between those forces. And those ratios govern the fundamental constants of physics.

Something like that.

Pael said, "That marvellous reflective coating of theirs is an example. Each Ghost is surrounded by a thin layer of space in which a fundamental number called the Planck constant is significantly lower than elsewhere. Thus, quantum effects are collapsed . . . Because the energy carried by a photon, a particle of light, is proportional to the Planck constant, an incoming photon must shed most of its energy when it hits the shell—hence the reflectivity."

"All right," Jeru said. "So what are they doing here?"

Pael sighed. "The fortress star seems to be surrounded by an open shell of quagma and exotic matter. We surmise that the Ghosts have blown a bubble around each star, a spacetime volume in which the laws of physics are—tweaked."

"And that's why our equipment had failed."

"Presumably," said Pael, with cold sarcasm.

I asked, "What do the Ghosts want? Why do they do all this stuff?"

Pael studied me. "You are trained to kill them, and they don't even tell you that?"

Jeru just glowered.

Pael said, "The Ghosts were not shaped by competitive evolution. They are symbiotic creatures; they derive from life forms that huddled into cooperatives collectives as their world turned cold. And they seem to be motivated—not by expansion and the acquisition of territory for its own sake, as we are—but by a desire to understand the fine-tuning of the universe. *Why are we here?* You see, young tar, there is only a narrow range of the constants of physics within which life of *any* sort is possible. We think the Ghosts are studying this question by pushing at the boundaries—by tinkering with the laws which sustain and contain us all."

Jeru said, "An enemy who can deploy the laws of physics

as a weapon is formidable. But in the long run, we will outcompete the Ghosts."

Pael said bleakly, "Ah, the evolutionary destiny of mankind. How dismal. But we lived in peace with the Ghosts, under the Raoul Accords, for a thousand years. We are so different, with disparate motivations—why should there be a clash, any more than between two species of birds in the same garden?"

I'd never seen birds, or a garden, so that passed me by.

Jeru just glared. She said at last, "Let's return to practicalities. *How* do their fortresses work?" When Pael didn't reply, she snapped, "Academician, you've been *inside* a fortress cordon for an hour already and you haven't made a single fresh observation?"

Acidly, Pael demanded, "What would you have me do?"

Jeru nodded at me. "What have *you* seen, tar?"

"Our instruments and weapons don't work," I said promptly. "The *Brightly* exploded. I broke my arm."

Jeru said, "Till snapped his neck also." She flexed her hand within her glove. "What would make our bones more brittle? Anything else?"

I shrugged.

Pael admitted, "I do feel somewhat warm."

Jeru asked, "Could these body changes be relevant?"

"I don't see how."

"Then figure it out."

"I have no equipment."

Jeru dumped spare gear—weapons, beacons—in his lap. "You have your eyes, your hands and your mind. Improvise." She turned to me. "As for you, tar, let's do a little infil. We still need to find a way off this scow."

I glanced doubtfully at Pael. "There's nobody to stand on stag."

Jeru said, "I know. But there are only three of us." She grasped Pael's shoulder, hard. "Keep your eyes open, Academician. We'll come back the same way we left. So you'll know it's us. Do you understand?"

Pael shrugged her away, focusing on the gadgets on his lap.

I looked at him doubtfully. It seemed to me a whole platoon of Ghosts could have come down on him without his even noticing. But Jeru was right; there was nothing more we could do.

She studied me, fingered my arm. "You up to this?"

"I'm fine, sir."

"You are lucky. A good war comes along once in a lifetime. And this is your war, tar."

That sounded like parade-ground pep talk, and I responded in kind. "Can I have your rations, sir? You won't be needing them soon." I mimed digging a grave.

She grinned back fiercely. "Yeah. When your turn comes, slit your suit and let the farts out before I take it off your stiffening corpse—"

Pael's voice was trembling. "You really are monsters."

I shared a glance with Jeru. But we shut up, for fear of upsetting the earthworm further.

I grasped my fighting knife, and we slid away into the dark.

What we were hoping to find was some equivalent of a bridge. Even if we succeeded, I couldn't imagine what we'd do next. Anyhow, we had to try.

We slid through the tangle. Ghost cable stuff is tough, even to a knife blade. But it is reasonably flexible; you can just push it aside if you get stuck, although we tried to avoid doing that for fear of leaving sign.

We used standard patrolling SOP, adapted for the circumstance. We would move for ten or fifteen minutes, clambering through the tangle, and then take a break for five minutes. I'd sip water—I was getting hot—and maybe nibble on a glucose tab, check on my arm, and pull the suit around me to get comfortable again. It's the way to do it. If you just push yourself on and on you run down your reserves and end up in no fit state to achieve the goal anyhow.

And all the while I was trying to keep up my all-around awareness, protecting my dark adaptation, and making appreciations. How far away is Jeru? What if an attack comes from in front, behind, above, below, left or right? Where can I find cover?

I began to build up an impression of the Ghost cruiser. It was a rough egg-shape, a couple of kilometres long, and basically a mass of the anonymous silvery cable. There were chambers and platforms and instruments stuck as if at random into the tangle, like food fragments in an old man's beard. I guess it makes for a flexible, easily modified configuration. Where the tangle was a little less thick, I glimpsed a more substantial core, a cylinder running along the axis of the craft. Perhaps it was the drive unit. I wondered if it was functioning; perhaps the Ghost equipment was designed to adapt to the changed conditions inside the fortress cordon.

There were Ghosts all over the craft.

They drifted over and through the tangle, following pathways invisible to us. Or they would cluster in little knots on the tangle. We couldn't tell what they were doing or saying. To human eyes a Silver Ghost is just a silvery sphere, visible only by reflection like a hole cut out of space, and without specialist equipment it is impossible even to tell one from another.

We kept out of sight. But I was sure the Ghosts must have spotted us, or were at least tracking our movements. After all we'd crash-landed in their ship. But they made no overt moves towards us.

We reached the outer hull, the place the cabling ran out, and dug back into the tangle a little way to stay out of sight.

I got an unimpeded view of the stars.

Still those nova firecrackers went off all over the sky; still those young stars glared like lanterns. It seemed to me the fortress's central, enclosed star looked a little brighter, hotter than it had been. I made a mental note to report that to the Academician.

But the most striking sight was the fleet.

Over a volume light-months wide, countless craft slid silently across the sky. They were organised in a complex network of corridors filling three-dimensional space: rivers of light gushed this way and that, their different colours denoting different classes and sizes of vessel. And, here and there, denser knots of colour and light sparked, irregular flares in the orderly flows. They were places where human ships were engaging the enemy, places where people were fighting and dying.

It was a magnificent sight. But it was a big, empty sky, and the nearest sun was that eerie dwarf enclosed in its spooky blue net, a long way away, and there was movement in three dimensions, above me, below me, all around me . . .

I found the fingers of my good hand had locked themselves around a sliver of the tangle.

Jeru grabbed my wrist and shook my arm until I was able to let go. She kept hold of my arm, her eyes locked on mine. *I have you. You won't fall.* Then she pulled me into a dense knot of the tangle, shutting out the sky.

She huddled close to me, so the bio lights of our suits wouldn't show far. Her eyes were pale blue, like windows. "You aren't used to being outside, are you, tar?"

"I'm sorry, Commissar. I've been trained—"

"You're still human. We all have weak points. The trick is to know them and allow for them. Where are you from?"

I managed a grin. "Mercury. Caloris Planitia." Mercury is a ball of iron at the bottom of the sun's gravity well. It is an iron mine, and an exotic matter factory, with a sun like a lid hanging over it. Most of the surface is given over to solar power collectors. It is a place of tunnels and warrens, where kids compete with the rats.

"And that's why you joined up? To get away?"

"I was drafted."

"Come on," she scoffed. "On a place like Mercury there

are ways to hide. Are you a romantic, tar? You wanted to see the stars?"

"No," I said bluntly. "Life is more useful here."

She studied me. "A brief life should burn brightly—eh, tar?"

"Yes, sir."

"I came from Deneb," she said. "Do you know it?"

"No."

"Sixteen hundred light-years from Earth—a system settled some four centuries after the start of the Third Expansion. It is quite different from the Solar System. It is—organised. By the time the first ships reached Deneb, the mechanics of exploitation had become efficient. From preliminary exploration to working shipyards and daughter colonies in less than a century . . . Deneb's resources—its planets and asteroids and comets, even the star itself—have been mined to fund fresh colonising waves, the greater Expansion—and, of course, to support the war with the Ghosts."

She swept her hand over the sky. "Think of it, tar. The Third Expansion: between here and Sol, across six thousand light-years—nothing but mankind, the fruit of a thousand years of world-building. And all of it linked by economics. Older systems like Deneb, their resources spent—even the Solar System itself—are supported by a flow of goods and materials inward from the growing periphery of the Expansion. There are trade lanes spanning thousands of light-years, lanes that never leave human territory, plied by vast schooners kilometres wide. But now the Ghosts are in our way. And *that's* what we're fighting for!"

"Yes, sir."

She eyed me. "You ready to go on?"

"Yes."

We began to make our way forward again, just under the tangle, still following patrol SOP.

I was glad to be moving again. I've never been comfortable talking personally—and for sure not with a Commissary. But I suppose even Commissaries need to talk.

• • •

Jeru spotted a file of the Ghosts moving in a crocodile, like so many schoolchildren, towards the head of the ship. It was the most purposeful activity we'd seen so far, so we followed them.

After a couple of hundred metres the Ghosts began to duck down into the tangle, out of our sight. We followed them in.

Maybe fifty metres deep, we came to a large enclosed chamber, a smooth bean-shaped pod that would have been big enough to enclose our yacht. The surface appeared to be semi-transparent, perhaps designed to let in sunlight. I could see shadowy shapes moving within.

Ghosts were clustered around the pod's hull, brushing its surface.

Jeru beckoned, and we worked our way through the tangle towards the far end of the pod, where the density of the Ghosts seemed to be lowest.

We slithered to the surface of the pod. There were sucker pads on our palms and toes to help us grip. We began crawling along the length of the pod, ducking flat when we saw Ghosts loom into view. It was like climbing over a glass ceiling.

The pod was pressurised. At one end of the pod a big ball of mud hung in the air, brown and viscous. It seemed to be heated from within; it was slowly boiling, with big sticky bubbles of vapour crowding its surface, and I saw how it was laced with purple and red smears. There is no convection in zero gravity, of course. Maybe the Ghosts were using pumps to drive the flow of vapour.

Tubes led off from the mud ball to the hull of the pod. Ghosts clustered there, sucking up the purple gunk from the mud.

We figured it out in bioluminescent whispers. The Ghosts were *feeding*. Their home world is too small to have retained much internal warmth, but, deep beneath their frozen oceans or in the dark of their rocks, a little primordial geotherm heat must leak out still, driving fountains of minerals dragged up from the depths. And, as at the bottom of Earth's oceans, on those minerals and the slow leak of heat, life forms feed. And the Ghosts feed on *them.*

So this mud ball was a field kitchen. I peered down at purplish slime, a gourmet meal for Ghosts, and I didn't envy them.

There was nothing for us here. Jeru beckoned me again, and we slithered further forward.

The next section of the pod was . . . strange.

It was a chamber full of sparkling, silvery saucer-shapes, like smaller, flattened-out Ghosts, perhaps. They fizzed through the air or crawled over each other or jammed themselves together into great wadded balls that would hold for a few seconds and then collapse, their component parts squirming off for some new adventure elsewhere. I could see there were feeding tubes on the walls, and one or two Ghosts drifted among the saucer things, like an adult in a yard of squabbling children.

There was a subtle shadow before me.

I looked up, and found myself staring at my own reflection—an angled head, an open mouth, a sprawled body—folded over, fish-eye style, just centimetres from my nose.

It was a Ghost. It bobbed massively before me.

I pushed myself away from the hull, slowly. I grabbed hold of the nearest tangle branch with my good hand. I knew I couldn't reach for my knife, which was tucked into my belt at my back. And I couldn't see Jeru anywhere. It might be that the Ghosts had taken her already. Either way I couldn't call her, or even look for her, for fear of giving her away.

The Ghost had a heavy-looking belt wrapped around its equator. I had to assume that those complex knots of equipment were weapons. Aside from its belt, the Ghost was quite featureless: it might have been stationary, or spinning at a hundred revolutions a minute. I stared at its hide, trying to understand that there was a layer in there like a separate universe, where the laws of physics had been tweaked. But all I could see was my own scared face looking back at me.

And then Jeru fell on the Ghost from above, limbs splayed, knives glinting in both hands. I could see she was yelling—mouth open, eyes wide—but she fell in utter silence, her comms disabled.

Flexing her body like a whip, she rammed both knives into the ghost's hide—if I took that belt to be its equator—somewhere near its north pole. The Ghost pulsated, complex ripples chasing across its surface. But Jeru did a handstand and reached up with her legs to the tangle above, and anchored herself there.

The Ghost began to spin, trying to throw Jeru off. But she held her grip on the tangle, and kept the knives thrust in its hide, and all the Ghost succeeded in doing was opening up twin gashes, right across its upper section. Steam pulsed out, and I glimpsed redness within.

For long seconds I just hung there, frozen.

You're trained to mount the proper reaction to an enemy assault. But it all vaporises when you're faced with a tonne of spinning, pulsing monster, and you're armed with nothing but a knife. You just want to make yourself as small as possible; maybe it will all go away. But in the end you know it won't, that something has to be done.

So I pulled out my own knife and launched myself at that north pole area.

I started to make cross-cuts between Jeru's gashes. Ghost skin is tough, like thick rubber, but easy to cut if you have the anchorage. Soon I had loosened flaps and lids of skin, and I started pulling them away, exposing a deep redness within. Steam gushed out, sparkling to ice.

Jeru let go of her perch and joined me. We clung with our fingers and hands to the gashes we'd made, and we cut and slashed and dug; though the Ghost spun crazily, it couldn't shake us loose. Soon we were hauling out great warm mounds of meat—ropes like entrails, pulsing slabs like a human's liver or heart. At first ice crystals spurted all around us, but as the Ghost lost the heat it had hoarded all its life, that thin wind died, and frost began to gather on the cut and torn flesh.

At last Jeru pushed my shoulder, and we both drifted away from the Ghost. It was still spinning, but I could see that the spin was nothing but dead momentum; the Ghost had lost its heat, and its life.

Jeru and I faced each other.

I said breathlessly, "I never heard of anyone in hand-to-hand with a Ghost before."

"Neither did I. Lethe," she said, inspecting her hand. "I think I cracked a finger."

It wasn't funny. But Jeru stared at me, and I stared back, and then we both started to laugh, and our slime suits pulsed with pink and blue icons.

"He stood his ground," I said.

"Yes. Maybe he thought we were threatening the nursery."

"The place with the silver saucers?"

She looked at me quizzically. "Ghosts are symbiotes, tar. That looked to me like a nursery for Ghost hides. Independent entities."

I had never thought of Ghosts having young. I had not thought of the Ghost we had killed as a mother protecting its young. I'm not a deep thinker now, and wasn't then; but it was not, for me, a comfortable thought.

But then Jeru started to move. "Come on, tar. Back to work." She anchored her legs in the tangle and began to grab at the still-rotating Ghost carcase, trying to slow its spin.

I anchored likewise and began to help her. The Ghost was massive, the size of a major piece of machinery, and it had built up respectable momentum; at first I couldn't grab hold of the skin flaps that spun past my hand. As we laboured I became aware I was getting uncomfortably hot. The light that seeped into the tangle from that caged sun seemed to be getting stronger by the minute.

But as we worked those uneasy thoughts soon dissipated.

At last we got the ghost under control. Briskly Jeru stripped it of its kit belt, and we began to cram the baggy corpse as deep as we could into the surrounding tangle. It was a grisly job. As the Ghost crumpled further, more of its innards, stiffening now, came pushing out of the holes we'd given it in its hide, and I had to keep from gagging as the foul stuff came pushing out into my face.

At last it was done—as best we could manage it, anyhow.

Jeru's faceplace was smeared with black and red. She was sweating hard, her face pink. But she was grinning, and she had a trophy, the Ghost belt around her shoulders. We began to make our way back, following the same SOP as before.

When we got back to our lying-up point, we found Academician Pael was in trouble.

Pael had curled up in a ball, his hands over his face. We pulled him open. His eyes were closed, his face blotched pink, and his faceplate dripped with condensation.

He was surrounded by gadgets stuck in the tangle—including parts from what looked like a broken-open starbreaker handgun; I recognised prisms and mirrors and diffraction gratings. Well, unless he woke up, he wouldn't be able to tell us what he had been doing here.

Jeru glanced around. The light of the fortress's central star had gotten a *lot* stronger. Our lying-up point was now bathed in light—and heat—with the surrounding tangle offering very little shelter. "Any ideas, tar?"

I felt the exhilaration of our infil drain away. "No, sir."

Jeru's face, bathed in sweat, showed tension. I noticed she was favouring her left hand. She'd mentioned, back at the nursery pod, that she'd cracked a finger, but had said nothing about it since—and nor did she give it any time now. "All right." She dumped the Ghost equipment belt and took a deep draught of water from her hood spigot. "Tar, you're on stag. Try to keep Pael in the shade of your body. And if he wakes up, *ask him what he's found out.*"

"Yes, sir."

"Good."

And then she was gone, melting into the complex shadows of the tangle as if she'd been born to these conditions.

I found a place where I could keep up 360-degree vision, and offer a little of my shadow to Pael—not that I imagined it helped much.

I had nothing to do but wait.

As the Ghost ship followed its own mysterious course, the light dapples that came filtering through the tangle shifted and evolved. Clinging to the tangle, I thought I could feel vibration: a slow, deep harmonisation that pulsed through the ship's giant structure. I wondered if I was hearing the deep voices of Ghosts, calling to each other from one end of their mighty ship to another. It all served to remind me that everything in my environment, *everything,* was alien, and I was very far from home.

I tried to count my heartbeat, my breaths; I tried to figure out how long a second was. "A thousand and one. A thousand and two . . ." Keeping time is a basic human trait; time provides a basic orientation, and keeps you mentally sharp and in touch with reality. But I keep losing count.

And all my efforts failed to stop darker thoughts creeping into my head.

During a drama like the contact with the Ghost, you don't realise what's happening to you because your body blanks it out; on some level you know you just don't have time to deal with it. Now I had stopped moving, the aches and pains of the last few hours started crowding in on me. I was still sore in my head and back and, of course, my busted arm. I could feel deep bruises, maybe cuts, on my gloved hands where I had hauled at my knife, and I felt as if I had wrenched my good shoulder. One of my toes was throbbing ominously: I wondered if I had cracked another bone, here in this weird environment in which my skeleton had become as brittle as an old man's. I was chafed at my groin and armpits and knees and ankles and elbows, my skin rubbed raw. I was used to suits; normally I'm tougher than that.

The shafts of sunlight on my back were working on me too; it felt as if I was lying underneath the elements of an oven. I had a headache, a deep sick feeling in the pit of my stomach, a ringing in my ears, and a persistent ring of blackness around my eyes. Maybe I was just exhausted, dehydrated; maybe it was more than that.

I started to think back over my operation with Jeru, and the regrets began.

Okay, I'd stood my ground when confronted by the Ghost and not betrayed Jeru's position. But when she launched her attack I'd hesitated, for those crucial few seconds. Maybe if I'd been tougher the Commissary wouldn't find herself hauling through the tangle, alone, with a busted finger distracting her with pain signals.

Our training is comprehensive. You're taught to expect that kind of hindsight torture, in the quiet moments, and to discount it—or, better yet, learn from it. But, effectively alone in that metallic alien forest, I wasn't finding my training was offering much perspective.

And, worse, I started to think ahead. Always a mistake.

I couldn't believe that the Academician and his reluctant gadgetry were going to achieve anything significant. And for all the excitement of our infil, we hadn't found anything resembling a bridge or any vulnerable point we could attack, and all we'd come back with was a belt of field kit we didn't even understand.

For the first time I began to consider seriously the possibility that I wasn't going to live through this—that I was going to die when my suit gave up or the sun went pop, whichever came first, in no more than a few hours.

A brief life burns brightly. That's what you're taught. Longevity makes you conservative, fearful, selfish. Humans made that mistake before, and we finished up a subject race. Live fast and furiously, for *you* aren't important—all that matters is what you can do for the species.

But I didn't want to die.

If I never returned to Mercury again I wouldn't shed a

tear. But I had a life now, in the Navy. And then there were my buddies: the people I'd trained and served with, people like Halle—even Jeru. Having found fellowship for the first time in my life, I didn't want to lose it so quickly, and fall into the darkness alone—especially if it was to be for *nothing*.

But maybe I wasn't going to get a choice.

After an unmeasured time, Jeru returned. She was hauling a silvery blanket. It was Ghost hide. She started to shake it out.

I dropped down to help her. "You went back to the one we killed—"

"—and skinned him," she said, breathless. "I just scraped off the crap with a knife. The Planck-zero layer peels away easily. And look . . ." She made a quick incision in the glimmering sheet with her knife. Then she put the two edges together again, ran her finger along the seam, and showed me the result. I couldn't even see where the cut had been. "Self-sealing, self-healing," she said. "Remember that, tar."

"Yes, sir."

We started to rig the punctured, splayed-out hide as a rough canopy over our LUP, blocking as much of the sunlight as possible from Pael. A few slivers of frozen flesh still clung to the hide, but mostly it was like working with a fine, light metallic foil.

In the sudden shade, Pael was starting to stir. His moans were translated to stark bioluminescent icons.

"Help him," Jeru snapped. "Make him drink." And while I did that she dug into the med kit on her belt and started to spray cast material around the fingers of her left hand.

"It's the speed of light," Pael said. He was huddled in a corner of our LUP, his legs tucked against his chest. His voice must have been feeble; the bioluminescent sigils on his suit were fragmentary and came with possible variants extrapolated by the translator software.

"Tell us," Jeru said, relatively gently.

"The Ghosts have found a way to *change* lightspeed in

this fortress. In fact to increase it." He began talking again about quagma and physics constants and the rolled-up dimensions of spacetime, but Jeru waved that away irritably.

"How do you *know* this?"

Pael began tinkering with his prisms and gratings. "I took your advice, Commissary." He beckoned to me. "Come see, child."

I saw that a shaft of red light, split out and deflected by his prism, shone through a diffraction grating and cast an angular pattern of dots and lines on a scrap of smooth plastic behind.

"You see?" His eyes searched my face.

"I'm sorry, sir."

"The wavelength of the light has changed. It has been increased. Red light should have a wavelength, oh, a fifth shorter than that indicated by this pattern."

I was struggling to understand. I held up my hand. "Shouldn't the green of this glove turn yellow, or blue? . . ."

Pael sighed. "No. Because the colour you see depends, not on the wavelength of a photon, but on its energy. Conservation of energy still applies, even where the Ghosts are tinkering. So each photon carries as much energy as before—and evokes the same 'colour.' Since a photon's energy is proportional to its frequency, that means frequencies are left unchanged. But since lightspeed is equal to frequency multiplied by wavelength, an increase in wavelength implies—"

"An increase in lightspeed," said Jeru.

"Yes."

I didn't follow much of that. I turned and looked up at the light that leaked around our Ghost-hide canopy. "So we see the same colours. The light of that star gets here a little faster. What difference does it make?"

Pael shook his head. "Child, a fundamental constant like lightspeed is embedded in the deep structure of our universe. Lightspeed is part of the ratio known as the fine structure constant." He started babbling about the charge on the electron, but Jeru cut him off.

She said, "Case, the fine structure constant is a measure of the strength of an electric or magnetic force."

I could follow that much. "And if you increase lightspeed—"

"You *reduce* the strength of the force." Pael raised himself. "Consider this. Human bodies are held together by molecular binding energy—electromagnetic forces. Here, electrons are more loosely bound to atoms; the atoms in a molecule are more loosely bound to each other." He rapped on the cast on my arm. "And so your bones are more brittle, your skin more easy to pierce or chafe. Do you see? You too are embedded in spacetime, my young friend. You too are affected by the Ghosts' tinkering. And because lightspeed in this infernal pocket continues to increase—as far as I can tell from these poor experiments—you are becoming more fragile every second."

It was a strange, eerie thought: that something so basic in my universe could be manipulated. I put my arms around my chest and shuddered.

"Other effects," Pael went on bleakly. "The density of matter is dropping. Perhaps our structure will eventually begin to crumble. And dissociation temperatures are reduced."

Jeru snapped, "What does that mean?"

"Melting and boiling points are reduced. No wonder we are overheating. It is intriguing that bio systems have proven rather more robust than electromechanical ones. But if we don't get out of here soon, our blood will start to boil . . ."

"Enough," Jeru said. "What of the star?"

"A star is a mass of gas with a tendency to collapse under its own gravity. But heat, supplied by fusion reactions in the core, creates gas and radiation pressures which push outwards, counteracting gravity."

"And if the fine structure constant changes—"

"Then the balance is lost. Commissary, as gravity begins to win its ancient battle, the fortress star has become more luminous—it is burning faster. That explains the observations we made from outside the cordon. But this cannot last."

"The novae," I said.

"Yes. The explosions, layers of the star blasted into space, are a symptom of destabilised stars seeking a new balance. The rate at which *our* star is approaching that catastrophic moment fits with the lightspeed drift I have observed." He smiled and closed his eyes. "A single cause predicating so many effects. It is all rather pleasing, in an aesthetic way."

Jeru said, "At least we know how the ship was destroyed. Every control system is mediated by finely-tuned electromagetic effects. Everything must have gone crazy at once . . ."

We figured it out. The *Brief Life Burns Brightly* had been a classic GUTship, of a design that hasn't changed in its essentials for thousands of years. The lifedome, a tough translucent bubble, contained the crew of twenty. The 'dome was connected by a spine a klick long to a GUTdrive engine pod.

When we crossed the cordon boundary—when all the bridge lights failed—the control systems went down, and all the pod's superforce energy must have tried to escape at once. The spine of the ship had thrust itself up into the lifedome, like a nail rammed into a skull.

Pael said dreamily, "If lightspeed were a tad faster, throughout the universe, then hydrogen could not fuse to helium. There would only be hydrogen: no fusion to power stars, no chemistry. Conversely if lightspeed were a little lower, hydrogen would fuse too easily, and there would be *no* hydrogen, nothing to make stars—or water. You see how critical it all is? No doubt the Ghosts' science of fine-tuning is advancing considerably here on the Orion Line, even as it serves its trivial defensive purpose . . ."

Jeru glared at him, her contempt obvious. "We must take this piece of intelligence back to the Commission. If the Ghosts can survive and function in these fast-light bubbles of theirs, so can we. We may be at the pivot of history, gentlemen."

I knew she was right. The primary duty of the Commission for Historical Truth is to gather and deploy intelligence about the enemy. And so *my* primary duty, and Pael's, was now to help Jeru get this piece of data back to her organisation.

But Pael was mocking her.

"Not for ourselves, but for the species. Is that the line, Commissary? You are so grandiose. And yet you blunder around in comical ignorance. Even your quixotic quest aboard this cruiser was futile. There probably is no bridge on this ship. The Ghosts' entire morphology, their evolutionary design, is based on the notion of cooperation, of symbiosis; why should a Ghost ship have a metaphoric *head*? And as for the trophy you have returned—" He held up the belt of Ghost artefacts. "There are no weapons here. These are sensors, tools. There is nothing here capable of producing a significant energy discharge. This is less threatening than a bow and arrow." He let go of the belt; it drifted away. "The Ghost wasn't trying to kill you. It was blocking you. Which is a classic Ghost tactic."

Jeru's face was stony. "It was in our way. That is sufficient reason for destroying it."

Peal shook his head. "Minds like yours will destroy *us,* Commissary."

Jeru stared at him with suspicion. Then she said, "*You have a way.* Don't you, Academician? A way to get us out of here."

He tried to face her down, but her will was stronger, and he averted his eyes.

Jeru said heavily, "Regardless of the fact that three lives are at stake—does duty mean nothing to you, Academician? You are an intelligent man. Can you not see that this is a war of human destiny?"

Pael laughed. "Destiny—or economics?"

I looked from one to the other, dismayed, baffled. I thought we should be doing less yapping and more fighting.

Pael said, watching me, "You see, child, as long as the explorers and the mining fleets and the colony ships are pushing outwards, as long as the Third Expansion is growing, our economy works. The riches can continue to flow inwards, into the mined-out systems, feeding a vast horde of humanity who have become more populous than the stars themselves. But as soon as that growth falters . . ."

Jeru was silent.

I understood some of this. The Third Expansion had reached all the way to the inner edge of our spiral arm of the Galaxy. Now the first colony ships were attempting to make their way across the void to the next arm.

Our arm, the Orion Arm, is really just a shingle, a short arc. But the Sagittarius Arm is one of the Galaxy's dominant features. For example it contains a huge region of starbirth, one of the largest in the Galaxy, immense clouds of gas and dust capable of producing millions of stars each. It was a prize indeed.

But that is where the Silver Ghosts live.

When it appeared that our inexorable expansion was threatening not just their own mysterious projects but their home system, the Ghosts began, for the first time, to resist us.

They had formed a blockade, called by human strategists the Orion Line: a thick sheet of fortress stars, right across the inner edge of the Orion Arm, places the Navy and the colony ships couldn't follow. It was a devastatingly effective ploy.

This was a war of colonisation, of world-building. For a thousand years we had been spreading steadily from star to star, using the resources of one system to explore, terraform and populate the worlds of the next. With too deep a break in that chain of exploitation, the enterprise broke down.

And so the Ghosts had been able to hold up human expansion for fifty years.

Pael said, "We are already choking. There have already been wars, young Case: humans fighting human, as the inner systems starve. All the Ghosts have to do is wait for us to destroy ourselves, and free them to continue their own rather more worthy projects."

Jeru floated down before him. "Academician, listen to me. Growing up at Deneb, I saw the great schooners in the sky, bringing the interstellar riches that kept my people alive. I was intelligent enough to see the logic of history—that we must maintain the Expansion, *because there is no choice.* And that is why I joined the armed forces, and later the Commission for Historical Truth. For I understood the dreadful truth which the Commission cradles. And that is why we must labour every day to maintain the unity and purpose of mankind. For if we falter we die; as simple as that."

"Commissary, your creed of mankind's evolutionary destiny condemns our own kind to become a swarm of children, granted a few moments of loving and breeding and dying, before being cast into futile war." Pael glanced at me.

"But," Jeru said, "it is a creed that has bound us together for a thousand years. It is a creed that binds uncounted trillions of human beings across thousands of light-years. It is a creed that binds a humanity so diverse it appears to be undergoing speciation . . . Are you strong enough to defy such a creed now? Come, Academician. None of us *chooses* to be born in the middle of a war. We must all do our best for each other, for other human beings; what else is there?"

I touched Pael's shoulder; he flinched away. "Academician—is Jeru right? Is there a way we can live through this?"

Pael shuddered. Jeru hovered over him.

"Yes," Pael said at last. "Yes, there is a way."

The idea turned out to be simple.

And the plan Jeru and I devised to implement it was even simpler. It was based on a single assumption: Ghosts aren't aggressive. It was ugly, I'll admit that, and I could see why it would distress a squeamish earthworm like Pael. But sometimes there are no good choices.

Jeru and I took a few minutes to rest up, check over our suits and our various injuries, and to make ourselves comfortable. Then, following patrol SOP once more, we made our way back to the pod of immature hides.

We came out of the tangle and drifted down to that translucent hull. We tried to keep away from concentrations of Ghosts, but we made no real effort to conceal ourselves. There was little point, after all; the Ghosts would know all about us, and what we intended, soon enough.

We hammered pitons into the pliable hull, and fixed rope to anchor ourselves. Then we took our knives and started to saw our way through the hull.

As soon as we started, the Ghosts began to gather around us, like vast antibodies.

They just hovered there, eerie faceless baubles drifting as if in vacuum breezes. But as I stared up at a dozen distorted reflections of my own skinny face, I felt an unreasonable loathing rise up in me. Maybe you could think of them as a family banding together to protect their young. I didn't care; a lifetime's carefully designed hatred isn't thrown off so easily. I went at my work with a will.

Jeru got through the pod hull first.

The air gushed out in a fast-condensing fountain. The baby hides fluttered, their distress obvious. And the Ghosts began to cluster around Jeru, like huge light globes.

Jeru glanced at me. "Keep working, tar."

"Yes, sir."

In another couple of minutes I was through. The air pressure was already dropping. It dwindled to nothing when we cut a big door-sized flap in that roof. Anchoring ourselves with the ropes, we rolled that lid back, opening the roof wide. A few last wisps of vapour came curling around our heads, ice fragments sparkling.

The hide babies convulsed. Immature, they could not survive the sudden vacuum, intended as their ultimate environment. But the way they died made it easy for us.

The silvery hides came flapping up out of the hole in the roof, one by one. We just grabbed each one—like grabbing hold of a billowing sheet—and we speared it with a knife, and threaded it on a length of rope. All we had to do was sit there and wait for them to come. There were hundreds of them, and we were kept busy.

I hadn't expected the adult Ghosts to sit through that, non-aggressive or not; and I was proved right. Soon they were clustering all around me, vast silvery bellies looming. A Ghost is massive and solid, and it packs a lot of inertia; if one hits you in the back you know about it. Soon they were nudging me hard enough to knock me flat against the roof, over and over. Once I was wrenched so hard against my tethering rope it felt as if I had cracked another bone or two in my foot.

And, meanwhile, I was starting to feel a lot worse: dizzy, nauseous, overheated. It was getting harder to get back upright each time after being knocked down. I was growing weaker fast; I imagined the tiny molecules of my body falling apart in this Ghost-polluted space.

For the first time I began to believe we were going to fail.

But then, quite suddenly, the Ghosts backed off. When they were clear of me, I saw they were clustering around Jeru.

She was standing on the hull, her feet tangled up in rope, and she had knives in both hands. She was slashing crazily at the Ghosts, and at the baby hides which came flapping past her, making no attempt to capture them now, simply cutting and destroying whatever she could reach. I could see that one arm was hanging awkwardly—maybe it was dislocated, or even broken—but she kept on slicing regardless.

And the Ghosts were clustering around her, huge silver spheres crushing her frail, battling human form.

She was sacrificing herself to save me—just as Captain

Teid, in the last moments of the *Brightly,* had given herself to save Pael. And *my* duty was to complete the job.

I stabbed and threaded, over and over, as the flimsy hides came tumbling out of that hole, slowly dying.

At last no more hides came.

I looked up, blinking to get the salt sweat out of my eyes. A few hides were still tumbling around the interior of the pod, but they were inert and out of my reach. Others had evaded us and gotten stuck in the tangle of the ship's structure, too far and too scattered to make them worth pursuing further. What I had got would have to suffice.

I started to make my way out of there, back through the tangle, to the location of our wrecked yacht, where I hoped Pael would be waiting.

I looked back once. I couldn't help it. The Ghosts were still clustered over the ripped pod roof. Somewhere in there, whatever was left of Jeru was still fighting.

I had an impulse, almost overpowering, to go back to her. No human being should die alone. But I knew I had to get out of there, to complete the mission, to make her sacrifice worthwhile.

So I got.

Pael and I finished the job at the outer hull of the Ghost cruiser.

Stripping the hides turned out to be as easy as Jeru had described. Fitting together the Planck-zero sheets was simple too—you just line them up and seal them with a thumb. I got on with that, sewing the hides together into a sail, while Pael worked on a rigging of lengths of rope, all fixed to a deck panel from the wreck of the yacht. He was fast and efficient: Pael, after all, came from a world where everybody goes solar sailing on their vacations.

We worked steadily, for hours.

I ignored the varying aches and chafes, the increasing pain in my head and chest and stomach, the throbbing of a broken arm that hadn't healed, the agony of cracked bones in my foot. And we didn't talk about anything but the task in hand. Pael didn't ask what had become of Jeru, not once; it was as if he had anticipated the Commissary's fate.

We were undisturbed by the Ghosts through all of this.

I tried not to think about whatever emotions churned within those silvered carapaces, what despairing debates might chatter on invisible wavelengths. I was, after all, trying to complete a mission. And I had been exhausted even before I got back to Pael. I just kept going, ignoring my fatigue, focusing on the task.

I was surprised to find it was done.

We had made a sail hundreds of metres across, stitched together from the invisibly thin immature Ghost hide. It was roughly circular, and it was connected by a dozen lengths of fine rope to struts on the panel we had wrenched out of the wreck. The sail lay across space, languid ripples crossing its glimmering surface.

Pael showed me how to work the thing. "Pull this rope, or this . . ." The great patchwork sail twitched in response to his commands. "I've set it so you shouldn't have to try anything fancy, like tacking. The boat will just sail out, hopefully, to the cordon perimeter. If you need to lose the sail, just cut the ropes."

I was taking in all this automatically. It made sense for both of us to know how to operate our little yacht. But then I started to pick up the subtext of what he was saying.

Before I knew what he was doing he had shoved me onto the deck panel, and pushed it away from the Ghost ship. His strength was surprising.

I watched him recede. He clung wistfully to a bit of tangle. I couldn't summon the strength to figure out a way to cross the widening gap. But my suit could read his, as clear as day.

"Where I grew up, the sky was full of sails . . ."

"Why, Academician?"

"You will go further and faster without my mass to haul.

And besides—our lives are short enough; we should preserve the young. Don't you think?"

I had no idea what he was talking about. Pael was much more valuable than I was; I was the one who should have been left behind. He had shamed himself.

Complex glyphs criss-crossed his suit. "Keep out of the direct sunlight. It is growing more intense, of course. That will help you . . ."

And then he ducked out of sight, back into the tangle. The Ghost ship was receding now, closing over into its vast egg shape, the detail of the tangle becoming lost to my blurred vision.

The sail above me slowly billowed, filling up with the light of the intense sun. Pael had designed his improvised craft well; the rigging lines were all taut, and I could see no rips or creases in the silvery fabric.

I clung to my bit of decking and sought shade.

Twelve hours later, I reached an invisible radius where the tactical beacon in my pocket started to howl with a whine that filled my headset. My suit's auxiliary systems cut in and I found myself breathing fresh air.

A little after that, a set of lights ducked out of the streaming lanes of the fleet, and plunged towards me, growing brighter. At last it resolved into a golden bullet shape adorned with a blue-green tetrahedron, the sigil of free humanity. It was a supply ship called *The Dominance of Primates.*

And a little after *that,* as a Ghost fleet fled their fortress, the star exploded.

As soon as I had completed my formal report to the ship's Commissary—and I was able to check out of the *Dominance*'s sick bay—I asked to see the Captain.

I walked up to the bridge. My story had got around, and the various med patches I sported added to my heroic mythos. So I had to run the gauntlet of the crew—"You're supposed to be dead, I impounded your back pay and slept with your mother already"—and was greeted by what seems to be the universal gesture of recognition of one tar to another, the clenched fist pumping up and down around an imaginary penis.

But anything more respectful just wouldn't feel normal.

The Captain turned out to be a grizzled veteran type with a vast laser burn scar on one cheek. She reminded me of First Officer Till.

I told her I wanted to return to active duty as soon as my health allowed.

She looked me up and down. "Are you sure, tar? You have a lot of options. Young as you are, you've made your contribution to the Expansion. You can go home."

"Sir, and do what?"

She shrugged. "Farm. Mine. Raise babies. Whatever earthworms do. Or you can join the Commission for Historical Truth."

"Me, a Commissary?"

"You've been there, tar. You've been in amongst the Ghosts, and come out again—with a bit of intelligence more important than anything the Commission has come up with in fifty years. Are you *sure* you want to face action again?"

I thought it over.

I remembered how Jeru and Pael had argued. It had been unwelcome perspective, for me. I was in a war that had nothing to do with me, trapped by what Jeru had called the logic of history. But then, I bet that's been true of most of humanity through our long and bloody history. All you can do is live your life, and grasp your moment in the light—and standby your comrades.

A farmer—me? And I could never be smart enough for the Commission. No, I had no doubts.

"A brief life burns brightly, sir."

Lethe, the Captain looked like she had a lump in her throat. "Do I take that as a yes, tar?"

I stood straight, ignoring the twinges of my injuries. "Yes, *sir*!"